D0410884

LATE NIGHTS
ON AIR

LATE NIGHTS ON AIR

Elizabeth Hay

MACLEHOSE PRESS
QUERCUS · LONDON

First published in Great Britain in 2008 by

MacLehose Press
an imprint of Quercus
21 Bloomsbury Square
London
WC1A 2NS

A CIP catalogue reference for this book is available
from the British Library

ISBN (HB) 978 1 84724 549 6
ISBN (TPB) 978 1 84724 5502

10 9 8 7 6 5 4 3 2 1

Printed and bound in Great Britain by Clays Ltd, St Ives plc

In memory of David Turney
1952–1988

HARRY WAS IN HIS LITTLE HOUSE ON THE EDGE OF BACK
Bay when at half past twelve her voice came over the radio for the
first time. A voice unusual in its sound and unusual in itself, since
there were no other female announcers on air. He listened to the
slow, clear, almost unnatural confidence, the low-pitched sexiness,
the elusive accent as she read the local news. More than curious,
already in love, he walked into the station the next day at precisely
the same time.

It was the beginning of June, the start of the long, golden summer
of 1975 when northern light held that little radio station in the large
palm of its hand. Eleanor Dew was behind the receptionist's desk
and behind clever Eleanor was the studio. She looked up, surprised.
Harry rarely darkened the station door except at night when he came
in to do the late shift and got away with saying and playing whatever
he liked. He paused beside her desk and with a broad wink asked
about the new person on air.

"Hired off the street," she told him. "The parting shot of our erst-
while manager."

"Well, well, well," Harry said.

Despite the red glow of the on-air light, he then pushed through
the studio door, only to be met by one of the great mysteries of life.
We look so very different from the way we sound. It's a shock, similar
to hearing your own voice for the first time, when you're forced to
wonder how the rest of you comes across if you sound nothing like

1

the way you think you sound. You feel dislodged from the old shoe of yourself.

Harry had pictured somebody short and compact with sun-bleached hair, fine blue eyes, great legs, a woman in her thirties. But Dido Paris was tall, big-boned, olive-skinned, younger. Glasses. Thick, dark, springy hair held back off a wide face. Faintest shadow on her upper lip. An unreasonably beautiful woman. She didn't look up, too intent on the newscast typed in capital letters on green paper, three-part greens, the paper-and-carbon combination the newsmen typed on.

He turned to check who was in the control room. Eddy at the controls and one of the newsmen standing at Eddy's shoulder. An audience, in other words.

Harry took out his lighter, flicked it, and put the flame to one top corner of the green. And still she did not look up.

An upper lip as downy as he imagined her legs might be. And yes, when she stood up later and came around the table, her legs were visible below a loose blue skirt, and the mystery of her voice was solved. She was European. European in her straightforwardness, her appearance, her way of speaking, which was almost too calm, except when the page was alight. Then her voice caught fire. She stopped turning her long pencil end on end, pacing herself. Stopped speaking altogether. Her eyes went in two directions – one leg on shore, the other in the canoe, but the canoe was pulling away from shore and *shit* – she picked up her glass, poured water on the flames, and read with jolting speed, repressed panic, to the very last word at the bottom of the page.

The news clip came on, she switched off her microphone and looked up wildly at the man with the boyish gleam in his eye. But he was not boyish, he was balding, bespectacled, square-jawed. She noticed his cauliflower ear.

"You're Harry Boyd," she said.

And she, too, had imagined another face – a big, bushy head to go with the relaxed, late-night growl that she heard only as she fell asleep. The man who had once been a big name in radio, she had been told. He was shorter than she had expected and his hands trembled.

Half an hour later, perched on Dido's desk, bumming a cigarette, Harry asked her how she had come by her intriguing accent. She studied him, not quite willing to forgive his outrageous behaviour, until he asked if she was Greek. Then out bubbled her easy and seductive laugh.

No chance. She had grown up in the Netherlands near the German border, the daughter of a Latin teacher who had listened to the B.B.C. and written questions to "London Calling" about expressions he did not understand. Her father had a reel-to-reel tape recorder and taped programmes off the radio. She learned English at school, she told Harry, but her pronunciation was terrible and so she had asked her father to make some tapes for her, and then she practised her English listening to Margaret Leighton reading Noel Coward and to Noel Coward himself, acquiring in that way her peculiar European-English accent, which she hated. "I figured marriage to a Canadian would solve my problem, but it hasn't."

"Two minutes," Harry said, "and you're already breaking my heart."

"It didn't last," she said.

"Then we have something in common, you and I."

He slipped her glasses off her face and breathed on the lenses and polished them with his handkerchief, then slid them back over her nose, saying, "And Dorothy Parker said men never make passes at girls with glasses."

"Parker?"

"Dorothy. A writerly wit who famously claimed to be 'too fuck-ing busy and vice versa'."

Dido was only semi-amused. To Eleanor the next day she called

Harry "the loser", a put-down softened by her accent; it came out "lose-air". She said he had taken a drag off her lit cigarette, then set it back on the ashtray. "So cheap," she said with a shake of her head and a faint, unimpressed smile.

"But not without charm," countered Eleanor. "Charm, sex, insecurity: that's what Harry has to offer."

Dido was more interested now.

"He's too old for you, Dido."

But his age was the last thing Dido minded.

Harry was forty-two. Winds of ill repute had blown him back up on these shores – a man with a nearly forgotten reputation for brilliance, one of those lucky luckless people who finds his element early on and then makes the mistake of leaving it – radio for a television talk show, where he had bombed. In short order, he was fired, his personal life fell apart, rumours rose up and settled down. A year ago an old boss stumbled across him sleeping in a hotel lobby in Toronto and pulled a few strings to get him a night shift in the Northern Service, the very place where he had started out fifteen years ago. At square one again, but with a difference. Now he was an *old* fish in a small pond.

And yet it suited him – the place, the hours, the relative obscurity.

Stories about him circulated: how he had numerous ex-wives, and a tremendous tolerance for liquor, and some dark deed in his past – some disgrace. Professional, certainly. Sexual? No-one was quite sure. His cauliflower ear suggested a life touched by violence. His trembling hands sent granules of instant coffee scattering in all directions. "Harry's been here," they would say in the morning, surveying the little table that held mugs, spoons, the electric kettle, the big jar of Maxwell House.

In that first conversation Harry asked Dido about her husband, tell me all about him, and she jested that she had married almost the first person who asked her, a fellow student at McGill, but when he brought her from Montreal through the gates of his rich Halifax neighbourhood, she saw his father in the driveway. "And we just looked at each other," she said, turning the oversized man's watch on her wrist in what Harry would come to understand was a yearning, nervous habit. "We just looked." Harry saw them, a man and woman unable to take their eyes off each other, and the picture cut into his heart.

After a moment Dido shrugged, but her face still ran with longing and regret. The situation became impossible, she admitted. She escaped the triangle by coming north.

"And your father-in-law let you go?"

She gestured towards the entrance of the station. "I half expect him to come through that door."

*   *

The radio station occupied a quiet corner a block away from main street. It had been an electrical supplies store once, Top Electric, and was that size. A one-storey shoebox in a town that had sprung up in the 1930s on the gold-rich shores of Great Slave Lake, an inland sea one-third the size of troubled Ireland.

Entering, the first person you saw was Eleanor Dew, who managed to be pretty even though no part of her was pretty. She had rather bulging eyes and a chin that blended into her throat, yet she gave off an idea of blondness, a sort of radiance that came from having her feet on the ground and her head in heaven. At thirty-six she was almost the oldest person in the station and a poet at heart, reading Milton between telephone calls – the community announce-ments coming in, the complaints and song requests, the mixture of personal and business calls for the six announcer-operators or the two newsmen or the station manager, who had run away with a waitress a week ago.

Her desk stood next to a plate-glass window that overlooked the dusty street leading up to the Gold Range, also known as the Strange

Range, and to Franklin Avenue, the main street with two stoplights. Turn left on Franklin Avenue and you passed on one side MacLeod's Hardware and the Hudson's Bay Store and on the other side the Capitol Theatre with its third-run movies and fifth-rate popcorn machine. Continue on in the same direction through the newest part of New Town, and then angle left, and eventually you came around to Cominco, one of the two operating gold mines that gave the town its initial reason for being. If, instead, you turned right on Franklin Avenue you passed the Yellowknife Inn on one side and the post office on the other, you passed the public library and the clothing store known as Eve of the Arctic. Proceed in a down-sloping northerly direction and you reached the oldest part of Old Town, an array of little houses and shacks and log cabins and privies, of Quonset huts and trailers and motley businesses, all of which seemed perfectly at ease on this rocky peninsula under the enormous sky. Well, they weren't competing with it. Yellowknife had only one high-rise and it was not on main street, it was a lonely apartment building in the southeastern part of town.

A rudimentary place of ten thousand people named after an indigenous tribe that used knives made of copper, and in many ways it was a white blot on the native landscape. But it was as far north as most southerners had ever come. It was north of the sixtieth parallel and shared in the romance of the North, emanating not mystery but uniqueness and not right away. It had no breathtaking scenery. No mountains, no glaciers, in the winter not even that much snow. But after a while it grew on them, on some of them at least, on the ones who would never forget, who would think back on their lives and say, My time there was the most vivid time in my life.

Only two stoplights, perhaps, but such a traffic in voices. That summer a small but steady parade of poets came through town, unconnected to the parade of experts addressing Judge Berger at his inquiry into what would be, if it went ahead, the largest single development project ever undertaken in the Western world, a gas pipeline running across the top of the Arctic and down the eight-hundred-mile-length of the Mackenzie River. Politics overshadowed poetry, as it always does. The poets came one at a time throughout the summer, a modest incursion and the first of its kind, organized by a local poetry lover and financed by the national council for the arts. The pipeline experts came in droves, it seemed, gathering at the gleaming white Explorer Hotel that dominated the road on the way to the airport. It was a time when Yellowknife was on the map, when the North was on everyone's minds, when the latest scheme to extract its riches had gained so much ground that this summer of 1975 took on the mythical quality of a cloudless summer before the outbreak of war, or before the onset of the kind of restlessness, social, spiritual, that remakes the world.

Harry went to a few of the literary readings at the public library. He went with Eleanor, who wrote poetry for her own pleasure, until he lost patience with what he called the empty wordplay. How can a poem last, he cried, if it does not touch your heart? You might remember the poet, he declared, but you will not remember the poem. To underscore his point he typed out verses from a poem he admired and taped them to the wall in the one and only announce booth, where their message about death and its haunting aftermath was like a skull sitting on the console. The poem was by Alden Nowlan, who came from Harry's part of southern New Brunswick, and it described the foolish time in the poet's life when he worked alone at night in a radio station and could not believe anyone was listening, for "it seemed I was talking / only to myself in a room no bigger / than an ordinary bathroom". Then one day he had to cover a fatal collision between a car and a train, and Nowlan the broadcaster turned into Nowlan the appalled listener. "Inside the wreckage" of the car, three young men were dead, but the car radio was still playing and "nobody could get at it" to turn it off. Across the

7

top margin Harry scrawled, *Do you ever wonder where your voice goes?*

The more personal question he avoided asking himself. How had he ended up back here, where he had started, in the little rabbit warren of rooms known as C.F.Y.K.? Sitting in the announce booth, feeling his own life collide with itself.

Eleanor was the station's gatekeeper. From her desk she controlled access to a single hallway that led like a short main street directly through the guts of the station to an exit that tumbled you back out into the northern summer – to a garbage bin full to overflowing with tape so edited, so beknuckled and thickened with white splicing tape as to be deemed unsalvageable, finally, by the head technician in his basement lair. Crusty Andrew McNab presided over the station's nether region of workbenches, labelled shelves, crowded corners, and his own tidy desk. For seventeen years he had practised frugality and extravagant disdain, "fathead" being his favourite term for anyone conceited enough to go on air.

Andrew's was not the only lair. The newsroom, just large enough for two newsmen and two desks and one editing machine, was another. Its firmly closed door lay directly in the line of fire between Eleanor's desk and the front door of the station through which the town's characters liked to come. Mrs Dargabble, for instance, with her lofty, loquacious, regular plea for classical music. I don't expect opera, but a little Mozart from time to time? Eleanor could not have agreed more. She wrote down the request, then tossed it sadly into the wastebasket as soon as the poor woman turned her back, since there was no hope, she knew. No hope for Mozart in Yellowknife.

Until Harry Boyd passed by one day recently and rumbled at the hefty, flapping, fragile woman, "Do you like Lucia Popp?"

"She sings the Queen of the Night," said the startled Mrs Dargabble.

"Tonight I'll play her for you. Turn on your radio at midnight."

"You *marv*ellous man. You under*stand*."

By now Harry was haunting the station at all hours and it was obvious to everyone why. He wanted to be around Dido Paris.

"How will I recognize him?" Harry had asked her, his voice a-growl with mock irony and serious intent. "This fancy man of yours. Your father-in-law."

She had a long, slow smile. "You're a romantic, Harry."

"I'm not ashamed of it."

He saw her face give way once again to such tender sadness that his lonely insides twisted and tightened. But then he took heart. "You like older men."

Dido leaned back and laughed at him. "Harry, you're so transparent."

He was not ashamed of that either. He recognized in Dido a deep streak of melancholy that he happened to share, and he was fascinated, not least by a childhood he guessed was partly to blame. Holland after the war. Not Holland, she corrected. The Netherlands. She told him her mother sewed warm winter pants for her from old army uniforms and she had to wear pyjamas underneath, otherwise the khaki chafed her thighs and made them bleed. At the look on his face, she smiled and touched his arm. It wasn't so bad, she said. In a way, I didn't mind. And you won't believe how much I miss what I ate then, chocolate sprinkles on bread, we put the butter on top of the sprinkles to keep them in place, and speculaas – you know? the Dutch windmill cookie? – between two slices of buttered bread. I bicycled to school and took that for my lunch. Her voice had a buoyant, velvety sound. Sensual, but not so sensual it lost energy or authority. Had her father been her teacher? he wanted to know. Not officially, she said, and she grew pensive again. Her father had died quite recently, in March, still listening to the B.B.C. At the time of his death she had been here, substitute teaching Maths and French at the local high school, a job that merely met her need to be as far away as possible from her romantic entanglements. After her father's death she felt impelled to rethink her life. In a first step, she came to the station offering to volunteer. "And the rest is history," Harry said.

9

He could not imagine this beautiful woman, whose manner he could only describe as regal, lasting very long in a town like Yellowknife. And when he asked about her intentions, she said she had no idea whether she would even stay in Canada. "Canada" she pronounced with a certain contempt. Canadians were spoiled, she said. Look at the size and weight of their overcrammed garbage cans, the number and newness of their cars, the houses standing unoccupied, the closets bursting with clothes, the daily showers. She did not go on, but she could have. Her ex-husband's family had used water as if there were no tomorrow, but with her sense of economy and quality – in the Netherlands even a tea towel was made to last for decades – with her sense of history, tragedy, and time, she knew better than these dishwashing guzzlers, these showering fools, these lawn-lovers and land-wasters. Yellowknife, however, was different. Here, she felt that she had stepped backwards into small-town life, especially in the unplanned old part of town where there was outdoor plumbing and the streets were unpaved and had names like Ragged Ass Road. Such a curious mixture, the city was, of brand-new and raw-old, of government buildings and beer parlours and bush planes and little shack-like houses close to the water, which seemed to lie in all directions, as did the vast wilderness. The place was full of opportunities, she said, especially if you were white and even if you were a woman.

Harry drew a map of Yellowknife for Dido, marking the location of his house on Latham Island at the far end of Old Town, not with an x but with a • like a beauty mark. And was it deliberate or unconscious, she wondered, that his rendition of the island (separated from the mainland by the narrowest of narrows) made it look like a penis with personality? An erect penis with a noticeable rightward curve. His house was near the base of the left-hand side of this curvaceous, prancing, happy, circumcised cock.

In watching him rapidly sketch the map, Dido Paris learned a few things and guessed a few others. Since Harry knew the coastline like the back of his hand, he must be a sailor, he must be happiest on water. His sketch was fast and deft and to the point. It showed no interest in the town itself, except insofar as Franklin Avenue ran down to the tip of the island-erection that bestrode the waters of Great Slave Lake. In manly capital letters he had written GIANT on the west shore of Back Bay and CON near Yellowknife Bay to indicate the two gold mines. But his focus was on the water and on inviting her, she assumed, to take an entertaining plunge.

THE DAY AFTER HARRY BRAVED THE STATION IN ORDER TO see Dido, a cloud of weather so warm had descended that Eleanor Dew went for a long walk before bed. She lived in the new part of town, in a basic but comfortable trailer home not far from Frame Lake. Occasionally that night she felt a cool breeze come off the water. Otherwise, warmth descended from the sky, then a little soft rain. The next morning the air outside was like one of those so-called white children – hair so blond it is white – a heavy mist obscuring the trailer next door. She was reminded of her grandfather, who had washed his fine head of white hair once a week with Old Dutch Cleanser.

This was the day Gwen Symon came into the station for the first time, and nobody noticed. It was the third day of June, a Tuesday.

Eleanor was caught up in playful banter with Ralph Cody, the freelance book reviewer. "You've drunk nineteen cups of coffee already. Do you plan to stay awake for a month?"

Ralph was a small man, about sixty, in a tweed jacket with patched elbows. His appetite for talk was barely whetted by the ten minutes allowed him on air. His teeth were darkly stained with coffee and tobacco. His nicotined hands were the smallest, daintiest hands Eleanor had ever seen on a man. The two of them were discussing discomfort, how much better everyone used to be at enduring it, but especially the voyageurs during the fur trade and all the storied travellers in the Arctic.

Gwen stood there. They were not aware of her. Or pretended they weren't. After a moment she said, "Some of those travellers weren't comfortable unless they were *un*comfortable."

Then they looked over and saw a pair of shocking blue eyes coming straight at them out of a young woman's white face. She had a large bruise on her throat – the size of a dollar bill torn in half, the purple ten-dollar bill. Dead-white skin (as white, thought Eleanor, as someone's feet, in shoes all year round, might be). A very bad haircut. And those blue eyes.

"Where did *you* come from?" Ralph said.

"I just arrived," she said, and pointed out the window to the soft-shaped, ten-year-old Volvo parked in the street. Attached to it was a very small trailer.

She said, "I was wondering. Who could I talk to about a job?"

They established that she was twenty-four, she had driven from Georgian Bay in Ontario, more than three thousand miles, camping in her trailer along the way, and if she could find work she would stay for a while. In Toronto she had been told that anyone as inexperienced in radio as she was should try the hinterlands first.

Ralph's lips twitched in amusement; he could just picture some bureaucrat with a grand vocabulary. "So you came all this way to be on air."

"Not on air," came the hasty answer. "In the background. And I came all this way for other reasons too. I've always wanted to see the North."

It turned out she was intent on becoming a script assistant for radio drama.

"I don't mean to be harsh," Ralph said, "but have you been listening to the radio up here? Have you heard any radio dramas? Have you heard even a skit?"

"I think you need them," she said quietly.

Ah, thought Eleanor. She had trapped a mouse in her trailer a few days ago and this girl was just as subtle in her camouflage: a buff-grey shirt with a pale brown collar, and darker brown trousers. No adornment except for the impressive bruise on her throat. An embarrassment, that, or something worse. But her sense of purpose was unmistakable, it cut through the static of her pale, brown personality. Someone else to watch. The girl's face was flushed now, the underarms of her shirt visibly wet. And Eleanor was reminded of her aunt who had to towel herself dry after she spoke on the telephone, the effort took so much out of her. Yet this same aunt had travelled cities the world over, and she had done it alone.

This place could be the making of you, Eleanor thought, smiling at Gwen. But then everyone thought the North would be the making of them, as she knew perfectly well. That is exactly what led to so many disasters.

Eleanor told young Gwen that she was not sure who she should talk to, since their station manager had absconded. Ralph cracked that where he came from it was the weather that was transient: all you had to do was wait five minutes if you didn't like it; here, all you had to do was wait five minutes if you didn't like the people.

Eleanor laughed and went on to say that head office had been talking to Harry Boyd and she guessed they would ask him to step into the breach.

"What if I watched in the meantime," Gwen said. "I could learn a lot by watching."

"Have you got a place to stay?"

Gwen indicated her little Boler trailer parked outside, and Eleanor offered her own backyard as a parking place until she found an apartment.

"You're brave to have driven all this way."

Gwen considered for a moment whether this made her brave. In truth, she was always afraid, always worried. She shook her head. "Like I said, I've wanted to come north for as long as I can remember."

"Three thousand miles!"

"Yes," still unimpressed by herself, "but I never went over fifty."

Eleanor gave Gwen Symon a tour of the station, and for the next couple of days Gwen sat in master control with silent Eddy the redheaded tech. and watched him operate the big console. She listened to the announcers, became familiar with their habits. There was the morning man, so prodigiously at ease on radio that it was like sleeping for him. The rest of his life was work – his troubled marriage, his full-time drinking – this was where he came to rest. There was the silver-haired treaty Indian, trim and immaculate and quiet, who did the news in Dogrib. There was the restless, fast-talking Metis sportscaster, who also hosted the late afternoon request show, since in the Northern Service announcers did more than one job and operated the equipment for themselves besides. There was the utterly reliable newsreader and host of Radio Noon, who was training Dido to take his place, since he would be leaving soon for a job in the south. And there was Dido, who struggled with pronunciation, but had the most beautiful speaking voice Gwen had ever heard.

As it turned out, Harry was indeed made acting manager. *Acting*, as head office took pains to point out, until a permanent manager was hired. Somebody had to cover temporarily, and Harry, despite his lamentable history, was the most experienced person at hand.

Gwen went to see him in his new office, the first room down the hall past Eleanor's desk. She arrived just as he swivelled in his chair and picked up his telephone, giving her his back, but not because he meant to. She hovered at the open door, having nerved herself to enter, and now was unwilling to go away. She knew his voice. She had heard him on her car radio as she drove the final leg to Yellowknife, drawn on by the endless light into a sunset that blended into sunrise, and accompanied for a while by this irreverent, handsome-sounding man who said things like, "The time may not be out of joint, but this joint is out of time". Now here he was in the flesh and her sense of letdown was part of a larger disappointment, since the North looked nothing like what she had expected either. It was not a dramatic scene of rugged simplicity, rather, mile after mile of stunted trees covered with dust from the gravel road.

From the door she had a good view of the back of his balding head and his fat left ear. He hung up the telephone, and she stepped all the way into his office, saying, "You don't look *anything* like how you sound."

Harry turned. He took off his glasses with one hand and studied her. "That," he said gravely, "is the tragedy of radio."

Gwen felt disarmed. Her face lit up, and Harry's relaxed into a smile. The old seducer, mutual honesty, had walked in the door and joined them.

"You remind me of Johnny Q.," she said, voicing her sudden thought.

Her favourite comic strip growing up. On her stomach, the Saturday paper spread wide and still warm from having been under her bum all through lunch (staking her claim before her brother did), she drank in the intoxicating smell of newsprint – a potent, throat-catching, alcoholic smell – and devoured "On Stage", the ongoing story of the actress Mary Perkins, who married the reporter Pete Fletcher, because he was handsome and reliable, even though she was deeply attracted to roguish Johnny Q. of the cauliflower ear. Johnny Q. came and went, other adventures intervened, but you always knew when he was back because his cauliflower ear appeared at the edge of the strip. Often his voice came first, a teasing sexy comment directed at a stewardess who was bringing him yet another drink. Then the back of his head appeared with the cauliflower ear jutting to one side. There was no greater pleasure in her childhood than knowing Johnny Q. would be around for several weeks at least.

Harry Boyd was not handsome, but he was appealing in his own idiosyncratic way. Polka-dot silk shirt, dress trousers, tennis sneakers. His face broad, underslept, middle-aged. Less a twinkle in his eye than an interested, half-irritated gleam. Like a pilot from the Second World War. Amused and thirsty.

"Sit down and make yourself homely."

She sat across from him in his little office, and he asked her why she wanted a job in northern radio. Her answer surprised and gripped him. When she was a girl, she said, she heard a radio programme about John Hornby, the Englishman who starved to death along with his young cousin Edgar Christian, and a third companion, Harold Adlard, when they overwintered in the Barrens in 1927. She had never forgotten it.

"'Death in the Barren Ground.'" He leaned back in his chair. "Alan King took the role of Hornby, Douglas Rain was Edgar Christian. I think Bud Knapp did the narration. An incredible story," he said, glad to be remembering it again. "George Whalley wrote the script."

"And the biography too," she said. "*The Legend of John Hornby*. I've read it three times."

Her eagerness made Harry smile. "Whalley's daughter lives here, you know. Just down the road from me on Latham Island. She told me her father's really a Coleridge scholar. His obsession with Hornby is something he pursued on the side. His 'love child', she called it. I made her promise to bring him round and introduce him if he ever comes to Yellowknife."

Gwen said, "I've wanted to make radio dramas ever since I heard that broadcast."

Harry cradled his glasses in his left hand. "I hate to break it to you, but we're a one-thousand-watt radio station. We don't do drama."

"Is that in the regulations?"

A simple question that scored a point without intending to.

Harry said, "You've got Hornby's eyes. Has anybody told you that?" He pushed back and swung his feet up on his desk, a sign

17

that he was interested, that she was worth his while. Harry had a weakness for shy, young travellers who had fallen in love with the North, having been one himself. "So what was it about Hornby's story that hooked you?"

Gwen did not hesitate. She told him it was Hornby's feeling for the Barrens. She understood the pull of that sort of desolate, rugged landscape; it's what had made her travel a year ago to Newfoundland. The Barrens were far more remote, she knew, and even more dangerously exposed in the treeless interior of the Arctic. She wanted to see them too. And Hornby himself fascinated her, she said. He went to such extremes, getting by on so little, pushing himself to the brink. And then there was the way he died. He was to blame for what happened, but young Edgar never blamed him. That's what she found so moving.

Harry was nodding. "It's one of those unforgettable northern tales that break your heart."

"But," she leapt in, "it was a tragedy that avoided a greater tragedy, since they never turned against each other."

His cigarette stopped halfway to his mouth.

"I just mean," and she stuttered a little and pulled at the jagged ends of her short brown hair, "I just mean sometimes people misunderstand each other after a while, and then they turn against each other. They don't want to," she said softly, "but they can't help it."

Harry felt suddenly alert. "That sounds like personal experience talking."

He saw her move back in her chair and suspected he was right. "So how did you get to be so wise?"

It seemed she might not answer his question, but she did. "I read," she smiled, and he chuckled. Small-town honesty. He could recognize it a mile away. Small-town honesty, and big-city drive.

The girl reminded him of somebody he had not thought about for a long time. Somebody he had met all too briefly at a reception years ago. A thin, young graduate student with short hair and a big shoulder bag into which she slipped food off the tables. She was making assiduous progress from the cheese to the butter tarts, wrapping the food in paper napkins, when he offered her a sausage roll for her collection, and her face crinkled with delight. How marvellous and rare, meeting a woman who liked to be teased. She made room for the sausage roll in her bag and he noticed the book tucked inside; the very book he was reading: Dashiell Hammett's *The Thin Man*. Then she gave him a warm smile and continued to the end of the table and then out the side door. He should have gone after her, but he let her go. He let her slip through his fingers.

Gwen Symon had the same kind of smile. She was telling him that Yellowknife was not what she had expected, but the light was remarkable and she was looking forward to the darkness and cold of winter. And she could see that it was a place where anyone could make a fresh start.

"Why would *you* need a fresh start?" he asked. "You look almost prepubescent."

Her sky-blue eyes stabbed him. She did not know the word, to her own surprise, and almost asked what it meant. Pre-what? Typewriters were clacking away on the other side of the wall and she was aware that his eyes had shifted to the bruise on her throat. "Why not?" she said at last.

A surprisingly self-possessed response. *Why not?* Harry straightened his shoulders, swung his feet back on the floor. A fresh start was exactly what he needed too.

"We have an opening, it so happens. Actually, two openings. I need someone to replace me on the night shift and soon I'll need a host for Radio Noon." He began to shuffle papers on his desk. "You're in luck. But whether we can *afford* to hire somebody else who needs to be trained is another matter. I know this will surprise the hell out of the c.b.c., but I'm a cheap bastard." Without looking at her, he spread his arms and lifted his shoulders. "I can't help it."

"Mr Boyd," she said. "Mr Boyd!" Leaning forward to get his attention.

"Harry's the name."

"I'm *cheaper*." Her eyes were bright, sharp, amused.

"You are?" His own eyes widened to take in this suddenly competitive girl. "*How* cheap?"

She was wearing sandals. Never in her life had she paid full price for sandals.

She raised her foot. "End of summer sale."

He pointed to his own feet. "Salvation Army."

That's where Gwen got her brassieres.

Harry said, "In Mexico I bargained so hard the street vendors turned their backs on me and walked away. I'm so cheap that when I go out with my buddies I forget to take my wallet."

"I've never sunk that low," she said.

"Honey, you don't know what my life has been like."

It was not hard, what she did next. Turning the conversation. Most men love to talk about themselves to women, even to a woman like her. "What has your life been like?" she asked, and he told her about what he called the violet hours of drinking that followed on the heels of his television disgrace, when he found himself eating corn flakes with a shoehorn since he did not own a spoon. "I was no good on television," he said, expecting her to contradict him. But she did not.

"My father was a drinker," she said.

"Then you know every sordid detail. You're not frightened."

"Not of that."

Harry waved her into the studio, the door of which was only a few feet from Eleanor's desk. He handed her the news story lying on the table, told her where to sit, lowered the microphone to her small, thin face. Then he went back out and down the hall to master control and asked Eddy to slap up a tape.

The studio in which Gwen sat at a big baize-covered table had an upright piano in the corner, and she wondered if musicians came in to play on air. The studio was connected by a picture window to master control, which was connected in the same way to the announce booth and the editing booth beyond that. She could see the length of the little station and into the hallway too. And thus she was inducted into the visibility and invisibility of radio, the intimacy and the isolation. Harry turned on his mike and spoke to her through the glass: Introduce yourself, then read the news story.

It was a story about a single car crash near Fort Rae, a settlement seventy miles west of Yellowknife. The car had skidded on loose gravel and had gone out of control on a lonely curve of bumpy road, the so-called highway she had driven on to get to Yellowknife. The man had been killed, the woman escaped with minor cuts. Five dogs were in the car at the time of the accident, one of them had still not been recovered.

Harry listened. He pulled a notepad out of his back pocket and jotted down: *Interesting. Monotonous. Worth a chance.*

"What do you think, Eddy?" he said.

"Not great," Eddy said.

"Not yet."

There was something about her voice. It sounded parched and boyish and defenceless, a little like Douglas Rain's voice – the eerie, naked, innocent quality he brought to Edgar Christian, the seven-teen-year-old cousin who accompanied Hornby into the Barrens and stayed loyal until his last breath.

The next day Harry offered Gwen a summer contract as an announcer-operator, thinking of it as a trial run, and she accepted.

* *

Gwen asked herself later why she agreed to the job. Why would someone who wanted to be in the background agree to be in the foreground? It was the only job going, she told herself. Then why

21

was she so ecstatic about the prospect of being on air?

She went for a walk down to Old Town and without her being aware of it the interviewing voice started up inside her head, asking, "As a child, did you realize how famous you were going to be?" And in a modest voice she answered, "Not as a child. Not then. Believe me, I've combed through my childhood looking for signs and there weren't any." An answer so honest and self-deprecating and gently humorous it provoked even more admiration from her imagined interviewer and she became aware that it was happening again, her mental tape recorder was on. She was being questioned about her long and famous life and she was talking easily, confidently, amusingly, without a trace of self-consciousness.

Gwen took over reading the news from the smooth-voiced favourite of the two newsmen, Roland Clark, who would be leaving in a week for Vancouver. Dido was given Radio Noon. The night shift would fall to a casual who regularly filled in on holidays, at least for now. Harry wanted to keep his options open until he saw how the women worked out.

Shake it up, he thought, when he leaned into the newsroom to announce the change, making his fresh start on Gwen's shoulders. How could she know that she had hitched her wagon to a murky star, to a man who had been written off by the real powers in the station as one more example of head office's ineptitude? But she discovered soon enough. The enmity of newsmen is no small thing.

IT WOULD BE ONE OF THOSE RARE SUMMERS WHEN THE light is crystalline, the sky deep blue, the air continuously warm. Yellowknife was like a summer residence, a northern resort. It was Summer itself. Children were in the playgrounds all night long.

Harry's little white house on Latham Island overlooked Back Bay, an extension of Yellowknife Bay, itself an arm of Great Slave Lake. One evening he enticed Dido to spend time with him by offering to take her sailing on the bay. Later the same week they went out in his canoe, paddling across Back Bay to the tiny abandoned cemetery on the opposite shore. Dido asked to get out and wander about, and it was there, in that spot, that she first smelled invisible apples.

"'Transparent fruit,'" nodded Eleanor a few days later when Dido thought it wise to bring her along as a chaperone. The pleasant odour, pervasive but without a source, made Eleanor think of other phrases that captured the North as it lit up the human imagination. "Garden of Desire." "Country of the Mind." She was sitting in the middle of the canoe as if she were a factor for the Hudson's Bay Company. "My father would have loved this," she murmured as they paddled her around, a woman who seemed older than she was, closer to fifty than forty, but she had always seemed older than she was, always an Eleanor, never an Ellie.

That evening Dido stayed alone in the cemetery, while Harry and Eleanor explored the shore. She was kneeling in the long grass, trying to make out the name on a weathered wooden cross and thinking of her father in his tweed cap and trench coat, an anglophile until the last. She had learned about his sudden death three weeks after it happened, in a letter from her mother, an act of casualness that still dumbfounded her. Now, in the sloping, overgrown shadiness of a faraway cemetery, something extraordinary happens. She hears him call her name. *Dido.* And she looks around, exactly as she did when she first caught the sweet smell of apples in the air. *Dido.*

Her heart opens wide and she trembles. The voice is real. Not old or quavery, but clear, unmistakable, as confident in her as ever. A steady, loving voice. Not wanting to break the spell, she stays kneeling for several minutes and says nothing to the others.

That night she sleeps a long, deep, uninterrupted sleep, and in the morning she dresses for work knowing she is equal to whatever lies ahead. At 5:30 p.m., when she reads the news, her accent is gone and each word seems to pronounce itself.

It was like putting my foot on firm ground, she marvelled a few days later when she confessed what had happened.

Gwen gave her a look of honest envy, keen and wistful. She had always wanted the same kind of miraculous release. To be caught up in something so remarkable that she was taken completely out of herself.

* *

Slender-hipped Dido. Who did not fall in love with her that summer? Who did not notice her habit of holding her mug backwards, embracing it with both hands and lacing her fingers through the handle? Or recall that she drank her coffee black? Or remember her boast that she had a Thermos of coffee at her bedside in order to indulge herself first thing in the morning before getting up?

Harry thought her voice sounded like a tarnished silver spoon. He listened for it coming down the hall, catching her unusual scent first. Patchouli, she told him. A heavy, dark-brown fragrance from the other side of the world.

Dido was slender despite having wide shoulders and thick wrists and big hands. Reliably kind despite being reliably hurtful. A long, pleasant evening might be the prelude to a single, crushing remark: "Harry, you grunt like an old man when you lift that canoe." Yet she was zealous in her compliments and capable of the most reckless intimacy.

That she would marry a man younger than herself, for instance, yet be more intrigued by his father even before she met him, her sense of attraction building from the son's initial description and abetted by his answers to her many questions, until she had a clear picture of the driven, moody, hugely successful businessman so good with his hands he had built his own forty-foot sailboat and named it *Nansen*.

Then she did meet him and he was brown as a nut from sailing – in a black polo shirt, white cotton trousers, bare feet. Immensely good-looking in his deep tan. Holding by the hand a nappied, towheaded grandson. Standing in the driveway as she drove up for the first time.

They walked to the beach together, they swam. He carried a bathing cap of sea water to wash off her sandy feet, put sun-warmed stones into her cold hands, took her sailing. Married, he was, to a woman who was afraid of water, whereas she of the soft, unshaven legs loved the sea.

In her father-in-law's home there were no rooms where they could hide, an open-concept, gravity-defying house on the side of a hill. A mistake, he said to her. If you do not have a door to close, you do not have a door to open.

Then move, she said.

You make it sound simple.

You're not *old*, she said.

She was twenty-seven, he was fifty-eight.

It was she who moved, leaving his son one day and coming north.

25

If her father-in-law loved her enough, he would find her. But a year had gone by.

Whenever Dido entered or left a room, eyes followed her. "You watch her just like a man," Eddy the tech. said to Gwen one day. Red hair, small eyes, tall, lean, older, in a town where "older" meant thirty-two, Eddy was an unsettling presence. He looked right through Gwen as she blushed, the innocent up and down of her scrutiny under scrutiny. "Your eyes were on her body," he said, "just like a man's."

Uncomfortable, uncomfortable. And just a taste of what was to come.

A station break. All she had to do was sit at the control board in the announce booth, lower the round dial – it was called a pot – that controlled the feed from the network, flip the switch, and open her mike by turning another pot, then give the local and regional weather.

Harry was with her. "Watch the clock," he told her. "At twenty-nine seconds, get the network back up."

At thirty-one seconds, Harry reached over her shoulder with experienced hands and lowered one pot (her mike) and raised the other (the network). Toronto came back in mid-word, and Gwen was giving the final temperatures to a dead microphone.

She turned around and located his face.

"The first time is the worst," he said. "I've known announcers who opened their mouths and nothing came out."

She clenched her hands. Cold, clammy.

Harry said firmly, "You've got to keep one eye on the clock as you read."

Then he took her hands, his own being warm, and held them for a moment. At his comforting touch, life came into her again and she said, "That was awful!"

She had been dropped in front of a microphone, like a child

dropped out of a sack: no mother, no father, all alone on the highway of sound.

"'Thro' the jaws of Death,'" quoted Harry, "'Back from the mouth of Hell.'"

"The Bible?"

"'The Charge of the Light Brigade.'"

"Kipling," she said.

"*Tennyson*."

And she buried her ignorant head in her hands.

* *

After two weeks in Yellowknife, Gwen managed to find a furnished basement apartment on an unpaved side street that ran off Franklin Avenue. She was told she was lucky. In general, decent housing was hard to find and rents were atrocious. In her small, anonymous living room, however, she missed the domestic companionship of Eleanor and her roommate. We shared suppers and breakfasts and the stories of our lives, she thought.

Dust drifted in through her open window and gathered on the books piled on the floor beside her bed. She wrote her name on the mirror. A block away was the public library, where she had gone to hear a visiting poet read. To the southeast, a five-minute walk away, was the radio station, where she was not doing very well at all. A place utterly contained, enclosed, yet voices carried beyond the horizon. She *was* the horizon to those listening.

One day Dido came upon her standing stock still in the record library, moaning to herself. "Don't think you're the only one," Dido assured her. "I cringe when I hear myself too."

But Gwen did not believe her. Dido lived outside embarrassment – in the free and easy woods of herself.

Dido was never slapdash, never in a hurry. She brought to every task the same care that Gwen's father brought to the repair of a wristwatch or necklace or alarm clock. After eating a sandwich at her desk, Dido would brush her teeth in the washroom in the basement, taking twice as long as Gwen would have taken had she bothered, plying her toothbrush like an artisan working with ivory.

"You're so good on air, Dido." Gwen was standing with her arms wrapped around herself. "You make it sound simple."

Dido smiled. It *was* simple. What could she say? It came naturally. "It's a piece of cake for me. Do I say it correctly?"

"You say everything correctly."

Dido smiled again. She liked Gwen – the way her face lit up and she stopped whatever she was doing to talk for a while, to ask her opinion, to listen.

"Try to slow down," Dido advised her. "You go too fast. But you sound better than you think you do." She pushed Gwen's hair off her troubled forehead. "You don't believe me. But I always say what I think."

Dido's unconventional beauty went hand in hand with the light. Officially, the June sun set close to midnight and rose three hours later, but it never got dark. Dusk, yes. Between sunset and sunrise there was a soft sort of dusk and the street lights came on, but nobody needed them or noticed them. The constant light was like endless caffeine.

One afternoon, as Dido stood talking to Eleanor, Mrs Dargabble came through the door, wearing a white-and-black scarf on her head. A wrap of sorts half fell off her shoulders and her red lipstick was in motion too, travelling like water through sand into the fine wrinkles above her lips and the deep fissures below. Mrs Dargabble exclaimed to Eleanor, "I had to see Dido here in Yellowknife!" Then she greeted the woman in question by quoting Shakespeare, "'In such a night stood Dido with a willow in her hand.'"

From her receptionist's desk, Eleanor watched Dido deal with one admirer after another. It was like being close to a beehive, the steady hum of light and attraction, and the mystery at the core. People were drawn to the North and in the North they were drawn to Dido, so it seemed, and Dido managed herself very well. It was an art, appearing interested while saving the main part of yourself for something better.

Mrs Dargabble was telling Dido that once upon a time she had been a hard-working seamstress with a lucrative business designing clothes. But then she met her husband – her first husband – a lovely man, from Boston like herself, who begged her to "jump". He urged her to be colourful and rambunctious and carefree, to shed her responsibilities and marry him instead. We came north together, she was saying, we set up a business raising dogs until – may he rest – he drowned ten years ago.

Gwen came out of the newsroom, and the old woman caught her hand as she walked by. "You're so soft," Mrs Dargabble said to Gwen with traces, still, of her Boston accent: yo-ah for you're. "So soft. My husband told me to jump. You must *jump*."

"Jump?"

"You must *jump*."

Gwen made an agonized face and continued on into the studio.

Mrs Dargabble had taken the chair that Eleanor always offered. It was on the side of her desk near the window and next to a small table of plants, avocadoes and oranges in pots, started by her from seed, and a handsome jade plant of uncertain age that Ralph Cody had given her after he saw her reading Ezra Pound's *Cathay*. She had heard his voice once, the poet who slowly went mad on the air. A short clip of one of his fascist broadcasts for Radio Rome. Young Gwen could not have sounded more different. She was reading the news now, coming over the speakers in the hallway. Her voice irritating, whispery. Like someone standing behind you and playing with your hair.

Dido was listening too, without comment, but she felt like stepping into the studio and taking over. She became aware of Eddy, who was leaning his long, sinewy body against Eleanor's desk, ignoring everyone except herself. He fixed her with his small, intent eyes. He wanted to know if she had ever been to Prosperous Lake. He was driving out there tonight.

"I'm sorry," Dido said, feeling and sounding invincible in her formality. "I have another engagement."

"What engagement?"

His expressive eyes – how small they were – did not let up, and against her will she laughed a little.

"What engagement?"

"We're going to the movies."

"Who's 'we'?"

Dido licked her dry lips. She did not like this man and did not feel the need to answer. He smiled and shrugged and headed out the door.

After he left, Mrs Dargabble said something so quietly Dido wasn't sure she had heard properly.

"Perhaps I'm wrong," Mrs Dargabble said. "But I don't think so."

"You don't think I should get mixed up with him." Dido looked thoughtfully out the big plate-glass window with its view of the street and saw Eddy heading up to Franklin Avenue. He carried himself with easy pride, like a professional soldier on leave. And she took away the image of a man pacing himself to outlast any number of wars.

IN THE LITTLE BOOTH OF LIGHT, SPEAKING INTO THE SILVER fruit hanging off the silver bough, Gwen struggled with the words on the greens. They twisted a little and moved away, capitalized, cagey. She tightened her grip on the page and stumbled. Alone, but heard for miles, she winced and stumbled again.

The news. Gwen Symon was reading the news. She heard herself make the mistake in her head and then she made it on air in a small voice flattened by panic. She remembered the fat actress with stage fright in "On Stage", who lost weight by eating lettuce without any salad dressing and got over her fright by imagining that everyone in the audience was a rabbit.

Her voice came over the speakers in the hallway and then she herself came out into the hall – greens in hand and white-faced – as white-faced, thought Eleanor, as George VI after the crown was put on his stuttering head. Gwen carried the greens back to the newsroom and gave them to one of the two newsmen, who took them without looking at her – she who had ruined their long day's work in fifteen minutes by booting one story after another.

Eleanor, from her safe perch, heard it all. Harry stopped on his way past her desk and said with a grimace, "I could hear the sheets rustling." He recognized the softness of uncertainty, of nakedness, of no confidence at all. The loneliest voice he had ever heard.

"You should help her," Eleanor said to him.

He jigged his head back and forth, as if considering it, and turned towards the door.

"You're helping Dido," Eleanor called after him, "who needs it less."

Alright. He would teach Gwen how to read, as he had taught his sister how to drive, how to navigate the lines of words, the lanes of vocabulary without embarrassment, accident. How to look ahead so that her voice flowed, rather than straight down at one stumpy phrase after another.

"I pretend I'm talking to one person," he told her the next afternoon in his office.

"I'm no good at that. I seize up. I run out of things to say."

She was watching his sensitive mouth. She would take away the memory of him smoking, and the spit-spit sound of getting the bits of tobacco off his tongue and lip. And of the three unfortunate things that were to happen to him that winter, one after the other, three months in a row.

The question she asked: How can you be a personality on the air when you have no personality?

That's good, came Harry's answer. Self-doubt is good. Most announcers are full of themselves, they're so in love with the sound of their own voices. You don't want a plummy sound. You don't want to be Henry Comor the second.

Gwen flared up. She loved Henry Comor, she told him. She had listened to "Hermit's Choice" every Saturday night when she was sixteen.

"Gwen, Gwen. Why weren't you out partying?"

Because nobody invited her. Curled up in the big armchair beside the varnished standing cabinet that contained the radio, she listened to Henry Comor interview well-known actors, writers, professors, journalists, politicians about what four books and four records they would take to a desert island, what in their solitude they would rely on for company. It was Robinson Crusoe-in-advance. Emotional seafaring on the airwaves.

She liked Comor's voice speaking *to* her, unhurried, and then to his guests. One of his guests, she remembered, was a professor of French who chose Stendhal's *Scarlet and Black* as one of his four books and talked about the very sad moment in his life when he discovered that Stendhal, who was short, fat, ugly, and too intelligent to be agreeable, died young, in his fifties, without having achieved his simple aim of being loved for himself. Then there was the Montreal poet Louis Dudek, who sounded like a farm boy and chose Joyce's *Ulysses*, since he wanted a book he could labour on. There was J. Frank Willis, the voice that reported the 1936 Moose River mine disaster with three-minute broadcasts every half hour for sixty-nine hours, day and night, without sleep. His breathing was heavy the night she heard him with Henry Comor, his voice like tyres on a gravel road leading to a summer lake. He chose George Gershwin, saying that the night Gershwin died, artists gathered at the Hollywood Bowl and played his music for seven hours straight.

Henry Comor's voice changed, depending on his guest. Anyone with an English accent, and his own voice got more posh. But she did not blame him, or any of them. She found it all too interesting. "It was wonderful company," she said to Harry.

Harry did not seem to be paying attention. But he was.

"How did you come by that bruise?" He pointed to her throat, and her fingers went to the fading colour. "If you don't mind my asking."

Outside, a car door slammed. A town where you could hear every sound. She saw a piece of paper fly across the street and wondered how much snow would fall in the winter and how cold it would get and whether she would still have a job in radio by then.

What happened, she said finally, still staring out the window behind Harry, was a scary encounter on her way to Yellowknife. She was north of Edmonton, near the Alberta–Northwest Territories border, when she asked a nice-seeming farmer, thirty or so, not old, about a campground and he offered his lane as an overnight camping spot. In the middle of the night he came into her tiny trailer and she jerked awake, sitting up with a pounding heart. He put his finger to his lips and whispered that he liked long hair on a girl. Then he bent over and pushed his mouth hard against hers. She shoved him away and his voice turned mean. *What's the matter? You don't like men?* He must have used the side of his hand. Striking her across the windpipe so hard she choked. But then, amazingly, he left. She got herself dressed and peeled out of there, and when it began to get light she pulled over to the side of the road and dug out her nail scissors and cut off her long hair.

Gwen looked over at Harry's concerned, assessing face and said, "I know. I know what you're thinking." He was thinking – she thought – that she had put herself in danger and was lucky to have escaped. That she was asking for trouble.

"What am I thinking, Gwen?"

"That I'll never get work in a hair salon."

He liked the joke. But that was not what had been in his mind. Gwen waited.

"I think you're intrepid," he said.

She ducked her head to hide her pleasure. Her face was warm. "Harry?" Looking at her hands.

"Gwen."

"That person you pretend you're talking to when you're on the air?" She looked up. "Who is it?"

Harry smiled. "My imaginary listener? He's a man in his sixties who comes home tired from work and he goes down to the basement to his workbench and builds model boats. And while he's doing that he listens with rapt attention to me."

"So it's not somebody you know?"

"Not somebody I've met," he said.

She nodded slowly, and Harry said, "Who do you feel comfortable talking to?"

You, she thought. "Nobody," she said.

"My favourite person. Now give him a hat."

She thought for a moment. "A fedora."

"Fine. What else is he wearing?"

Into Gwen's mind came a middle-aged man puttering around a kitchen. He wore a wedding band, but he lived alone. A widower. He cooked for himself. His radio sat on the kitchen table. He had it on whenever he ate – it was always on. Before he went to bed he cleaned up, doing the dishes, setting up his coffee for the morning, sipping a final glass of Scotch. I could talk to someone like that, she thought.

*　*

In the quiet house in Ontario where Gwen grew up, her father used to sit at the head of the table and crack Brazil nuts so painstakingly they came out whole, while her bruised and fractured walnuts whizzed through the air. Nearby was Owen Sound, which gave her the notion that you could be stuck in a certain sound for the whole of your natural life.

Her mother's throat music, for instance. Those purring sounds of affection meant to reassure Gwen's dad. And her soft throat clearing whenever company came and awkward silences fell. It was what "not being able to think of anything to say at the moment" sounds like.

Gwen had a radio in her room, installed the summer she got poison ivy. 1961. In that little town of woods and rocks, trails and leafiness, it had been her fond habit when small to pull leaves off the mock orange and stuff them as money into her dead grandpa's old tobacco pouch that closed with a zip. Her homely, slight, small-bodied grandpa from Manchester, who had wanted to go to China as a missionary but ended up in Canada instead – a spiritual man, an odd duck. One day, out and about with the family dog, Gwen forgot to think – forgot to look out for the three glossy leaves, and besides, where she was they were everywhere. She pulled down her shorts to pee, and her bottom was tickled by the leaves she was not paying

35

attention to. Then, in an excess of affection for the dog, she hugged him, this well-travelled connoisseur of every poison-ivy patch, and rubbed her face against his fur.

The itching began several hours later and had a visual equivalent. For dinner her mother served sausages, fat fingers with a grease-gagging flavour that brought tears to her eyes. Two halves of one misery. She shifted in her seat, her bottom crawling, but wasn't allowed to rise until the sausages were gone. (One day, in her late twenties, she would meet someone – her future mother-in-law – who would say, If I knew my kids didn't like something, I didn't serve it. Gwen would look at her with the wonder most mortals reserve for sightings of God.)

From ankles up to and across her bottom, then up to her face and into her eyes, she was soon ablaze and oozing with rash, blisters, torment. Her mother had her lie naked on the bedsheet, where she was too far gone for books or even the ink-induced spasm of excitement that came with the arrival of the *London Free Press* and the ongoing story of Mary Perkins.

A solution of cool water and baking soda, everywhere but on her private parts, which also raged, since her fingers had wandered there too. Her mother wrapped her hands in strips of flannel and Gwen ran her swathed hands across her chest, and the gentle relief of that light scratch, followed by the renewed, Job-like escalation of itching, made her understand the word torture.

Then one day came the radio. Installed beside her bed, turned on. She escaped on the highways of the air. The Archers, John Drainie (reading a story she would never forget about a woman strangled by her long scarf when it caught in the wheel of her convertible), Max Ferguson as Rawhide, the weather, the farm broadcast. Once, as part of the farm broadcast, there was a horse auction with all the sounds of buying and selling, while in the background a young girl sobbed. There were suffering people in the world besides herself, Gwen learned. There were people who were heartbroken.

Thinking back, it was a childhood of warts, wens, carbuncles, poison ivy, and trench mouth, this last affliction treated with gentian violet, her gums painted an astonishing violet-blue. Buttons were lost in the schoolyard. Shirts torn. All this was before television, though not technically. But her parents remained in the pre-television era, doing without one, eventually cancelling their subscription to the *London Free Press*. Living in silence, except for the radio.

The dusty pale pink of calamine lotion.

In her bedroom loose white curtains moved in the breeze. A sleeping-porch spacious with lack of anything but a white bed and bedside table and straight-backed chair and chest of drawers – and the movement of air through screened windows as gauzy curtains swelled inward. In another part of the house the telephone rang. But not here. Not in this outpost of quiet.

And over the radio one night came the story of John Hornby, and something happened that she had almost despaired of ever happening. From having been locked in (at the end of a chapter, the poison-ivy chapter), she entered somebody else's life and saw it from beginning to end. A man who starved to death. A man whose mistakes caused the death by starvation of his two young companions. A blue-eyed, soft-voiced, lucid madman, who courted hardship and seemed absolutely fearless. Gwen liked him enormously and fell under the spell of the desolate North.

"YOU CAN TELL SO MUCH ABOUT A PERSON BY HEARING his voice," said Dido. She was in Eleanor's kitchen, drinking up her coffee. The radio was on in the background, an announcer introducing choral music.

"I wonder," replied Eleanor, who had gone to church that morning, reviving a habit she had given up years ago. "I wonder how much you can really tell." She remembered what her father had said about hearing Stalin on the radio in 1943: he had the warmest, sturdiest, most trustworthy voice he had ever heard.

Dido's hands were wrapped around her coffee mug. Her hair was loose, her reading glasses in her pocket. "Gwen sounds like she's falling asleep on air. I can't listen to her."

"Give her time," Eleanor said.

She knew more about Gwen's past than Dido did, she knew Gwen had been having troubles with her family, she had run away in a sense. But even if Gwen had not confided in her, she would have assumed something was wrong. There was her strange pallor, which made Eleanor think of Byron's ivory-pale skin, the result of overeating, then eating nothing, and since she had watched Gwen starve herself at breakfast only to overindulge at dinner, she guessed the girl might be self-denying and gluttonous, in turn. There was her consistently drab wardrobe, and not a trace of makeup or a bit of jewellery.

"She seems to want to erase herself," Eleanor said, "so it's strange she's on the radio. It must be hard to have everybody listening to you."

"Or does she want to draw attention to herself?" Dido, impatient, swept her dark hair off her face. "She's always talking to me about how bad she looks. I don't mean to say," altering her tone, "that she's aware of how she talks. I don't think she knows herself very well, actually. Anyway," she said abruptly, "let's get back to me."

Their eyes met – amused – and Eleanor forgot about Gwen for the moment.

"When can I move in?" Dido said.

"Tomorrow, if you like."

Lucky Dido. For almost a year she had been sharing a small bungalow with two other women who did not know the meaning of the words *quiet* or *clean*, and it was more like camping out than living. Tomorrow she would move her things into the small and tidy bedroom left vacant by Eleanor's previous roommate, who had decided suddenly she could not face one more day in Yellowknife, let alone one more winter. Dido would have the run of the mobile home, the use of Eleanor's books, the pleasure of her civilized company at a monthly rent that was lower by a third than what she had been paying. I'll stay here one more year, Dido thought, and then I'll go somewhere entirely different.

*   *

One night in mid-June Dido and a former teaching colleague went to a party in Old Town that featured caribou burgers and kegs of beer. On a big deck overlooking a rocky slope with the bay in the distance, she discovered a crowd of strangers, men with huge bellies and heavy-handed hospitality and horrible opinions. She wondered if Texas was like this. She heard someone say, "If you're a white man, vote for a white man." She heard someone else say, "Any girl can type. We'll just drag a squaw in off the streets."

Dido saw the racism more clearly, seeing it with a newcomer's eyes. These were businessmen who believed the North belonged to them. They smelled money, she thought. They couldn't wait for the gas and oil to flow, and so they had no time for the inquiry into the proposed Mackenzie Valley pipeline. They hated the tax dollars it was soaking up and the delays it was causing. They resented the platform it was giving to natives, environmentalists, do-gooders of every stripe. They belittled the government-appointed judge who was running it. *Berger*. She heard the name being bandied about with contempt. But the pipeline was going ahead, she also heard them say, nothing would stop it. Government was behind it, big money was behind it, real northerners like themselves, who put their shoulders to the wheel and prospered, they were behind it.

Overhead were ravens and lake gulls, all around were low hills made of the oldest rock in the world bathed by the most beautiful light on earth, and lovely miniature birches, and small flowers clinging and spreading. Dido had learned recently that this rock was the very rock she had failed to drive tent pegs into three thousand miles away in Ontario, on an ill-conceived camping trip with her ex-husband: it was all part of the great Canadian Shield, a connection that ran deep and underfoot, though on the surface it failed to bring even two quarrelsome people together.

After a while, she gravitated towards a less crowded corner of the deck and saw Eddy leaning on the railing, his loose hips, long legs. He was staring off into the distance. She glanced his way several times, but not once did he acknowledge her. She went to stand next to him. She rested her arms on the railing beside his, and he said to her, "These people are despicable."

"Then we agree about something."

He looked her in the face, his eyes full of anger. "Racists run the show up here," he said.

"I know."

His harshness appealed to her and surprised her. She began to ask him about himself, and he responded and not with small talk.

He had grown up in California, the son of a house builder who died at the age of thirty-eight, leaving his mom with three kids and no money. Now his troubled boyhood had been stirred up again by the sudden death of his sister-in-law, who had left behind a little girl, only five years old. He had been five, too, when his father died.

"How did he die, your father?"

"He was up on a roof and they say he lost his balance."

His voice was quiet and clean, she thought, unlike Harry's fleshy growl. Eddy was leaning back now, against the railing, his fingers pushed into the front pockets of his jeans.

"Tracey asked me how you spell disappointment," he said.

His niece, she thought. "Disappointment," she repeated softly.

"I helped her sound it out and she got it all except for the second *p*."

Dido made her excuses to her friend, and she and Eddy left the party together. It was midnight. A car went by, having no need of headlights despite the hour. They walked south on Franklin Avenue, uphill, for they both lived in the new part of town. A drunk in a white shirt came weaving down the hill towards them. On his way by he reached out and grabbed Dido's arm and brought his dazed, liquored-up face to within a few inches of hers. Eddy stepped neatly between them and the man reeled off. "Incredible," Eddy muttered, "that he'd do that when I'm right here."

They walked on.

Dido was touched by his account of his niece. She could picture him sitting on the floor beside the little girl, helping her spell out her state of mind, and the girl would feel protected, cherished.

They reached the Yellowknife Inn and Dido said she would take a taxi the rest of the way home. Eddy offered to drive her. He had a truck, his place was just a couple of blocks away – he had not driven to the party, he had ended up there, he did not bother to explain how. No, she smiled, this was fine. He opened the taxi door for her, and once she was safely inside he asked her where she lived, then told the driver where to go, and in the back seat Dido felt a little amused but not displeased. Eddy was looking out for her.

The next morning she was in the bank. Another perfect summer's day, and she was congratulating herself on having come to a part of the world that was dry and light and vast. I understand infinity now, she was saying to her father in her head. From my base point I've come a huge distance to a place consisting, in itself, of infinite distance.

She was at the side counter, signing a money order for her mother in Nijmegen, when a single red rose was set down beside her right hand. She stared at it, then turned, and there he was. Unsmiling, aggressively gallant, intent on being understood. Eddy touched his hand to his heart and held her gaze. And then he turned and walked out of the bank.

Dido followed him with her eyes, then looked down at the long-stemmed rose. And again, from nothing, or almost nothing, her attraction grew.

That night she lay beside Eleanor on Eleanor's double bed, listening to music on the radio, turning the big watch on her wrist and think-ing aloud "about a day on the beach when I was as close to my father-in-law as I am to you, watching all these little birds race along the water's edge". They had found a sheltered place in between the sand dunes, she said, and her father-in-law had told her about the first time he made something with his hands and discovered he was good at it, and it surprised him, not that he was good, but that anyone could be who was interested enough in what he was doing. "'Find something you're really interested in and everything else falls into place.' I was lying on my side, watching the light on his face, and I said, 'O.K., what about some*body*. If you find somebody

42

you're really interested in, does everything fall into place?'" Her voice dropped a little, moved into another register. "I remember the hour exactly, because he spotted this watch in the sand and picked it up and slipped it on my wrist. Half-past-four and he said, 'This is what I think about at night, if you ever wondered,' and he bent down and began to kiss me through my blouse, everywhere, not just my breasts, everywhere.

"Like this," and Dido demonstrated on Eleanor's sleeve. Eleanor giggled.

He had drawn her blouse into his mouth, sucking it up with light puffs of air, a sort of reverse kiss, warm, amazing, the most arousing thing she'd ever felt.

To Eleanor the demonstration felt like being vacuumed by a little vacuum cleaner. "And then?"

"Then he stopped himself. 'I can't do this to my son.'"

The rose was in her room down the hall. Being given a rose should not make such a difference, and yet it did. "Father and son," Dido said. "That's what mattered." She was remembering how every Friday her father had brought fresh flowers home from the market to her delighted mother, whatever was in season, gladioli, dahlias, margaritas, lilies, tulips.

"You mattered," Eleanor said. She was trying to read the changing expression on Dido's face.

"Not enough."

Their heads were inches apart. For another moment Eleanor studied the faraway look on the face beside her. Then she turned on her back and stared up at the ceiling. Dido's words – candid, confiding, self-absorbed – had come so easily that they infected Eleanor with the same ability to touch upon things normally never spoken about. And so on this June night filled with light, when so little sleep was required or attainable, she divulged the secret of her own failed marriage.

She was teaching English in those days and she had fallen in love with a colleague, a married man whose wife was mentally ill. He was very good to his wife, very kind, but always sad. "He talked to me about her all the time, and now and again I went to visit them. He always called her 'sweetheart'. Sweetheart, here's Eleanor. This went on for years, but then she got worse. Well, she became violent. She tore up his clothes, one day she threatened to kill him. In the end she was institutionalized and a year later he got a divorce. I thought he was right – not everybody did – but he had a life to live and so did I. After the divorce I persuaded him to marry me. On our wedding night we lay on the bed – like this – side by side, and he let me touch him, but he didn't touch me back. On our honeymoon he removed his wedding ring. When we got home he wouldn't tell anyone we were married. And then he began crying, he couldn't stop crying."

"Are you saying you never made love?"

"We never did."

"How long were you together?"

"About six months, in 1970."

"That's the year I came to Canada. I arrived in August and in October there was the War Measures Act. I couldn't believe it. I thought Canada stood for peace, and suddenly, tanks in the streets."

"It was a bad year," Eleanor said.

Dido raised herself on one elbow and looked down at her. She smoothed the long wisps of blond hair off Eleanor's forehead, then bent down and kissed her briefly on the mouth, an act of affectionate sympathy that moved Eleanor and took her aback. Then Dido said, "We both came north to escape love affairs. At least you left him."

"No. He left me. I would have stayed."

Dido flashed her a look of disbelief, and Eleanor said, "Sex isn't the most important thing to me."

Dido responded by once again turning the watch on her wrist. She seemed to Eleanor miles away. In another world.

"Tell me," Eleanor said quietly, "where was your husband while you were on the beach with his father?"

Dido looked directly into her face. "Danny adored his mother. He pretty much forgot about me when he was with her."

Eleanor did not think that could have been possible. But she said, "My husband doted on his mother too. What's his name? Your father-in-law."

"Daniel Moir."

"And you're still thinking he'll come to find you one day?"

"I don't know any more."

"But he knows you're here."

"He knows."

Eleanor woke up the next morning and discovered she was not alone. In the night Dido had slipped in beside her; she was curled up on her side, sound asleep. Eleanor lay still for a moment. Then she got out of bed and made coffee. From the kitchen she heard Dido stretch and yawn. She filled another mug and took the two mugs down the hall, aware of the sound of her feet on the carpet. Dido plumped up her pillows gratefully. Eleanor sat at the foot of the bed and watched her friend take her first sip.

Dido smiled at her. "I couldn't sleep."

"It's alright."

"I don't like sleeping alone," she admitted. "I fall asleep, but then I have bad dreams." She sipped her coffee and said slowly, "I woke up from a dream about Nijmegen and I had a real feeling of home-sickness."

"I don't mind. It's like having a sister."

"I knew you wouldn't mind."

Dido intended a compliment and Eleanor took it as such, benign flattery. But it was not really like having a sister, she thought. It was not quite like anything she had experienced before.

* *

She remembers as a girl climbing into an apple tree with a cushion and a copy of Palgrave's *Golden Treasury of Poems*, and staying there till tea time. Her pretty mother had so wanted a pretty daughter, but Eleanor had her father's unfortunate chin and needed thick glasses before she was eight. She was fifteen when they moved to Canada, propelled by the legendary moment in her father's life when he stumbled into a news theatre on Piccadilly, escaping one of London's killer fogs, and saw "The Romance of Transportation" – a jazzy, funny, animated film about a northern country so clean and simple and fresh and refreshing that he asked himself what they were waiting for. It was 1954.

Her father had been an impetuous man, a poetry-loving physician as beguiled by bad verse as by good. McIntyre's deathless ode to the Ingersoll cheese never failed to cheer him up. *We have seen thee queen of cheese / Lying quietly at your ease, / Gently fanned by evening breeze, / Thy fair form no flies dare seize.* He had read aloud to her. Walter de la Mare, Tennyson, Christina Rossetti, Shakespeare. The trouble with Othello, he told her, was that he had no sense of humour, poor wretch. Even Macbeth had a sense of humour.

Her father bought a house near the Ottawa River, then a canoe and an old Hillman, following in the strokes of his beloved explorers in one, retracing the steps of early settlers in the other, and instilling in his reluctant wife and eager daughter a sense of Canada as a northern country. That is what made it special. He had a library of books about the Far North and an old dream of seeing it with his own eyes. Eleanor knew all the names: Franklin, Ross, Peary, Cook, Rasmussen, Stefansson, Samuel Hearne, David Thompson, John Hornby.

On their local travels it was usually just the two of them, since the motion of the car made her mother sick. Eleanor was navigator, co-pilot, chronicler, copying into a notebook words and dates on plaques, such as, AUGUST 28, 1955. *In memory of the services, self-devotion and tragic death of Charles Lennox, Fourth Duke of Richmond, a gallant soldier and governor in chief of Canada, who died here, 28th August, 1819.*

Self-devotion? He was devoted to himself? That couldn't be good, she remembers saying, and her father told her she was quick to pick that up. But no, devotion of self to duty.

Spreading the picnic rug near the stone cairn, setting out the Thermos of tea and the bread and butter and hard-boiled eggs, he had then told her the sad and remarkable story of the fourth Duke of Richmond, who went mad after he was bitten by a pet fox. Nothing happened to him for a little while, but there came a night when he could not swallow his mulled wine and a morning when the sight of water in his shaving basin sent him into a convulsion. At the time, he was travelling by bush trail from Perth back to Richmond, and he kept travelling, careful to avert his eyes from streams or any running water, hydrophobia being a classic symptom of what he was suffering from, namely rabies. His final hours were eked out on Chapman's farm, close to this very spot. Not in the cabin, which overlooked the unsettling waters of the Jock River, but in a dimly lit barn, where he lay on a pile of corn shucks suffering excruciating pain and delirium. At dusk, when the river was hidden from view, they moved him into the cabin and he died soon after, poor wretch.

"Wretch" was one of Ring Lardner's favourite words, her father informed her. Mr Funk, the poet and dictionary publisher, had compiled a list of the ten most beautiful words in the English language, namely: mist, hush, luminous, murmuring, dawn, chimes, lullaby, melody, tranquil, and golden; and the American humourist had responded with a list of his own: gangrene, flit, scram, mange, wretch, smoot with a small "s", guzzle, McNaboe, blute, crene. A blute being a smoker who does not inhale, and a crene a man who inhales but does not smoke.

"Those aren't real words," she had said, "blute and crene."

Her father sucked happily on his pipe.

"*Your* favourite word is knucklehead," she said.

"No. My favourite word is daughter."

"Don't be a blute," she said.

They were thick as thieves.

One December day, close to Christmas, her father invited her to come with him into the country to see a patient, which is how they found themselves driving down a lane at the end of which stood something of a miracle. A tall maple tree in full leaf. Closer, and the tree appeared to be hung with clumps of sod. Closer still, and Eleanor asked what they were. They were partridges, sixteen in number. Sun-seekers, her father said, and he stopped the car. The Burnt Lands of Almonte were behind them, an area of flat, scrubby heath, a natural home for partridges, pheasants, quail. It was a mild December with what the weatherman on the radio called "snow-licking temperatures". As they watched, the sun came out and the tree shone with its unusual fruit. Like something out of antiquity, her father said.

There was another time she remembered as vividly. They had gone one Sunday afternoon for a walk in Rockcliffe Park above the Ottawa River, when suddenly the wind rose and her father, putting his hand on her shoulder, told her to listen. Do you hear the different sounds in different trees? They stood entranced. The wind whispered through the pines and roared through the elms, mournful then tumultuous, reminding him of a line from the past, and he quoted it: *like a lost wave seeking a forgotten shore*. His fine Dew memory often retrieved quotations without identifying them. There would be plenty of time for that. They had a lifetime of poetry to look forward to.

But less than a year later, on the evening of October 22, 1957, her father closed a book halfway through. He had been reading to her as part of his campaign to improve his boyhood French "at your expense", he'd say, since she was near the end of high school by this time and her French was better than his. *La fille qui était laide*. A picture book about a girl so ugly no-one in her village would have

48

anything to do with her, and so she ran away to the forest, where, day after day, one page at a time, the fresh air brightened her eyes, the sun bronzed her skin, the wind lifted and ruffled her hair, and she became beautiful.

But her father closed the book. He was not feeling well. He needed to lie down.

"Sorry. Tomorrow."

He went upstairs to bed and at nine o'clock he died.

There was a day, a few weeks after the funeral, when she put her grief to one side and tried to do something for her mother. She took her for an outing, a change of scene. They went to the National Gallery in the east wing of the Victoria Museum at the end of Metcalfe Street and stood in front of Rembrandt at his less-than-best. The doughy face of Esther, her skin so obviously the product of a cold, northern climate – its range of splotchy colour – and the thin, awful hair. It could be a portrait of you, thought Eleanor, turning to look at the parent she had been left with.

She had been her father's daughter, and she consoled herself by spending long hours at his L-shaped desk in a corner of his second-floor study, surrounded by volume after volume about the North. The faded spines of blue, green, red, and gold were like an ancient springtime that took her back to the earliest scenes of affection. She would always be living her life backwards, she realized, trying to regain something perfect that she had lost.

Her mother, frantic about money, sold the library a year later to Gladys Pyke, owner of Ye Olde Book Shoppe on Gilmour Street. They moved to the small town of Almonte, where everything was cheaper, including their rented bungalow on the highway. Among the books her mother packed up and sold were a Japanese marine book tied together with shoelaces that showed coastlines and islands and clouds and rain, and a book about Japanese artists who would go out into the weather and observe it, absorbing it in every level of their being, before coming back inside to paint. *La fille qui était laide*

Eleanor never found. It must have come from the library, her mother said. It must have been returned. But no librarian then or since had ever heard of the tale.

Finally, Eleanor went north herself, and now in the summer of 1975, a variation of the story was about to unfold in front of her eyes.

ON THE SHORTEST NIGHT OF THE YEAR, A GOLDEN EVENING without end, Dido climbed the wooden steps to Pilot's Monument on top of the great Rock that formed the heart of old Yellowknife. In the Netherlands the light was long and gradual too, but more meadowy, more watery, or else hazier, depending on where you were. In her part of the Netherlands, the rolling and agricultural southeast, winds from the west brought a marvellous, sea-swept clarity, while from the east came all the dust of landlocked Europe. Here, it was subarctic desert, virtually unpopulated, and the light was uniformly clear.

On the road below, a small man in a black beret was bending over his tripod just as her father used to bend over his tape recorder. Her father's voice had become the wallpaper inside her skull, he had made a home for himself there as improvised and unexpected as these little houses on the side of the Rock – houses with histories of instability, of changing from gambling den to barbershop to sheet metal shop to private home, and of being moved from one part of town to another since they had no foundations. All the little and large efforts of settlement intrigued her. Down the shore from the old cemetery on Back Bay there used to be market gardens. Some of the log buildings remained; it was not impossible, with greenhouses, to produce melons and tomatoes in Yellowknife. We Dutch would have stopped at nothing, she thought, we would have turned this place into a northern garden. And that is what pained her most about her Canadian father-in-law, how easily he had given up on her. She remembered one of her father's questions to "London Calling". "What did you mean by the phrase 'a month of Wednesdays'?" And the answer came over the air: "The expression is 'a month of Sundays', but in the particular context 'a month of Wednesdays' made sense." Her father-in-law was not going to come after her, not in a month of Sundays, and not in a month of Wednesdays either.

The man in the beret was Ralph Cody, she realized. She had seen him around the station when he came in to do his book reviews. He folded his tripod and moved along Ingraham Drive, as it was fancifully called, since the narrow little roads on and around the Rock were more cow path than grand driveway. She had read that the Ingraham of Ingraham Drive had been an early settler and hotel-builder who lost both feet and most of his fingers in a terrible boat accident on Great Bear Lake: fire then frostbite then amputation. All of these pioneer families were colourful, storied, and a diversion, Dido firmly believed, from the real story of the First Peoples, displaced and impoverished and now having their audience with Judge Berger, who would not be radical enough in his recommendations. That went without saying.

Dido turned 360 degrees to take in the west, north, east, south of Back Bay, Giant Mine, Latham Island, Yellowknife Bay, Willow Flats, New Town, Peace River Flats. Then she made her way back down the flight of wooden steps to Ingraham Drive and took a side road to another road that led past float plane bases and around to the government dock on Yellowknife Bay. Here there were small warehouses and from one of them came the sound of gentle hammering. She poked her head in the open door, surprised to see Eddy sitting at a workbench. He did not look up and she could have stepped away unseen.

She went in.

He was working on a big old radio set, adapting it to his own purposes, he said when she asked. What purposes? His smile came suddenly, transforming his small eyes. Their depths came alive with an amused, seductive light that went right through her. He told her he knew about electronics from the U.S. army, he had been in the communications corps. What purposes? she asked again, but again he did not answer. So she confessed she had grown up on war stories, or stories of liberation, to be accurate; her father adored both England and Canada.

Eddy had rented one corner of this warehouse, the rest of the space was occupied by rolled-up carpets. He did not have the room in his apartment or the freedom at the station to spread out, and he indicated the array of tools and parts on the long table beside him.

"I wish I knew even half as much as you do," she said, conferring praise, singling him out as special. "Where are your people from?" she asked, and spoke his last name. *Fitzgerald*.

"Ireland originally," he told her. "We don't adore England."

She smiled too and turned the loose watch around her wrist, but she was not finished with her questions or he with his evasions. She asked him where he got the parts he needed. He ordered them, he said. And they arrived in the mail? Exactly.

"What are you doing, Eddy? What are you up to?"

"Do I have to be up to something?"

Their eyes met and it was clear that she hoped he *was* up to something, and he knew it and did not mind.

For a few minutes she watched and said nothing. He was working with the tiniest of screws, using tweezers to pick them up. Eddy's fastidious hands and the rolled-up carpets behind him worked on her receptive mind, and she was brought back to her home in Nijmegen, to their practice of spreading heavy and valuable rugs over tables rather than across the floor. Strangely, she smelled apples again as a light breeze came in through open windows.

Eddy asked her what her plans were for the next few hours.

"Do you want the truth?"

"Always," he said.

"I think I'll stay up all night. I want to see all the changes in the light, the sequence from sunset to sunrise."

He offered to keep her company, if she liked. He would make a pot of coffee at midnight, and he indicated the hot plate on the table. If she got tired he would unroll one of those carpets and they could lie down together for a while. Dido laughed and shook her head. No, she said, she would be fine alone. But her heart quickened and her body opened and ached.

"I'll have the coffee on," he called to her departing back. He could not see her face and the big, shining smile she could not keep from her lips.

Eddy was still at his workbench a little after midnight. She came in and stood close to him. Without looking up, he reached for her wrist and circled it with his hand.

She said, "I've come for my cup of coffee."

*   *

Eleanor no longer found Dido in bed very often now – neither in her bed nor her own.

The first time she noticed her absence she got up and wandered outside, unable to sleep, and looked for Dido's brown car. The shortest night of the year, and no sign of the woman or the car. She had to wonder at the loneliness she felt. Eleanor, Eleanor, you're almost forty, working in a lowly job, writing poetry you don't publish, essentially alone. What are you doing with yourself?

At the station the next day, Dido was as friendly to her as ever, but less talkative. Apparently, Dido was not a woman who felt the need to explain herself, and Eleanor was left to read on her own the signs of something new between her friend and Eddy.

That night, once again, Eleanor could not sleep. She had made a mistake with the measurements when she had ordered new window shades for her bedroom, and light poured in on all sides, giving her what she called Marilyn Monroe nights, they were so blond and sleepless. Finally, she went into her windowless bathroom, closed the door, rolled up a towel and shoved it into the crack between door and floor. Then she sat on the floor in the perfect darkness and suddenly tears were rolling down her face and she did not understand why. I'm not unhappy, she thought. I'm really not unhappy. I've been much unhappier in the past.

About three in the morning she made tea and took her cup outside. She sat on the steps and fell to brooding about her ex-husband, his life with poor Barbara, his life with her, his unresolved life. Then her thoughts drew her back to childhood, to her father, to their joy in each other, their mutual devotion. Moved by some impulse, Eleanor went back inside, crossed to the bookshelves in the living room, and pulled down the first book her hand landed upon. Where the book fell open, she began to read, and the first words were "like imperfect sleep".

"Like imperfect sleep, which instead of giving more strength to the head, doth but leave it the more exhausted, the result of mere operations of the imagination is but to weaken the soul. Instead of nourishment and energy she reaps only lassitude and disgust: whereas a genuine heavenly vision yields to her a harvest of ineffable spiritual riches, and an admirable renewal of bodily strength."

Eleanor read the passage a second time. Saint Teresa was justifying her visions, saying they came from God, not the devil, because they left her changed for the better: not feeling as one feels after imperfect sleep, but renewed and strong.

A lovely coincidence, thought Eleanor, but it doesn't lead anywhere.

Nevertheless, she kept reading. The book was *Varieties of Religious Experience* by William James, and she found herself especially affected by the chapters about sick souls, the divided self, conversion. She came upon the old, recurrent phrases in use for centuries, "inexpressible joy took hold of my heart", "a great change came over me", and thought, These people who find God assume a new flesh tone. Instead of being clothed and lumbered with self, they step naked into a new world. She thought she understood how it worked. Just as you can know by the wreckage of a moment that life will never be the same – your father dies one night when you are eighteen – so an awakened soul understands that from this moment on everything will be different, but rather than pain and sorrow, a reliable joy will be yours. If you take up the challenge.

Eleanor set down the book and closed her tired eyes. Such a big "if".

Later, as she stood under a hot shower, she wondered whether any of her feelings would ever be consummated, or if she were one of those people who is religious without ever having a vision, just as she had been married without ever making love.

WHEN GWEN WAS FOUR YEARS OLD, SHE HAD A YELLOW summer dress with an ice cream pattern. To eat an ice cream cone in that dress, to watch her cone melt and disintegrate while the pretty cones on her dress remained frozen, perfect, gave her a sensation not unlike this one, of seeing typed words on the page turn into a great big mess in her mouth.

She tried to describe to Eleanor what it was like being on air – feet dangling, heart pierced with doubt, head all tangled. And Eleanor thought of Absalom in the Bible – Absalom fleeing an angry King David by riding his mule through the woods, dodging trees and ducking under boughs, until his mass of curly hair got so entangled in the low branches of an oak tree that he hung there, suspended; then along came Joab and thrust three darts through his heart.

Eleanor did not burden Gwen with her recent Bible reading, she just listened and sympathized and understood that time was running out for Gwen. She knew the two newsmen, Bill Thwaite and George Tupper, had stormed into Harry's office, demanding he get rid of her as the newsreader.

Harry had fobbed them off, telling them to have patience, the girl had been reading the news for two weeks, what did they expect? But privately, he began to alter his plans.

A week later, he took Gwen to the Gold Range for a beer. The bar had its own atmosphere. Winter or summer it was the same seedy, over-lit, smoke-filled, hotdog-smelling tavern of small round tables covered with fitted dark-red terry cloth and glasses of beer. "You have to let yourself enter the story," Harry told Gwen with a new note of impatience in his voice. "Enter it and let your eyes move ahead to the end of the line and down to the next line, and your voice will pick up and follow. Read as if you're searching out the meaning of the words."

"But you have a great voice," she told him.

"I've never cared for it."

"It's great."

She noticed Jim Murphy, the morning man, at a table in the corner. He had been there for hours by the looks of it. Jim had given her a couple of lessons in editing tape. Tight-lipped and rushed, but not unhelpful, he had sat in front of the old Studer in the editing cubicle and threaded the dark, slippery, quarter-inch tape through the playback head and up onto the take-up reel, then pressed fast-forward until he reached the part of the interview he wanted to cut. He liked to jockey the reels back and forth by hand, rather like a man screwing lids on two jars at the same time, his ear attentive to the dragged-out whump and thump of words on tape. Having located the precise end of the word he wanted to keep, he marked the tape at that spot with a red grease pencil, then let the expendable sentences spool onto the floor until he came to the next word he wanted, backed up to the intake of breath, marked the spot, smoothed that portion of tape into the grooved cutting slot of the editing block, and sliced the tape with his razor blade. He did the same with the earlier spot he had marked, then he made the two ends meet, butting them up against each other, before pressing an inch-long piece of white splicing tape over the join with his fingertip. Jim was fast, Gwen quite slow at first. But she found the handwork restful and took pleasure and pride in making cuts that no listener would be able to decipher, and in eliminating the stumbles and repetitions and bad grammar of voices on tape. It felt like kindness and a form of magic.

Gwen sent a tentative smile Jim's way and got back something less, a raised-eye acknowledgement followed by a hostile glance at Harry. For the first time, she felt worried not for herself, but for Harry. One of the newsmen, it was skinny Bill Thwaite, joined Jim and then the dirty looks directed Harry's way became double-barrelled.

"Harry?"

He stopped drumming the table with his fingers and smiled at her, an honest shambles of a man who could not bring himself to tell her what he had to tell her.

"Is it hard being the manager? I mean, going from the night shift, when nobody bothered you, to all the hassles of running the station."

"Acting manager. I have no illusions. I've got the job while they figure out their long-term plans for television and the new station they've got in mind. But I'm going to use my time to do a few things."

She watched him tap another cigarette out of his pack, grateful for his faith in her so far, dubious about how much longer it could possibly last. "Such as," she prodded.

"I'm going to defend radio from TV."

His mood became more expansive, and she relaxed a little, believing he would not bother to tell her these things if he had written her off. Radio was like poetry, he told her. At its best it could be, while television was like a blockbuster novel: one made you think and feel, the other dulled your mind. "A radio programme isn't a 'show'," he went on. "It's not showbiz, it's not an assault. It's about one person learning something interesting and telling it to somebody else. You're speaking to one person, remember that. And don't say who you are every fifteen minutes, or give time checks to the second. Is there a listener alive who really cares if it's going to be 5:28 ten seconds from now? Just say it's five-thirty. We're not in Toronto, for Christ's sake."

She looked over at Jim and Bill, who were ordering more beer. "Jim never makes a mistake," she said, her voice envious, wistful.

59

"He's so sure of himself."

"That's his problem."

A remark that made her eyes glisten with interest, for she had had exactly the same thought. Jim was too smooth. He was so smooth you tuned him out.

Leaning forward, "What's his problem?"

"He doesn't think it's hard. To be any good you have to believe it's hard. It's called creative tension." Harry looked at her pale, intense face and read her mind. "And you won't be any good until you're dedicated to something outside yourself."

Gwen considered this. "Is Dido dedicated to something outside herself?"

"Dido's ambitious." His voice was bleak. "She won't stick around radio very long."

"You haven't answered my question," she said.

Harry smiled. He was impressed by these young women, who seemed to know what they wanted, and it was not marriage and children. They seemed smarter and more aware of themselves than men. On the other hand, they lacked what he would call proper arrogance – the arrogance necessary to succeed at something over the long haul, despite your insecurities. Not that he was one to talk, of course.

"You're competitive," he allowed.

"I don't think I am," she answered slowly. "Except maybe in an ingrown way."

Harry laughed and drained his glass. He felt his pockets, patted himself front and back.

"I suppose you've forgotten your wallet," she cracked.

"Hang on." He located it in his back pocket, slapped it on the table, then narrowed his eyes. "But I bet my mother is cheaper than your mother."

"That's impossible."

"My mother was so cheap," he said with energy, "that when she made raspberry jam it was mostly rhubarb. And she never turned on the oven unless she had several things to bake. 'Not for twenty minutes, for *one* thing.'"

"Mine too," Gwen cried, "mine too. She had to have something in every corner of the oven or the heat was going to waste. We used to make a game of hunting for the chips in her chocolate chip cookies. 'Mom? How can you call these chocolate chip cookies?'"

Harry sniggered. "They don't call them chocolate *chips* cookies for a reason, Gwen."

They became aware of the bar again – of Jim Murphy and Bill Thwaite on one dark horizon, while from a nearby table came the low and thunderous rumble of a female voice talking about all these well-meaning left-wing lawyers from southern universities coming up here and telling the natives what to think and what to say to Berger. She personally thought, she did, that everybody should cut the dramatization and stop talking about the past. What matters is now and tomorrow.

"Who's that?" whispered Gwen as the voice blared on about all the bullshit being shovelled around, since who in his right mind would give up clean water from a tap and a centrally heated house and food at the Bay to go back on the land? Why not talk about all the good things we've brought them, all the benefits that make life a lot easier?

"She's been around for years. A settlement manager for a while. A teacher before that. She's a pain in the neck, but she's no fool."

Years ago he had paid a visit to her classroom in Nahanni Butte, where the children, using plasticine, had made uncannily accurate models of every kind of animal and every make of snowmobile. To her credit, she even had them writing haiku.

Harry paid the waiter for their beers, then studied Gwen for a moment. She was chewing her nails, staring at the floor.

He said, "I used to be scared too."

She looked up.

"But then I learned that making a mistake is just something you

61

go on from."

Gwen's eyes did not leave his face.

"I don't mean I felt secure," he said. "Feeling secure makes you lazy. You have to have an edge. The good ones are always nervous."

But you weren't good on television, she thought, you were terrible. She had realized rather suddenly one day that it must have been him, must have been Harry, that night years ago when she was watching television. On her small screen he had been a blurry figure, who seemed out of focus he was so out of place; she saw him stumble and thought oh no, he's going to fall, and she switched channels.

How it perplexed and disturbed her, this question of good nervousness versus bad nervousness.

They headed back to the station. This part of town was no different, really, to the place Harry had known in 1960, when he started out. In those days there were only three thousand people, instead of ten thousand, and there were no subdivisions in New Town, no high-rise, no Explorer Hotel. He had arrived at the end of summer, a refugee from graduate school, and for a few months he had worked at Cominco, one of the two gold mines in Yellowknife. Then he began to do some freelance radio pieces, and before he knew it he had been offered a permanent job. Now, all these years later, he could not approach the station without feeling nostalgic and depressed, both, about life in general and himself in particular. At the corner he noticed a dog limping towards them, and knelt down. A small husky, who allowed him to lift and examine her sore paw. A shard of glass from a beer bottle had lodged between two badly scuffed pads: he removed it.

"If only you could fix my problems so easily," Gwen observed dryly, looking down at the top of his balding head and at his big hands, gardener's hands, she thought.

He let out a short laugh and stood up. Gwen wasn't bad company.

He wondered if the dog might be the one missing from the car that skidded off the gravel near Fort Rae; he would hold on to her and call the police. The dog followed them across the street and into the radio station.

On Eleanor's desk lay the pile of community announcements broadcast three times a day in five-minute time slots, a listing of events and of personal messages.

> Would Henry Wandering Spirit please contact the R.C.M.P. as soon as possible.
>
> Helen Jumbo, you have a C.O.D. parcel in the Ft Simpson post office.
>
> The paediatrician will be at the nurses' station in Ft Smith on Thursday afternoon from one to four o'clock.
>
> To Albert Drygeese: The plane won't be coming in today because of the fog. It will come tomorrow at three in the afternoon. Dad.
>
> The Gene Bertoncini Jazz Trio performs in Yellowknife in the auditorium of Mildred Hall Elementary School this Sunday at 8 p.m.
>
> To the Chocolates in Fort Rae: Debbie Lynn had a baby boy, six pounds, eight ounces. Both doing well.

They glanced at these and other announcements typed on the half sheets of yellow carbon paper. Nobody was looking for a lost dog.

Harry went searching for a water bowl for his new buddy, while Gwen reread the announcement about Saturday night's Raven Mad Daze All Night Golf Tournament on the town's nine-hole golf course, infamous for being made of sand and for having a special ground rule to cover the ravens that swooped down and stole your ball. Seize the moment, Gwen thought to herself. Time to jump. She went down to the technical shop in the basement to ask about signing out the Nagra tape recorder, and that's when she heard what

Harry had been meaning to tell her.

In the basement Andrew McNab gave her a careful lesson in operating the Nagra, a beautiful Swiss machine, he said of the heavy reel-to-reel tape recorder encased in black leather. "You might as well," he allowed when she explained that she wanted to tape part of the midnight golf tournament. "You'll be getting used to late-night hours."

It turned out Harry had consigned her to the night shift, the radio wasteland of 6 p.m. to 1 a.m., but he had not quite got around to telling her.

The dog lay at his feet on the floor of his office when Gwen positioned herself in the open door. "Harry, there's something you haven't told me."

He looked at her over his glasses. She had seen this look before on her father's face when she had come in tenth in a foot race, having previously done rather well in the hop, skip, and jump. Then he removed his glasses and asked her to sit down.

"I'm thinking of calling her Ella," he said, "if the police don't call me back to say someone's got a prior claim."

They both gazed at the dog, who did not take her eyes off Harry.

"Old Eller," he quipped.

Having made Gwen smile, he said, "Don't take the night shift personally. It's where every apprentice starts and where some of us choose to end up." He was working the arms of his glasses, tapping them together. "Let me put it this way, you'll be able to work out your kinks a lot more easily." And he told her how much he had enjoyed the solitude and freedom of being the only one in the station, hour after hour. He had found his feet in radio again, regained some of his old confidence. After seven o'clock the station was pretty quiet, he said. There was a certain amount of busywork, tapes to set up, the logging machine to maintain, sound carts to record, sometimes a news feed to send or receive, weather stats to be gathered by telephoning the weathermen at the airport, and the live station breaks every hour. But there was plenty of time to listen to music; he had needle-dropped his way through innumerable records, selecting songs for the hour from midnight to 1 a.m., when local radio took over from the national network. At 1 a.m. you signed off and shut down the station. He missed it, he said. It was a great place for trying things out, you could be as creative as you liked. Besides, he added, she would be doing him a favour; the casual who had been filling in for a month had taken full-time work elsewhere.

Gwen listened and adjusted, and by the end of their conversation felt almost pleased. Until the next day, that is, when she learned that Dido, who among other things had been doing Radio Noon, would become the permanent newsreader as well.

Later that day, Gwen took the gradual slope downhill to Old Town. To have water on both sides, to know which way was north, to be walking towards it – this was comfort by any measure.

It came to her suddenly that what she missed most was frankness. So much of the time you were not allowed to say certain things. You were not allowed to say you were lousy. Nobody wanted to hear it. You were not allowed to say you were jealous. As she walked along, the voice started up inside her head, asking her about the biggest obstacle she had ever faced. Probably my own jealousy, she confessed to the shadowy, sympathetic, ever-impressed voice. In my early years in radio, I was very bad. I know, it's hard to believe, but something about radio made me even more self-conscious. In Yellowknife I worked with Dido Paris and she was such a natural. The name means nothing to you? Well, she was wonderful on air. I wasn't like that at all.

"You're deep in thought," Ralph Cody said.

She had slowed down and was saying these things to herself, so busy being a famous old woman looking back on her past that she was not aware of anything else.

Ralph had his camera bag over his shoulder and was heading to the causeway that joined Old Town to Latham Island, so Gwen went along, glad of the company, and learned that in the 1930s, before they built the causeway, a woman named Bertha used to row people across the narrows for a nickel a head, and that a family named Cinnamon had moved up from Vermilion and become prominent in Yellowknife, "creating a veritable rainbow of names", Ralph crowed. In those days, he said, you could meet a woman in the Wildcat Café and get married by a priest who doubled as a magician and have your wedding in the Squeeze Inn.

Ralph's fine grey hair blew about and his small, nicotined hands were deft with tripod and camera. To Gwen he seemed old and thin and irresistible, like her high school English teacher who taught her to love Shakespeare. Mr Smiley had been a pilot in the war and had lost his sense of smell, a stroke of luck, he liked to say, since thereafter he was spared the smell of women's perfume. A cynic. Yet for all that, you knew he loved women, perhaps too much.

Gwen wanted Ralph to know the reason she was free in the middle of the day, and Ralph asked how she felt about it, being moved to the night shift. He himself was something of a nighthawk, he confessed, working on his educational contracts after dark, when he was not reading the books he reviewed for radio; daylight hours he saved for photography, though in the summer he could photograph around the clock. Gwen said she felt alright, but she wished she were better on air. Ralph told her she sounded fine.

Gwen considered this. "I wonder if you mean that." And her bleak challenge made him smile.

"A woman trolling for compliments," he said. "You sound fine. But if you *want* to be jealous," he added mischievously, "you're not as good as Dido."

He set up his tripod on a flat rock that extended into the water, then stepped back. "Take a look."

Gwen bent over and peered through the lens at weeds in water. To her eye the sinuous grasses were like long filaments of silver drowning in a watery sky. She came from a family of jewellers, after all. Her father and uncle, and a great-uncle too. The great-uncle had gone west from Ontario and opened up a jewellery store on the Prairies, and she liked to imagine him working with tiny, intricate objects under a vast Saskatchewan sky.

She said, "I don't want to be jealous, but I am." So jealous she had even gone shopping for the kind of scoop-neck T-shirts Dido wore. She was wearing one now, as well as a short necklace of blue beads.

"I don't photograph people as a rule," Ralph said. "But I'd make an exception for Dido."

The hair on his head blew in the other direction and his scalp shone as he bent over his tripod. Thinning-haired Mr Smiley used to lean against his desk and read Shakespeare's sonnets aloud, weaving in jokes about beautiful women losing their looks. We aren't here for long, he would say. And that turned out to be true, for he died very suddenly in his sixties.

"Dido's my first Dido," Ralph added after taking several shots. "Apart from the opera."

Gwen folded her arms. "Well, don't enlighten me. See if I care." And it relieved her feelings to speak with rough humour.

Ralph looked up and chuckled. So she wasn't a pushover, he thought, and he eyed her with more respect.

The opera he'd meant, he said, folding up his tripod, was *Les Troyens* by Berlioz – about the tragic passion of Dido and Aeneas, and the founding of Rome and the fall of Carthage. "Dido was the Queen of Carthage and Berlioz learned her story at his father's knee. He was reading Virgil when you were reading Dick and Jane."

Ralph liked to talk, liked having a curious and attentive listener. He said the opera was not popular but it was very powerful, especially at the end when Dido kills herself, since in her dying moments she has a terrible awareness of what is to come – not only has Aeneas ruined her life by leaving her and sailing off to found Rome, but in founding Rome he has set in motion the last days of her beloved Carthage. "Do they teach you about Carthage these days?"

Gwen waved her hands to indicate vaguely, she knew vaguely.

"The Romans razed it to the ground. Then they sowed the surrounding fields with salt. That's the North, if the pipeline goes through." He was struck by his own analogy. "Not bad, Ralph. Write that down. Building the pipeline is like sowing the ground with salt."

They walked back to the road, and he told her that last year, during the opera season, he and Eleanor and Lorna Dargabble went into the station on Saturday afternoons and Eddy fed the broadcast from the Metropolitan Opera in New York into the lobby, since C.F.Y.K., in its wisdom, pre-empted the Saturday afternoon opera in favour of a country and western request show. "Bring on Merle Haggard," he intoned, revving himself up. "Get down with Johnny Cash. Let's hear it for Conway Twitty."

Gwen laughed, but she could not picture Eddy listening to opera, and she said so.

"Eddy's a surprising guy," Ralph said. "Eddy's the kind of guy who could be running guns for Angola or writing odes to his mistress."

"I don't think he likes women very much," she said, expressing a reservation she had never articulated before. "On some level he *dislikes* them. Except for Dido, of course. He can't take his eyes off her. Any more than Harry can."

"*I* like women."

"I know you do." She smiled. "I've seen you flirting with Eleanor. I don't mean Eddy's interested in men," she went on, "I don't mean that at all. I just have the feeling he's got contempt for women."

"I would never underestimate a woman's intuition," said Ralph easily. But later, he would have reason to think back on young Gwen's assessment of Eddy.

Gwen got bounced – out into the midnight woods. And there, night after night, through the month of July, she improved. No-one was watching, few were listening, the light was entirely different. Alone in the announce booth, she turned off the overhead light and operated in the jewel-like glow of the little diodes and v.u. meters. She used headphones, since Andrew McNab was not around to chide her about announcers being addicted to the sound of their own voices, and thus she heard herself close by, not ricocheting around an empty room and careening out over empty wastes, but here, in the dark warm woods that resembled in a wonderful way the darkness backstage.

One night in the basement she found a little sound-effects door. Constructed of wood and about the size of an old-fashioned wall telephone, the wee door turned on a hinge and had a bell and a door knob of regular size. With Andrew's permission, she brought it upstairs into her snug little booth, where the control board was carved out as if to accommodate a well-filled belly. Sliding her wheeled chair into its embrace, she operated switches and pots, rolling to the left or right to work the turntables on either side, or to reach the standing rack equipped for reel-to-reel tapes and sound cartridges, the latter carrying station i.d. and music stings: press the square green button to start the cartridge and the yellow button to stop it. In the privacy of her late-night show (in her mind she called it "show" with apologies to Harry), which displaced the network from midnight till 1 a.m., she tried out the sound-effects door, shutting it hard on songs she did not like and opening it wide on its squeaky hinges to welcome singers she enjoyed.

She gave herself a new name. Stella Round. And used it on air.

She experimented with sound. "Can you identify this bird?" she asked into the night, playing a persistent, rather eerie bird call she had recorded through an open window in the early morning hours, not expecting an answer and not getting one either. She recorded Eleanor's impish, girlish, delighted laugh. She recorded a Venetian blind clicking in the wind and Bill Thwaite typing in the newsroom. Ella barking and a raven answering. Then she organized the sounds in a formal way, like music. A phrase, then a repeat of it, then a new sound, and a repeat, then back to the beginning, looping around her neck the long necklaces of dark-brown tape that she moved about and reinserted.

Jim Murphy, listening at home, telephoned her at the station. "Let me air that what's-it, that sound thing again in the morning." O.K. But let her do some fine editing first.

At the old Studer, working with grease pencil, razor blade, splicing tape, and a few take-up reels, she made seamless joins between ambient noise and particular sounds, like a shoemaker leaving behind a flawless shoe for the morning.

With time she had grown more accustomed to the bracing experience of the microphone. It no longer felt like plunging into cold water – in and out – before towelling herself off. She could stay in much longer. A burka for the shy, the nighttime announce booth. A dark tent that covered her up as she crossed the wide desert of late-night radio.

IT WAS HARD TO SAY WHEN THE LARGER SUSPENSE BEGAN. At first, like almost everyone else, Harry had thought there was not much Judge Berger could do. His inquiry was window dressing and everyone knew it. But then Harry realized that the denigrators were missing the point. It was not Berger's job to decide whether or not a pipeline was to be built, but what conditions should be imposed if construction went ahead. Those conditions could be minor or they could be major. At stake was something immense, all the forms of life that lay in the path of a natural gas pipeline corridor that would rip open the Arctic, according to critics, like a razor slashing the face of the Mona Lisa.

Harry and Berger were the same age. In fact, although he hated to admit it, Thomas Berger was a year younger. Harry had met him and sized him up as casually formal, serious, unconceited, tireless, aware that he was facing the biggest challenge of his life and not about to blow it (the way Harry had), the sort of man who listened, the sort of man women could not get enough of. Harry came away impressed and nothing ever happened to make him less impressed. Berger was doing more to bring the issues of the day to the fore than anyone else he knew.

Now, voices that had never been on the radio had their chance to speak. Plain-spoken, same-spoken, tentative yet clear, young and old, in translation or speaking English, usually soft, sometimes strident, native people were convincing Judge Berger that the land gave them life, it was their flesh and blood, they were born and raised on it, they lived and survived by it, they loved and respected and belonged to it, as had their ancestors for thousands of years. Louis Caesar of Fort Good Hope, Lazarus Sittichinli of Aklavik, Fred Widow of Willow Lake, John Steen of Tuktoyaktuk, Jane Charlie of Fort McPherson. Up and down the Mackenzie River Valley the message was overwhelmingly the same. The past had never gone away, had no intention of going away.

The testimony was not unplanned (the native organizations were active in every settlement, urging everyone to speak out and speak with one voice), it was not left to chance, it was *almost* unrehearsed. Roy Fabian of Hay River told Judge Berger, "there's very, very few white people that will be friends with native people. Any of these white people that are friends with native people, it's like a pearl in a pile of gravel."

Tom Berger was a pearl. He listened with grave, courteous, uncommon openness, being a careful speaker himself, and one who took his time. Reporters questioned him about his seemingly infinite patience, his ability to listen for hours to highly technical presentations on the one hand, and to meandering life stories on the other. He explained that from each speaker he tried to learn something new, and indicated that he felt at home with the way native people talked. If the Dene had nothing to say, they did not say it, and the not saying could go on for a long time. "You often just sit there looking at the river."

Berger's distinctive voice became familiar to everyone in the North. Those who heard it would recognize it immediately, no matter how many years had gone by, his firm, thoughtful, soft-spoken voice soliciting expert testimony about the social, environmental, and economic impact of the pipeline, but also the opinions of anyone who would be affected by what would be the biggest project ever built in the history of free enterprise, if it went ahead. Every evening the opinions, arguments, voices were carried by all the stations in the Northern Service in the hour-long coverage prepared by the C.B.C.'s special team of six reporters working in English, Dogrib, Slavey, Hareskin, Loucheux, Chipewyan, and Inuktitut. "Let me put it this way," Berger would explain in his unhurried, tempered fashion, "we have never before in our country had an inquiry before large-scale frontier development was undertaken. So this inquiry is unique in the Canadian experience and really unique in the experience of any industrialized country in the West." And he invited everyone in "this vast Territory where we have people of four races speaking seven languages" to be a part of history in the making.

Although based in Yellowknife, where lawyers for the pipeline companies and the native organizations set out their formal positions, the inquiry would travel over the course of two years to settlements up and down the Mackenzie Valley, to communities on the Beaufort Sea and in the Yukon, and even to major cities in southern Canada, since at issue was the future of the northern wilderness, alternately considered a last frontier by developers and an indispensable homeland by the native people, but undeniably one of the last wonders of the earth.

With July came the smell of smoke in the air from distant forest fires. Trees and ground were tinder-dry after weeks of unbroken warmth and no rain.

Harry walked the thirty minutes home in the evening, his dog, Ella, bounding along beside him as she had in the morning when he had gone to work. They followed Franklin Avenue to Old Town, then crossed the causeway to Latham Island, and the walk gave Harry time to ponder the struggle taking shape on his own small turf. A fancy new C.B.C. station was in the works, to be built on the southern edge of town and to house the new regional television venture, with radio taking second place. In a few years T.V. would reach beyond

73

Yellowknife to every remote settlement in the Arctic and produce a generation addicted to instant gratification – the final death knell, in Harry's opinion, for native language and culture. But did it have to be that way? He knew he was fighting a rearguard action, but so was Berger, and so were the settlements voting in favour of prohibition to turn back the tide of drunkenness and abuse. Harry could not stop the new station from being built, but he could champion radio as more flexible, more forward-thinking, far cheaper than television, and a natural home for northerners.

Most of the time, when he turned into his driveway, his neighbour Louise Corrie was sitting on her stoop next door, smoking her pipe. Louise in her bandana, her brown stockings and ankle socks, mukluks and low rubbers, old skirt and blue jacket. Black Louise, she was called, for her various illicit activities, making home brew for one, and certainly she had a steady stream of visitors, mostly men, at all hours of the day and night. But what she seemed to like best was to sit in the sunshine on the spot of lush green grass directly in front of the door of her shack. Harry would see her there and think "pigeons on the grass, alas," since gulls would land and pick about, drawn by the food she scraped out of her pot. This was where she had sat on the morning a few weeks ago when she had opened a can of paint and to Harry's wonderment and delight painted her brown cane entirely white.

Harry went inside, made himself some supper, fed Ella, and then listened to Dido's voice on the sly. He had made a tape of her reading the community announcements on Radio Noon, and though he tried to ration himself, still, every night her voice filled his house. It was not true that he never tired of it. He tired of it as one tires of even a beautiful song. But to reach that point took a lot of listening. There was a moment when she announced a call for local "thespians" to audition for the drama society, and she giggled, for all the world like a lamb kicking up its heels.

Late one night he telephoned her. "I thought of dropping in to see you."

She was silent on the other end of the line.

"Silence," he said.

"No. It would be nice to see you. But tonight isn't a good night."

The next night, by chance, he happened to see her without being seen. Restless, he had whistled for Ella and they had gone out into the light-filled road around eight o'clock. Louise and her lopsided friend, Andrew, were sitting in front of her shack, Louise with her pipe, and Andrew lopsided, they said, from his habit of throwing himself in front of moving cars in the hope of collecting on the insurance, but never without a huge, goofy, good-natured grin for Harry, or anyone else, who greeted him.

Harry had nothing in mind except following the narrow road to the gently rising hill that overlooked Rainbow Valley at the end of the island – from the hill he would be able to see the valley and the big lake beyond. As he walked along, he passed the snug, well-designed home that belonged to the daughter of George Whalley. Farther on, also on his left and in a clump of trees, was Father Fumoleau's little house, the political priest who had spent years documenting the history of Treaties 8 and 11 to prove the natives had never extinguished their claim to the land. Harry stood just above the priest's house and looked down at the multi-coloured little dwellings that gave the valley its name. Officially, it was Lot 500, fifty-six unsurveyed and unserviced acres set aside for the Indians, the people who had lived on this land for hundreds, if not thousands, of years and now managed on the scraps tossed their way. Harry shifted his gaze to the vast, shining waters of Great Slave Lake.

It seemed to him that spiritual changes come like a gust of wind on a quiet day, blowing a door open or blowing it shut. He was think-ing about Eleanor, who had told him she was going to church again, and he knew she was reaching out for something and it touched him, but he felt more in tune with his mother, who had tried to pray for her sister's recovery from a stroke and suddenly realized there was no point; no-one was listening. His mother had been a better mother

75

than a minister's wife, a wonderful mother, really, despite her threats to feed him ground glass and arsenic if he didn't eat what was on his plate. Well, she should have lived here, he thought, where arsenic was all too plentiful from the milling of gold. For years rumours had circulated about native children eating snow and dying of arsenic poisoning. About children eating the plentiful red berries near Giant and Con mines and getting sick. About horses in the very early days drinking the spring runoff water lying about in puddles at Giant Mine and dying in the autumn, and of a similar fate befalling the cows that were brought north in the late 1940s by a Mr and Mrs Bevan.

Harry was about to turn around and head back to the fork in the road, following it to the less occupied side of the island, when he saw Eddy and Dido come out of a faded blue house down below. They crossed the road together and got into Eddy's white truck. The other day he had watched Dido scratch her head with a pen. She had run the end of the pen through her thick hair at the back of her head, repeatedly and from different angles, like the long handle of a comb, languidly, unconsciously. After she left her desk, he went over and picked up the pen and held it to his nose, pathetic man that he was, trying to smell her hair.

But now he turned and walked fast to get himself around the corner and out of sight. What were they doing there? he wondered. Dido and Eddy.

The curving road on this side of the island was lined with trees, the few houses were hidden, or not so hidden, and most of them occupied by white northerners, a somewhat anxious breed, he had always thought, composed of transients, newcomers, long-timers, old-timers, pioneers – they were the rungs on an ascending ladder of possessive pride about one's stamina and attachment to the North. Who had Dido and Eddy been visiting? he wondered. And why?

*

That night he was lying on his bed thinking about the station – his station – and radio people he had known. Quarrelsome as sparrows guarding their territory, but what issued from them was song, birdsong being proprietary and exclusive. What were people imagining as they listened to radio? How friendly everyone was. How well they must get along, how intimate they must be. Not knowing how they fought to get air time, resisted anything new, stewed in their own jealousy and ill will.

These were Harry's jaded thoughts. He knew he was too friendly with some of his staff, too cantankerous with the rest; it came from being an announcer himself, and from not having his heart in management – programming, yes, but not management. For his own sake, and the station's, he should court the newsmen, bolster them, encourage them, make them feel valued. His radio was on, a low-level irritation at the moment with its yap yap yap of excessive information and mediocre music coming from Toronto. Ella lay on the floor beside him, awake, alert, always ready for a walk. He reached over and rubbed her ears and an idea came to him for a programme, of old songs, old tales, old remedies, old places. He heard the wind and the familiar thudding sounds of ravens on the roof, and stroked his dog's thick coat. His grandfather had been a furrier. Edgar Farnham, his mother's father, a man with wide-set eyes, floppy ears, floppy moustache, a man who liked to talk but only in a quiet room. As a small boy, Harry loved going into his shop in Winnipeg, loved all the fluff on the floor, the pigeon feathers in the windows, the girlie calendars on the walls, the winking men bent over their sewing machines. In the back office, he learned some bits of fur terminology: a thin pelt that crackles is called a "paper", a thick pelt a "heavy". He learned that you can clean fur by tumbling it with sawdust inside a drum; that mink is much cleaner and easier to work with than fox or coyote – shake a coyote pelt and you get clouds of dust. On his fifth birthday, his grandfather gave him a small swatch of mink and it became precious. Without it rubbing back and forth under his nose he could not fall asleep.

He was seven when they left Winnipeg. His father took over the Presbyterian parish in Woodstock, New Brunswick, and Harry drifted naturally into a friendship with a boy who made him think of his grandfather. The two things got mixed sentimentally in his mind: leaving his grandfather, then finding Mark Green, whose family had the only fur store in town.

Not surprising that the first he saw of his wife was her hair. Several long black hairs on the back of a chair. He had picked them off distractedly, thinking they looked oriental, but they turned out to belong to the head of a dark and temperamental Scot.

After she left him, he opened a book one day and noticed a long pencil mark down the page. But it was one of Evelyn's long, dark hairs.

Later that night Harry had the idea of giving a party as a way of seeing more of Dido. He would invite everyone at work and then she would come too. He chose a Saturday in mid-July and spread the word around the station. However, news got bruited about the Strange Range that there was a party on Latham Island at the white house with the red canoe out front, and all sorts of people Harry had never seen before turned up.

Jim Murphy got particularly drunk and had to utter each word very carefully. He kept saying, "You're missing the whole point. Everything you do ought to be bilingual. Every programme ought to be bilingual." And Eleanor listened, surprised he would even have thought about it, and agreeing with him, though why he was telling her rather than Harry was a mystery.

She turned with relief to Ralph, who asked if the name Agnes Deans Cameron meant anything to her. It didn't mean a thing, so Ralph told her about the fascinating schoolmarm from Victoria who wrote a book about her travels to the Arctic in 1908. She visited Hudson's Bay trading posts along her route and read their logs, he said, and discovered in the process an account of the two starving Indian women who attacked and killed a pair of mail carriers on the Mackenzie River, partially devoured them, then made the leftovers into pemmican. Ralph said, "The Hudson's Bay factor asked the women what the flesh tasted like and they replied that 'one of the men was very good but the little red Scotchman tasted of tobacco'." And he roared with laughter.

For his part, Harry watched Dido. He took heart when she needled Eddy about being a teetotaller. Eddy, without rising to the bait, filled her glass whenever she held it out: his wrists narrower than hers, more wiry. They were never more than a few feet apart — if Dido moved away, Eddy was soon at her side, and if Eddy moved away, it was the same.

But there came a moment when Eddy set the wine bottle on the coffee table, and the hard, neat sound of glass on wood marked a shift in the party. In his abrupt, inscrutable way, Eddy stood up to leave, and Harry had all his suspicions confirmed. Between Dido and Eddy things were more advanced than he had wanted to believe, more advanced, more aggressive, more potent.

He growled, "Eddy," halting him in his progress to the door. "How did you end up in Yellowknife, anyway?"

Eddy stayed where he was standing. The music had stopped and the noise of the party had fallen off for a moment. "It's a long story, Harry."

"I'm not going anywhere."

With mild contempt, "Is that right?"

A pause, and then Eddy deigned to give a cold sober account of his movements. About a year ago, he said, leaning against the wall, he was driving around one day, aimless and bored, and he came to a fork in the road. He was in Montana at the time. The sign had two arrows, one pointed north, the other south. He could have gone either way. But the singer on the car radio was Neil Young, so he turned north, and then he decided he might as well follow the road until it ran out, which it finally did on the north shore of Great Slave Lake.

"Are you always so impulsive?" asked Dido, who by now had joined them.

"Try decisive," Eddy said.

"So what was Neil Young singing?" she persisted with a faint smile.

Harry, through the pain in his heart, saw exactly what he was up against. Eddy had no sense of humour, and Dido, serious Dido, did not care. European to the core, she had fallen for the lean, sardonic, tight-lipped cowboy in jeans.

Eddy flipped through Harry's records – then dropped the needle directly onto the first note of "Helpless".

After that Dido stopped giving Eddy a hard time, she yielded her rights to tormenting him. And Harry, watching the play of feeling on her face, understood the power of a song to advance a man in a woman's heart. Songs, he thought, were the seven-league boots of romance.

Dido did not leave with Eddy, though. She stayed, and the party went in another direction. Rapidly downhill. Harry would stand in the bathroom doorway an hour later, and in a state of marvelling despair watch while one person threw up in the bathroom sink, a second put his head in the toilet, and a third vomited into the bathtub. Not long after that, all of the afflicted had passed out on his living-room floor.

Rocking in his rocking chair, Harry presided over the aftermath of his own poor judgment, since he had been the one to open the bottle of tequila. Gwen was sound asleep on the sofa. Two strangers were sleeping next to her on the floor. Eleanor had nodded off in a chair, waiting for Dido. And Dido sat on the floor in the lotus position, awake, alert, wired.

Then began the conversation that Harry would return to whenever he tried to understand Dido and what happened to her. Had he only said something different, had he issued the right sort of warning, had he offered her some other view of herself – who knows, he might have rescued her in time. It was three o'clock in the morning and the rising sun began to touch everything in the room, rosy light on ashtrays, bottles, glasses, bodies. Dido was asking him what he thought of Eddy, what he knew about him. At the time Harry was so busy following the passage of light across her skin, and so disinclined to ponder anything or anybody else, that he simply said he barely knew the man. Dido pressed him, she asked if he thought Eddy was good at what he did. Then he had to admit that he was, that Andrew McNab considered him the best radio technician he had ever had. A look of pleasure lit up and relaxed her face. That look – of basking in what she had wanted to hear, perhaps without even knowing she had wanted to hear it – made Harry realize that Dido was talking herself into something, talking herself into being serious about Eddy. So he said acidly that Eddy was obviously a reformed boozer given the way he turned down anything stronger than Pepsi. She smiled. "Did you know he served in Vietnam?" He nodded. He did know.

Silence. Till Harry hoisted himself to his feet, asking what she wanted to listen to, and Dido said he had done well in choosing the previous record, she'd be curious to see what he chose next.

Gwen sat up with a groan at that point and rubbed her eyes. Eleanor and the strangers on the floor slept on.

"This is the last record for tonight," Harry said, searching for the bagpipe music he favoured whenever he wanted to blast everybody out of his house.

"He won't tell us what it is," Dido said to Gwen. "He likes to hold his chest to his cards. Do I say it correctly? Harry?" He looked over at her. "Do I say it correctly?"

She was so beautiful. Even at this hour she looked elegant, perfect. She was wearing a yellow sweater and he felt old.

"I've got to go home." Gwen was on her feet, swaying.

"You're white as a sheet," Dido cried, and she followed Gwen to the door. "Wait. Your shoelace is undone."

Then Gwen sat on a chair while Dido, quite tenderly, as if Gwen were a child, tied her shoe.

OVER THE SUMMER AIR CAME FOOTSTEPS IN THE SNOW. Gwen had learned from Jim Murphy the trick of kneading cornstarch in a plastic bag to duplicate the sound. Also, how to make ocean waves by sloshing the contents of a hot-water bottle back and forth. Generally, she was alone at the station as she aired her playful sound effects, but sometimes Eddy haunted the record library until she signed off at one in the morning. He had a key to the station, too, and a few times she had gone home, leaving him to lock up.

"The mistakes don't matter," he informed her one night after she stumbled over a station I.D. and apologized on air. "It's the recovery that counts."

If she had a nickel for every one of his smiles, she would have ten cents. She nodded sheepishly, preferring Harry's way of phrasing the same point. *I learned that a mistake is just something you go on from.* Harry's advice gave her a route to follow, a path forward. Somehow Eddy managed to exchange one form of stress for another.

He leaned against the doorway, a paperback Faulkner under his arm, a pen in his hand. Frequently, he brought her records, slipping them in and out of their covers as he introduced her to Lester Young, Dexter Gordon, John Fahey, Sarah Vaughan. With Eddy she always felt even younger than she was. Not *disliked*, revising what she had said to Ralph, not held in contempt, that was too strong. Just examined in passing and discarded. Sometimes Eddy answered her questions, sometimes he did not.

"Harry's in love with Dido too," she said bravely, curious to see his reaction.

"Harry's not good enough for her."

"Are you?"

He had a way of working the clip on his pen with his thumbnail, making a series of aggressive click click clicks. "Why don't you ask if she's good enough for me?"

Something in his manner reminded her of her brother, whom it was never wise to cross. Her brother did not rest until he got his own way; then, having won, he would sweeten. Countless, countless, countless times, she had been sucked in by his forceful personality, his general indifference to her, his occasional delight in her, and then, how did it happen? It was harder to breathe, because she was breathing his air.

"So what's it like to have a third-rate boss?" Eddy asked her, still in the doorway.

"Second-rate," she bristled, then had to laugh since her defence was hardly a ringing endorsement.

"No. Third-rate." Not giving an inch to Harry or to humour.

Then he reached over and began to stroke the back of her neck. "Relax," he ordered, moving directly behind her and massaging with both hands. "*Relax.*" His fingers dug into her neck, hurting her.

She let herself be experimented upon. Or so it felt to her.

"I've got a great record for you," he said.

"What."

"It's perfect for your show."

"Are you going to tell me. Or am I supposed to guess."

"Promise you'll play it."

The record turned out to be *Kind of Blue* by Miles Davis, cool melodic jazz forever ruined by the feel of Eddy's fingers pressing into her neck.

A few days later Gwen went to the town dump near the airport to record the extensive vocabulary of the local ravens, their rasping croaks and rattles and gargles and gulps, their metallic *toks* and *awks* and *ku-uk-kuks* and *quorks*. She discovered in the process how to avoid the wind noises that wrecked the clear sounds she was after. An old umbrella lay on a heap of shoes. She held it open in front of her microphone and it worked like a charm, defeating the wind without blocking the weird and wonderful squawks, or the strong wing-beats overhead.

Eddy appeared while she was there and she asked him what he was looking for, since he did not seem to have anything he was getting rid of. He didn't bother to answer. She took another tack. "Do you mind?" she asked, and she turned on her tape recorder and picked up the sound of their footsteps as they crossed the crunchy ground. Then she directed her microphone towards his mouth. "What brings you to the dump?" she asked. He frowned, but told her he was looking for bicycle spokes. Then he went on. He told her you could furnish a house with what got thrown into this dump. He had found window frames and unbroken panes of glass, perfectly good doors and shelves and kitchen cupboards. He had found radios and television sets and cameras – an excellent camera that he had fixed in an hour.

"People are getting stupider with each passing day," he said. "It used to be that every little town had its repairman who made a nice living mending anything that broke; now something breaks: pitch it." Waving his hand at the dump, "I wouldn't mind if every corporate executive was put in jail."

"You want to be different," Gwen said.

"I *am* different. You want my view of the future? I see a handful of people. A few survivors. The Dene will be O.K. Indigenous cultures. They've still got the basic skills. But the rest of society? Down the toilet."

The ravens croaked and Gwen smiled. "Have I finally found somebody cheaper than my mother?"

She saw his face stiffen. He did not like the word *cheap*. Neither did her mother.

Gwen took the tape back to the station and put together a short radio piece that began with the hoarse and garrulous ravens, proceeded to steely Eddy, and ended with her own impression of what the dump looked like: a shipwreck on dry land. The station had become her workshop, reminding her not just of the backroom in the family jewellery store, but of camping, since everything she needed here was also close at hand. On air, in the dusky light of the booth, she was walking through homes with her voice, along leaf-covered trails, under a canopy of trees, and nobody minded. Listeners in pyjamas took themselves down the path past the outdoor pump to the screened-in toilets, where long-legged insects spent the night on walls and ceiling, around the light fixture, batting at the screen door.

*   *

Everyone noticed the change in Gwen. The girl had laced up the soft shoe of her voice. Now she spoke rather more confidently and not so close to the microphone. Her voice did not make the same sad dive at the end of every sentence.

One night, towards the end of July, Harry appeared in the doorway of the announce booth. "I've been listening to you. You're getting better."

She fastened him with skeptical eyes.

"There's a new warmth to your voice, Gwen."

"I've always preferred the coolth. But thank you, Harry."

Seeing him like this, suddenly, made her ache a little, the way her teeth ached after she flossed them.

He had come to tell her that an old radio hand from Toronto would be arriving the following week to give a six-day training workshop. A good friend of his and a veteran announcer. Abe Lamont. Harry had leaned on him to give up a week's holiday for the good of northern broadcasting. It would mean long hours, he said, doing her regular shift at night and the workshops during the day. But it was a great chance. She was doing fine, but it could only help.

"Harry?"

He was watching the way she sat sideways at the control board, shoulders hunched up around her ears like a kid in school just before an exam. He had not thought about school for a long time and now it flooded back, all his early doubts and vulnerabilities that seemed of a piece with his feelings for Dido. "What?"

"You said to be good you have to be afraid. But I'm better because I'm *less* afraid." She sat a little straighter and her shoulders dropped an inch.

He took the empty chair. She was monitoring the network, doing the hourly station breaks, there was plenty of time to talk. "You make me want to go back and start all over again," he said heavily.

And to her surprise the skin around his eyes went a subtle pink, as it does when you speak well of someone dead. At her mother's funeral she had noticed this – that deep feeling comes in reds and blues, and in movement across the face. The tone of Harry's skin changed, the area around his eyes reddened, the rest of his face went pale, bluer. His eyes were suddenly too gleaming.

"Did I tell you this is where I started out?" He looked around the booth. "The clock is different. Everything else is pretty much the same."

Then his eyes settled on her again. The suggestion of tears had subsided, and the colour.

"Harry," and her voice was earnest, curious, "have you ever thought about going back to Toronto and doing radio there?"

"They don't want me," he said.

"That can't be true."

"They don't want anything to do with me, Gwen. Believe me."

*

That night she played a heartbreaker by Emmy Lou Harris. It ended, and she said, "That was so beautiful, let's hear it again."

And Judge Berger called out of the blue to thank her.

He agreed to go on the air for a moment, and Gwen introduced him as The Great Listener. She asked him what he did with his free time, and he confessed he had gone to see "Shampoo" at the Capitol Theatre, Warren Beatty exposing all the pitfalls of being a certain kind of male. "Really it was a very good movie," he said with a wonderfully amused laugh.

There were times that summer when she found herself talking to Berger on air. That is, she imagined him listening as sympathetically to her as he listened to the witnesses in small settlements who were speaking for the first time into a microphone.

THE TRAINING SESSIONS HARRY ARRANGED LED TO A SEA change at the station, opening wounds, fanning grievances, inspiring ambitions, and creating the alliances that would pave the way for his eventual downfall. His old friend, bearded, big-bellied Abe Lamont, set himself up in the studio at the baize-covered table, and that first day Abe saw every member of staff who worked on air, one at a time, for half an hour. It was easier if you had no illusions and little experience. Jim Murphy, a broadcaster for fifteen years, emerged from his initial meeting looking sour and asking Dido what "fatuous" meant. Dido went in eagerly, but also came out chastened and annoyed. Abe had told her that her delivery was almost too perfect, he had warned her against sounding antiseptic. *Antiseptic?* She drew herself up and his eyes glinted in response. Dido joined Jim in the office where the announcers had their desks, and he told her not to pay any mind, Abe Lamont was as over the hill as Harry. Where they got these people was a mystery.

The station had to keep running, of course, so everyone fitted their sessions with Abe around their regular shifts. Gwen came in at noon. She read the script he provided, and when he played her voice back, her body contorted in embarrassment. Abe would have none of that. It's a discipline, he told her, holding her gaze with blood-shot eyes, working his hand through his beard. No horror allowed. No self-revulsion. It has nothing to do with *you* per se, and everything to do with what you're trying to achieve. If you're going to be a professional, he told her, then you have to listen to yourself in a detached way and work to correct what is wrong. He asked her to read the page again with as much energy and passion as she could muster. "You'll never overdo it," he said. "It's not in your nature."

Different instructions for the men. I'm going to take an octave off your voice, he told them. Put your head between your knees. Open your mouth. Are you drooling yet? When you're drooling, come back up, and you'll sound like you've got a third ball. Now let's record the last syllable of time, he would tell them. Let's have a little sound and fury.

But the same basic assignment for everyone. Go out into the field, as he called the world, gather tape, edit it, write an introduction, present it to me. Nothing longer than ten minutes.

Gwen headed to the post office, intending to ask people what letters they were dreading to get, but on the way she saw Lorna Dargabble seated on the steps of her house, her shoulders shaking with laughter. Gwen went up the walk, tape recorder running, but the laughter turned out to be heartbroken sobbing and she stopped her machine. Then she sat down beside the sorrowful woman, who took her hand and fingered and kneaded it as she might a seam – as she did a seam, the frayed state of her sofa being all too apparent when Gwen passed through the living room on her way to a cup of coffee.

"You know, my dear," declared Lorna sadly, "you'd be beautiful if you made a little effort. Come downstairs and I'll cut your hair."

It turned out that Mrs Dargabble had a hair-styling shop in one half of her basement and no, she didn't mind if Gwen taped the snipping and the running commentary: "Dear girl, all your clothes are brown. What are you afraid of? With skin like yours you need blues, lavender, off-white. Show some spirit."

"You mean jump?" smiled Gwen, remembering the elderly woman's advice.

"I mean *leap*. And you can start by calling me Lorna."

Next to the space occupied by chair, sink, mirror, and shelves was a standing cabinet like the one Gwen grew up with. Inside it, a radio with its large golden speaker and a record player with a deep shelf for records. Lorna confessed that she came down here to listen to music and to be alone. "But you'd better turn that thing off," she said, and once again Gwen pressed PAUSE. Then Lorna confided that she had had dozens of records until he broke them in a drunken fury. Her husband. For a moment, she looked around herself in despair. Also in the basement were boxes upon boxes of financial records – a painstaking paper trail of every one of her expenses, she said, and every bit of the income she had earned in this second marriage that was destroying her. She said, "He'll take everything he can."

"I'm thinking," Gwen said gently, meaningfully, "that perhaps you jumped into the wrong marriage." She was sitting on a padded stool in front of a mirror with a hairdressing cape over her shoulders.

Lorna took up her long scissors. "*Touché*, my dear. Just remember there are worse things than loneliness and you won't make my mistake. But winter here does terrible things to people. You'll find out." The old woman's Boston accent came out in her vowels. "Winter leaves a lasting mark, my dear," and it sounded like "lasting mack". "You discover you're not so strong, after all."

"I'm looking forward to winter."

"Not so strong and that's a fact."

Lorna's breathing was heavy and she stopped in mid-snip to say there was something else she had learned, something worse – "But let's have some music." She went to put on one of her few surviving records, then returned to her thought. "It's a terrible thing. But even the nicest people get corrupted by the company they keep."

Gwen guessed that Lorna was talking about marriage in general and her husband in particular.

"I mean to say," she continued, "you put an onion next to butter and you get butter that tastes like onion."

"You're talking about your onion-husband," Gwen said.

"Yes." Laughing. "My onion-husband."

But now it was Brahms who made her cry.

Gwen listened too, less moved by the music than fascinated by its effect on her friend. In the mirror Lorna's old chin began to wobble and work like a little machine of emotion, quite independently and alarmingly, all its pistons firing. And then the tears flowed down her cheeks. She stopped to mop her eyes with a towel and to blow her nose. The sad heaviness of her face reminded Gwen of thick frosting badly applied and shored up with stiff scrapings from the bowl. She stood up and put her arms around her. Lorna hugged her back, and then recommenced cutting.

Half an hour later, Gwen looked at herself in the mirror and thought, *Is that really me?* Lorna had shaped her hair and lifted it somehow so that her small face looked wider, prettier.

Opening a closet, Lorna began to pull out clothes. "I used to be as skinny as you are. Try these on. I told you I used to make clothes."

To Gwen's surprise they were simple tailored garments of cotton and linen in white and cream and blue and chocolate brown. A shift, a few pairs of trousers, tunics with pockets. She gazed into the mirror again – new clothes, new colours, new haircut – and couldn't take her eyes away.

An hour later, Gwen approached the doorway of the announcers' office, then hung back for a moment, suddenly self-conscious. She could see that Dido was absorbed in conversation with Harry and Jim, but Dido looked up and let out a whistle. The other two turned around, and Harry said, "Oh no!"

"Don't listen to him," Dido said.

"What have you done?" Harry raised his hands to his ears to indicate her hair, but he was play-acting, exaggerating.

Dido examined Gwen from the back as well as the front. "It's a vast improvement," she said decidedly.

And it was. But something about Gwen would get on her nerves in the coming days. Dido had seen similar types in the classroom when she was substitute teaching, fresh-faced girls trying too hard to succeed, feigning surprise at their good marks, being disingenuous. Girls who were more ambitious than they ever let on or perhaps ever realized.

Gwen would feel Dido's coolness and be puzzled, not sure what she had done wrong. Perhaps she had just been herself. Anyone might tire of that, she thought. It would take time before she realized that she and Dido were locked in one of those personal misunderstandings that has no clear entrance and no exit either.

Later that same afternoon, their first day of training at an end, they all went to the Strange Range and occupied a table in the corner. Harry told Gwen that he had known her hairdresser when she was still Lorna Palliser. "Doug Palliser used to volunteer at the station. A wonderful guy. He was running a rapids on the Back River when his canoe flipped over and he drowned. Lorna's been a lost soul ever since."

Abe Lamont of the golden pipes and caustic opinions held forth – first about his days producing Harry's television show, then about his return to radio announcing. His week here was a favour to Harry, he said, though he had done training before, he wasn't a neophyte; he had gone into other stations and coached the staff on how to write, perform, interview, edit: radio skills, in short. Then, having established his credentials, Abe left the subject of radio altogether. He said he had seen "Last Tango in Paris", finally, having missed it when it first opened. A great movie. They should see it if they ever got the chance.

"Great, if you like creepiness," challenged Dido, who had not seen the movie, and who would recoil from it when she did. She turned her big watch on her big wrist, unaware that it clunked against the table. Gwen sat to her right, listening.

"I didn't find it creepy," Gwen said quietly.

The others looked at her in surprise, but she did not say more.

"Go on," Harry said.

For a second she hesitated, gathering her thoughts. "I didn't find it creepy," she said again, "just interesting and very sad. You understood why she shot him in the end. He wouldn't let go."

She had found the movie profoundly disturbing but enchanting. She did not know if she fully understood it. The movie was sad, but even sadder, she thought, would be to never experience that sort of all-engulfing love. She was almost twenty-five. She wondered if it would ever happen, if she would ever be passionately in love with someone who was passionately in love with her.

A pause, during which Harry caught Abe's eye and saw Gwen rise in his estimation. Then Harry stood up. He reminded Gwen that her regular shift started in forty minutes and he headed off. Jim Murphy muttered something about a wife on the warpath, and he left too.

The others watched the two men thread their way past tables and Dido reached over and poked Abe Lamont's arm with one finger. "So, how long have you known Harry?"

"We were in high school together."

She put her elbows on the table then, and smiled. "Then you can tell us what the man is really like."

Gwen leaned forward.

Abe Lamont's bulk overspread his chair, his beard doubled the size of his face and gave his hand something to burrow into while he weighed how to answer this gorgeous, prickly woman who was not unlike Harry's ex-wife. Evelyn Boyd had also been dark-haired and bossy and built.

"He's a wonderful cutter, a wonderful editor. Better at that than being a T.V. personality. We did a history of jazz series together and I remember how elegantly he cut from 'yes' on page three to the top of page seven, bridging the cut by inserting 'but'. Of course, he operates best on three double Scotches and on three he's cold sober, but it makes him irritable."

"He's not irritable with *me*," Dido said.

94

"No," giving her an appreciative look, "he wouldn't be irritable with you."

A pause. "I find it hard to imagine," Dido said, "what his wives were like."

"There was just one wife. She was nice enough."

"Oh, Abe," her voice low and commanding, "you can do better than that."

Her words dislodged an uncomfortable smile – he had good teeth, she thought, for a man who couldn't be bothered with the rest of himself. Take care of your teeth, he had advised them all earlier in the day: false teeth will end your career on air.

He said, "You're annoyed with me. Don't be."

"Am I annoyed?"

"By the end of the week you'll see the value of what I'm doing. Trust me."

"All I'm doing," she said with a small hard smile, "is trying to find out about Harry."

He took another swallow of beer, then wiped his mouth and the beard around it with the side of his hand. He was thinking she could not take criticism and that was too bad.

"Harry's a minister's son," he said. "A son of the manse. So he's a complicated man with lots of hang-ups. He's brilliant and he's proud and he's touchy. They said he needed a co-host on T.V. and he refused. He said co-hosts don't work, they talk to each other instead of to the viewer or the listener. He had a point. But they had other ideas, so they fired him."

"He detests television," Dido said.

"He doesn't understand it." Abe rocked his empty beer glass with his free hand. "He's sneering and condescending about it, about anything he can't stand."

In Abe's opinion, Harry was unreasonable about television. A smarter man – not smarter, Harry was smart – a *wiser* and less vulnerable man would have taken his T.V. failure less personally and not gone around painting all television with the same bitter brush.

Dido chose her words carefully. "Harry is what I would call an anachronism, actually."

"Anachronism?"

"You like big words." In no hurry to forgive him for *antiseptic*, to say nothing of *fatuous*. "You know what anachronism means, I'm sure."

They were at a standoff – until Gwen interceded, her voice oddly emotional. "*I* think Harry's *shy*."

Abe nodded and looked pleased. "You're right. I was shy too."

The word ignited a connection between them, an identification, a deep interest. Shy. For Gwen it was a tiny, precise, potent word like air, like loam, rock, sand, clay, marl, silt, mud, one of the basic building blocks of the world she lived in. An old word, wonderfully adapted to what it described. Being shy. Which meant shying away from oneself and from others, from life itself.

Abe claimed that his shyness arrived when he was seventeen and he remembered the exact moment. He was standing beside an orange car parked in the street, looking back at his house, when he felt a wave of shyness followed by a wave of depression. What flooded through him was exactly the opposite of whatever it was – the ecstatic joy – that swept through gloomy Proust when he tasted his madeleine biscuit and recaptured his past.

Gwen's eyes did not leave his face. She wanted to know what kind of shyness he meant. Did he feel that everybody was looking at him?

"No. I was alone in the street. Just suddenly I felt mediocre and worthless." His rich radio voice made his words sound even more singular. "A guy without a future."

Gwen was trying to put her finger on the same shift in herself. In her case, shyness arrived at puberty and shut down her carefree childhood. After that, everything was hard: talking, being with people, being in the world. "According to my mother, I was loud and boisterous when I was little. I know it's hard to believe."

"I don't believe it," Dido said.

"I do," Abe said. "I was like that. Gregarious and reasonably confident. But then everything changed. For one thing, I avoided people and they took it the wrong way."

"There's a *right* way?" The word *shy* rankled with Dido too. What did it really mean? Everybody was shy from time to time. But the two of them – Gwen and big, boozy Abe Lamont – seemed to be of one cozy mind on the subject.

"Except for Harry," he said, ignoring the sarcasm. "We fell into walking to school together. He didn't talk and I didn't talk."

"And you both ended up in radio," Gwen said.

"Harry has a great face for radio," Abe cracked.

It was a good line. Gwen would use it from now on. *I have a great face for radio.*

"You get to be invisible," Abe went on. "You control the inter-view, you ask the questions, you say when it's over. The theatre world is packed with the same kind of people. Extroverted introverts."

Dido was biting her thumbnail. "That's different. On stage you lose yourself in a part, in radio you have to be yourself."

Abe leaned back. "It's still a performance, Dido. You can't just be yourself on the radio."

"I thought that's what everybody was trying for."

"No. You're trying to be *almost* yourself. You see the difference? You're giving a performance as your natural self."

"It's not you," Gwen said, thinking aloud, mulling it over.

"It's almost you," Abe said.

That night Gwen was speaking on the telephone to the weather office at the airport, gathering weather stats, when Eddy stuck his head into the booth. His chiselled face and mouth looked extra-hard somehow. He wanted to know if she had seen Dido.

"She was in the Gold Range when I left."

Without saying a word, he turned on his heel, and she assumed he had left for the night.

Later on, Harry appeared. He pretended to barricade the door of the announce booth with a chair, as if seeking refuge from all the nutcases hounding him, and Gwen felt agreeably flattered. She said, "Abe told me he used to be shy, and so were you."

"That can't surprise *you*."

This sounded like a compliment. She too sought out corners, or spots behind doors, much as Harry had done just now.

"At bottom we're afraid of people, you and I," he said, collapsing into the only other chair. "Or maybe intimidated's a better word."

Not a compliment, then.

At that moment Eddy reappeared – he walked into master control, not having left the station, after all. Through the glass window they saw him take off his black leather jacket and drape it over the back of a chair.

"Eddy's the sort who could intimidate me," Harry said.

Eddy was intent on the equipment, taping something off the network. They had a view of his lean, muscled back. He was a man in control, running things, daring you to contradict him, quiet in a way that made you feel anything you said would sound foolish. Once, late at night, Gwen had witnessed him in master control take his wheeled chair and slam it into the wall – the impact more than the sound made her look up. Something had infuriated him. But when she asked him later what it was, he shrugged it off, said he had just wanted to give her another sound effect – if you ever want the slam of a steel door, that's how to get it.

"The alpha male," Harry said. "What does he do here at this hour?"

"He's often here. I don't think he sleeps."

Eddy caught sight of them, and stared for a moment without any expression, then went back to what he was doing.

"Stoned," Harry murmured.

"I thought he'd gone. He was looking for Dido a while ago."

"The mystery couple," said Harry, and his voice was so low-spirited, so defeated that Gwen did not know how to respond.

Then Harry shook himself and brightened a little. He told her he had got authorization to hire a woman to present the news in Dogrib. Teresa Lafferty would replace silver-haired Sam, who had joined the special team of reporters covering the pipeline inquiry fulltime. Teresa had grown up in Fort Rae, he told Gwen, and gone south years ago, but she had come back for her mother's funeral, then decided to stay on. An older woman, Harry said, but a real live wire. It was Sam who had suggested her name, he had known her family for years, and described her as smart, fluent in both languages, conscientious. "She starts tomorrow," Harry said, "so she'll get the benefit of Abe's training too."

Her full name was Teresa Dolorosa Lafferty, the Dolorosa for Mary's seven sorrows. But Teresa was not sorrowful. She had a sweet brown face with eyes almost hidden by laughter-induced wrinkles and sun-darkened pouches of skin. Teresa was fifty-three, and she would turn out to be a completely natural broadcaster, moving back and forth between English and Dogrib, and speaking softly and persuasively in a somewhat nasal, low-pitched voice. She would start out by translating the news into Dogrib and reading it twice a day, but within weeks she was doing two hours of talk and music on Saturday afternoons, ad libbing without effort as she cued up records, and sounding irreverent, down to earth, utterly human.

Gwen learned all about Teresa's past when Abe Lamont had several of them sit around the table in the studio and interview each other. Think about the best first question, he told them. Ask something that will make listeners *wait* to hear the answer.

Gwen looked at this vibrant, independent woman, and asked what she had been like at twenty-one, and instantly Teresa was full of mirth. She had spent her twenty-first birthday in a nunnery, she said, shaking her head, laughing. Inspired by the local priest, she and her older sister Audrey entered together, though her sister lasted longer. "As children we would say fifty rosaries each. Audrey insisted we hold our arms out like Jesus on the cross, and alternate. So we'd stand, arms outstretched, for as long as it took to say one hundred rosaries. First our hands would go numb, then our arms, then our shoulders. I had to throw myself into a state of holy detachment," she laughed, taking undivided pleasure in the telling.

Teresa rolled her smokes from Player's tobacco and smoked while she talked, the paper clinging to her lips like skin you're trying to pull off. Short dark hair without a trace of grey, light-blue jeans, pressed white shirt. Gwen admired her astonishing levity, her ability to rise up into a seventh heaven of teasing and being teased, a woman who had a way of defanging anyone else's intemperate remarks. Teresa did not take offence when Abe told her that her reading skills were questionable. "Questionable," she chortled. It wasn't a matter of thick skin, but of this lightness, Gwen thought. A balloon, genial and serene, floating in the air, and not pulled down by the small, nervous people around her.

Under Abe's eye, Gwen practised her interviewing skills, and got an outpouring of stories – about Teresa's days teaching in Old Crow in the Yukon, teaching on a native reserve in Saskatchewan, running a roadside restaurant, getting busted for trafficking marijuana, spending three months in jail. First, in a holding cell in Regina – a bunk with a filthy mattress and one thin blanket that she arranged so her face would not touch the mattress, her body shaking with the cold and with shock. "Michelle, just a kid," she said, "came in at midnight for murder." By then, in order to escape the insults of the police, the humiliation, she had "retreated to the moon", practising a version of the same holy detachment that brought her through the marathons of hundreds of rosaries.

It was in jail, she said, where she became part of a native healing circle. "And that changed everything. That's when I gave up my life of blaming. You claim your mistakes," she said, "you claim your good qualities, and you don't get stuck. You move around the wheel of life from one level to the next, from the emotional level to the spiritual, making room as you move for something else to enter."

That night Gwen was in the announce booth when she heard her name being called. She opened the door and Teresa was standing in the hallway. She had something to give her – a rosary she had found while unpacking boxes in her apartment. Gwen slipped it into her pocket and pulled it out the next afternoon in the Gold Range café. She and Eleanor and Teresa had gone there together for coffee. It was about three in the afternoon. Outside, the perfect summer weather held, hour after hour. Gwen would remember back to this time and it seemed to her it rained only once; a place where you had no need of an umbrella.

Unaccountably, the rosary had broken inside her pocket, and Teresa hooted. "You're going to hell. You'll have to buy a *big* indulgence for that."

Gwen and Eleanor laughed. Then Gwen, a little alarmed despite herself, laid the rosary flat on the table. She tried to refasten the broken wires, but two of the beads were missing. "Hell twice over," Teresa said.

As Gwen and Eleanor watched, Teresa went around the rosary showing them how to count off ten Hail Marys and when she came to the missing beads, instead of "Hail Mary," she said, "Roast in hell, Roast in hell."

Eleanor, with arms leaning on the table, was smiling at the banter. She confessed she had been reading the Bible lately. "It's been coming on me gradually," she said.

Gwen stared at her soft and tired eyes, and Eleanor went on. "I'm talking about belief. The belief that Christ is a source of perpetual grace."

With these words Gwen's antipathy to religion came back. It was

101

like a moth's antipathy to cedar, it filled her whole being. "I wish Christ didn't have to come into it," she groaned. "Why does grace have to be personified in Christ?"

Eleanor stared down at her hands. "Because Christ is a *person*," she said. She knew it sounded simple-minded. But Christianity was not a system, it was person-to-Person.

Dido and Eddy had come in while they were talking, they were at a table near the front. Teresa spotted them and said, "Nobody works. I love it."

Between spoonfuls of ice cream, Teresa claimed she had no regrets about her years as a nun. There were concepts like Devotion and Respect that she did not know how she would have learned about otherwise. All religions had something to offer. Even the Jehovah's Witnesses. When they knocked on her door, she invited them inside for a cup of coffee. "To be rude is just not part of my diet."

Teresa had been watching Dido and Eddy out of the corner of her eye. When they stood up to leave, she watched as Eddy put his hand on the back of Dido's neck and guided her through the door. "Those two are cooking up a train wreck," she said.

Eleanor and Gwen swung round and saw the pair through the restaurant window. Teresa asked how long they had been together, and Eleanor told her it had started in June, so a month.

Teresa said, "I've seen other couples like that. He won't let her do things and she likes that. He'll get her to do other things, and she'll like that too."

* *

The same afternoon Ralph Cody dropped into the station. The tobacco-stained bibliophile traded books back and forth with Harry. Today Ralph was returning *The Big Sleep*, hard-boiled reading for a hard-boiled town, and bringing Harry an issue of *Blackwood's*

Magazine of interest for its engrossing article about stammering Frank, the fifth son of Charles Dickens.

"Dickens had seven sons," recounted Ralph with energy, "every one a disappointment. They all had what the great man called 'a curse of limpness' upon them. It must be the worst luck in the world, don't you think? Having a father who's a literary genius."

Harry had reached into a bottom drawer of his desk and pulled out a bottle, and now he and Ralph sat back and enjoyed the fruit of Scotland, while Ralph continued the tale of stammering Frank. Dickens tried to cure the boy by making him read Shakespeare out loud, but young Frank grew up tongue-tied and deaf to boot; he got work eventually, with the Bengal police, a job that paved the way to sunstroke, deep depression, full-scale dissipation. Then strings were pulled, Ralph said, and he came out to Canada in 1874, taking a post in the newly formed North-West Mounted Police, where his superiors immediately rated him an officer of "no promise". Over the years he saw many things, including the decline of buffalo herds and the consequent emaciation of the Indians, and some of their more desperate battles, and in the end, concluded Ralph, he acquitted himself rather well. "He said if he himself ever wrote a book, he'd call it *Thirty Years without Beer*."

Harry laughed and stared into his glass. "'The curse of limpness'. That sounds like a manager I could name."

Then he remembered to tell Ralph something not unrelated. On Saturday morning Abe Lamont would be playing "Death in the Barren Ground" for anybody on staff who was interested, a copy from radio archives in Toronto, and he'd be welcome to join them. It was the narrative drama of Hornby's last journey written by George Whalley. Harry knew that Ralph had copies of Whalley's biography of Hornby and of the diary written by Hornby's young cousin, Edgar Christian – a diary published in 1937 with a title Harry admired, *Unflinching* – and he was right to think Ralph would be eager to come.

Harry waved his big hand to take in the station. "I should have prepared everybody for Abe. Warned them not to expect flattery. I don't know how to manage egos. I alienate people."

"You've heard rumblings of discontent?"

He had. He had even heard himself referred to as the crunchy granola dictator. Bill Thwaite, not bothering to keep his voice down. "It's too bad I can't be a bit more charming," Harry said.

Ralph snorted with laughter. "You're charming."

"Who have I charmed?"

"Who do you want to charm?"

Harry rubbed his eyes and readjusted his glasses, then shifted the conversation back to safer ground. "What's got you reading *Blackwood's Magazine*?"

Ralph smiled and went along. He said it had been a command performance when he was young, his family all read it from cover to cover and his father stored every back issue in the attic in Vancouver. His father was a great character, he added, the one who had got him interested in languages by introducing him to the Cyrillic alphabet. They had spent hours together poring over stamps, enchanted especially by anything Russian.

"My old dad was something of a mystic," he added. "Like the Celts, he believed we're made up of invisible currents. He used to say there are 'thin places' where we're closer to the unseen world."

"Name a thin place."

"The ocean. You stand next to the sea and you're in touch with all your longings and all your losses."

"Longings and losses," Harry repeated. "That does sort of sum it up."

Ralph took in Harry's rumpled face. "Dido came to see me the other day."

"Lucky you," Harry said.

"She wanted to borrow a book."

"A book," said Harry.

"*Rules for Radicals.* I sent her home with a year's worth of reading. Her arms were full, lumbered, aching with books."

"Saul Alinsky," Harry said slowly. "A smart man."

"They've started a study group."

"Who has?"

"Dido and Eddy. You know. 'Concerned whites who oppose the pipeline and want to support the native cause.' Solidarity. Brother-hood. Resistance. They asked me to join."

They had not asked Harry to join.

"She's a serious woman, Dido. I told her I wasn't the studying type."

"I like serious women," Harry said, and in his mind he saw Dido and Eddy come out of the little blue house in Rainbow Valley, and thought, So she's into politics. Then came the second thought, and it was bitter. Not politics – love.

"IN THE SPRING OF 1926, JOHN HORNBY'S PARTY, THREE MEN *and one canoe, left Fort Resolution and travelled to the site of Fort Reliance at the eastern end of Great Slave Lake. Here they were delayed for a time by heavy ice. Then by the classic route of Pike's Portage, they entered Artillery Lake. After that there was silence.*"

So began the hour-long radio drama "Death in the Barren Ground". A handful of staff had come to listen. In the studio were Harry and Dido, Eleanor, Gwen, and Ralph. Eddy and Abe were in master control.

The narrator, marvellous Bud Knapp, described how two years later, in July of 1928, a party of geologists led by Harry Wilson was travelling by canoe from Great Slave Lake to Hudson Bay. They were aware that Hornby and his two companions had gone into the Barrens the previous summer, intending to overwinter there as Hornby had done once before, and that the three men had not reappeared, and there was some anxiety about them. Thirty-five miles below the junction of the Hanbury and Thelon rivers, Wilson discovered the derelict cabin and two bodies "apparently sewn in blankets" to the right of the cabin door, and, inside, a third body on a bunk. A note on top of the stove directed them to the papers and diary laid in the cold ashes inside, papers that would identify the three men as John Hornby, Harold Adlard, and Edgar Christian.

Knapp's voice then took them forward to the Mounted Police

investigation and the conclusion of "death due to starvation not foul play", and then he took listeners back to the beginning, to the man at the centre of the story, the small, wiry Englishman, the son of a famous cricketer, who came to Canada in 1904 and fell under the spell of the Arctic, soon acquiring a reputation for incredible physical endurance, for surviving against the odds, for considering the Barren Ground "his destined element". At the age of forty-six, he had determined to make at least one more journey into a part of the world that only a few people had ever travelled through.

Here were Hornby's own solitary, musing words taken from his writings and spoken by actor Alan King. "I'm jealous, I suppose. Jealous of that country. Jealous of any man who goes in there without me." To Harry, the man sounded compelling, candid, clear-headed. "The trees end at Artillery Lake. The timber doesn't straggle off, it just ends in a distinct line that cuts diagonally across the lake. Beyond that, the Barrens . . . I've seen it go down to eighty below. There are no cabins, no trading posts, no human beings. But in the season, and if you're lucky, there's plenty of game . . . The caribou! Wonderful. I've seen tens of thousands of them in the open and at the shallow river crossings. At a narrow ford they may take hours to go by, trotting in a solid mass, their eyes glazed, the air shaking with their funny gruntings, their hooves grinding the ice to a fine powder. There's no sight like it."

And here were Edgar Christian's perceptive, accepting young thoughts about his much-admired cousin whom he called Jack. "He doesn't talk very much and when he does it's as though he were talking to himself." Edgar's voice, as spoken by Douglas Rain, was haunting, milky – *I am as safe as a house with Jack.* The boy was only seventeen.

Harold Adlard, the third member of the party, who had joined up with them in Edmonton, out of eagerness to see the North, was twenty-seven.

The three men travelled slowly that summer of 1926. It was not until October that Edgar's diary began in earnest, by which time they were putting the final touches to their cabin on the Thelon River and contemplating a last push to get caribou. But the effort to get meat failed and winter set in. Hornby, quixotic, eccentric, confident he would survive because he always had, was guilty of defying "the immemorial custom of the North; he had not laid in his winter's meat in September". Their food ran low, then it ran out, and the three men turned into Hansel without Gretel, starving in a winter cage. Hornby had always planned to write a book and call it *The Land of Feast and Famine*. Now his notes for the never-finished volume took on the colour of tragedy. "My life has been finding out how to eat when there's nothing to eat, finding game when there isn't any, crawling on hands and knees to find food when you aren't strong enough to stand up and when your will to live has shrivelled away . . . In the Barrens starvation is an intensely active process. You are more likely to die of exhaustion than of starvation. As your strength goes you become more methodical and remorseless. A kind of creeping obsession entirely focused on the need your body has for food, and you set about finding it with the ingenuity of a deliberate, cold-blooded murderer."

Time and again, they hunted desperately and unsuccessfully, their days a succession of blizzards, frostbite, enforced idleness, injury, slow starvation, quiet valour. Triumphs of composure offset their bodily sufferings. Young Edgar was devoted to Hornby, Hornby was as selfless as he was reckless, the two were alike in their courage and resolve, which seemed inhuman, sublime. Hornby died first, on April 16. Harold Adlard died next, on May 4. Edgar Christian lasted another month, all by himself, until early June. By then there was still no northward migration of birds or animals, and for several days it had been blowing a snowstorm. His last diary entry was June 1. *9 a.m. Weaker than ever. The sunshine is bright now. Make preparations now. Left things late.* He would write to his father, then to his mother. *Dearest Mother. Feeling weak now. Can only write a little. Sorry I left it so late. Please don't blame dear Jack.*

Make preparations now was heartbreaking shorthand. Making the preparations for imminent death that Hornby had failed to make to preserve their lives.

Whalley's script put it beautifully, Harry thought. "For in the end most of what can be said about John Hornby is outweighed by the record of his unrelenting courage in the face of a disaster that he must have known his own irresponsibility had produced." An enigma during his life, Hornby was fortunate after death in having the best of biographers.

It seemed to Harry as he listened that everyone had fallen under the same spell, except Dido, whose blank face he could not read. Now she caught his eye and his heart sank. She did not like this documentary he loved, this unfolding drama of fascination. He shifted his gaze to Gwen, who had heard the programme when it was originally broadcast, as had he, and from her expression he could see that she recognized certain voices, remembered certain turns of phrase, and was caught up all over again in the overwhelming pull of the story.

But *why* had Hornby dallied so long, so inexplicably? Why had he let September slip by without laying in the winter's meat, thus leaving himself and the others short of food as early as November? Harry had his own explanation. To him, Hornby was a George Orwell type, even in appearance. The two men shared an enormous appetite for doing without. *Down and out in Paris and London. Down and out in the Arctic.*

The programme ended and Harry broke the silence with a resonating afterthought: he would like to see the spot where Hornby died. It would be worth the trip, he said, casually setting in motion the events of the following summer.

Dido, listening to Hornby's story, remembered her father. She was back in their house where he was grading papers as he listened to the radio, pausing in his correction of a mangled line from the *Aeneid* to drift over to England in his mind. Their house a house of maps and books and foreign sounds, of coffee every evening at eight, of fresh cut flowers, of salty liquorice. Her father would have liked this documentary, it would have appealed to his melancholy mind. She wished he had done more with his life. But what her mother used to say was true. He did not have a fighting temperament. Nothing could arouse the battling instincts of that mild and gentle man. His voice was not unlike the actor's who played Hornby, she thought, the same ruminating style and pace of someone who seemed to stand outside life – a kind of baffled backwards sound, as if the future was already in the past.

She glanced through the window at Eddy in master control and knew what he was thinking: the programme was well and good in its minor way. This was not the North that interested him, these old tales of the glories and disasters of English travellers. The present called out for justice, not for nostalgia over another extravagant failure on the part of blind and incompetent white men. Teresa Lafferty was not here. Why would she be? Dido looked around at all the pale, absorbed faces and felt like an atheist in church. These Canadians, she thought, these old-fashioned, colonized Canadians. She saw Gwen's fingers steal up to her eyes and Eleanor's gentle smile of too easy, too automatic appreciation lingering on her face. Abe Lamont's beard jutted out like a furry flag. And Harry, she knew without even looking, Harry was watching her, measuring her reactions, wanting something she was not about to give. Don't look at me like that, she had told him once, you'll wear out your eyes. She glanced at him now and raised her eyebrows and his face had that hungry look of special pleading – fill my bowl, give me seconds – that made her lose patience. Earlier in the week she had complained to him about Abe. Said that in calling her antiseptic, he was being racist. It was an anti-Dutch slur, she said, and no, she was not kidding.

In this moment (this parting of the ways) she made up her mind to be more uncompromising, less like her father. She remembered something Eddy had said about Berger. The man was too *reasonable*.

Afterwards, they remained in the studio and talked. Dido said Hornby must have been a masochist. "He was demented," she said, enunciating too clearly, this habit of over-enunciation that made Abe Lamont call her too perfect on air.

Gwen flared up. She hated words like *masochist* and *narcissist* and, and, and – she tried to think of another such label and couldn't. "Call someone a masochist," she spluttered, "and there's nothing left to say. It's the end of the story. You've written him off. Explained him to death."

Dido replied in a steady, even tone. "You haven't explained everything maybe, but almost everything."

"No! Those labels just give you a fancy reason to stop thinking about people."

"What would *you* call Hornby then?"

"Complicated." Gwen could not bear the criticism – she never could bear it when anyone she treasured got pilloried and dismissed. "What did Whalley say?" she cried. "'Brave, desolate, and haunted.'"

Dido pursed her lips. "Poor Edgar," she murmured. She was tired of Gwen's vehemence. All week, whenever she had floated a new idea, Gwen had leapt in with a differing opinion, as if she had some privileged understanding of radio. They had made a ten-minute documentary together about a Dene play on alcohol abuse, it was being performed on an outdoor stage, and they had interviewed the actors and the director, who said, "Mostly we don't really tell them how the play is, but we want them to make the story to themselves of how the play is." Gwen had overruled Dido's intention of running music below the interviews, shaking her head dismissively, not even considering it.

Eddy weighed in now. Usually you could count on his silence. He said that Edgar, without Hornby, was nothing; he would have lived

111

an ordinary life and been completely forgotten. He was talking to Dido, asking her which she would choose if she had the choice. "A long, steady, unexciting life or a brief spurt of intensity?"

Dido traced circles on the table with her fingertips. A small smile parted her lips. At last she admitted it. "Intensity."

Harry could not help himself. "And you accused me of being a romantic!"

But Dido and Eddy were not paying attention, not to him.

Eleanor tried to say that surely the two were not incompatible, intensity and a long life, but nobody was listening and she did not go on. The words that kept ringing in her head were Hornby's *I've come to love the silence*. After the others had left, she said to Harry that Hornby's description of the Barrens as sudden, featureless, endless, as land ground down and scoured by glaciers, put her in mind of the holy men of the desert starving themselves in order to have visions. Hornby had been drawn to a place that almost nobody had ever seen, where everything was severe, but where suddenly the air shook with life, with the sounds of tens of thousands of caribou. Eleanor said visionaries and mystics are always drawn to emptiness and silence as the necessary preconditions for an upwelling of the spirit. No wonder George Whalley turned to the Bible when he tried to describe the power of this world at the end of the world. "Stones of fire" was one of his phrases. From Ezekiel.

She said, "If you go to the Barrens, Harry, I'd give anything to go with you."

* *

On the afternoon of the same day, several of them went canoeing on Frame Lake, the protected inland lake on the western edges of New Town. It was a day soaked in sunshine and threaded by blue damselflies, in twos, mating. Darning needles, Harry called them. They lit on everybody, but especially on Gwen's shoulders and hair, stitching her with colour – blue, delicate, darting, iridescent – mending her mental aches and pains and errors and embarrassments. She was in the bow of Harry's canoe, Eleanor was paddling with Ralph. Ralph called out, *Gwen, they like you. You're a flower*. And she turned around with a wide smile.

Eleanor caught her breath. *La fille qui était laide*. Gwen looked beautiful.

What would happen next? wondered Eleanor. Love would happen next, as it always does, she thought, even to the old heroes. She had been reading her beloved Edith Hamilton, refreshing her memory about the twelve labours of Hercules and thinking, as she turned the pages, about what a long, eventful, exhausting life he had, poor wretch, only to be reminded that yet to come were all the complications of love. First for Iole, then for Deianara, this latter ending in unendurable pain and death.

The canoes carried the canoeists and the canoeists carried the damselflies and everything seemed weightless. They were heading towards the first day of August, the street lights were noticeable again, and a few leaves were turning yellow, indicating in their minimal, elegant way an end to this long, warm summer and the beginning of a darker chapter.

Harry and Gwen went for a walk later on, all the way to the lip of Rainbow Valley, at the end of Latham Island. Gwen's voice was animated as she told him what she had learned from Abe about lifting words off the page. He had coached her to raise her eyes as she read, and it was hard to do, she was not relaxed enough, but a few times she had succeeded in delivering the words as if speaking directly to the listener, and it was wonderful, she said, to feel unlocked from the tyranny of the page.

She had had a good week and he was glad. Her professional progress was a small part of what he was after – a new flow of languages and information on air. He wanted one long street of sound that would be interesting to anyone, white or Dene, at any time of day. If radio could be more relevant than ever, he reasoned, then it stood a better chance against television. He was sure of it. He had also been thinking that if head office was going to waste money on an elaborate new building, then it could be argued they should spend generously on crucial new programming. Already he was picturing Teresa Lafferty's hour of blended Dogrib and English; he wanted to hire another Dene woman, young Tessa Blondin, to do reports in Slavey; and he was tempted to curry more disfavour with the newsroom by carving five minutes off the regular local newscasts and adding them to the Dene allotment.

He and Gwen reached Rainbow Valley. They stood together looking down at the colourful curve of poverty, the small prefab houses painted in pastel blues and greens and pinks. Scruffy children played in the road, an old woman hauled a pail of water up her steps, smoke rose from several chimneys. The scene of settled displacement pulled from Gwen a wistful, pointed question. "Are you ever lonely?" she asked Harry. Tacitly confessing, she knew, that she herself was lonely and glad for his company.

Harry did not hesitate. He said yes, he knew he would always be lonely. "But I always have good friends wherever I am."

And Gwen knew exactly where she stood. She was meant to feel included in that company – one of many. She fell silent as they walked back to his house, disappointed somehow in Harry's answer. He made tea, moving a large box off his kitchen table to make room for teapot and cups. The box was addressed to Harry, she saw, and had a return address in New Brunswick. But he had not opened it.

"Why not?" she asked, dumbfounded that anyone could receive a package in the mail and resist its mystery.

He laughed and said that opening boxes made him sad. "I get lost in them, Gwen. All sorts of ghosts pour out."

114

IT WAS ABE LAMONT'S LAST NIGHT IN TOWN BEFORE FLYING back to Toronto. Harry had arranged to join him in the Gold Range, and he found him there, soused and voluble, bending Dido's ear about the old days when thousands of geese shot in the Mackenzie River Delta were piled high on barges and shipped south. Travelling the other way by barge came Pete, the Lebanese peddler from Alberta, selling oranges at every stop for a dollar apiece.

Dido was wearing a necklace of red coral beads, and in Harry's mind the colours took over, the creamy-grey breasts of the geese, the precious oranges, the reddish beads. Eddy was not with her and Harry took heart: perhaps she was not so attached to him, after all. He kept looking at her, but she was having none of his glances, none of his big, obvious, smitten heart. He felt old and raw with wanting her and not having her. A few weeks ago he had invited her to a cabin on Prosperous Lake for a day of what he imagined might be seclusion, confessions, concerted wooing, but she had declined to go.

"Then have dinner with me in town. I'll cook for you."

"If you insist."

"Oh, I never insist."

That made her smile. "Alright, then."

He had made his signature dish, cauliflower soup so delicious (a touch of curry powder, and thick cream) that Dido had a second helping. "You're young," he had said, looking at her but speaking of himself, "you're doing something really interesting, you think your future holds more of the same, but better. Then you discover that the highlight of your working life occurred at the beginning. And you can't go back."

Dido had laughed his comments away. "You want me to believe the best is now, things will never be better than this. Of course they'll be better. Of course I'll try television if I get a chance. Who wouldn't?"

"Let me see your palm." He had stroked her palm with his fingertips. "Is television in Dido Paris's future? I see mansions, tropical trees. A lot of water."

"Swimming pools."

"A flood."

"You can't drown me just for wanting to go into television, Harry."

She had spoken from a mocking distance that kept him very effectively at bay.

Now he watched, bemused, as she chummed up to the man she had derided earlier in the week. She was plying Abe Lamont with questions about the legendary lost valley of orange trees in the Arctic. Abe the windbag, he thought indulgently, Abe the big tub of talent gone awry; no wonder the two of us get on so well: we could have set the world on fire, but neither of us is going to.

"Lamont! You're full of shit!"

Abe made a show of glowering back. "I feel sorry for you," he said to Dido (who seemed to like nothing better than the blood sport of male one-upmanship, the fondly savage insults). "I pity you having the great Harry Boyd as your boss. As I was saying," and he deepened his studio voice in order to mock himself and amuse her, "explorers found the tropical valley, but couldn't *re*locate it. There's an old trapper, Gus Kraus, he lived on the Nahanni River for years, and in the summer he grew melons and in the winter he walked across his cabin floor in bare feet, that's how warm it was from the hot springs below.

I expect the Nahanni gave rise to the legend."

"Or it could have been the place where Hornby died," she said. "The Thelon River."

"It could have been," Abe agreed.

He had made peace with her the day before. She was the equal of any announcer on the national network, he had told her in the end, and he had offered to recommend her to a producer he knew in Toronto.

*   *

That same night, much later and on the spur of the drunken moment, Harry hammered on the door of Eleanor's trailer, hoping Dido would be there. He was lucky. She opened the door, a glow of white night-gown and loose hair.

"Save me from my insanity," he pleaded.

Inside, he fell into an armchair and she curled up on the sofa.

"Are you alright?" he asked her. "I worry about you, I want you to know that."

"I was asleep," she said.

His face looked hollowed out, she thought, as though he had false teeth and they weren't in. His glasses had slid down his nose.

She said, "You should worry about Eleanor. You probably woke her up."

"Shhhh." Finger to his lips. "Sorry." He took out his unfiltered cigarettes and offered her one. She shook her head, then changed her mind.

"I almost killed myself twice," he said, "I want you to know that."

She held the cigarette between her fingers. His accent was different when he was drunk. It went Irish, maudlin. His face reminded her of an open book that had fallen into a puddle.

"Why do you want me to know that, Harry?"

"The first time I saw you," he said, and he fumbled for words, "the first time I *heard* you, you made such an impression on me. I felt such a connection." He heard his voice, the pleading, but could not help himself. "Was it only me?"

She gazed at this man, who sat in a cloud of smoke. He made her feel tired and cruel. Vulnerable men did not appeal to her, they never had.

Without answering his question, she got up and went into the kitchen, which was an extension of the living room. Harry stayed where he was. When she came back with a mug of coffee for him, he said, "I was watching you."

"That's new."

"Ah, Dido. Be kind to an old man."

She sat beside him and straightened the collar of his shirt as if he were an old man. "So what did you see when you were watching me?"

"A bird hunting for a worm. A woman looking this way and that for a coffee cup." He paused. "A beautiful woman."

But she had been called beautiful before.

"It's time for you to go," she said after he took a few sips and set down the mug.

"You're right."

He stood up and looked around him, patting his pockets, and that's when he saw Eddy's leather jacket hanging over a chair in the corner. Then he sagged.

"I'm too old for you, aren't I?"

"You're not too old, Harry. You're too needy."

* *

Eddy picked up his leather jacket in the morning, and in the afternoon he and Dido were on the hill near School Draw watching immense clouds roll in from the north. Below them lay Old Town, glittering in the low-flung light like an inviting bed of nails. Dido wanted to take cover, but Eddy put his arm around her and held her in place. Eddy, so relaxed, talked about being a kid when it seemed every time he and his brothers climbed Blueberry Hill the sky churned up a wild and violent storm. They played chicken with the elements, their fingers going after the blue, almost-black berries on the open hillside until the first close CRACK sent them skidding down to lower ground, laughing like fools. Beautiful berries, hanging full and ripe and surprisingly heavy on the underside of bushes as low as these ones. And he bent down and with his pocket knife hacked off the tip of an arctic willow and put the willow twig in Dido's hand.

That morning they had driven to the Yellowknife River, and once they were well underway, miles from town, he said casually that the gas tank was empty and smiled at her alarm. Eddy always knew what he could get away with. That was the lesson of the drive, and of his lingering now on the exposed hilltop, his arm around her as the first strokes of lightning flashed across the sky and she trembled. "Loon at three o'clock," he said.

A moment later, when he looked into her face, she seemed a million miles away. He asked her what she was thinking, and she said the North Sea.

She said, "My mother. I think she's losing her memory."

"She's old."

"Sixty-one."

"Well, that's too young."

Dido turned to look at Eddy's hard, steady face. "Why didn't she telephone me when my father died? I have this terrible feeling she forgot."

"To telephone you?"

"Forgot she hadn't telephoned me. Her letters are full of half-explained things she expects me to know about, but there's no way I could know about them."

"Don't worry about it," he said, his arm firmly around her, his response practical, definitive. "There's nothing you can do from here."

After the wind fell away, and just before the rain began, they came down off the hilltop and saw Gwen hurrying home. So they swept her up with them into Eddy's small truck and he drove her to her door.

Later, out of curiosity not unmixed with jealousy, Gwen said to Dido, "Well, I can see what you'll bring to him. But what will he bring to you?"

Dido didn't answer, stung by the very question that was in the back of her own mind, and irked by Gwen's presumption. She thought fiercely, defensively, about Eddy's kindness to his motherless niece, how he telephoned her every week and was sending her gifts of toy animals, a seal, an ookpik, a polar bear, a caribou, one at a time, until soon the little girl would have a perfect northern menagerie. Ordinary people had no idea how attentive Eddy could be.

"She's so judgmental," Dido complained to Eleanor during a quiet moment at the station several days later.

"She's young."

"She's not much younger than I am." Dido was making herself a cup of instant coffee, and Harry walked in to do the same. "She'll be twenty-five tomorrow. You heard her say it the other day."

"I know all that. But compared to you she's inexperienced and unsure of herself. She's shy."

"Is she? Or is she perfectly sure of herself?"

Harry lifted his head. "There's something to that." Gwen could be surprisingly self-possessed, an odd mixture of crippling modesty and immodest determination. "She's improved a lot since she began."

Dido said, "I think she knows it. I think she knows exactly how good she is."

In the hallway Gwen had stopped a few feet from the door,

brought up short. Her arms were full of record albums.

To hear herself spoken of disparagingly – it hadn't happened since she was a child at camp. At the age of ten she'd stormed into the tent with her objections: *I heard you. I heard what you said.* And all the other girls looked at her, embarrassed, but also sorry for her. And what had come after the anger? More anger, but in a different form. Anger with herself for having spoken out, and with the situation that goaded her into speaking. After the illicit blaze of indignation, there was the long, dark walk to the shore.

She heard Dido's damning, dismissive voice. "I think she's the type that gets called shy and isn't shy at all."

She heard Harry clear his throat, then say, "Well, most of us don't have your confidence and poise." Ingratiating himself with Dido, not coming to her defence at all.

One of the albums slipped out of her grasp and hit the floor with a bang. She swooped to pick it up – aware of the sudden, awful silence.

"Shit." Dido drew her head in from the open doorway. She had glimpsed the back of Gwen beetling into the record library.

"Did she hear us?" Eleanor whispered.

She must have. She must have heard every word.

＊　＊

In the record library Gwen's eyes smarted, a wounded bear with voices in her head, *she knows exactly how good she is . . .* The voices lifted her up off her chair and out of the station and into the low wide town. They transported her over rocky ground, but not high enough to avoid the rocks. So bang and drag and jostle and bump she went on her way through Old Town, which was barely older than she was. She passed the vagabond-like disarray that was Peace River Flats on the left and Willow Flats on the right, then made her way around the base of the Rock to the causeway to Latham Island. On the island she walked past Harry's house and came to the little dirt road on the left that led to the shore of Back Bay.

Agitated, she went down to the water.

And there she saw a vision of happiness. A young woman with her hair in a braid was throwing a stick for a big, handsome dog. He tore back and forth on the narrow shore, bounding and leaping with pleasure. *Stan*, the woman called. *Good dog*, she praised.

Not far away from the woman and her dog was Ralph Cody. Once again, he had his tripod set up at the water's edge, and when he saw her, he waved. Her grateful heart propelled her feet. She went over to him.

"They're always changing," he said of the watery weeds he was enamoured of. "The light, the current, the wind, the way they float and move. I've taken dozens of pictures and each one is subtly different."

The events of the following summer would make these pictures of Ralph's almost intolerably moving. But Gwen could not know that now. The two of them stood together on the strip of sandy shore under high clouds, white and grey, feathering across a blue sky.

Ralph manoeuvred to get another angle and she asked him what he was looking for and he considered for a moment. "Energy. I recognize energy when I see it. It's more than just the scene in front of the camera," he said, peering through the lens. "It's a kind of electric connection. Almost a union between your intuitive side and your rational side." He looked up from his Nikon. "I heard Abe Lamont talking about how to shape an interview and write for radio. It's not so different, is it? One thought in each sentence. Not too many adjectives. Simplicity. Intimacy. Directness. That's what I'm after too."

She nodded and heard Abe's commanding voice in her head: "It's not about you, it's about the script, the story; think of that." And thinking of that, what did she see? Dido. Something the matter between Dido and her, something she did not understand. What Abe had dinned into her over the course of the week was the need for excellence, the need to take risks to get excellence. She had felt excited, raised up, inspired. Maybe she had even seemed sure of herself. Maybe that's what Dido was talking about. And Gwen felt lost in the enormous gap between how she felt inside and what others thought of her. Dido was wrong. Wrong about her. Unless, of course, she was right.

On the way back to the station, she made a detour to the Explorer Hotel. Teresa had mentioned that the formal hearings of the Berger Inquiry were instructive and more interesting than you might expect. She went whenever she could to sit in the audience and listen. Now Gwen made her way through the hotel lobby and down the hall to the big meeting room, and Teresa was there, in one of the chairs set out for the public. Gwen sat down next to her. A lawyer for one of the pipeline companies was talking, a large man in a perfect suit and tie. "Arctic Gas," Teresa whispered with a grin. "Watch out." He was cross-examining an expert witness, an engineer employed by his own oil and gas consortium, to explain and defend what they were proposing – a pipeline that would be bigger in diameter than any existing gas pipeline in North America, that would be operated at a maximum pressure of 1,680 pounds per square inch, and designed to withstand this pressure, and reinforced, besides, with steel bands or "crack arrestors", meaning it could not ever crack, rupture, burst. "Ha, ha," Teresa said, loud enough to turn a few heads.

Judge Berger sat alone at a small table at the front. He listened and made notes by hand. In keeping with the official nature of these formal sessions, he wore a navy blue pinstripe suit. Gwen was more familiar with his relaxed appearance in newspaper photographs taken at community hearings. Here, she gathered from Teresa, the expert witnesses sat at a table on his right. The reporters who covered the inquiry fulltime sat on his left at an extended table that was spread, as were all the tables, with a white cloth. The lawyers –

for Berger's commission of inquiry, for the pipeline companies, for the native organizations, for environmental groups – sat at other tables, their backs to the audience. When the hearing stopped for a coffee break, Teresa said she supposed she should get herself to work. Gwen left with her, and a moment later they were outside in the afternoon light walking back to the station. "Malarkey," Teresa said, and laughed. No purpose was served, she said, by all the malarkey that happens when people are not honest.

"In white culture, people are so busy lying through their teeth. So busy thinking about getting ahead and making money, so busy thinking about how they come across, that they can't be themselves in a natural way. It builds up such a complicated and depressing web."

Teresa was not laughing any more. To Gwen she looked tired, uncharacteristically worn out.

Teresa went on, "If someone is sitting across from you and says, 'I want your land'. And you say no, I happen to like it here and I've been here forever, then they should respect what you've said, and that's an end to it. They shouldn't try to get around you. They shouldn't read something else into what you've said. They should *respect* you."

In the coming months, Gwen would often attend the inquiry. She noticed other townspeople who came regularly, a grey-haired woman who was always knitting, a wide-faced mother who breastfed her baby. They heard the native organizations push their moral high ground, and the pipeline companies don the cloak of thoughtful realism, and church and environmental groups attack the amorality of multinational oil. Of equal interest to Gwen was the science. All the types of snow, all the complications of the soil, all the varieties of wildlife she had never given much thought to. Everyone addressed Berger when they spoke, and he guided them forward, passionate about every aspect of the issue, you could tell, but sober, balanced, Leonard Bernstein as parson, a force field of quiet attention. If something was not clear he asked a question, and every single person listened.

After they realized they had been overheard, Eleanor and Dido and Harry stood frozen in place for a moment until Dido began to laugh – embarrassed, shocked, working up a kind of carelessness to ease her guilt. Harry went over in his mind what he had said – what the other two had said – not so bad, really, no great harm done, he hoped. But he had better find Gwen. He went to the record library. A pile of records on a chair, but no Gwen, as he told them when he came back.

Eleanor wished that she had nipped the whole thing in the bud. And yet she knew these regrettable conversations happened, were even necessary entertainment of a kind. Friends, good friends too, take the measure of each other behind the other's back, pronouncing with injudicious yet satisfying finality. They do it to make themselves feel better, only to end up feeling rather ashamed. They do it as a form of emotional release. They do it, in some way, not to bury the relationship but to keep it alive.

But there were consequences. No-one who hears ill of herself quite trusts the friend again.

What were they to do? Harry said he would talk to Gwen the next time he saw her, he would joke her out of it. But Eleanor said some gesture of friendship was needed, and Dido was the one who suggested they celebrate Gwen's birthday. It seemed to the others a generous thought, and Eleanor offered her place for the party.

"A *surprise* party," Dido specified. "Otherwise, she'll find an excuse not to come."

Eleanor was dubious, but she agreed to be the one to invite Gwen home for a drink without divulging what lay in store.

Later that afternoon, when she saw her come into the station with Teresa, she called to her and Gwen came over to her desk. Eleanor searched her face and said quietly, "You've been gone quite a while."

The sympathy in Eleanor's voice picked at the thread of her

self-pity, and tugged, and Gwen felt herself unravel childishly. She bit her lip.

"You overheard us talking," Eleanor said.

Gwen looked down, her face a study in embarrassment, and a phrase came to Eleanor's mind: proud flesh. In an old medical book of her father's, its yellowed pages smelling of sweet dustiness, like an old church, she had read among other things about burns and scalds, about suppuration, pain, excessive granulations or "proud flesh", and, unless skilfully treated, ugly scars.

"People say all sorts of things, Gwen. It doesn't mean much. It doesn't mean they aren't fond of the person, very fond."

Gwen still could not meet her eyes, and Eleanor reached across her desk and touched her hand. "Listen. Your birthday's tomorrow. Let's have a drink together."

Gwen looked at her then, a look of gratitude. She nodded and smiled. Then, fingering some of the papers on the desk, she said, "Dido," and stopped.

"Dido isn't as confident as she looks. And you can seem very sure of yourself sometimes."

Gwen stared back at her amazed. "I don't *feel* sure of myself."

"I know."

GWEN TURNED A QUARTER OF A CENTURY ON HER DAY off, Friday, August 1. Nothing from her brother, not a telephone call, not a card. She thought of him in the jewellery store he had taken over after their father died, her father a jeweller who never looked up, her brother a businessman who never stopped glancing around for another sale. Being on the radio, she had discovered, was easier than dealing with certain people. There was a restfulness, an intimacy, a wonderful privacy when you did not have to speak to someone face to face. She had fallen into the habit of reading out a bedtime poem "for all you lie-awakes" before she signed off at night. Then afterwards she liked to take her time going home, roaming around on summer nights that at their darkest were still light enough to pick berries by. But things were changing now it was becoming cooler, duskier.

Friday evening, she arrived for her birthday drink with Eleanor at seven o'clock, and Dido was there. Dido, making an effort, she could see that. A measured effort, a measured welcome, and as they worked at making conversation, and nothing was easy, Gwen understood that she was going to have to live with this – her negative effect on someone who used to like her, someone she still admired.

Between glasses of wine, and during an awkward pause, Gwen took herself to the bathroom. She followed the beige-carpeted hallway, pausing to look in through the door of the small spare bedroom,

Dido's room, and it looked barely inhabited, its narrow bed more a shelf for books and papers than a place for sleeping. So she was spending her nights with Eddy. The second door was the bathroom, but a third door – the open door to Eleanor's bedroom – offered another view, another way of stalling, of avoiding Dido. Idly, she gazed in at the unmade double bed, the armchair, the window shades, when something caught her eye. A few feet away, a bottle of patchouli on top of the dresser. An unattractive scent, she had always thought. She noticed a pair of Dido's slingback shoes on the floor.

As Gwen retraced her steps to the bathroom, a penny dropped in her mind.

At eight o'clock the bell rang, the door burst open, and in came Harry and Ralph and Teresa with overzealous cries of "Happy Birthday".

Gwen felt tears spring to her eyes, and she smiled. She embraced everybody. "Thank you," she said, and her voice was husky. But, in truth, she hated surprise parties. She could not help feeling that it was cruel to string a person along, to say nothing all day in order to give her a hard, brotherly punch of affection at night.

For an hour or two she did her best. She mingled, listened, asked questions. She ate cake. After a while, she hid for a time inside a book she found on Eleanor's shelf, Rasmussen's *Observations on the Intellectual Culture of the Caribou Eskimos*. While Harry doctored himself with Scotch and Ralph satisfied his sweet tooth, Gwen was out in the arctic wastes and fifty years back in the past when the Inuit were still living much as they had for hundreds upon hundreds of years. *Small flocks of caribou were extremely shy and could not be hunted on the creaking snow in good weather, but only in a snowstorm, when it was sometimes possible to stalk quite close up to them.*

Rasmussen had entered the Barren Grounds in the spring of 1922, having heard as he travelled "many harrowing tales of the privation that had prevailed that winter". Everywhere Eskimos were starving. He followed the Kazan River looking for inland tribes, "the people of the whirlpools" and "the people of the willow thicket". The months of March and April were always the most dangerous time. Winter food caches had been used up, the May caribou migration had not begun.

"Hornby wasn't the only one who starved to death," Gwen thought, and she looked up to see Ralph watching her indulgently. "A serious reader," he said. "A woman after my own heart." He, too, liked to retreat behind a book or a magazine at parties, especially now that he had no wife to accuse him of being unforgivably and boyishly rude.

Gwen smiled and relaxed. She put the book down and returned to a party that seemed more complicated in its social tensions than the straightforward business of starving to death. A party she found touching and baffling and tiring and hard to navigate.

Dido was dancing by herself in bare feet. Teresa kicked off her shoes and joined her. Gwen watched from her armchair, fascinated by both women, afraid she would be expected to dance too, charmed by their lack of inhibition, and envious. Would she ever be like that? Dido was much the bigger of the two, yet her hips were almost as narrow as Teresa's. They were dancing to the Beatles – Dido reached over and jacked up the volume, she slipped her loose watch off her wrist and set it on the stereo – flirtatious, girlish, free, encouraged by applause from Ralph and Harry, who seemed as disinclined to dance as Gwen, and over the din Eleanor heard the doorbell.

It was Eddy on the doorstep. An entrance that changed everything. A visit in the manner of a visitation from an uninvited guest, although Eddy had been invited. He apologized for arriving late, he acknowledged Gwen with a squeeze of her shoulder. But the playful mood vanished, the women stopped dancing, and the music changed. Eddy had a new recording he wanted them to hear. Soon Joe Turner was singing slow, funky blues backed up by wailing trumpets. "I Know You Love Me Baby."

Eddy and Dido were dancing, and Gwen could see exactly what

Eddy brought to Dido. Dido moved differently with Eddy. She was slower, unhurried. Her breasts looked heavier, riper, her hips wider, lower, fuller. She shone with a different glow, a dark, erotic radiance.

By now Teresa was sitting cross-legged on the carpet beside Gwen's armchair, rolling a smoke, her hands trembling. Looking down at her, Gwen could see the traces of grey that she had never noticed before in the dark hair on top of Teresa's head. She could see the side of her face, and was struck by what seemed to be a sad and knowing smile. The other day Teresa had told her that although she had followed her sister into the nunnery, she had never followed her into a bad marriage. That was the great sadness of her life, she said. Her sister's terrible marriage.

It was late. Harry lay semi-sprawled on the floor. He gave up trying to make his point, having forgotten what it was. Gwen was curled up in an armchair, reading again. Eleanor's eyes rested on the birthday girl and a memory came back of a boy she knew growing up, Ronny Ferguson, a strange boy: other kids would be playing outside and he would be inside reading Marvel comics; even at his birthday party he kept on reading. His mother let him, that was the wondrous thing.

Gwen closed the book and asked what time it was. She asked the room at large. Everyone, except herself, was at this point sitting on the floor.

Dido, across the room with her back against the wall and Eddy beside her, waited a moment before she replied. "What time do you want it to be?"

Dido had slipped her shoes back on, low heels, black. Her bare arms were the colour of peeled almonds. Her watch was conspicuous again on her wrist.

Gwen wanted it to be very late. She wanted to go home. "I want it to be the time it is."

"But what time do you *want* it to be?"

130

Gwen felt herself being toyed with, baited by Dido's amused, provocative, subtly hostile tone, and her own voice came out hard and strained. "I. want. it. to. be. the. time. it. *is*."

Eleanor leaned her head back against the wall. It seemed to her that something was going on here that was closer than friendship, just as the scratchy label of a sweater is closer than the sweater.

The smile widened on Dido's lips. She shifted and looked at her watch. Then she looked at Gwen. "Why are you sitting on a chair? All the rest of us are on the floor."

"I'm comfortable on the chair." But she did not feel comfortable. And didn't look it either, she knew that.

"You don't look comfortable," said Dido with that slightly mocking smile.

"I'm as comfortable as I ever am."

"But you're apart from us, sitting up there. You've set yourself apart."

"I know. I know I'm sitting on a chair and everyone else is on the floor."

"Do you *feel* apart from the rest of us?"

"Maybe a little. Is that a crime?"

Dido was watching Gwen, but nobody else was. "It's not a crime. I just wonder what's going on. And why you're so angry."

Somebody had to break the silence, but nobody did.

Then Harry spoke, his voice low, conversational, a little slurred. "What's the book, Gwen?"

She looked down at the book in her hands.

"Show me."

She stood up then and handed him the book. And that's how she got off the chair-island on which she had been stranded. She knelt on the floor beside Harry. From here she could see partway down the hall and picture the rest – the barely used small bedroom, the fully used big bedroom. She could scarcely credit it. Yet it nudged her again. The eerie feeling that she knew something she could use against Dido.

Only in a snowstorm, she thought, a flurry of stuff in the air, was it possible to outwit the caribou. Outwitting people, however, that was easy. They were at the door. Eleanor embraced her and soothed her heart by saying, "Let's have lunch tomorrow. I'll ring your bell at noon." But brazen Dido took her face between her hands and kissed her on the mouth. "Happy birthday, birthday girl."

Dido's lips felt thin and over-soft, innocent yet all wrong. Harmless, but not harmless at all.

* *

It was 1 a.m., and Dido and Eleanor were listening to Billie Holiday sing good morning to her heartache as they emptied ashtrays, stacked dishes, began to wash up after the party.

Dido dried a plate. She reached for another, and as she did so, she remembered something, and the towel went still.

"I had a terrible dream last night."

Eleanor stopped too, and turned to look at Dido, who stood transfixed. She was back in the dream.

"I was in a big city and it was very dark, pitch dark. It felt like Eastern Europe somewhere. Pitch *black*, I mean. A taxi pulled up and I got into it, and we began to drive down this old, narrow street. There were two men in the front seat in black suits. They were staring straight ahead. I couldn't see their faces. I had no idea who they were, I didn't know where we were going either, I didn't know where I was." Dido rubbed her forehead with one hand. "There was nothing in here," she said slowly. "I had no memory. I had no mind. I didn't know anything. It was as black in here as it was outside." She looked at Eleanor. "It was terrifying."

She's describing a hearse, thought Eleanor. She's describing her own journey into death.

She took the tea towel out of Dido's hand. "You're tired, honey. It's late."

Dido turned to stare at the clock on the kitchen wall. "Eddy said, 'Loon at three o'clock' the other day. I didn't know whether to turn my head right or left. I couldn't remember where three was on the clock."

Eleanor put her arm around Dido and drew her away from the clock. "I get confused by things too and I'm not trying to juggle two languages and two countries the way you are."

*   *

Gwen had driven Harry home. On the way they did not talk and were comfortable not talking. They came down Franklin Avenue, named for the man who ate his boots, the explorer who managed to lose the lives of all one hundred and twenty-nine of his men in one of those foolhardy attempts to find the Northwest Passage. Proof to Harry that if your disaster was on a large enough scale, your incompetence would be forgiven.

In passing the Capitol Theatre, Gwen saw "The Godfather Part II" on the marquee, and she said, "Eddy has cruel lips."

"Women go for that," Harry said with a dry laugh.

She knew he meant the movie male aggressiveness that was undeniably exciting. "Dido has cruel lips too," she said.

Harry pretended not to hear this quiet remark. It was August 2 now, and the darkness was like a partially open drawer.

"There's Mrs Dargabble," Harry said.

Lorna Dargabble was on the other side of the street, out for a walk at one in the morning, hands in her pockets, oversized *chapeau* on her head. A lonely figure, slow, heavy, troubled. The last time Gwen had knocked on her door, no-one had answered, but she had heard a radio, faintly; Lorna always had the radio on – it was her life-line, she said. In the hallway Gwen had called out her name, and up came Lorna from the basement, full of apologies for not having her teeth in and dressed in much the same style as the half-renovated kitchen: she wore the most elegant shoes, green suede with straps at the back, a long green velvet skirt, and a lumber jacket. The kitchen had insulation but no drywall, a new stove not yet installed, and a true boarding house smell of none-too-clean.

"I don't see her at the station any more," Harry said.

"Oh, she still comes in. She's been talking about moving back to Boston. She says Yellowknife is no place for an old woman."

Harry nodded. Or an old man, for that matter.

When Gwen pulled into Harry's driveway, she turned off the motor and sat back, unwilling to end a night she had held steadfastly at bay. There was something she wanted to ask.

"Harry?" She ran her necklace of blue beads back and forth across her lower lip.

The gesture reminded Harry of his ex-wife, who used to draw forward a strand of her long hair and curl it around and around her finger.

What she wanted to ask was why Dido had kissed her on the mouth like that. What was she trying to prove? And why were her personal things in Eleanor's bedroom when she was obviously sleeping with Eddy? She wanted to say, What's going on with Dido, this woman you're so in love with?

But an easier statement slipped out. "I'd like to live down here," she said.

Then she said something else. "I don't really like living alone. I liked it better when I lived with Eleanor. I mean, lived with her, sort of."

"Too bad she doesn't have more room."

She looked at him. "There's enough room. Dido's bedroom doesn't seem to get much use, even when she's there."

For a second his eyes drilled her. Then he looked ahead with a bleak little smile.

It had slipped out innocently enough, cloaked in honesty, even delicacy. She had observed something. How could she not take credit?

Iago. Iago had bobbed up inside her.

"It's late, Gwen." He reached for the door handle. "Thanks for the ride."

But she was Iago and Othello in one: insinuating and sorry. "I'm sorry. Forget what I just said. I don't know what I'm talking about." She was looking over at him. "I shouldn't have said that. I don't mean to be nasty."

Harry remained silent.

"Or maybe I do," she said.

Harry heard the misery in her voice. Now she was staring at her hands in her lap. It was cool enough that he was surprised she was not shivering in her light jacket.

Later, he would ponder on what she had implied. *Dido's bedroom doesn't seem to get much use.* A shock – if it was true. But his world was not destroyed by the thought of Dido in Eleanor's bed. It is not the thought of a woman with another woman that makes a man unhappy, it is the thought of a woman with another man. Anyway, he didn't buy it – although he'd give anything to see Eddy's face if it were true. No, the remark said more about Gwen than it did about anyone else. She had leapt to a conclusion for reasons of her own, and then she had had the decency to regret it.

GWEN FOUND HERSELF THINKING ABOUT THE VULNERABLE rivers and birds and plants and animals and old ways of life – all of it unprotected, much of it wary. At the Berger Inquiry she had heard that snow geese in late August gathered in the thousands on the arctic coast, feeding for several weeks on berries and sedges before flying eight hundred miles non-stop to northern Alberta, then on to the wheat fields farther south. On these August staging grounds, said the biologists, the birds were easily frightened by planes overhead and activity on the ground – the noise of a compressor station at a distance of a mile and a half, or a small aircraft at the same distance, was enough to flush them into the air. Similarly, the white whales of the Beaufort Sea were wary of man, yet increasingly exposed. To give birth they came into the warmer, shallow waters of Mackenzie Bay, now the site, and increasingly so, of offshore drilling for oil and gas.

Then there were the caribou. In March they left their winter range among the trees and travelled slowly north across the tundra, arriving at their calving grounds near the arctic coast in late May. In early June, after the calves were born, the cows joined together in small, timid clusters, then larger bands, then greater herds that culminated in the post-calving aggregation, the gathering en masse in July that forms the sight over which everyone marvels, a spectacle equal to the long lost flights of passenger pigeons, or the once glorious massing of buffalo. But disturb them while calving, fly a helicopter low in the fog, and you cause the females to be separated from their young, with drastic results. At the same time these creatures were enormously resilient, able to withstand extreme cold and hunger, epic distances and plagues of maddening flies.

She learned the word *albedo*. An oil spill, in turning the ice black, ruins its albedo or reflective capacity, causing it to absorb light rather than reflect it, and to melt, thereby changing the environment in unforeseeable ways. Albedo like albino, went her connecting mind, like bezel – a ruby-eyed albino. Jewellery terms came back to her, and her father's slender explanations, his reticence. He would sit at his jeweller's bench, using a brush to sweep up piles of silver dust, or lemel, which he kept and melted up for reuse. He had little boxes of gold dust too. Every so often the big jewellery makers would take everything up, he told her once, all the floorboards, all the shelves, and burn them for the gold. He would bring his magnifying loupe to his eye, then raise the jewel to the loupe, checking for imperfections. It's all illusion, he had murmured once as he fine-sandpapered a brooch: you make something smooth with a series of scratches. Cabochon was another old word used in the trade; it referred to any stone that was flat on one side and round on the other. In little drawers her father had cabochons of amber and turquoise, in other little drawers loose pearls, garnets, amethysts. Anneal. She loved to watch the process happen, the metal relax and change colour, soften and become supple under the steady heat of the gas flame. Her father would have said that Dido had a jeweller's hands and wrists and shoulders, square and strong and capable. It was not hard to imagine Dido doing what she herself had never managed to do, polish silver and gold on the rouge wheel without ever blackening her long, competent fingers.

In the coming months, Gwen formed an image of the North as an open page in a book of wonders illustrated and illuminated with rare animals and subtle plants. The North was the tropics made simple and cool. A rather more knowable place, since it held on to all traces of passage, to every weathered bone and fire-cracked rock. One scientist talked about the length of time it took anything to decay in the arctic air, on the one hand, and to grow, on the other, since food supplies were limited, summer was short, reproduction rates were meagre. In some parts of the North an arctic char did not produce ripe eggs until it was twelve years old, and even after that it spawned only every second or third year. A world, where if you were a child and the world was a plate, then the plate would be huge and have lots of space between a few select foods. She had been that very sort of child, wanting everything kept separate, and not a lot of different things at once, or much of any one thing at all.

The inquiry was making so much visible and noteworthy. Something quickened inside her when she heard native testimony on the radio about living on the land, about existing in makeshift shelters as you went storm-tossed and sun-warmed through life. Many native people still spent May and June in their spring camps trapping muskrats, and summers at their fish camps in the Delta catching and drying fish or harvesting white whales, and parts of the winters inland, hunting and trapping. Berger was going to their doorsteps, settlement to settlement, thirty-five in all. He was visiting summer camps and fishing grounds, like the itinerant preachers of old, in his corduroy jacket with the leather patches on the elbows, wearing his large school-boy glasses on his pleasantly wide face. And people, of course, were coming to him. Countless witnesses were speaking into the microphone in a gathering, an aggregation if you like, of informants and information. A remarkable time of hope for anyone opposed to the pipeline, for anyone in favour of the present learning from the past.

*   *

Around Yellowknife, the miniature birches and poplars changed colour in August. For about two weeks they were a ravishing yellow-gold. It was quite astonishing, but so fast: every single leaf was on every single tree and every single leaf was yellow. Farther south, colour gathered on some leaves as others fell, and you only ever got a piece of the whole, but here you had all of the glory all at once, and then it was gone. In September, it snowed enough to cover the ground, and the roads turned icy. They would not see water on the streets again until April.

Towards the end of September, a large package arrived at the station addressed to Gwen Symon. A round-shouldered bundle of heavy brown paper, bigger than a big sleeping bag, she thought. No return address. She had thought immediately of a peace offering from her brother in Ontario – they had not spoken in months and months – but the postmark said YELLOWKNIFE.

Opening it, while Eleanor looked on, Gwen recalled Harry's comment about ghosts pouring out of boxes. He was right. It was a fur coat, a ghost of sorts.

She lifted it out of its wrappings, her expression open-mouthed and astounded, and Eleanor said, "We're going to remember this for the rest of our lives. You'll remember the look of the coat and I'll remember the look on your face."

Gwen held the coat by its shoulders and shook out its folds. She examined the dark, brownish-grey fur that seemed to shed light. It felt as soft as talcum powder. She checked the label, "Wright Furs", then looked for tags and found none, looked for signs of wear on the brown silk lining and found not wear, but the softness of having been worn. She slipped it on, bringing it close around her neck, and stepped up to the studio window to see her reflection.

"You look wonderful," Eleanor said.

Gwen put her hands in the pockets and pulled out a small card. *From a secret admirer.* Now her insides were as transformed as her outsides: she felt flattered and stunned. The first snowfall had worked a similar change on the town itself. It dazzled interiors by transforming the external world.

The beauty of fur. The coat was light in weight but warm and luxurious. And Gwen did look wonderful. Even she could see that.

Teresa was able to identify the fur. Her father ran a trapline, and so she knew sheared beaver when she saw it. The coat had been perfectly cared for, she said. It was as good as new.

Dido had appeared too, drawn by all the fuss. She fingered the coat enviously. "It's beautiful, Gwen."

"Try it on."

Dido tried it on. She had to hunch her shoulders and when she stretched out her arms, inches of bare wrist protruded. "Whoever sent it knows your size," she said. "Maybe somebody's watching you. Did you think of that?"

Gwen took the coat back from her, and slowly, carefully folded it. She had not thought of that, and what had been latent, a twinge of alarm and suspicion, now overtook her joy. She stroked the fur. What a shame if she could not wear it.

"Come on," Teresa protested. "Who cares where it came from?"

Then quite suddenly Gwen knew. In her childhood a big basket of precious blueberries from Manitoulin Island had been sent to a family down the street, the Johnsons, a gift from their island relatives. But the berries never arrived – they were delivered by mistake to another family with the same name – a story pieced together only after the relatives wondered aloud at never having been thanked. "There must be another Gwen Symon," she said.

But then why was the package addressed to her at her place of work? No, she realized, she was the one it was intended for.

In the end, Gwen would take Teresa's view. She wore the coat. She called it Dolly. Come on, Dolly, let's go for a walk. And she would take long rambles, warm as toast and reasonably worry-free. She never ceased to puzzle over who might have given it to her, but no-one stepped forward, and the riddle remained unsolved for more than a year.

A few days later, in the parking lot next to the liquor store, Harry pulled up behind Dido's parked car. She sat alone behind the wheel, so still that he wondered why, and then the light dawned. No doubt she was listening to the radio, and he turned his on to see what might have captured her attention.

It was Eliza Doolittle's spirited invective against Henry Higgins, but what Harry could not know was that Dido was reliving the skip on her childhood recording, a skip ingrained in her memory as much as the music itself. She heard it coming, then heard it happen, even as the song on the radio sailed smoothly on. It brought her whole childhood back. Her father would lift the needle and place it, delicately, a fraction of a centimetre ahead. As precisely as Eddy had located "Helpless". "My Fair Lady" had been a recording for daytime. At night, her father frequently put on "Harold in Italy", and she would fall asleep to those glorious, haunting strains, learning to love the viola because of Berlioz, because, in truth, of her father. Sitting here now, suspended with music that flooded her with the past, she wondered what her father, who had been drawn to strong women, not to strong men, would have thought of Eddy. Eddy was so private, intense, possessive; he wanted to have a child with her, he wanted a son; and yet there were things he kept entirely to himself, and there were times when she did not seem to matter to him at all. The radio news came on and she turned it up. Gravesites were being prepared for the winter, not at the old cemetery on Back Bay where she had heard her father's voice, but at the new one near the airport, twenty-five graves that would be covered with wooden cribbing to protect them until needed, after which the ground would freeze so hard it would be impossible to turn it over with a spade. The innocence of these arrangements struck her. Nobody expects anything bad to happen, she thought, anything out of the ordinary. She, on the other hand, had been having one violent dream after another and they coloured her days with vague apprehension.

Harry's tuneful whistle greeted her when she got out of the car. He was leaning against his van, whistling "I've Grown Accustomed to Her Face", and she had to smile. She recognized the compliment, understood the connection; he had been listening to the radio too.

Harry was delighted to see her, delighted to catch her in an unguarded moment. He was thinking that the age difference between them was not as vast as that between Higgins and Eliza. He in his forties, Dido in her twenties. But Dido must have read his mind because she said, "Harry, I'm not Eliza Doolittle, you know."

He watched her head into the liquor store and admired her more than ever for seeing through his foolish self.

* *

Radio mattered more as the days grew shorter. Gwen, broadcasting at midnight, had more calls and more complaints about the music she played. There were times when she put her disgruntled listeners on the air and defended herself, using the little sound-effects door to good effect. "Thank you and good night!" Or, "You think that's opera? Let me introduce you to opera. Here we are at Joan Sutherland's door." She rang the doorbell and invited Joan to sing an aria from *Norma*.

At the end of her summer contract, Harry had called her into his office and extended it for a year. For Gwen, that was more than enough. She felt a new surge of confidence that helped to balance other worries, like her ongoing estrangement from Dido. Their paths rarely crossed any more, and when they did, nothing transpired except the briefest of greetings. She had more contact, really, with Lorna Dargabble, who often telephoned during her late-night show, almost pitifully grateful for some of the music she played.

Sometimes when she closed down the station at one in the morning and stepped outside, she would see the elderly woman coming back from one of her solitary walks. In the summer, Lorna said, she ventured as far as Frame Lake, and walked along the shore, or went down to Old Town and circled the Rock. In the colder months, however, she stayed in the downtown area that was scented by the warm, stale, greasy puffs of air that issued from Jason's Chicken.

On this occasion, as Gwen accompanied Mrs Dargabble home, they saw Eddy and a young Dene man ahead of them, the latter identifiable by his long black braid and a posture even more erect than Eddy's.

Lorna said, "I don't trust those two. I don't know what they're up to, but they're up to something."

Gwen looked at her, surprised to catch a hint of prejudice. "Do they have to be up to something? I mean, here we are, you and I. Would you say we're up to something?"

Lorna chuckled and put her arm through Gwen's. But soon she let out a heavy sigh. "My days of being up to anything are over," she said.

Gwen asked what was weighing on her mind, and Lorna told her that she had almost decided to see a lawyer about getting a divorce.

"But that's good," Gwen encouraged.

"No," Lorna said. "Nothing's good."

*   *

Gwen's breakfast was everyone else's lunch; she got into the habit of joining Teresa in the Gold Range café around noon. One day, when Eleanor was with them, Teresa split her egg roll down the centre, poured the sweet sauce inside, and said, amused and mischievous, "Love is like a Chinese menu. It's not a question of meeting the one and only. There's infinite choice. All you have to do is pick."

"Listen to you," Eleanor said, who shared Teresa's side of the booth. Teresa leaned into her, capsized by mirth.

The café was busy and warm, dank with steam and grease and cigarette smoke. A framed photograph, "Lunchtime Atop a

Skyscraper, 1932," on the wall: workers with lunch pails in their laps, balanced on a high beam above New York City. Teresa's relaxed work ethic meant for longer than usual lunch breaks and later than usual hours to make up for it. That suited Gwen, who did not begin her shift until 6 p.m.

This was the day when Teresa let drop quite casually that she used to volunteer at the gay crisis line in Vancouver. "A thirty-five-year-old woman called up," she said, "and I suggested we have coffee together. I told her don't worry. I'm an ancient Chinese washer-woman. I won't come on to you." Teresa recognized the look on Gwen's face, the controlled shock, and added with a small smile, "I try not to hide anything about myself."

A pause. Eleanor said, "That's what I love about you."

For Gwen, Teresa's revelation brought her birthday party into focus. She remembered Teresa's trembling hands after Eddy claimed Dido for himself, and realized she had been right about something, after all, just wrong about the someone.

Eddy came in, and with him came not Dido this time, but his Dene friend. The two men passed the three women and nodded. Eleanor greeted them by name. "Eddy. Paul." They took a booth at the very back of the restaurant. Eleanor said, "Paul came to our northern support group to explain the native land claim."

Teresa's face had darkened. Suddenly she looked every inch her age.

"I wonder if *you'd* come one night," Eleanor said to her. "We'd love to hear your views."

There was something wonderfully innocent and generous about Eleanor Dew, thought Gwen on her side of the booth as she watched her kind, lived-in face become animated with the issues of the day. Eleanor filled Teresa in on the northern support group formed by Dido and Eddy, a workshop of like-minded whites who wanted to discuss the native land claim, understand it better, support it publicly, offset the usual white ignorance and mistrust of native rights. The

North of Sixty Support Group, they were calling themselves, and it wasn't meant for journalists, she said with an apologetic smile for Gwen, just ordinary people in town. "Well, Dido's the exception. There's just a handful of us. We meet once a week in my trailer. There's a teacher. An architect. There's the United Church minister. One woman's a nurse. There's a painter. There's me. We're tasting the pleasures of radical thinking," she said with a gently ironic smile, "Going to the root of what Eddy likes to call 'present reality'. But it's good. Paul spoke to us a few weeks ago," indicating him with a movement of her finger, "I found it interesting, helpful."

Teresa said, "I know Paul Julien." She pushed her plate to one side. "He's a cousin of mine." The food she had not eaten would go into the garbage cans behind the restaurant and be squawked over by the flapping, theatrical ravens.

"We deserve a land claim settlement," Teresa said. "We deserve to have control of this country. But Paul's what I'd call a man on the prowl. He's bad news."

*   *

Late one night, Gwen, wearing Dolly, stood in the middle of the street, head craned back, awestruck, listening. She had finished her shift and put on her borrowed finery, the mysterious loan, as she chose to think of it, that had fallen into her lap from the amazing sky. A sky that on this night towards the end of October was filled with a moving white fog, which began to shimmer and ripple downwards in long, shaggy icicles, then sideways in draperies of pale green and violet – a huge, heavenly version of the gas flame of a jeweller's torch shooting out to the side and shifting in colour from white to blue to green to orange. If she had been outside the city, somewhere in the arctic wastes, she might have heard the northern lights swish and whisper as everyone said they did, Dene, Inuit, trappers, prospectors, everyone except the dreary scientists.

Earlier the same night, there had been earthly fireworks of a milder sort on Latham Island. Judge Berger was holding a community hearing in the hall a hundred yards or so from Harry's house. These community hearings, as distinct from the formal hearings in the Explorer Hotel, were casual and open-ended, continuing until everyone who wanted to speak had spoken. It was Berger's contention that every person who lived in this part of the world had a right to say what he or she felt about a pipeline.

Harry sat at the end of a row of chairs, listening to a smart, young Yellowknife doctor utter a series of warnings about the next southern invasion of the North. Look at Alaska, the doctor was saying, where the Alyeska pipeline was built *after* a land claims settlement with the native people, and even so, the effect has been catastrophic on rates of suicide, divorce, alcoholism, mental illness, violent crime: a horror story, and we haven't heard the final chapter. Here, said the doctor, the natives don't *have* a land claims settlement. So what's going to happen? For three winters a few of them will be hired as part of a big pipeline force and they'll receive high wages. Then what? They'll drift south looking for the same wages, they'll drift into unemployment and welfare in Vancouver or Winnipeg or Toronto, and the North will have lost its best young men just when the Dene are trying to establish their right to self-determination. Young native women will be enticed and sexually exploited by transient white labourers with lots of money and easy access to alcohol and no thought for the consequences of their actions. "Who is going to pay for all this?" he wanted to know. "The pipeline company? The oil company? The people of Canada? These people may pay the dollars; we already know who is going to pay the price in human misery."

The little hall was bright with lights and cameras. The possibility for spontaneous, unscripted drama made these informal hearings of special interest to journalists. Nothing went unnoticed.

Harry saw Eddy and Dido at the back, their coats over their arms.

Lorna Dargabble sat in loose disarray at the end of a middle row. Berger, in jacket and tie, was at the front, seated at a small square table, a pedestal mike directly in front of him. On his left were the transcribers, getting down every word that was spoken. At another table were representatives from both pipeline companies, who were there to answer questions. Behind the judge, and tacked to the wall, was a huge map showing the proposed routes for the pipeline, there being two proposals, as Berger took pains to explain in his opening remarks. The one that was 2,200 miles long had been put forward by an international consortium (Arctic Gas). It was to bring gas from Prudhoe Bay, along the north slope of Alaska across the Yukon to the Mackenzie Valley, then pick up Canadian gas from the Mackenzie River Delta, and in a single pipeline bring it to markets in the south, Canadian and American. The other was an all-Canadian proposal (Foothills Pipe Lines) to bring Canadian gas from the Mackenzie Delta south to Canadian markets only. This one was 800 miles long. Arctic Gas claimed their bigger venture would be more economical in the long run, and gas would cost less than it would if the Foothills project went through. "Well, that's the argument between them," Berger said, setting himself apart from the companies even as he explained their intentions to the audience of about seventy people. No matter which pipeline project went ahead, he said, there would be thousands of men needed to build it and it would take years to build. And if a gas pipeline was built, an oil pipeline would surely follow. It was logical, then, for his inquiry to address not just the impact of a gas pipeline, but all the development that would come thereafter. Listening to him speak, Harry appreciated just how much Tom Berger had managed to turn his inquiry into an exercise in democracy, informing, questioning, teaching, listening. "I hope you'll feel free to speak up and tell me what's on your mind," Berger would say to the local people at these informal hearings, "just as if there were only yourselves and myself here tonight."

After the doctor finished speaking, a pilot for one of the small charter companies in Yellowknife went to the microphone, a man skeptical about the value of the inquiry, who referred to "the proposed, and it would seem from all accounts, inevitable pipeline". He said he would welcome the boost to the economy, the extra business, but he felt depressed about what was bound to happen to the relaxed and easy-going town he loved.

After the pilot, Eddy got up to speak.

Teresa Lafferty had come in by then, and was standing at the back, curious to hear what these townspeople had to say. She would not speak herself until Berger brought his inquiry to her hometown of Fort Rae the following summer. She wanted her relatives, her grandmother especially, to hear her voice added to theirs; she wanted them to be together on that historic day. Then she would say that what the pipeline companies were asking for was enormous and what the people were asking for wasn't much at all. It wasn't asking a lot to have the land claim settled first. If the pipeline should burst, what would happen to their traditional hunting grounds, to the animals and all the food they depended on? My people don't have any money at all, she would tell the judge, and I don't think they care to make money. The only ones who stand to benefit from a pipeline are the big oil companies and southern Canada and the United States. I'm afraid of the pipeline, she would tell him. I'm afraid for the elders, for all my relatives, for their traditional way of life, and for the land itself.

Tonight Teresa looked around at the mostly white faces and wondered where these people came from – where you came from being the question put to everyone in the North (everyone except the Indians, she thought). From outside, but from where outside?

Harry was motioning to her, asking if she wanted to sit down, and she took the chair beside him. Then Harry was holding his glasses, closing and opening the frames as he listened to Eddy.

"A Dene friend of mine," Eddy was saying, "told me he'd been to Vietnam too, and I thought he was joking. But we drove out to

Fort Rae, and I wonder if you know this, Judge, that seventy miles from here there's a place they call Vietnam. Crappy houses, broken windows, dust and dirt and misery. Fort Rae isn't much, but part of it's so bad they call it Vietnam. A real skid row. So what I want to say tonight is that I think you have good intentions, but good intentions aren't enough. Some friends and I started a northern support group to add our voices, in a very small way, to the call for social justice for the native people. We called ourselves the North of Sixty Support Group. Then a couple of weeks ago a few rednecks, I can't think of any other word for them, stole our name, registered themselves legally, and set about printing ads in favour of the pipeline. What can you do against people like that?" Eddy addressed his question to the audience at large. Then said to Berger, "You're an employee of the Government of Canada. You're part of the system. I've been living here for over a year, I've got a white boss, most of the folks I work with are white. That radio station I work at – it should be Dene-run. This inquiry should be Dene-run too. They're the majority, they should be in charge. But it's never going to happen, not by having nice, polite meetings."

Teresa shifted her embroidered parka in her lap. She thought, In a year he'll be gone, back to where he came from. All the white people went home eventually.

"Look," he gestured with both hands, his jaw working with suppressed anger, "you've already had some Dene witnesses say they'll lay down their lives to stop the pipeline and the whites all squawked about it. *They're threatening violence.* But I'm saying there's already violence. The conditions in the settlements. That's a form of violence. Why aren't the whites up in arms about that? Why aren't they up in arms about the underhanded disrespect and back-room wheeling and dealing that does violence to goodwill and good intentions? So I want to go on record as opposing the pipeline and supporting the Dene taking control by whatever means necessary."

149

There was a smattering of applause. One of the native reporters raised his fist and grinned with glee, one rabblerouser congratulating another. Dido saw Harry Boyd tug on his ear, left-handed, good-hearted, ineffectual Harry. But Eddy was right. The world was divided into the majority who wanted to believe everything was O.K. and the radical few who knew it was not and were galvanized by that fact. Eddy had energy and so did she. She had an immigrant's energy and impatience and sense of purpose, and so did Eddy. Privately, they were both coming to believe you had to do something drastic to stop corporations from violating the land. Something to convince them the North would not be a safe place to put their money.

Lorna Dargabble was on her way to the microphone. Harry glanced back at Dido. She was standing in front of Eddy, leaning against him. His hands were on her shoulders. The two of them shone with a powerful, self-righteous glow, it seemed to Harry, who considered self-righteousness a sin in itself, not that the thought made him feel any better. Lorna Dargabble was wishing everybody would stop romanticizing the past. She was an old woman, she was saying, and she had seen what men do to women late at night and it did not matter if they were white or native, or if it was ten years ago or today. There's a lot of ugliness in the North and a lot of abuse. We need kindness, she was saying, jobs and kindness. But she was losing her train of thought, and Harry noticed Eddy whispering in Dido's ear and Dido smiling and nodding. They seemed to be amused by the old woman. Not only self-righteous, he thought, but cruel. Then he was called back to Lorna, her voice suddenly clear as a bell. "I heard on the radio this man telling you the pipeline companies will rape the land. Well, this man ought to know. I mean to say, he's been up on rape charges more than once. There's a lot of talk about the terrible degradation the pipeline will bring. Oh, yes. And I'm worried too. But don't believe everything you hear, that's all I'm saying."

Lorna's short testimony was greeted by a shuffling of feet, a certain embarrassment. Berger, unfailingly polite, thanked her. At every one of these hearings the atmosphere was serious, unhurried; people wanted to express themselves. Frequently, someone would say, as a young woman was saying now, "I didn't intend to speak tonight, I just intended to listen. However, after listening to the last person, I felt I had to speak. I think it's time we believed in the native people. This is their land." A Dene fellow went to the microphone after that. "Like myself," he said, "I'm a young man. I'm only twenty-three years old and I'm thinking about my kids." Harry would see this man again on a cold winter's day under circumstances so different he would not recognize him at first. "Today I was parking my truck downtown. Yes, I parked my truck because I was going to be gone about half an hour, but I was gone forty-five minutes. When I got back to my truck I got a ticket and it was going to cost me three dollars. I was thinking, well, this is Dene land. They should at least ask us before they do their regulations. At least they should ask the chiefs. They should say, what do you think?" There was a murmur of sympathy from the audience, some nodded their heads. "Before the white people came to Yellowknife, kids used to be learning lessons from their parents. Our kids don't listen now and even the dogs, we don't have any good dogs now. All the white people came and brought their small dogs around, they're all mixed up now. Everything they're spoiling. They spoiled the water too. They spoiled the land." The hall was quiet now. "I just hope the government listens to us," he said, and pushed back his chair. "So, this is all I wanted to say."

Harry ought not to have stood up. He knew better. But he cradled his glasses in his left hand and went to the microphone. He had expected somebody else to take issue with Eddy. Had they been uptown in the Elk's Hall, rather than here in Old Town, there would have been any number of businessmen and local politicians ready and eager to defend the pipeline. He had no intention of being pro-pipeline, but he felt he had to speak. "Judge Berger, I'm the white boss referred to earlier. I'm the manager of a radio station soon to be dwarfed by a television station. So as bosses go, I'm pretty small potatoes." He heard the door of the hall bang shut and wondered if that was Dido and Eddy leaving. "This isn't going to make me popular with my own bosses, but I feel I have to say it. I'm speaking for myself as a resident of the North, you understand. Here we have an inquiry about the effects of the pipeline, what you, sir, in your opening remarks called the most expensive project ever undertaken by private enterprise anywhere in the world. But Judge, let's say you're able to recommend ways of keeping the pipeline far away from the communities. Let's say you're able to do that," Harry said. "Then it could be argued that its impact will do less harm in the long run than television beamed in from the south. I don't mean to trivialize the pipeline. My real point is that some things we can't escape, television's one of them, the pipeline's probably another. But we can slow them down and we don't have to resort to violence to do it. An example. Last March the settlement of Igloolik rejected television in a referendum. They chose instead to have a radio station they control. In my view the best thing your inquiry is doing is waking everybody up so they're on guard against being rushed and pushed and bullied into things. For the record, I don't want the pipeline, and I don't want it because the native people don't want it. After all, we white people from the south are in the minority up here. We should stop trying to get our own way all the time." Harry thanked the judge, and returned to the back of the hall, hoping for what? Not Dido's semi-smile, her look of cool appraisal, if that was what it was. That was certainly what it felt like. Teresa touched his arm when he sat down. "Thank you, Harry."

Not long afterwards, as Harry was leaving to go home, a reporter from the local newspaper stopped him at the door, wanting to be sure he had his name and job title right. Once he was home, Harry made a pot of coffee, and then he went for a long walk and came upon Gwen, in her fur coat, staring up at the northern lights.

"Aurora Borealis," he said. "Electrically charged particles in the solar wind collide with molecules in the Earth's upper atmosphere, and the collision gives off light."

"You should be in bed," Gwen said.

"The green is caused by oxygen and the violet by nitrogen."

They continued to stare at the colours in the sky, Harry recalling the moment last summer when Gwen had been decorated head and shoulders in blue damselflies. Here she was again, glad to be out in the elements. It made him feel better just to see her.

"I did something I shouldn't have tonight," he said.

"What was that?"

"I took a political position. I said where I stood."

"That's commendable."

"Not for the manager of a public radio station. We're supposed to be objective, not take sides, especially in a political climate as charged as this one."

It became known as the Harry Boyd incident, and it caused him more grief with his own newsroom than with head office. Head office merely rapped his knuckles and warned him not to do anything like it again. But Thwaite and Tupper were furious with him for making their own lives more difficult. Here they were trying to present themselves as unbiased, which they were, and their station manager had to run off at the mouth at a public meeting. They sent a letter of complaint to the head of the Northern Service in Ottawa. There would be a later letter, too, signed by others.

ONE DAY IN EARLY NOVEMBER, DIDO CAME TO WORK IN dark glasses. That evening Gwen found her staring out the window of the empty office, lost in thought. She had pushed her sunglasses to the top of her head, and Gwen saw the bruised and puffy left eye.

Between the two women there sprang up a momentary, unbridgeable silence. Dido's cool glance. Gwen's stock stillness. Dido had not turned on the overhead light. Except for one desk lamp, the room was dark. Fleetingly, Gwen remembered sitting in the shade of a plum tree after her mother's funeral. A neighbour, attending to his garden on the other side of the fence, scraped a trowel against a clay pot, and the earthy sound cut through all her troubles and made her aware of the grass and plums and birds.

"Dido?"

"I'm right here."

Gwen hesitated. Then she took a step forward. "We don't talk much any more. Something went wrong. I don't know when it all began."

Dido smiled a little. She was wearing a close-fitting leather jacket over a black top. Her hands were expressive and lean and white as she took her dark glasses off her head and folded them and set them on the desk in front of her. "I knew we'd end up talking about this."

"And you don't want to." Gwen had settled gingerly on a chair about eight feet away. There was the smell of old coffee. A dark purple iris on the calendar on the wall.

154

Dido smiled again. "You're hot and cold."

Gwen absorbed this, the surprise of it, the weight of it. "I don't think so," she said, puzzled. No-one had ever said such a thing to her before. If anyone was hot and cold, it was Dido herself.

"I used to go home at night and slam the table and yell your name, I'd be so mad at you."

Gwen stared at her in amazement. "But what for?"

"For some snub during the day. I'd say something and you'd answer something back as if to say I was stupid."

"No." Gwen was shaking her head. She felt like a child caught doing wrong, cold and sick in her stomach.

"Yes. That's exactly what you do. You say by a look, or just your tone of voice, that the idea someone's talking about is ignorant. You can be so contemptuous."

"Dido, I don't feel *any* contempt for you. If I seem to, I'm sorry."

"Are you sure?"

Gwen sat there, dumbfounded. She scanned back through the past, trying to resurrect incidents, but she and Dido, working their separate shifts, hadn't seen each other much at all. She wanted to say, Are *you* sure you've got the right person?

She said, "I get nervous. I know that puts me in a bad mood. Usually I'm so uncertain about what I'm doing." She stopped. Then deliberately she quoted Dido back to herself. "Some people know exactly how good they are. Some of us aren't like that at all."

But Dido did not appear to catch the reference. "Well, you shouldn't make *me* suffer for it. I expect to be treated differently by you."

Gwen sat back in her chair. Dido was being unreasonable. She wanted to be treated with kid gloves. A queen. But she was a slipping queen. There she was with a black eye.

"Does it hurt?" Gwen said. "How did it happen?"

Dido gave her a long look. "I don't feel I can trust you." She delivered her deadly verdict in an even voice. "Not with anything really important. You're too unpredictable."

"You can predict what I'm going to talk about," Gwen said carefully. "You knew we'd end up talking about this."

That is when Dido's face softened somewhat and she backed off. "I suppose you're right." She reached over and turned on another lamp.

In the extra light, Gwen saw how vulnerable she really looked. It was more than the black eye, it was her skin, which looked paper-thin instead of creamy, and the way she rubbed her thumb with the fingertips of the same hand, repeatedly, but seemed unaware she was doing it. The way she dug her teeth into her lower lip, leaving tooth marks.

For a while they talked about other things, but not about anything really important: not about Dido's eye, for instance. What they talked about was work. Gwen had taken it upon herself to dramatize a series of northern legends about Raven, trickster and creator of the world, and she asked Dido to be the narrator, something she had been meaning to ask for days. "That is, if you don't mind working with me."

"I don't mind," Dido said. "If you treat me with respect."

"Dido, everyone respects you. Don't you know that?"

Although Dido did not respond, Gwen could see by the way she swept her hair off her face – an old and confident gesture – that she was pleased, and Gwen felt almost forgiven.

Before Dido left for the night – leaving the station in Gwen's hands – she hugged her, then stood back and surveyed her wary, appeasing face. Then leaned forward and kissed her, for the second time, on the mouth.

"Don't be afraid," she said in response to the alarm in Gwen's eyes. "I won't rape you."

* *

In fairy tales there is the fairy who is not invited, the child who is not protected, the princess who is wooed by the wrong prince. These shocking moments are lifted whole into the light, drawn up out of a deep well, and there they hang, glistening and floundering, all exposed.

The first time Eddy and Dido got stoned together, Dido learned what *the body electric* meant: they were their own northern lights, murmured Eddy, who kept up an intoxicating riff of suggestive, explicit words as he made love to her slowly and expertly. Dido had walked away incredulous, then gone back for more. Eddy had a basement apartment on a street two blocks south of the radio station. His furnishings were meagre, provided by the landlord, but he kept it very clean. Once the weather turned cold, he had stopped using his space in the warehouse in Old Town and moved all his transmitters and radio parts and cameras into the spare bedroom. He took photographs of Dido and developed them in the bathroom until a photographer at the local newspaper let him use their darkroom instead. He showed Dido his shots of her and pinned several to the wall. She did not know about the other photographs he was taking, and when she did find out – and viewed them – she made the same excuses, offered the same rationale that Eddy would.

His place had no curtains and the light that came across their bed was like moonlight from outer space. Their bodies glimmered against the sheets. Then came the early morning when she wanted to leave and he would not let her. He pinned her less than playfully to the bed. The next time he got rough with her, she got rough back, and that aroused her in a way that shook and sickened and excited her.

Dido's confusion deepened after an interview she did – a native linguist in his fifties recalled his experience in residential school. He began to tell her in a calm voice what happened.

His mother died when he was three, he said into the microphone, and for a while he was raised by his grandparents, but one day his grandfather put him on a horse-drawn wagon and said in their language, "You are going away". He was sent to Elkhorn, Manitoba, to a boarding school run by an Anglican mission. In school they were all warned not to speak their own language, but the day came when he had been caught too many times, and he was punished. The Anglican missionary slapped his face until his cheeks were red and hot, but he did not cry. Then he was told to take off his clothes, his coveralls, and he was smacked on his bare behind, and then he cried. His hands were strapped behind his back, his ankles were tied, and he was put on a tall stool and left there until he fell off the stool and messed himself. Again, he was spanked. He was ordered to fill a basin with warm water, to stir a bar of soap, cut in half, into the water, then to wash his mouth with it. Soon his mouth was raw inside and he felt the most violent thirst. Then he was put into an empty room. After a time the priest came back and brought out his penis, "but I was five, and I didn't know what he meant, so he shoved it into me, and I fainted".

The man's story of childhood horror triggered a personal memory – pulled from somewhere deep inside her – of a child spanking a younger child's bottom, and she was the child. She was five, the younger child was two or three. They were upstairs in her house, a group of them, playing. And what prompted it? All she remembered was pulling down the little one's panties and the suffusion of feeling that accompanied the application of her bare hand to that bare bottom. It rushed through her untrammelled, a sense of dirtiness, excitement, and guilt.

She had forgotten, she had forgotten, and now it flooded back. A five-year-old's upwelling sexuality. Maybe it was not untypical, she told herself, maybe it was something all but a few outgrew, all but a few celibate priests who got it off by spanking bare bottoms and more, the unutterable things the native linguist spoke of, until she said to him, "This is too hard to listen to."

"Yes," he agreed, and he stopped, and did not seem to mind stopping.

She asked Harry what she should have done and what they should do next. Harry told her she had done the right thing by listening until it was too painful to listen any more.

"I feel like a coward," Dido said.

The telephone calls to the station were mostly from offended listeners who did not believe the man. He had come to Yellowknife to appear before Berger, testifying to the long destruction of native languages and what was likely to happen in that regard if the pipeline went through. Dido had known only that he was respected in his field (Ralph Cody had told her how highly regarded he was) and had asked him, innocently, about his background.

"What should I do in the way of follow-up?" she asked Harry, sounding at once agonized and prim, sounding quite unlike her old self.

Harry suggested she take it on as a project, not doing piecemeal interviews from time to time, but gathering information for a documentary about abuse. "It's time the schools and churches were held to account."

"I'm not sure I have the heart for it," she said.

Harry nodded. "I don't blame you."

*   *

It happened bit by bit, over the weeks, as the nights grew longer. Dido's troubles gathered around her. She began to look seedy, sallow, unwashed. Beside her mouth pimples blossomed. Her voice had the same calm, thrilling energy on air, but in person she seemed distracted and people remarked on it. Is something the matter with Dido? Is she ill?

It was strange to see her briskness vanish and her confidence recede. At the dinner table, on the occasions when they ate together, Eleanor noticed how Dido's hands were always in restless motion: she would pick up both fork and knife and roll them endlessly

159

between her fingers, or smooth both sides of the placemat repeatedly, giving the impression of agitated competence, of a newly spawned nervousness. At work, there were days when she had to force herself to pick up the telephone and line up an interview. Dido, who had formerly brimmed with life, was not faring well with love.

Dido did not confide in her any more, and so Eleanor was left to brood about the eloquent stillness that came over Lorna Dargabble's face when she saw Dido's black eye, and her quiet questions about Dido's personal life, not to be prying, she said, but out of concern. And then Lorna's words with Eddy, her little confrontation. Lorna was sitting beside the jade plant when Eddy appeared with his coat on, heading out. She called to him and he stopped. "I've seen you half a dozen times and you haven't seen me," she said. His eyes narrowed. He studied her. "I'm on my break," he said.

"Your mother would be ashamed of you."

Eddy shoved his hands into his pockets. "I don't know what you're talking about."

Lorna followed Eddy's progress up the street by watching him through the big window, and Eleanor said, "What was *that* about? Lorna?"

"I've just made an enemy. But it can't be helped."

"Lorna?"

"I don't care for sneaky men who can't keep their hands to themselves."

One late November morning, Harry found Dido standing on the shore of Back Bay, looking across at the cemetery, chilled to the bone. She smiled at him when he approached and said she had been thinking about her father.

"Have you heard his voice again?"

"I hear it very often. I should say, I remember hearing it. It keeps me sane."

"What's wrong, Dido?"

"Nothing. Nothing's wrong." But she could not stop shivering.

Harry took her home and wrapped her, fully dressed, in a blanket and set about making coffee. "I would give you a fur coat if I could," he said.

"Would you?"

"In a minute."

After a pause, "Who do you suppose gave Gwen the fur coat?"

He glanced at her and did not answer. Then busied himself putting out milk and sugar, forgetting for a moment that Dido drank her coffee black.

"Your mother must have had a fur coat, Harry. What happened to it?"

"She wears it," he said. "Every winter."

He poured the coffee and she laced her fingers through the handle of the mug and stared down at it.

"Drink," he coaxed.

She lowered her head and sipped.

He looked at her pale face, her hair damp and pulled back as if she had been swimming in the wrong season. "You're deeply loved," he heard himself say, but she did not respond. He pulled out a chair and sat next to her. "Leave him," he urged. "He's not right for you."

Her voice was quiet. "Why don't you like Eddy?"

"He has no soul." For a moment he held his own against her glittering eyes, but then he backed down. "Maybe I'm wrong."

"You *are* wrong."

Her face had colour again. That much he had accomplished – putting the blood back in her cheeks.

"You deserve so much more," he said.

"Are you so much more?" She would punish him for pitying her. "Should I settle for you?"

Harry winced and rubbed the back of his neck. He stood up. "Let me run a bath for you," he said.

161

Ten minutes later, alone in the bathroom, she sank under the hot water, remembering how Eddy had once bathed her, every limb, every inch of her.

That was the day Harry fed her hot drinks and hot food, made up the spare bed, tucked her in. She slept. When she woke up in the middle of the afternoon, feeling rested for the first time in weeks, she gazed around the peaceful room and heard Harry in the kitchen, talking to his dog. Suddenly, also for the first time in weeks, she felt safe. And she stayed.

To Dido's great surprise Harry was uninhibited and appreciative in bed. His vulnerability descended like a wave from his balding head to his yielding eyes and responsive mouth and down to a softly furred chest and belly, to sturdy hips and to a penis more narrow than wide – more Oh Henry! bar than chocolate slab, more spring rhubarb than autumn gourd, more canoe than motor boat.

He appreciated everything Dido did. He responded to everything. He was animated, uncritical, and ardent.

For six weeks they lived together in Harry's house on Latham Island, the little white house he had been renting and just recently had managed to buy. He planned a party for the new year, complete with champagne and roast caribou, to celebrate his new house and new life with Dido. But there would be no roast caribou, no champagne.

*   *

Harry would remember Dido's big wristwatch, not least because she continued to wear it after he bought her a new one. At Eldonn Jewellery, in the first week of December, he selected an elegant watch with a narrow band that looked like beaten gold. But Dido put it away in a drawer and continued to wear the watch her father-in-law had found on the beach and slipped onto her wrist. Her large hand was always turning it, as someone else might turn a wedding band. It clicked against tabletops, including the one in the studio covered with baize for that very reason, to mute every rustle and thud. The green baize was like the winter footgear that muffled the sounds of your feet. Harry wore caribou-hide mukluks with felt liners, and the only time they failed to keep his feet warm was after he walked across the wet floors inside the doors of the Hudson's Bay Company store. Nothing else, not front hallways or vehicles or other stores, or even the floor of the Strange Range, had enough meltwater to soak through the hide-and-wool combination and interfere with his footwear's capacity to insulate. In a frozen world you dressed for the cold. Mukluks, snow trousers, parka, parka shell, fur hat, fur-lined mitts. None of the barehanded, bareheaded going-without of southern Canada.

On the coldest days and nights, chimney smoke rose straight as a plumb line. One of those days was Dido's birthday. She was twenty-nine on December 5, the date, she told Harry, when children in the Netherlands put a shoe beside the stove to be filled in the night with gifts from Sinterklaas. Dido put her hands on Harry's face and looked into his eyes. "I'll leave my shoe beside the stove tonight and you can put a gift into it. I don't want anything else."

"What about a cake?"

"I love cake."

He made her a glorious Black Forest cake. He started at eight o'clock in the evening, little realizing how much time he would need. Four layers, and his oven too small to hold more than two at a time. The last layers came out of the oven at midnight. Dido was in bed, the dog curled up beside her. The bedroom door half open and the fragrance wafting in. Nothing could be cozier, she said, when he came in with a tray and on the tray the whipped cream beaters and the bowls, the cake itself too warm to assemble. They had a little picnic of tastes and lickings. The next morning she had a piece of triumphant cake with her coffee in bed.

"You would make a wonderful mother," she smiled.

He would, in fact, like to be a father. "Have you ever wanted children?" he said.

"I cannot seem to picture myself as a mother, Harry."

After the cake and coffee, she inspected her shoe and found the gold watch she said was too good to wear. He asked her if everyone in Holland set out their shoes for gifts, and she said, "The Netherlands, Harry. There are two provinces, north and south Holland, inside the Netherlands. And yes, we put a shoe by the stove or fireplace with hay and carrots in it for Sinterklaas' white horse. No, your ordinary sturdy leather shoe, and in the morning the hay and carrots are gone and there are the presents: toys, books, sweets, chocolate letters. The initial D in thick Droste chocolate. I used to eat it between two slices of buttered homemade bread, and if it was raisin bread, even better. My mother made the best raisin bread. We never had to bicycle between the raisins, my father used to say."

Later that week, all-too-transparent Harry tried his hand at several loaves of raisin bread. He left work at noon, and when he returned at six o'clock to pick up Dido, he walked into the station carrying the smell of hot bread on his wintry clothes. Together they went out to his van and it was like stepping into a heavenly bakery. All the way home Dido breathed in the homey fragrance, touched by Harry's devotion, but impressed even more by the enduring nature of certain evanescent things. The sound of her father's voice. The taste of Christmas marzipan. The smell of Eddy's skin.

The air crackled whenever she and Eddy passed in the hall or were in the same room. As far as anyone could tell, Dido did not avoid him and he did not seek her out.

It was a source of considerable interest, this new pairing of Dido and Harry, even as the man she had left for Harry continued to work in master control. Eleanor and Teresa talked about it more than once,

Eleanor struck by the apparent civility amongst the three: Eddy's and Dido's work did not appear to suffer from their proximity, and their proximity continued without incident, day after day. Harry, she said, looked ten years younger.

"You mean," Teresa laughed, "that instead of looking as old as I do, he finally looks his age. The man tells me he's only forty-two."

Another time Eleanor said, "I underestimated Eddy. I never imagined he'd let Dido go so easily."

"Just wait," Teresa said. "They haven't reached shore yet."

Teresa had some experience in this line, she said, having watched her sister leave her husband several times. Audrey had come to her during their separations and Teresa could almost time the stages. Her sister would have a short period of determination and peace of mind, followed by a bout of waiting for the telephone to ring, followed by a third phase when she tried not to telephone her husband, but did. Audrey was addicted to him, perhaps they were addicted to each other, and there was nothing she could do except be there to pick up the pieces. "I wonder how long Dido will hold out against Eddy."

Eleanor cocked her head. "Eddy's manipulative. I've known that for quite a while."

"She might be too," Teresa said.

* *

On the shortest day of the year, a mother of young children told Dido on the air that she was able to see the sun rise and set outside her small kitchen window. Her window faced south, she said, the sun came up on the left and went down on the right, staying well within the window view all the while, and taking four hours to complete its journey. The poor woman was trying to set up a mothers' co-op in a church basement to give kids a place to run around screaming and mothers a place to talk with others over the age of six. Dido listened with sympathy. She recognized fraught nerves when she heard them.

Her own life was calmer now, but only on the surface. Underneath, everything that mattered was unresolved. Eddy had closed himself off. He ignored her as completely as he had in the very beginning after she had spurned his invitation to go with him to Prosperous Lake. She admired his steely self-assurance, of which he seemed to have an unlimited supply, but she felt sure he was hurting inside. One afternoon, moments after congratulating herself on having stayed away from him for three weeks, she walked into master control and touched his shoulder. How are you, Eddy? He turned around and looked at her – a look that told her everything she needed to know. He had been suffering too. And so they were right back where they had started, except that now Harry was in the picture.

Harry was so amazed to have Dido in his life that he had stopped drinking in order to savour every moment. Last winter's habit of emerging on his nights off from overheated bars into temperatures that were thirty below Celsius, of standing drunkenly under a ravishing sky as his eyelashes froze together and the insides of his nose got seared by the desiccating air, of thump-thumping home in a van whose tyres had frozen flat – all that belonged to the past. Now he stayed home every night to be with Dido, who was frequently pensive and restless, but also companionable and sometimes caressing. He left her only to take his dog for a walk on the frozen bay. Outside, the air had a certain smell, sweet, from wood smoke, and pure, from the cold. The snow, so dry and brittle underfoot, sounded like fingernails screeching on a blackboard, but rhythmic, evocative, fascinating: the most northern of sounds. *You're breaking my back, you're breaking my back*, squealed the snow as he trod upon it. His parka hood rustled against his ears, the fur trim extended several inches beyond his head like a woman's hair blown forward in the wind.

One particular night would stay in his mind, for its eerie and unnerving quality. He and Ella were on the bay, and Ella had bounded ahead full of rapturous doggy-spirits. His own feet were playing a squeaky duet on the violin-snow, when for some reason he looked behind him and saw two huge dogs on shore. They stood perfectly still, watching him. He walked on and glanced back and there they were, gliding along, keeping pace. Uptown, there would have been a few cars on the road, taxis. Not here. He shouted to Ella and she bounded over and stayed close. He looked back a third time. The dogs were still keeping pace, tracking him, stalking him, and his blood ran cold. A few months later, a small boy would trip and fall directly in front of a chained-up husky and within seconds his head was torn open. A hundred stitches to close the wounds, his round scalp like a football laced with zips. Harry looked back a fourth time, and the dogs were gone.

*　*

A few days before Christmas, Eleanor flew to Ottawa to spend the holiday with her mother. She had not looked for another roommate. She would have, but she had suspected that one day Dido would need a place to come back to from Eddy. Instead, Dido had turned to Harry. But how long would that last? Only yesterday she had seen Dido and Eddy walking down the street together, and Dido had a vibrancy about her, like a plant watered after a drought.

On the long flight home Eleanor thought about her and Eddy. About the evening when she had come to appreciate his lethal but understated anger. Their northern support group had gathered in her trailer. She had been the one to spot the ad in the local paper by the pro-pipeline group that had swiped their name, and she showed it to Eddy. He took a pair of scissors and clipped the ad, then laid it on the kitchen table and studied it, his right hand crumpling the rest of the newspaper until his knuckles were white. Dido sat away from the table, silent, while the others expressed outrage. But then Eddy

167

began to talk. He said this was not a walk in the park. If they were going to play dirty, then so should we. That was the night their little group disbanded. Eddy was too scary, too contemptuous of the rest of them for not being radical enough. Only Dido seemed to agree with him. Eleanor pondered another moment too. She had had a copy of *The Diary of Anne Frank* on her desk, and Eddy had picked it up and said, "Any teenager could have written this." His dismissiveness, his crassness. He enjoyed being inconsistent if it kept you off balance and made him look ahead of the game. But somehow Dido had fallen under his spell, the spell exerted by strong men through the centuries, perhaps.

By the time she reached Ottawa, Eleanor had decided that on Christmas Eve, when she took her mother to church, she would light a candle for Dido.

Christmas Eve in Yellowknife was warmer than usual, about twenty below Celsius, and snow was expected before morning. Gwen had persuaded Harry to be her special guest on air from midnight till one. *Christmas Eve with Stella Round.* He could use a pseudonym too, she told him. He could be Johnny Q.

She sat in master control, wearing headphones. Harry was on the other side of the glass, in the studio, and they were discussing favourite songs when he startled her by saying, "Let me demonstrate." Tilting the microphone towards the corner, he stood up and walked over to the piano, making a rapt listener of Gwen and of anyone who was tuned in at home. They heard his footsteps cross the studio floor, the creak of the stool, the pause before he began to play, and the fumbling start. Then his pretty decent version of Irving Berlin's "What'll I Do?"

Gwen was completely charmed by Harry, by the song, by the surprise of hearing him at the piano. She had not even been aware that he knew how to play. The "liveness" of it transported her, and she wished that all radio could be so spontaneous and simple, that all nights could be like this one.

The rest of the hour unfolded in the same relaxed spirit of music and impromptu recollections, including hers of hearing Kathleen Ferrier sing Brahms over the car radio one summer when she and her parents were held up for nearly an hour at a lift bridge in Hamilton. His "Alto Rhapsody", or as the announcer had called it, the "Rhapsody for Dark Voice". Harry responded by telling her that Kathleen Ferrier had been a telephone operator for a while, "Did you know that?"

"In England?"

"Can you imagine calling the switchboard for a number and getting Kathleen Ferrier on the other end? In northern England, while she studied music. She was only forty-one when she died, poor thing. Maybe you know this, in that rhapsody Brahms is pouring out his longing for two women, Clara Schumann and Clara Schumann's daughter, who's about to be married."

"I didn't know." And something occurred to Gwen that had not occurred to her before, except as foolishness. The real possibility of a man loving two women, first one, then both.

"Mr Q., how did you get that cauliflower ear? I ask, because I've been admiring it for months."

"You're after my secrets. Well, never play rugby if you value your ears."

"I promise," Gwen said.

Harry slipped out of the studio, returning a few minutes later with two cups of Maxwell House Instant spiked with Hudson's Bay overproof rum, which he had liberated from his desk bottom drawer. Also a recording of Kathleen Ferrier singing nineteen songs. Gwen dedicated "Blow the Wind Southerly" to Lorna Dargabble, "my favourite hairdresser", who did not call afterwards, as Gwen expected her to; but it was Christmas Eve, after all.

Gwen and Harry were in such good spirits themselves that they did not sign off as required at one in the morning, but went on for another half hour. Gwen coaxed Harry back to the piano, where he played "Autumn Leaves" and sang the words, forgetting only a few, and afterwards remarked that the lyrics were good, especially about missing the girl's sunburned hands, but Johnny Mercer made a serious mistake about the weather, did you catch it? And Gwen said yes. Days grow shorter as the leaves fall, they don't grow long. "They're growing longer *now*," she added. "Today we gain seven more minutes of daylight."

After they finished for the night, Harry telephoned Dido to say he was on his way, he'd be home in a few minutes. "I thought she'd be asleep," Gwen said, suddenly forlorn in the doorway.

"Not Dido. She's making a cheese fondue."

Harry helped her on with her fur coat, looking her up and down, she thought, with all the romance of a sales clerk. He got his parka from his office and drove her home through the falling snow. It came down gently, fine, dry, and in surprising quantities.

*   *

Lorna Dargabble went for a walk that night and did not come back. Her husband reported her missing on Christmas Day, but her disappearance did not become common knowledge until two days later when it was broadcast on the news. Eleanor returned from Ottawa that evening to all the speculation.

Her husband told the police that she had gone for a walk, she was always going for long, solitary walks late at night. She had not taken her handbag. It was on the table in the hallway. Her coat was gone, her boots were gone. She had left behind her hat, but no note of any kind; he had looked. Irving Dargabble was a handsome man in his ruddy, white-haired, thick-tongued way. He had been a foreman at one of the mines and he was a heavy drinker. Anyone acquainted with him suspected he was in the habit of roughing up his wife. The police knew it for a fact, having been called to the house more than once. They brought him in for questioning. Then for lack of evidence to hold him, he was let go. They questioned the neighbours on either side. They appealed on the radio for anyone who knew anything about the missing woman's movements that night to come forward.

The search for Lorna took in the areas her husband suggested, places where she usually walked, and extended beyond them to School Draw, to the other side of Frame Lake, to the area known as Tin Can Hill, to the shoreline. But the Christmas snowfall had been followed by another, a day later, and this one was also undisturbed by wind. Whatever tracks Lorna had made had been covered and wherever she might have gone lay hidden by snow.

AT ELEANOR'S KITCHEN TABLE AT THE END OF DECEMBER, Gwen was making a circle with her fingertip, gathering up crumbs.

"She was so unhappy," Gwen said. "I keep wondering if it was suicide. I think it was."

Eleanor did not reply. She was remembering how Lorna had confronted Eddy, and wished she had asked more questions while she had the chance. It seemed to her the frail, old woman must be dead, if the husband was to be believed, and even if he was not. There was talk that she might have gone back to Boston, slipped away on a plane without anybody knowing. But how could she have gone without her bag? There was talk about the husband, too.

Gwen said, "I keep seeing all those boxes in her basement full of papers and receipts. She was so worried about money."

"It might have been foul play," Eleanor said.

"The husband, you mean?"

"I guess so."

Across the table Gwen rubbed her hands free of crumbs. She sat back in her chair, then leaned forward and started again on the irresistible toast crumbs, gathering them off the table with her fingertip. "One of her neighbours thinks she went to Edmonton, just because it's the nearest big city. That's what he told the police. But I don't think so. I think she went for a walk, as her husband said, as she always did."

"Well, it wouldn't be hard to get lost at night if you turned the wrong way."

"Or if you went too far. I mean, she was old. She might have fallen, I suppose. Or just become tired. It might not have been deliberate," Gwen said, but she sounded unconvinced, especially to herself.

Then she added, "I knew something was wrong when she didn't telephone me after I played Kathleen Ferrier for her."

*   *

On New Year's Eve, Gwen was alone at the station doing the late shift as usual. Shortly after nine o'clock she went into the record library, and minutes later she heard voices and footsteps. A whiff of patchouli, pungent, exotic, weird; a nasty smell, she thought. She crossed the hall to the editing cubicle and saw them at two removes: Eddy and Dido in master control. The mystery couple, mysteriously together.

What she saw next reminded her of scenes from the romantic comic strip she had loved so much as a girl. Though comic was hardly the word – a saddie rather than a funnie. They had their coats on, they looked to be quarrelling. Dido wheeled around to leave and Eddy grabbed her by the wrist, jerked her back to him with a hard twist of the arm and she retaliated by slapping his head. Gwen stood rooted to the spot. Dido's perfume was still in her nostrils and it made her feel queasy, sickened and not herself, as she watched Eddy take Dido's head between his hands, and tipping her head back, kiss her mouth with such tenderness that Gwen thought *nobody will ever love me like that*. She felt doubly returned to girlhood. An almost shameful sorrow for her undeveloped self.

She retreated to the record library across the hall and stayed among the records until just before the hourly station break, when she went down the hall into the announce booth and did the thirty-second I.D. and weather, and saw that master control was empty. She went out to the front, to the reception area. They were not there either. Poor Harry, she thought. I wonder if he knows.

There would be a light, firm tread on Harry's front steps and a knock on the door. Dido recognized the footsteps and felt herself cave in, a landslide of feeling that left her barely able to stand. Eddy knew her hours, he knew Harry's whereabouts, he wanted her to come away with him and she was making him wait.

In Eddy she saw a fine recklessness based on having nothing to lose. He came through the door as if she were his, and it was the nerve of it that appealed to them both. Partly the nerve, partly the secretiveness, mostly the physical pleasure. She led him, not to Harry's bed, but to the spare room, which had the advantage of anonymity spiked with risk.

Every day Harry thought of Dido lying in his bed at night – the feel of her skin, the curve of her bottom, those dark, tanned-looking nipples erect against creamy skin – never less than incredulous at his good fortune and never unaware of her tolerance. She was sexually knowing and relaxed, she knew what pleased her, she could direct him, and she could turn away. Sometimes she did turn away. He would run his hand down her back and she would move perceptibly further from him, as if to say *I don't like to be touched there.*

And it was this that held him. Her little bit of physical disgust with him that made her, yes, the love of his life.

One night there were his usual jokes in bed and even though he was exhausted – amorousness; but so short-lived this time, so train through a tunnel, that Dido went still with disappointment. Harry felt her lying there, slipping out of his hands.

"Don't leave me," he begged, and she was touched and repelled. "What are you thinking?" he said, and a sad half-laugh reached his ears.

174

She was thinking that she didn't know what to think. Eddy was on her mind, he always was. She wondered why he was willing to share her with another man for so much as a minute.

"I used to know what I wanted," she said. "I never thought I would be like this."

"You're perfect."

"I'm fucked up, Harry." Her voice was flat and distant. He had almost never heard her swear.

"We're all fucked up," he said. He was remembering a tape he had heard years ago, Japanese, of course, of female orgasms from around the world, and the cries of Western women seemed forced and overdone, while Asian women were quiet and intense and finally uncontrolled. And as he lay beside her he knew he would not be able to hold on to her. Peter Peter Pumpkin Eater. Had a wife and couldn't keep her.

She said, "I don't like myself very much at the moment, Harry."

*   *

Towards the middle of January, Harry and Dido were in the penthouse of the only high-rise in town. It looked like a waiting room for Air France, dark leather chairs, a kind of airless faux luxury. From some of the windows you could see Con Mine's property, a desolate wasteland of rocks and stumpy trees that extended a long, snowy distance to the shoreline of Yellowknife Bay. Harry, looking out the window, remembered years ago having a picnic with an old sweetheart on a bit of a cliff right along the water's edge. He told Dido that he would take her there in the summer, and she smiled. "I'd like that," she said.

The occasion was a territorial government reception, and Dido had come hoping to meet Tom Berger, but he was not there. Laid out were wine, cheese, arctic char. Harry was speaking to the vice-commissioner when Dido came up to him and said she had to leave.

175

He accompanied her to the lift. She was wearing a yellow sweater draped over her shoulders; her parka was over her arm. She got into the lift and took his breath away by saying very quietly, before the doors closed, *I love you*. The doors began to close and she mouthed the words a second time. *I love you.*

Harry stood there, watching Dido say she loved him, and then down she went – into the underworld, he thought when he got home. She was gone, she and Eddy too, as he found out later.

HARRY WAS ALONE NOW IN HIS LITTLE HOUSE. THE INSIDE surface of the front door and the doorknob itself were feathered with frost. The windows had a thick build-up of ice on the inside. He was drinking and in his muddled mind it occurred to him that he should have given Dido flowers. But a woman friend once confided that the worse things got, the more European her husband's gestures became. Dozens of roses, she said, rolling her eyes.

He had given her a gold watch instead, which he found in her bedside table along with a key chain and a letter. The letter was addressed to Dido at Box 853, Yellowknife. It had a Halifax return address with the last name Moir and a December postmark. Harry held it, suddenly aware of what he had picked up. The slim envelope came alive in his hand. He hesitated, then drew from it the single sheet of notepaper. His eyes flicked from salutation to signature, from *Dear Dido* to *Daniel*. Then he read the letter itself – a bold, tidy script saying that his new wooden skiff had lovely lines, that his grandson was turning into a sailor in his own right, that apart from these two pleasures he found things as they were intolerable, but he saw no way forward at the moment. He thought of her constantly and loved her.

Harry could see that Dido's father-in-law was not about to "walk through that door" any time soon, but he still wondered why she had left the letter behind.

*

On a Sunday in late January, two weeks after Dido had left him, the police came to his house not once but twice.

Around noon, there was such insistent knocking on his front door that his heart leapt. But it was a Dene fellow wavering on his doorstep. He had been shot in the foot by somebody who was in the house across the road, and another guy had been clubbed on the head with a rifle butt, and would Harry help him out and call the police?

Harry brought the man into his kitchen. His name was Arthur, he said. And that was when Harry recognized him. He was the one who'd complained at the inquiry about getting a parking ticket on Dene land. Harry drew out a chair for him, then went to the telephone, and in the time it took him to make the call, a pool of blood had formed around one of Arthur's leather boots.

Harry poured a glass of orange juice for him and gave him an ashtray. Then he hushed Ella, who was growling, sent her off into the living room and told her to stay, and saw through the window the other man stumbling past Louise's shack next door, holding his head in his hands as he lurched forward through the snow.

He put on the kettle for coffee and the police arrived before it boiled. They showed up in three cruisers with bullhorns and rifles. They made a show of loading their rifles, but it was not necessary. Four men and two women trooped out of the house in question and stood passively at the side of the road, no longer arguing or drinking. Harry went out to help. The man with the wounded head was now in the back seat of one of the cruisers, and when the ambulance arrived Harry helped him onto a stretcher, helped lift the stretcher into the ambulance. There was a lot of blood, and the poor man was crying.

After that Harry took the police into his kitchen. The kettle was boiling away, the juice in Arthur's glass was gone. Two policemen lifted Arthur off the chair and half-carried him outside, a third took the cigarette from between his fingers and dropped it in the sink on his way past. Harry would find it there, soggy, later when he went to do the dishes. After the police were gone, he cleaned up the glutinous puddle on the floor and discovered what congealing powers blood has. Only then did he feel sick, quite sick and shaken. They will have to cut Arthur's boot off his foot, he thought, his brand new leather boot with the high heel.

Later that day, the police were at his door again. Not about Arthur, it turned out. About Eddy. They were following up a complaint and they wanted to talk to Harry as Eddy's employer.

Harry listened to what they had to say.

"I don't believe it," he said.

After they left, he sat still for a while. The police were investigating something sordid. Men giving Indian girls booze for sex in a motel on the road to the airport. One of the girls had wandered outside and nearly frozen to death.

He had told them they were barking up the wrong tree. Eddy didn't drink, for one thing. For another, he wasn't that kind of guy. For a third, he'd left town before the incident occurred. Harry wanted to know who had fingered Eddy, but the police would not say.

He stood and went over to the window. Outside, it was thirty-one below. The willows between his house and the bay were full of ptarmigan, feathery plops of white balanced on slender branches. He remembered Eddy saying we're too soft; fucking Eddy, running his hands through his wiry red hair and boasting that he slept with a window open all winter. So where did fucking Eddy do all his fucking?

On the lake the ice was green, the snow lavender. On the far shore the gold mine nestled into the bay. Smoke flapped out of chimneys.

He thought of a phrase, something he had read in one of Ralph's northern books: *to have felt snow and ice forever, and nothing forever but ice and snow*.

The cold gathered. It was just beyond his window. He could feel it

179

pressing in. All the cold from all over the Arctic pressing against that pane of glass.

* *

At work, Harry leaned against Eleanor's desk, idly lifted a few papers, then looked into her face.

"I haven't heard a thing from her," she said quietly. "Nobody has."

Harry had instituted Monday morning story meetings for everyone on staff. Just once a week, he said, to keep one another generally informed of what we're doing. And still he met with sullen resistance from the newsroom. If anything, they were more openly mutinous. Bill Thwaite attended against his will. "What have you got this week?" Harry would ask. And Bill would fold his arms and answer, "Not a thing."

They were in the studio, gathered around the big table. Harry peeled an orange over the metal wastebasket, the scent reminding him of lost Dido. The explosive fragrance. After she had left him, his private drinking spree had cost him a week of work and earned him another black mark on the list of sins that would before long be used against him. Gwen watched his hands, fascinated by the way his fingers dug under the skin of the orange and ever so neatly peeled it back.

She had been brought in from the night shift to take over from Dido, a casual had been hired to do the night shift in her place, another was rapidly being trained by Andrew McNab to be a technician.

Harry looked around for Jim Murphy. But Jim, it would seem, could not be bothered to show up.

He turned to reliable Gwen. She mentioned having lined up an interview with a bush pilot who had discovered the remains of a beer keg on one of the high arctic islands, probably left behind in the

1800s by a search party looking for Franklin, and Bill laid into her for poaching on his territory: That's *news*, he said, jabbing his ink-stained finger at her.

Turf wars, thought Harry. Inside the station, and out. "This is why we have story meetings," he said wearily, "to coordinate current affairs and news. If you want a clip of Gwen's interview for the newscast, all you have to do is ask. And Gwen, you won't air the full interview until after Bill's run the clip. O.K.?"

He turned to Teresa. Teresa had in front of her the newspaper story that related the case of a young Dene woman wandering naked and blind-drunk in the street after being locked out of a motel room; two men who worked at one of the mines stood accused of rape. She tapped the paper with her finger and said she wanted to do a series on violence against women. She had in mind an on-air manual in English and Dogrib of anecdotes, advice, information – what women faced, what they could do, who they could turn to. Gwen expressed immediate interest and they agreed to work on it together.

Before the meeting ended, Gwen asked Bill if he had heard anything more about Lorna Dargabble. What were the police doing, anyway?

"They're doing their job," he said. Then, a little less grudgingly, he added, "I'm guessing we'll learn what happened in the spring, after the snow's gone."

In the background, providing a wealth of material for Gwen and Teresa, were quietly impassioned witnesses at the Berger Inquiry presenting what amounted to a catalogue of northern pathologies. Anthropologists outlined the history of prospectors, traders, whalers, and miners pouring into the North with their diseases, their alcohol, their licentiousness. Medical experts and social workers methodically outlined what happens when the traditional pattern of life breaks down and individuals, families, whole communities lose their way. They described the particular burden for women, their isolated and vulnerable lives during the long northern winters. And in the Dene communities, witness after witness told Berger about a close-knit culture increasingly fragmented by the white frontier mentality. Everyone, Dene and white, agreed that booze was the most destructive force in the unravelling of lives that ended either in the slow violence of apathy and despair, or in the sudden violence of death by accident, murder, poisoning, suicide.

THIS WAS THE WINTER, THE WINTER OF 1976, THAT GWEN would remember in part for the three unlucky things that happened to Harry, three months in a row. January robbed him of Dido. February brought a second loss, which unfolded far from town. March would have its own misfortunes.

On a Saturday in late February, Harry and Ralph went ice fishing. They took Harry's van and drove an hour to Prelude Lake, Harry's dog riding in the back with the gear. Normally, Ella rode up front with him, leaning into his side "like a hot date", in Ralph's amused estimation.

They parked at Powder Point, skied across the tip of the snow-covered lake to a small rapids and followed the portage around them, then skied across a stretch of frozen river before climbing a steep hill, crossing a small lake and following another portage into Hidden Lake. From the edge of the lake rose rocky outcrops dusted with snow. Slender birch trees and taller spruce had footholds near the shore and more haphazardly on ridges and between rocky hills farther back. Every so often a raven spoke to them, cr-awk, cr-awk, and flew from one tree to another.

Ralph took note. The raven's call had a little pop or pong sound, it seemed to him, an oval-shaped noise more appropriate for a mouth than a beak. He had helped Gwen assemble and dramatize her programme of Raven tales, lending her his books and doing much of the writing of the trilingual scripts, since he knew a basic, uninhibited Inuktitut from his days of teaching in the eastern Arctic. From Teresa he was now learning some basic phrases in Dogrib – Teresa had written and delivered the Dogrib repartee for the Raven tales, as natural an actor, as uninhibited and relaxed, as she was a broadcaster. The beautiful Dido had narrated, but she had not stuck around to hear the broadcast.

Long ago, went the central tale, man and the wild animals lived in utter darkness, for the great Chief hoarded the light. Raven, inspired by his own dark cunning, devised a plan to steal it. He turned himself into a pine needle, set himself afloat on water, and was swallowed by the Chief's daughter, who became pregnant, giving birth to a boy. The boy grew up playing with his grandfather's bags of light, biding his time, until finally he was old enough to fly up through the smoke hole and with a triumphant squawk empty the bags into the sky, thus giving light to the world.

A book of northern legends weighed down one of Ralph's pockets, a flask of whisky weighed down another.

Ella, in her glory, bounded along beside them, darting off into the bush, darting back. Such easy travelling, wind and bug free (unlike last summer on the same lake when Ralph applied his hand to the back of his head and felt about twenty little bodies smear into his scalp; this he had done every few seconds, it seemed, with unvarying results). In a sheltered cove, they used an auger to cut through the three-foot depth of ice, making four holes about half a foot in diameter each. They dropped in lines baited with the small fresh-water herring called cisco. Each line was attached to a short stick propped up in the snow: when the stick fell over they had either a bite or a trout. To keep warm, they built a fire on shore and made tea and ate Ralph's ham sandwiches. Once, Ella broke through the thin ice that covered a fast-running stream. The dunking soaked her fur coat, which froze immediately, making her look like a four-legged wraith. But her spirits were undampened.

With bare hands Harry and Ralph pulled up their lines, landing a total of five fat trout. They warmed themselves at the fire and talked about the summer expedition they were planning to the Thelon River. The trip was rapidly taking shape. A group of four was best, Ralph believed. More than that would be cumbersome. Fewer would be risky. "You say Eleanor is keen to go," he said.

"She's motivated," Harry said. "And steady. I've never seen her lose her cool."

"I like her," Ralph smiled. "She puts up with me."

"There's Gwen. She's avid to go too, even though it means two weeks without pay."

"But I wonder if she's got enough muscle," Ralph said, "enough heft."

"She's wiry. She's a worker. You'd get your money's worth, I think."

"She's got physical courage," Ralph conceded. "It's not a mean feat, driving by herself all the way from Ontario."

"There's holiday time for her to work out. Eleanor, too. Six weeks is a long stretch."

"Can *you* get away?" Ralph said.

"I'm the boss," Harry said with a mock swagger.

"Shall I tell them we're on, then? Or will you do the honours?"

"I'll leave that to you," Harry said.

The conversation turned to Eddy. Harry had told Ralph when it happened about being visited by the police. But there was no reason for Eddy to be mixed up in that kind of thing, he said again, still puzzled, still disturbed. He was a strange guy, but if he had anything it was a sense of morals.

"No reason you can think of." Ralph rubbed his hands together close to the fire. He remembered Gwen's view that Eddy had a problem with women. "Why I wonder did he and Dido take off so suddenly."

"I don't know. I don't know."

About three o'clock they headed back to the van. Under the overcast sky, they had trouble seeing any contours until they were upon them, the snow deceptively flat in the fractional light. Harry kept a concerned eye out for leg-hold traps, having seen snowmobile tracks leading across the lake and knowing that trappers were about. He kept his dog close to him. But within sight of the road Ella bounded far ahead, suddenly stopped, then went after something.

Harry, coming alongside, shouted at her until he saw that it was not a trap, just some dark indecipherable thing sitting above the snow. Not a body, animal or otherwise, but a piece of meat or skin. He called Ella away, she refused to come.

He skied on, paused, called her again. This time she came, but reluctantly.

They stowed their skis and packs, took swigs from Ralph's flask, surveyed the dim sky. They were about to get into the van when the dog began to act strangely. She let out a whimper, turned in circles, then fell to the ground and lay writhing. Harry knelt beside her, his hands on her jerking head, until she quieted, then he lifted her into his arms. The dark something must have been baited with poison and left in the open for wolves, probably, or foxes. A trapper hunting fur with poison.

Harry gave the keys to Ralph. In the passenger seat he held his nearly spent dog in his lap, while Ralph stepped hard on the accelerator. After about ten minutes, the second fit took hold, her limbs kicking, her whole body convulsing. Again, she quieted. Harry spoke to her, soothed her, stroked her.

Ralph kept the accelerator to the floor, but after a while Harry said what Ralph already knew, that there was no need to speed any more.

In the weeks that followed, watching Harry's sadness, Eleanor found herself talking to Dido in her head, *You left somebody in the lurch, you know*. She wondered if she would ever get the chance to say it face to face.

It was Eleanor's fourth winter in Yellowknife. For the duration of it, all eight months, she missed the tiny flowers and richly coloured lichens that dotted the rocky outcrops, but she wasn't sorry not to see the quantities of garbage that surfaced everywhere in the spring. She missed the long grass that shone whitish-gold with a purple tinge in the setting sun; the wild, small, misshapen raspberries sufficient for a modest pie; the occasions when half a dozen Dene children tore up and down the street, tumbling about at midnight, having a loud and happy time. But at the same time she was glad not to have to look at the cowering, cringing, beaten dogs that spent the summers chained to willows and covered with flies.

One afternoon, when she and Gwen were in the Gold Range café talking about how to prepare for the summer expedition, Gwen said to her, "Sometimes I see Lorna out of the corner of my eye. At night I catch glimpses of her grey fur coat. It's never her, of course."

Eleanor did not answer. She felt a helpless anger about Lorna and her sad life and no doubt sadder end. About Dido she felt a different sort of anger. Cavalier Dido, who had also left suddenly, without saying goodbye, then chosen to inform the station she was gone by calling at around seven in the morning, when she knew Jim Murphy would be the only one there. She had told him that she and Eddy were in Hay River already, and they would not be coming back.

Suddenly Gwen looked up and asked, "Do you think I'm hot and cold? Too unpredictable to be trustworthy?"

"I wouldn't be going on a canoe trip with you if I did."

Later that afternoon, Harry came to Eleanor's trailer, having offered to mend the worn patches on her kitchen floor with some left-over linoleum he had in his house – a pattern of black and white squares that he measured and cut, showing more dexterity than she had given him credit for. His grandfather had been good with his hands, he explained, passing on the information that the old man had been a furrier in Winnipeg. In Eleanor's mind something clicked.

"Did *you* give Gwen the fur coat?"

He looked up from where he was kneeling on the floor. For a moment he was silent. "It was my grandmother's," he said. "Gwen looked to be the same size." He shrugged. "It's a loaded gift, a fur coat, that's why I don't want her to know."

"You thought she might take it the wrong way."

He bent to his task.

"You're an unusual man, Harry Boyd. How did you happen to have your grandmother's fur coat?"

"I had my mother put it in the mail."

"That's a lot of trouble to take," she said quietly.

"She didn't mind. It didn't fit her. The coat was going to waste."

"I mean a lot of trouble for *you* to take."

Harry knew what she meant. A trace of a smile crossed his face. "It was an act of charity. I know Gwen. She'd never spend money on a good parka."

"I'll say it again, Harry. You're an unusual man."

He ran his eyes from corner to corner of the black and white linoleum. In a quarter of an hour he'd be finished and have to return to his own house, for which he no longer had the slightest enthusiasm.

Eleanor poured him a Scotch when he was done. "You signed the card 'your secret admirer'."

"Did I? I suppose I wanted to put her off the scent."

He took his drink and went to look out the window. Eleanor came over and stood beside him. No-one was outside. Nothing flew by. Or moved.

"One of these days," Eleanor said, "this winter's going to end."

"Right. Why should love last when nothing else does?"

"Poor wretch," she said, and put her arm around him. She said there was a beautiful ode by Horace to that effect. It made the very point that earthly love turns with the seasons, and there is nothing we can do about it.

"The seasons return, though," she said after a moment, "and so can love."

"It didn't for Horace," he said.

At the end of March, when Harry was thinking that only one month of winter was left, his third stroke of bad luck occurred. It was a bright and sunny Tuesday. He sat at his desk going through the mail.

A bit later, when he saw Gwen pass by the door of his office, he called her to come in. He had his feet on his desk and a letter in his hands. His glasses were on his desk, too, beside the telephone.

"You didn't sign this," he said, waving the letter.

She looked mystified, and he said, "I thought so. You didn't know about it."

"About what."

He handed her the letter and she read it, then sat down and read it again. It was dated March 18, 1976. It was addressed to the head of the Northern Service in Ottawa and it was signed by George Tupper, Bill Thwaite, Jim Murphy, and Andrew McNab. Calling themselves the most senior employees at the station, they said they had heard that Harry Boyd was going to be appointed permanent manager and they wanted to express their views about his unsuitability before it was too late. Then followed a list of Harry's deficiencies and errors of judgment: his autocratic style, his anti-news bias in favour of current affairs, his inappropriate public statements, his infringement of union rules that prohibited management touching the equipment, his negative attitude towards television, his trouble with the bottle. It would be a grave mistake, they said, to appoint to the job someone who did not understand the role of manager or the future of the c.b.c. in the North.

Gwen looked up. Harry was watching her. He pointed at the

letter, and said it was a copy of the original; his buddy in head office had sent it to him so that he would know what he was up against.

His eyes looked old and worked over. He ran his hand slowly down the side of his jaw. "I wouldn't have taken the job anyway, not that I think they were about to offer it to me."

"Harry, I'm sorry."

"It just makes it awkward as hell."

"Let *them* feel awkward. They don't know what they're talking about."

He smiled. "That's my girl."

"But you'll stay on."

He looked out the window. "I just called Ottawa. I made them swear they'd have my replacement here by the first of June. Not a day later." The sun was shining and he squinted his eyes. "Whoever takes over, it won't be me." Still looking out of the window, still squinting, "Anyway," he said, "this makes three."

She understood. Dido, his dog, his job. It had to be the end of his run of bad luck.

BY LATE APRIL, THE LONG HOURS OF LIGHT WERE BACK. IN town all the snow was gone, and all the garbage, so thinly but effectively disguised, had resurfaced, soft and soggy and in unbelievable amounts. It was the time of year when winter secrets got revealed.

The foursome who would be canoeing the Thelon River were already in harness, walking miles in the early morning or in the evening with brick-filled rucksacks. They were meeting regularly to plan the expedition, the maps, supplies, equipment, freeze-dried foods, mosquito nets, new tents, extra-warm sleeping bags, life preservers, extra paddles. Firearms, given the likelihood of grizzly bears. But none of them knew how to use a gun, and they agreed that having one with them would endanger them more than a grizzly would. They read books on canoeing skills. Only Ralph had done extensive trips with whitewater—he had special paddles he was attached to, his favourite one having been made by a native wood carver in eastern Ontario from a single piece of cedar. But all of them had paddled, Harry and Gwen since childhood, and Eleanor since her early twenties. Ralph, with his customary relish, became the chief organizer. Had they ever formally chosen a trip leader, had they ever agreed that it would be Ralph, then some of their initial difficulties might never have arisen. They were going forward with a kind of informed innocence, with the naïve faith that they had the physical and mental resources to make the journey and come back unharmed.

191

Teresa could not resist ribbing them. Only you white people, she said, approach the land like it's some great undertaking. You have to do fifty miles a day with your maps and your compasses. You have to count up the miles. Are you sure you don't need a guide? she smiled. Babes in the Barrens, she called them. At least take a gun, she advised. I'm serious.

They were gathered at Harry's house one evening when Ralph Cody arrived late. They heard him before they saw him, his familiar, humour-filled voice talking loudly to itself as he came up the driveway.

"Ralph!" Gwen called from the front door.

He saw her waving.

"I feel like Odysseus," he shouted.

He came striding in, jacket unbuttoned, beret in hand. He had walked to Frame Lake and back, a distance of several miles, and this after jogging five miles earlier in the day. Even Harry was lifting weights, though he had no small estimate of his own strength, being stocky and able to lift heavy things with ease. Without fanfare, he had cut back on his drinking.

That evening Gwen took one look at Ralph's tentative list of supplies – the thirty salamis, the forty bars of chocolate, the forty-two rolls of toilet paper – and accused him of going wild. How much liquor was he planning to bring? A case?

Ralph called her a cheap Scotswoman.

Her retort was brisk. An aunt of hers used to write down all the things she wanted and could not afford, and then burn the list. It was very effective.

Eleanor agreed. She had used the same method for losing weight: write down all the foods you want to eat on a sheet of paper, then burn it.

Ralph accused them of being female missionaries to his bold adventurer, and Eleanor promised not to sing "Jesus Loves Me", just to think it.

Gwen's thoughtful, emboldened eyes remained on Eleanor.

"That's what you really believe." It was almost a challenge.

Eleanor smiled and did not take the bait, and Ralph saw and approved. Harry was right. Eleanor had the necessary temperament for a trip like this. Even-keeled, unruffled, steady.

The two women had spoken privately about what it would mean to spend six weeks in Ralph's and Harry's company. Gwen had wondered aloud what sort of lover Ralph might be, and Eleanor surprised her by saying she thought he might be rather good.

"He eats so fast," Gwen said thoughtfully. "That's never a good sign."

"He would *enjoy* sex."

"But would I?"

Eleanor smiled. "What about Harry?"

A cloud came over Gwen's face. "Fast, furious, drunken," she guessed.

"That's not what Dido implied," Eleanor said.

Harry read books about the Barrens to take his thoughts off Dido. Whenever he stopped reading, she floated into his mind – the sandal markings on her swinging bare foot, the winter imprint of a knitted sock, the memory of thinking that nothing wants to be forgotten. Summer doesn't. The sock doesn't. I don't.

One day his eyes rested on Gwen and she understood his bleak expression perfectly. He was brooding about Dido. Wishing she were Dido.

He had a book under his arm and a fresh mug of coffee in his hand. They were in the announcers' office and he said to her, "Silence is an incredible weapon".

Gwen had suspected as much: Harry had not heard a word from the fugitive pair. She had thought of asking him once or twice if he had had any news, but it would have been cruel if it turned out he had not.

"I'll show you," he said.

They took facing chairs. He fastened her with an intent look, then pulled a question out of the air. "Why do you hate your father?"

She lifted her hands and shrank back in her chair. A long pause, and then she struggled to say something.

"I suppose because he preferred my brother to me. And because he never asked me a thing about myself. And because he wasn't too kind to my mother."

"See? Silence is an interviewer's greatest asset. All you have to do is wait, and the person feels obliged to fill the vacuum with a serious answer."

But it did not seem entirely fair, what she had said. Certainly it was not the whole story.

"Why do you love Dido?" she asked.

Harry glared at her, but she held his glance. Fair is fair.

"That's a dirty question."

"So was yours."

Slowly, Harry's face gave way, and Gwen felt gratified and sorry, fascinated and pained.

He said, "I think I loved her before I ever saw her. I loved her voice, first of all. Then I loved the way she looks. Then I loved the way she entered a room –" He stopped. "I don't need to teach you a thing."

In the beginning Dido did not change when she entered a room, that is what Gwen remembered. She did not gulp for air and something to say. There had been a smoothness to her entries and exits. Rather than the winter of shyness and the summer of over-effort, she was all of a piece and natural. But then she did change. Her personality darkened and shifted before Gwen's eyes, and reminded her of Ralph's grasses moving under water, of words dissolving on a page.

Gwen did not miss her, or Eddy. The station was easier without them. She had even read the news a few times, on days when Jim Murphy could not, and the usual had not happened; she had not stiffened; her brain had not slammed into the hard, cold fender of nervousness. But it was wrong to say Dido and Eddy had left. They were here, she thought, present in every sad ounce of Harry's body.

In his office Harry was reading about John Hornby. There were nights when he did not bother to go home. In a grim and sardonic act of defiance, he had had a La-Z-Boy installed. His successor would have the chair removed in a month's time, and would discover on the floor, gathering dust, a multitude of balled-up memos about television and the impending new building.

There were two ways of looking at Hornby, Harry thought. If you took his life as a series of disasters in rapid succession, if you saw him as a distillation of his shortcomings, then you would call him a loser, feckless, under-prepared, dangerous. If you saw him, instead, in all his complexity, in the fullness of his extraordinary life, then he was no less irresponsible, but he was also astonishingly vivid, driven, solitary, intense, endearing. Harry was all for seeing people in their complexity and having them return the favour. But what spoke to him most was the duality of the man – his courage and his foolishness, his loyalty and his carelessness, his shyness and his poetic, almost erotic attachment to the land. Also the size of his mistakes, and the way death spared him from having to live with the consequences.

Harry set aside Whalley's biography, and thought about what lay ahead. Ralph, he suspected, wanted to prove himself – prove that at sixty-one he was still youthful. And Eleanor had indicated that she and the Barrens might be a good spiritual fit. And Gwen had the young person's all-consuming desire to see a place for the first time, especially since it would complete a story that had captured her imagination as a child; she would see with her own eyes where its final chapter unfolded. As for himself, he was looking forward to a clean break from old dissatisfactions, a summer that would help him forget his winter.

A week later, as it happened, George Whalley's daughter brought her father in to see him, as she had promised to do when he came to town. Harry chatted with George Whalley, only a little surprised by the mid-Atlantic accent, neither Canadian nor English, but cultured, the sort of voice that used to be the only voice on C.B.C. Radio. Whalley looked to be in his late fifties, tall and grey-haired, forthcoming yet reserved, a professor poet. He told Harry how he had first read Edgar Christian's diary in 1938, soon after it was published in England, where it caught everyone's imagination to the extent that it was reprinted several times. Like many other readers, he could not forget the events it recorded. He had thought of writing something at the time, but it took fifteen years before he saw how to do it, making a radio version of Edgar Christian's diary, a broadcast that was then heard by people who had known Hornby and got in touch with him to fill out the picture. What followed was the seven years of research and writing that produced the full-length biography, *The Legend of John Hornby*. Harry listened and thought of his own life, his years in Toronto when things had gone from bad to worse to bizarre to desolate, until the moment his old friend Max Berns stumbled upon him and put his hand on his shoulder and said *Harry? Harry?* and he had snorted awake into what he knew was a rescue. How much better to have encountered something as a young man, to have been ignited as Whalley had, and to have remained on fire ever since.

Harry asked him if he was willing to be interviewed. Later, listening to Whalley's dialogue with Gwen, what struck him most was how the professor responded to the question of whether he and Hornby were alike. He hesitated, then said he supposed he shared with Hornby a tendency to approach life "crabwise", meaning sideways and backwards rather than head-on. The man was gentle, serious, fascinating. Gwen fell for him instantly, he could hear it in her voice, and Harry took heart from Whalley's own view of himself. The man was not on a forced march, but rather on a wandering route notable for its "digressions and divagations", as the old explorers liked to say. A route of the soul, perhaps.

Judge Berger was not moving in lockstep either. Back in March, the news had reported that he was under pressure from the federal government to complete his inquiry by June and have his report ready for them in September. But Berger would not be pushed. He was planning to take his inquiry south, to big urban centres like Vancouver and Winnipeg, and involve the larger Canadian public in the debate about the competing claims of the indigenous peoples and the pipeline companies to the same land. He wanted everyone to ask themselves seriously what gave them the right to exploit the North, to subject its shifting terrain of sea coast, tundra, boreal forest, rocky hills and marshy plains, permanently frozen ground and discontinu- ous permafrost to a development project that scientists were saying could not be completed without ugly consequences, certainly not in the time allotted and at the cost predicted. According to one soil scientist, as soon as they started to dig into soil that was held together by ice, it would melt like ice cream.

Berger had spoken of the arctic wilderness as "the last of North America, the eighth wonder of the world". This was after having flown by helicopter along the arctic coast and seen migrating cari bou, three grizzlies and several wolves, and dozens of seals on the sea ice. Harry knew that where they were going on their canoe trip was even more remote, in the sense of less settled, less visited, less on the human map, than where Berger had been.

IN THE MIDDLE OF MAY, A YOUNG WOMAN IN BRAIDS, WALKING her dog near Con Mine, stumbled upon a body. She was on an old road the mine had not used for years. Every winter it got snowed over, and in the spring two or three dog walkers usually trod out a path. The young woman's dog had wandered off, fifty yards, and was making his way through trees and low brush when he began to bark. He did not stop barking until she came over to investigate, tripping over tree roots, sinking into a surviving patch of snow.

The evening news said that after almost five months, the mysterious disappearance of Lorna Dargabble had apparently ended with the discovery of a woman's body on Con Mine's property. Police said they were almost certain the body was that of Mrs Dargabble, who was last seen in Yellowknife on Christmas Eve and was reported missing Christmas Day. The body had been found by a city resident. It would be flown to Edmonton for lab and X-ray tests. At present there were no indications of foul play. The body had been found spread-eagled on the ground, with one arm above the head, clothed in a fur coat and slacks similar to those worn by Mrs Dargabble when she was last seen.

After the newscast, Gwen stood in the doorway of the newsroom, looking at Bill Thwaite. He was frowning over a page in his typewriter. "What does 'spread-eagled' mean?" she asked. "Was she facing up or was she face down?"

His eyes went to her. He leaned back in his chair. "Facing up," he said.

All day a rumour had flown about the station, and so Gwen asked, "And was there a liquor bottle beside her or is that just talk?"

He did not answer for a moment. Sudden death changes everyone, at least for an hour or two. He did not send Gwen packing as he might have done.

He said to her, "If you put what I'm about to tell you on the air, I'll skin you alive."

"I'm not going to say anything on air."

Bill scratched the back of his neck. He had seen Lorna Dargabble many times, bending Eleanor's ear and Gwen's ear, and he had thought of her as a pest, a nuisance. She was easy to ridicule. The husband he knew by sight, well enough to say hello to. A hard drinker, always in the bars. He and his buddies liked to sit at a table and make vicious fun of women's lib. He had heard Irving Dargabble refer to his old lady as a perfect punching bag. He said, "She had something in her hand, but it wasn't a bottle."

Gwen came all the way into his office. She moved some newspapers off a chair and sat down. She waited.

He held up his open hand and closed it. "A hank of somebody's hair," he said.

Gwen stared at him. She tried to picture the hair in Lorna Dargabble's old fist. "What *colour* was the hair?"

Bill rubbed his nose and looked at her closely. "You sound as if you think you know."

"White," she said, thinking of the onion-husband.

"Try again."

She looked into his sly, shrewd eyes. "I can't. I don't know."

"About the colour of your hair. Light brown."

The local newspaper had a gentler account of the discovery. Eleanor read the article several times, especially the final paragraph. "Lorna Dargabble was known to take long, solitary walks. Her body was found to be in a peaceful, reposing position as if she had lain down to rest."

As if she had lain down to rest, she repeated to herself, "*like a lost wave* finding *a forgotten shore*". She was back in Rockcliffe Park, listening to the wind move through the canopy of trees, hearing her father utter a quotation she had never been able to identify, and thinking that we only ever get *part* of the story. By its very nature Lorna's death would always be a mystery. More searching might provide more parts, but never the whole. Though, of course, that was part of the whole – this partialness. On Sunday she went to church and found herself weeping for Lorna Dargabble. The phrase "the kingdom of God" had come to have enormous meaning for her, though. It summoned up a wide and widening realm.

That night Eleanor's telephone rang, and it was Dido.

She was calling from California and her voice was buoyant, jarring. "We're here among the orange groves."

"Dido." And Eleanor sounded sharper than she intended, but perhaps no sharper than she actually felt.

"Don't be angry."

Eleanor pictured the glow and weight of southern fruit, she pictured Dido and Eddy bronzed and unaware. "You left somebody high and dry," she said.

"How is Harry?"

"He's well enough. He's busy. We all are." A pause. "I'm glad to hear from you, Dido. I really am. But I'm curious to know why you're calling me now after all these months."

"I meant to call a long time ago. I should have called."

"You should have, you're right." Then, struck by a possibility, "Is Eddy behaving himself?"

"Eddy's being a very good boy."

Boy. As if Dido were his mother. Just possibly, thought Eleanor, Dido and Eddy deserved each other.

"Don't be angry," Dido said again. "I didn't intend to hurt anybody. Certainly not you."

With these last words Eleanor felt seen through and silenced. But after a moment she asked, "So why did you take off the way you did? In the middle of the night?"

"It wasn't the middle of the night."

"It might as well have been."

Eleanor heard Dido take a deep breath before answering. "I suppose it was a test, to see if I loved him enough to go with him. An old friend of his called and said there was work down here. Eddy wanted to go and he wouldn't leave without me."

"It felt as if you ran away from something." There was no response at the other end. "Dido?"

"No. We just wanted to get away from all the complications and to be together."

Eleanor reached for a chair. She dragged it close to the telephone and sat down. "So what am I supposed to tell Harry? You took off, you left him in the lurch, you left the station in the lurch. What am I supposed to tell him?"

"He doesn't have to know I called. I just wanted to hear your voice and to find out how you are. To find out what's new."

"Well, I'll tell him you're alright. It's simple kindness," Eleanor said.

"You can tell him I'm sorry."

"No. That's something you would have to tell him yourself." Eleanor studied the kitchen floor, Harry's handiwork. Then said, "They found Lorna Dargabble's body last week near Con Mine. I haven't been able to think about much else."

A certain stillness came down the line. And in the same way that a telephone call bearing bad tidings has a different ring, a slightly more urgent tone, this silence felt charged.

Yet Dido's voice, when she spoke, was unaltered. "Was she murdered?"

"We don't know. We won't know till after the autopsy." Eleanor paused. She weighed her words. "Lorna and Eddy didn't care for each other, did they?"

Dido replied easily. "I don't think Eddy knew who she was."

If you say so, thought Eleanor. "You haven't told me what you're doing with yourselves down there."

They were learning about film, Dido said, both of them were. Eddy was spending time with his little niece, but making contacts too. Also organizing an exhibition of photographs he had taken in Yellowknife. She herself had found work as a script assistant. This last caused Eleanor a moment of *déjà vu*. That's what Gwen had wanted, she remembered. To be in the background.

Eleanor said, "I wasn't aware that Eddy took any photographs, let alone enough for an exhibition."

"He didn't make a big deal of it. They're very political, very disturbing. Hard to describe, really."

Then Dido asked what else was new, and Eleanor told her about their imminent canoe trip, which was three weeks away now. Dido's response startled her. "Have you got room for me?" she said.

Eleanor did not know what to say. She heard Dido's tone of voice, plaintive, flirtatious, knowing, sad. As if the trip were something she did not deserve, yet knew no-one could deny her if she chose to come.

Dido said, "The trip will probably change your life."

Eleanor absorbed the yearning behind Dido's words. A car went by and children were yelling in the distance. "You sound sad."

"I am sad sometimes."

Then, in a different tone, as if returning to safer ground, Dido said, "I have something I'm going to send you. A little something to take along on your trip. That way," Dido said, "you'll remember me."

"Did you think I would ever forget?"

*   *

Eleanor stepped into Harry's office the next day and closed the door. He had not begun to clear out his desk, even though this was his final week. On his last day, Eleanor would bring in a cake and round up the willing and the unwilling in a farewell gesture that was notable for its awkward brevity and for Harry's parting shot. "When it comes to television," he would say, "listen to radio, and when it comes to managers, don't listen at all."

But now Eleanor leaned her back against his door and hesitated a moment, taking in his defenceless morning face, then told him Dido had telephoned. "Last night. She's fine. She's with Eddy. They're in California."

Harry took off his glasses and leaned back. "She's well, you say."

"As far as I could tell. They seem to have jobs in film. I should have asked more questions. She gave me her telephone number, though."

Harry heard what she had said, but all he could think was that Dido had telephoned Eleanor, not him. Apparently, she had not even asked about him, or Eleanor would be telling him.

To Eleanor he looked so defeated suddenly, and so hurt, that she was afraid he might collapse into dust – as in the fairy tales. She almost said, Dido asked me to tell you she's sorry, but then held back, knowing how empty it would sound.

She said instead, "Maybe I shouldn't have mentioned it. But I thought you'd want to know."

Harry looked up. "Of course, I want to know. Of course, you should have told me."

"Good. That's what I thought."

He said firmly, a flicker of anger in his eyes, "There's nothing worse than being in the dark."

Eleanor and Gwen arranged a gathering in Lorna Dargabble's memory. They wanted somehow to commemorate Lorna's passing, given that no funeral seemed to be in the offing. They ran a note on the community announcements: anyone who would like to remember Lorna Dargabble's life would be welcome to come to Eleanor Dew's mobile home in Forrest Park on Sunday, June 6 between two and five in the afternoon. They had no expectation that the husband would come, and he did not. Others came, however. Lorna had not had a wide circle of friends, by any means, yet she was well known, and Eleanor's home barely had room enough for everyone. The memorial was never meant to be anything but simple. There was wine and tea and coffee and pastries. Mortality in the air. And not that much talk, at first.

Almost everyone was grey-haired, veterans of the magic five years – it being thought that if you lasted that long in Yellowknife, you might stay for decades. They had known Lorna from her previous, happy life, with her first husband. They had known that in her second marriage she was abjectly miserable. One woman spoke about Irving Dargabble as a horrible drunken lout, and said she knew Lorna had been "holding it together", just barely, for years. Another older woman, wearing a bright red vest, said she suspected Lorna just wandered off into the night "which is so easy to do up here". She herself had been in Igloolik one time, she said, and started to walk back to the hotel and thought if she turned right instead of left, she would never be found. "The vastness really hit me," she said with feeling.

There was a young woman who came, too, a young woman in braids. She turned out to be the one who had stumbled upon Lorna's body. "Actually, it was my dog who found her. He deserves the credit." She had tied him up outside before coming into the trailer and pointed to him now out of the window, a big brown and black dog named Stan, she said. The young woman joined in the conversation about wandering off and getting lost. She had heard about blizzards in the eastern Arctic where the wind blows for three days, then stops, and you can be fooled into going outside, only for the wind to swing around from the opposite direction and disorient you totally. Ralph recalled stepping outside into a blizzard in Fort Simpson, and not being able to breathe; the wind sucked his breath out of his mouth. Everyone agreed, however, that on Christmas Eve, when Lorna went missing, conditions were peaceful. A gentler night, Lorna's last night. No wind at all. But cold, certainly cold.

Gwen listened, haunted by the unexplained light-brown hair Lorna was holding in her hand. A chilling detail that was not common knowledge. She had mentioned it to the others, though, to Harry and Ralph and Eleanor, thereby learning about Eleanor's lingering suspicion of Eddy, even as she put it to rest.

*   *

In the middle of June, just days before they left for the Barrens, the local coroner issued his long-awaited news release. There would not be an inquest into Lorna Dargabble's death, after all. As reasons, he gave the following: there was no evidence of wounds, injuries, poison, or disease on the body; the pathologist in Edmonton had given the cause of death as exposure to the cold; and the investigation by the police clearly absolved all individuals who might have had something to gain by her death. He concluded that there was absolutely no suspicion of wrongdoing or complicity on the part of any person.

The four canoeists were in Harry's house, repacking, rearranging, jettisoning a few things (like the hip waders Ralph had intended to use when he fished in the rapids for trout, like the second bottle of Scotch Harry had planned to bring along). Now that they were within forty-eight hours of having to hoist everything onto their backs, they were being realistic. The evening light poured into the living room as Harry packed an extra sweater and woollen socks. So suicide then. Lorna had walked out on Christmas Eve and consigned herself to the elements. As for the hair clenched in her hand – the investigation had shown it was a lock of hair, cut from somebody's head, not torn out by the roots. It could have been anybody's light brown hair. She was a hairdresser, after all. But whose hair? he had to wonder. And why had she taken it with her that night?

He went on organizing his supplies. The day after tomorrow they would fly to the eastern arm of Great Slave Lake, and in a few weeks they would reach the Thelon River and view the remains of John Hornby's cabin, the spot where his body had lain undiscovered for more than a year in that wooded oasis in the Barrens. Harry heard Ralph across the room remark that the western sky looked clear, promising, but he felt too preoccupied to respond. The fact of Dido's telephone call had stirred up more unanswered questions, which worked on his mind. At times, the thought of her father-in-law's letter was consoling. She had left behind two loves, he thought. His and Daniel's. Possibly she was saying, It's not just you, Harry. I'm leaving everything behind. He could feel almost reconciled then, able to carry what he felt for her and carry it easily; he would hear from her in time, he would see her again. But then he would picture her with Eddy – think of her leaving without a word – think of her tele-phoning, finally, but not telephoning him – and his reaction was so intense it stopped him in his tracks. And so it went, back and forth, between feelings of love and feelings of anguish.

Just days ago something else had brought her back in an unex-pected way. A small package from California had arrived in the mail for Eleanor, who had shown him and the others what it contained. A Saint Christopher medallion on a chain. Eleanor was wearing it now. It fell forward as she leaned over her impossibly heavy knapsack. *St Christopher, protect us.*

ON THE MORNING OF JUNE 17, THEY LOADED THEIR CANOES and packs into a float plane and took off from Yellowknife Bay. The pilot flew them to the rugged, uninhabited eastern end of Great Slave Lake. They planned to camp there for two nights, on Charlton Bay, breaking themselves in slowly. Then, following in Hornby's foot-steps, they would undertake the classic route of Pike's Portage into Artillery Lake, and from there continue on to the Thelon River.

By afternoon they were on a rocky sunlit point of land in Charlton Bay, setting up their tents, judging which spots were warmest and most sheltered by the depth of the moss and lichen. They were alone now. About three hundred miles below the Arctic Circle in almost continuous daylight, facing six weeks in the wilderness.

Chunks of ice floated by. Candled ice, the long vertical ice crystals that form when meltwater on a frozen lake works its trickling way down to the water below, had bunched against the shore. The candles tinkled and chimed, and Gwen taped the sound. Ralph headed off in his canoe, eager to test his muscles and to take his first photographs. Harry gathered wood for a fire, and Eleanor listed birds in her note-book. Lapland longspurs, gone from Yellowknife two weeks ago, were with them here, where it was colder. The little birds let her walk noisily over stones to within two feet of them, before they hopped away. Twice, Hornby had overwintered nearby, building himself a small cabin, and nearly died both times.

Although they had what seemed like all the space in the world and all the time, they were committed to a definite destination: the Twin Otter would come back for them on July 27 at Beverly Lake, five hundred miles from here. And so time and space were in potential conflict.

The next day, their first full day, they deliberately took it easy, exploring the site of old Fort Reliance near the mouth of the Lockhart River. They paddled to the ruins after breakfast and discovered a site of great loveliness. It was like a park of white and green moss and lichen, with spruce trees arranged as though planted. They followed a path, and then a wider one, almost a driveway through the natural park. The trees had tiny buds. They were heading backwards, they realized, into a much later spring of lingering ice, and fresh snow on the hills in the morning, melted by early afternoon. Eleanor said she could picture Jane Austen walking here it looked so civilized, so groomed. There were three perfectly shaped birches and two graves, fenced with weathered slats, one a child or infant's grave, tiny, the other larger.

"The past is as close," Eleanor said to Ralph, "as I am to you."

Ralph, a man of books and pockets, and pockets stretched out of shape by books, opened George Whalley and read the quotation from J.W. Tyrrell, the land surveyor and mapmaker who had stood in this spot in 1900 and sung its praises. "Five stone chimneys only now remain of what were 66 years ago three substantial buildings . . . situated on a lovely level green terrace about twenty feet above the harbour, and two hundred feet from the shore." Back's Chimneys they were called, after Captain George Back, who came through in 1833 and used the fort as his winter quarters. He and his men were a relief party on the trail of Sir John Ross, who was on the trail of the North-West Passage (*to have felt snow and ice forever, and nothing forever but snow and ice*), though in the end Ross, unlike so many, needed no rescuing.

That afternoon Ralph pulled Gwen up the sandbank laughing,

and a few minutes later Harry accused him of taking his cup.

"That's my cup you're drinking out of."

"No. It's mine." Ralph's voice was even, easy.

"No, it's not," he growled back.

"I brought it up with me from the canoe."

"No." And Harry was about to battle on when he saw his own cup sitting a few feet away on the moss. He reached for it, attempted a laugh, and turned to see Eleanor eyeing him critically.

She said, "Watch you don't slip a cog."

Afterwards, he asked her to repeat that expression, the one she had castigated him with.

Slip a cog. "Poor Ralph was sitting there quietly and I knew it was his cup because I saw him bring it out of the canoe."

"I don't feel as cantankerous as I sound." He managed an apologetic smile.

"Well, it's good you can laugh about it now."

He felt reproved and childish and he was not laughing. The mosquitoes were nimble. Wilder, or it was just earlier in the year; they escaped before he could slap them.

Pike's Portage was twenty-five miles long, a series of small lakes and trails that led to Artillery Lake, itself fifty miles long. An Indian route from time immemorial. Its first leg (to Harry Lake, of all places) was brutal, as they knew from trip reports by other canoeists, three miles long with a climb of five hundred and ninety feet, rocky and wooded, when their packs were heaviest and they were least in shape.

The feeling of release once Harry reached the end and sank to the ground and extricated himself from the eighty pounds of torture on his back, was like sprouting wings and floating up to heaven. But the feat had to be repeated three times, first with one pack, then with another, then with a seventy-pound canoe on his shoulders. He portaged one canoe, Ralph the other. Five trips, if you counted the there and back, and more taxing than anything he had ever done before or ever imagined. The only thing that kept him going was stubborn pride. Arms at his sides, fingers swelling up like stubby sausages, he trudged along under his burden, listening for Ralph behind him and trying to keep ahead, or at least not fall behind. He heard footsteps and after a minute Eleanor appeared around the bend, on her way back for another load. Then Gwen. The women had to carry packs that weighed sixty pounds or more. He had hoisted Gwen's pack onto her back and she had swayed and he had steadied her, and then she had stepped forward – all five-foot-three of her and 120 pounds – Hornby's size, he thought – and started up the trail. Now here she was going back for the second round. Eleanor was a bigger woman, taller, heftier, but they shared the same look of exhausted, dazed determination. The women disappeared and he stopped for a moment, and still he heard the thumping of feet, then realized it was the blood pounding in his head. Mosquitoes abounded. He felt something on his tongue, explored with his finger, and came out with a drowned mosquito. At the end, his legs gave out. Going into the little hollow and across to the rocks, where he could ford the last stream, he felt them go rubbery and only just managed to totter to the finishing line of open water, where he let the canoe fall from shoulder height into a cradle of willow bushes. Again, the sweet release.

At the end, after everything had been transported, they bathed in the warm evening sun, their bodies bone white, stone white at the water's edge, scooping aching-cold Harry Lake over their heads.

The next day, June 20, the fourth day of their trip, Harry had an early-morning dream about Gwen. Of coming into her house through the back door and she was in her dressing gown, having called him for help. A stalled car? She went upstairs to change and after an interval he followed and entered her bedroom through the half-open door. She was sitting on the edge of her bed, still undressed, except for panties that were in tatters (her drastic underwear he would see set out to dry on the arctic willows, waist pulling away from elastic, saggy brassiere) but no brassiere in the dream, her breasts round and warm as she turned an undershirt right side out, her eyes concentrating on the cat's cradle of what had become a lacy camisole – the undershirt had become pretty in the dream – and all of her alert, attractive, attracted, naked. Was he not about to reach for her breasts and she about to respond when he woke up?

Harry could not recall ever dreaming about Dido, which surprised him. Perhaps if all of your waking thoughts are taken up with someone, then your sleeping mind has to catch up. He found himself carrying the dream about Gwen through his arduous day.

But it was Ralph, who would bury his face in the tundra heather and say he wanted tundra tweeds, a full suit made of the stuff and bearing its array of muted colours and its smoky, subtle smell, it was garrulous, poetic Ralph who would score.

They moved across the wilderness like a ragged troupe of toiling actors, it seemed to Harry, transporting sections of a colourful banner, namely the tents and canoes and packs. Ralph the gentleman duke. Eleanor the wise Queen. Gwen the moody princess. And he, the blistered and bitten and disgruntled fool. After a mere four days, he was so stiff that to get up he had to roll on his side and push with his aching arms. He took the huge blisters on his heels to Eleanor, who bandaged them. Took his aching shoulders to Gwen, who pressed and rubbed and kneaded. Gwen he began to call Kate, "Kate like the hazel twig", since against the backdrop of so much immensity her small body seemed not fragile but intensely delicate, her eyelids like petals, her small ears astonishing.

On the fifth night, he assumed a new identity, haughty chef Rodrigo. "Pork chops Rodrigo" became the first of many such dishes. "Grayling Rodrigo" and "trout *Béarnaise*" and "*boeuf* ha ha ha", all served with flourishes of theatrical bad temper. "My kingdom for a garlic press," he would snarl. Or, with a snap of his fingers, "The Great Rodrigo must have curry." And he would rummage in his pack and pull out the unexpected spice, earning genuine applause for his gastric foresight.

Gwen burned her mouth on his bedtime cocoa. "That's the point of cocoa," he told her. "I've lost half my taste buds!" she said. "You have far too many taste buds anyway," he told her.

Ralph had brought along Farley Mowat's *Tundra*, a fine collection of excerpts from the accounts of great arctic travellers, and that night he passed it to Harry, suggesting he read them to sleep. Harry's voice recounting the adventures of Samuel Hearne (who coined the phrase "the Barren Ground" for the arctic expanse of treeless plains that he toiled across between 1769 and 1772), Harry's voice carried from their tent to the women's tent a dozen feet away. *From the 20th to the 23rd of June, we walked nearly twenty miles a day without any subsistence other than a pipe of tobacco and a drink of water when we pleased. Early on the 23rd we saw three muskoxen, and the Indians soon killed them. But to our great mortification it rained before we got them skinned, and the moss could not be made to burn to make a fire. This was poor comfort for people who had not broken their fast for three or four days . . . The weather remained so bad, with rain, snow, and sleet, that by the time we were again able to make a fire of moss, we had eaten the amount of one muskox quite raw. I must confess that now my spirits began to fail me a little. Indeed our other misfortunes were greatly aggravated by the weather, which was cold and so very wet that for three days and nights I had not one dry thread on me. But when the fine weather returned, and we had dried our clothing by a fire of moss, I endeavoured, like a sailor after a storm, to forget past misfortunes.*

From above, in the never-ending light, their canoes and tents looked like separate fruits on a flat tree espaliered against a grey stone wall. Gwen's orange tent, shared with Eleanor; Harry's, lemon-yellow, shared with Ralph; Harry's red canoe; Ralph's silver canoe. Aircraft, or anyone at a distance, would have spotted them easily, which was the point, and became the point.

They were proceeding from lake to lake in the string of eight lakes that comprised Pike's Portage into Artillery Lake. Harry Lake then French Lake then Acres. "This is where we can get lost," Ralph said, examining their map repeatedly. Then Kipling Lake.

By now they were moving into the Barrens. The north-facing side of Kipling Lake had stunted trees or none at all, and any leaves they saw were tiny. It should have occurred to them then what lay ahead, but by day it was so warm. Their faces and hands burned, their fingers and lips cracked and split. They tied the canoes together in the middle of the lake for lunch, catching the wind which kept away the mosquitoes, and drifted gently to shore, where they finished their salami, cheese, bannock, peanut butter.

After Kipling came Burr Lake, large and surrounded by round hills, all of a height and bare, except for a few boulders sitting on top, dropped by a retreating glacier 8000 years ago. In the simplified landscape you could see a very long distance. It was rather like a kept golf course, Harry thought. Beautiful lines, beautiful details – silver-grey lichen, tiny pink flowers. Easy to walk on, the growth ankle-high.

That evening he watched Gwen wash her hair. She knelt on a rock and bent her head forward, exposing the tender ring around her neck formed by the chafing collar of her wool shirt. She dipped her head into the punishingly cold lake, quickly swept water over her head with one hand, rubbed in shampoo, rinsed, lowered her head into the lake again, again swept water over it. "Still soapy," he called to her, and with both hands she scooped water and splashed it more vigorously over her hair, then grabbed a towel and wrapped it around her head, achieving sweet and immediate relief as he could tell from the relaxation of her shoulders, which were bare, her upper body clad in a faded blue undershirt, soft from use.

Birds sang in the background, white-crowned sparrows. One

called nearby, a long summer call, another answered faintly on the other side of the hill, declaring its territory.

"My little trout," Ralph said smilingly when he looked up from the fire and saw Gwen.

"Quasimodo," Harry grinned, thinking of her hunched shoulders at the edge of the freezing lake, and wanting to be contrary and humorous and remembered.

It wasn't the change of scene that was making things easier, Harry decided, or the hard labour, or the distraction of sore shoulders and a sore knee. It was being removed from all possible contact. No mail, no telephone.

On their sixth day they reached Artillery Lake, only to experience what would be the first in a series of shocks ending in something far worse. The lake, fifty miles long, turned out to be covered in ice.

They were at the southern end, a narrow fjord of open water that turned an ominous white in the near distance. Ralph climbed a ridge with his binoculars and did not return for some time. When he came back he was subdued and would only mutter, "a lot of ice".

They had moved still farther back in time to pre-leaf catkins, red-tipped, on the dwarf willows, and to the first subtle blush of green on the miniature birches and alders. Yet it was June 22.

At nine-thirty in the evening, Harry retreated to his tent, away from flies and light and consciousness, away from people and things to do, away from Ralph's indefatigable drive. Already they were crossing swords about how early to get up each morning and when to pack it in each day. He heard more birds and a stream in the distance. Then Gwen boasting about the dessert she was cooking. "Come and look." He did not stir. He wanted a drink, not a bloody dessert. But his bottle of Scotch, wrapped with care in a sweater, and siphoned little by little into his hip flask, was going to have to last the whole trip. He held off.

With fiendish energy Gwen had made a version of strawberry shortcake: sweet bannock scones topped with freeze-dried strawberries boiled and sweetened and thickened with cornstarch, and topped in turn with thick cream from a can. She brought him his portion on a plate and he had to admit it wasn't bad. He lay in a corner of his tent, by himself, out of harm's way, licking his fingers.

But Gwen's achievement was a direct challenge to The Great Rodrigo, and so he redoubled his efforts, concocting in the morning a deluxe porridge to seduce her, the confirmed porridge-hater. A bowl of oatmeal covered with freeze-dried peaches, brown sugar, a dab of butter, his own special cream of powdered milk and Coffee-mate, a sprinkle of cinnamon. She ate his "porridge *à la crème pêche*" out of kindness and would not be coaxed a second time.

The next day, their seventh day out, they took as a day of rest, exploring and photographing, napping and reading. Eleanor sat quietly, waiting for creatures to appear, fingering the St Christopher medallion, cool to the touch, and shaking herself every so often to keep away the flies. She began to feel like a cow in a lichen pasture. She and Gwen had pitched their tent on a flat bed of lichen. When she crawled inside, the floor of the tent scrunched like wrapping paper. She lay on her thin mattress of insulite, away from bothersome mosquitoes, and listened. Harry and Gwen were drinking coffee by the fire, washing dishes, talking. She heard an intimacy beneath the banter, and saw without closing her eyes the landscape they had been looking at for days – rocky slopes covered with all manner of lichens, silver-grey, mustard, lime-green, soft-green; the exquisite balance of boulders left perching thousands of years ago; tiny leaves, gold, red; and pink flowers in clumps, scattered, as were antlers left to bleach on the side of the hill, and animal droppings. The air holding the warmth.

She had been so very tired yesterday, especially around supper time, trying to drive tent stakes deep enough into the ground – quite a wind then; but now the air was perfectly still, and a second wind was inside her. Lying on the ground, being reshaped, was like lying awake beside a new husband. Inside the orange tent the light was eternal sunshine no matter the hour, her burned face and hands gave off rays of heat. She closed her eyes. Pink flowers against lichen flashed in a near irritation of feeling, an over-arousal; the wedding bed again.

At first, they stayed in the narrow leads of open water between ice and shore, making progress of a sort. Sometimes the leads turned into wider channels and they paddled in smooth water under a hot sun. Where the ice was tight against the shore, they portaged, or if the ice happened to be smooth, they pushed their loaded canoes across it, but carefully, wary of falling through. Whenever they could, they lined the canoes, guiding them forward with ropes through shallow water until they got caught up in rocks, and then once again they were carrying everything on their backs over uneven ground.

Impatience made them bolder. Instead of hugging the shore, they began to push their canoes over long frozen stretches of Artillery Lake farther away from land. Ice-canoeing, they called it: one foot in the canoe, the other on the half-rotted ice, they scooted forward, ready to hop into the canoe if the ice gave way, and once it did. Harry and Eleanor, who always paddled together, managed to hop aboard in the nick of time. But then they were wedged in place, surrounded and pinned on all sides by ice. Eleanor leant forward, she was so tired, and cried for a moment. They got free, finally, by rocking the canoe and breaking up the ice around them until they reached a portion that was solid enough to take their weight. Then off they went again, pushing forward with one foot, like Scott and Shackleton and all the other polar lunatics.

Deep water below, and ptarmigan off to the right – in three hours the only sign of life. By late afternoon, they were exhausted.

In Harry and Ralph's tent, the larger of the two, all of them huddled in awkward silence, since ten minutes earlier Harry had pointed a finger at Commander Ralph and told him to fuck off.

"Harry, *do* something," Ralph had barked when he saw Harry standing immobilized. The rain starting to fall, their packs uncovered, Ralph busy with tarps and with stones to weigh the tarps down. "Do *something*."

Harry pointed his finger. "You, fuck off."

And so it was ice, rain, headwind, bad temper. Harry's felt hat, beaten about by the weather, no longer looked quite so dapper. Yet when they walked across certain patches of sun-warmed ground, they inhaled the perfume of small pink flowers and it was the lightest, most papery, most northern of scents. Harry stopped and breathed it in, burying his troubled mind in a tree full of apple blossoms. A fragrance as different from patchouli as anything he could think of. If it came to that. And it did. It was a sudden thought.

Inside the tent, out of the wind and rain, they risked making tea on their little butane stove, and Eleanor took a restorative sip.

"'Sweet are the uses of adversity,'" she murmured into the tension-filled air.

"'Which, like the toad, ugly and venomous,'" Ralph supplied, "'wears yet a precious jewel in his head.'"

Earning himself a wide and appreciative smile. He had picked up and finished the quote, just as her father would have done.

*　*

Although they were locked in ice, the air flowed – the bright, bitter light of June. For two days they stayed put on Artillery Lake, hoping the ice would loosen and move away from shore. It was too cold for flies, that was the blessing. Rain fell, then slowed to a drizzle, then turned into low cloud, then lifted.

Harry climbed a butte and saw goshawks and cliff swallows, a hill covered in purple flowers, and through the binoculars infinite ice. Eleanor knelt next to a rock to be out of the wind and pulled out her flower book: the purple was Lapland rosebay, while around her blossomed low white clusters of small-leaved Labrador tea. Gwen made doughnuts, her arm coming floury out of the bannock bag, her face delighted by the boisterous encouragement from all sides, the cries for jelly filling and chocolate icing. She rolled the sweetened dough between her palms, formed rings and fried them, several at a time, in melted lard, then rolled the hot doughnuts in a mixture of cinnamon and sugar, and Harry offered up his joke. "So a guy goes into a restaurant and orders a hamburger. The waiter brings it to him and the guy takes a bite and pulls a long hair out of his mouth: 'Hey, what's *this*?' So the waiter takes him back to the kitchen and there's the cook pressing meat patties in his armpits. 'That's *disgusting!*' 'You think that's disgusting?' says the waiter. 'You should see how he makes doughnuts.'"

* *

They gave up waiting for the ice to improve and on June 28, they set off again, battling their way down Artillery Lake, skirting ice, or hauling themselves up and across it, or paddling in any open leads. Harry boiled over at the incessant headwind and slammed his paddle on the ice, almost breaking it, and he did not care.

"I almost broke my paddle," he stormed.

Eleanor looked around from the bow of their canoe. "Slam your head into the ice instead, not something we depend on."

He refused to go on. They were considerably behind the other two, in what would become their standard pattern, but he beached the canoe and stood next to a rock. Eleanor stood beside him. He said, "I'm not going any farther till the wind dies down."

She felt an involuntary smile come up on her face, so she bent her head and walked to the canoe.

"Say something," he said.

"I will. I'm just thinking."

She said it might take a long time for the wind to die down. They had not moved for two days. They all wanted to get ahead.

He did not answer, and they went on.

At Crystal Island the tree-line cut diagonally across Artillery Lake as visibly as a long dark pencil mark on a blank page. They passed over the line into a world without walls, a land of rolling plains as exposed as the open sea. Their backs were sudden trees. Their hats were leaves the mosquitoes rested upon. Birds flew past their shoulders, like familiars. And at night their quiet talk around the little bannock fire was similar to the voices of the trees that spooked the early Eskimos, who ventured down in search of wood for their sled runners, but never stayed longer than ten days among the whispering, groaning wood spirits.

That evening they fell into recalling their first memories. Hers, Eleanor said, was of being blamed unfairly by other kids for breaking the eggs in a robin's nest, and this was an English robin, smaller than Canadian robins, with bluer eggs. That might be why a recent thought had taken the particular form it took: the robin in the egg does not know the robin's egg is blue.

"Meaning what?" Gwen said.

"Meaning that we're blind to our own blind spots."

Gwen nodded slowly, picturing the robin inside the blue egg and herself inside her small world. "Like my blind spot about religion."

"If you want. Or like being in love with someone and not knowing it."

A pause. "Who are you talking about?" Gwen said.

But Eleanor was not prepared to say, and then Ralph was confessing a first memory so personal and out of the ordinary that her point got lost for a while. Ralph's first memory was taking the dry little turds out of his nappy and lining them up in a careful row on the windowsill. "I had a collector's eye even then," he laughed.

"But what was your mother feeding you?" Eleanor cried.

Gwen remembered a piece of white satin fluttering in her grand-mother's mahogany wardrobe, though it might have been a dream, she was not sure. Eleanor suggested that perhaps she was seeing the future. Her own grandmother was a little girl when she dreamt about a soldier's cap, then years later she saw the cap on her daddy's head as he lay in his coffin.

They were carrying wood with them, having left the trees behind. Gathering up whatever driftwood they could find, keeping an eye peeled for any dry sticks. Gwen, Harry noticed, looked like a young girl in her red wind jacket and running shoes, one trouser leg turned up, bending over the fire or gathering wood. One evening she sat on a rocky outcrop above Ralph, who was fishing from shore. Ralph set down his fishing rod, turned around, and began to pelt her with snowballs. She giggled and shrieked, hands in front of her face, then scooped up the same snow and fired it back at his head. Soon after-wards he gave up fishing and went over to the fire. Gwen came down off the rock innocently: Ralph? Want any help? No, he was just letting the fire burn down to have coals for bannock. Then a blood-curdling yell as he felt snow shoved down the back of his shirt and rubbed against his bare skin.

From his perch several yards away, Harry lit another cigarette. The spit spit of tobacco off his tongue. He heard Gwen offer to tend the bannock so that Ralph could take his evening hike. Ralph leapt at the chance and Eleanor went with him. Then it was Gwen and Harry by the fire. Every evening one of them made bannock, a thick, wide, pancake-biscuit of flour, salt, baking powder, powdered milk and water. They cooked it slowly, patiently, in melted lard in a frying pan, providing themselves with a ready-made and speedy lunch for the following day.

Old worries had followed her into the Barrens, Gwen confided to Harry, lifting the bannock with a spatula to make sure it was not getting scorched. Being all alone on the tundra – as exposed to the weather as she had been exposed on the air – made her brood about certain things, like the flimsy shelter of personality. She was beset by radio dreams, she told him. She would be on a bus leaving town, for instance, and suddenly remember she had forgotten all about preparing her programme and she would have to telephone the station in a panic and tell them to play music.

"There was another dream," she said. "About Dido."

Harry lifted his head. "What about her?"

Gwen did not answer. She looked down at the soft-green lichens adhering to the rock, impervious to any wind, at the little twigs clinging to her woollen trousers. She was seeing the two loons that swam ahead of them earlier in the day. Most elegant red-eyed birds. Dressed in black stockings, it seemed to her, soot-black, pulled over their heads and down their long necks. And the white of their breasts, where breast met water, so white they might have been pushing snowbanks ahead of them. Immaculate, until they opened their beaks and sounded like nothing else you had ever heard. Sorrowful calls that reached to the horizon. Or rippling, demented laughs.

"What about Dido?" Harry pressed.

"Just that she had taken all my stuff out of the filing cabinet and replaced it with her own things." It sounded pathetic. She gave her shoulders a shake.

"She can't take what you have," Harry said quietly, "unless you let her."

Such a lot to unpack from that slender gift of a sentence. Harry was on her side, but only if she was on her own side, and there were no sides, really, unless she chose to look at it that way. But Harry understood the dream and did not blame her, which was a comfort.

The contrast between comfort and discomfort was their daily bread – the pain of portaging and the bliss of lying in the evening sun, warm, fed, rested. A light wind to keep the flies somewhat at bay.

But the sun was not shining, and had not been for days. ·

And then it was. On June 30 the sky turned blue and a canal as wide as a wide gateway (three canoes wide) opened in the ice on Artillery Lake. They paddled forward and it seemed biblical, blessed and childlike all at once. A pathway opened up through life. Winds could not trouble them here, where there was not enough open water to allow for any waves. For one enchanted hour the lake was less ice-infested than ice-enriched. On the bottom of the lake were stones so clear to the eye they could count every one of them, on either side was the endless surrendering ice, beyond them the canal snaked around the very corner that would take them where they wanted to go, while above, in the blue-blue sky, one low and narrow cloud hung close to the horizon, a soft repetition of the ice on either side.

Cool air came off the ice and mixed with warm winds offshore, a combination that recalled for Gwen a summer job sorting strawberries inside a refrigerated truck.

Pieces of loose ice crunched under the canoe.

And then they were beyond the ice. The colour of the water changed – deep blue, violet, green – platinum where it was shallow over sand. The two canoes pulled apart. Gwen and Ralph, always in the lead, continued at the same pace, while Harry and Eleanor fell far behind. Bewitched by the bright shore of white sand, they stopped to photograph a line of small green clumps of moss on which tiny pink flowers described a pattern. Pale-lilac, and Eleanor identified them as moss campion, a cushion plant. "Look how it protects itself from the wind. So clever," she said. "So persevering." She looked up and smiled at Harry with such affection that he felt restored.

They paddled on. The open water was calm and shiny, the mosquitoes abundant again; in the bow Eleanor felt like a splattered windshield from all the bugs knocking into her. Gazing into the clear water she and Harry spotted a big trout with a silver lure hanging from its mouth. Also, a goose walking across the ice – walking, walking. Was it hurt?

By evening the two of them were at the far end of Artillery Lake, looking for the exit. Rain clouds had blown in. They could see where it was pouring to the left and right. Around them the country was the same as it had been for some time, low and flat, except now they were working their way through back channels, and they were lost.

They had last seen Ralph and Gwen quite a while ago, and the maps were in Ralph's canoe. Ralph had misplaced his camera bag a few days back, setting it down on undifferentiated ground as he stalked a ptarmigan; it had taken half an hour of searching by all of them to find it. And to her chagrin, Eleanor had forgotten Dido's medallion while bathing one morning. She had removed the chain from around her neck so it would not slap against her skin, then not thought of it again until lunchtime when they were miles beyond where she had bathed. She tried not to see the lapse as a bad omen.

They had come too far. Or so they thought. They turned back and retraced their route and became even more confused and alarmed. Harry confessed he had no sense of direction. He told Eleanor about the infamous night in Toronto when he went to play poker at a buddy's house for the umpteenth time, but walked into another house entirely, on a different block. "I was hanging up my coat when the owner came out of the kitchen. I figured he had to be the new poker player. So I said, 'Where's the booze?'"

Eleanor took the compass out of his hand and studied it herself. But it seemed wisest to stay put and let themselves be found. She suggested they pitch his tent in order to make themselves more vis-ible. They did that, and the bright yellow material fluttering in the air reminded her of what Ralph had said the other night about the frailty of arctic explorers. Dehydration was the biggest danger, the desiccating winds. If they lay down, Ralph said, it was "bye-bye, butterfly".

A raven croaked as it flew overhead. Eleanor was grateful for the company. She said, "Why is it that ravens don't turn white in the winter like ptarmigans?"

"Ptarmigans are like us," said Harry. "They need all the help they can get."

An hour passed and a grim fear worked its way into his bones. He pulled his flask out of his jacket pocket, unscrewed the lid, and handed it to Eleanor.

"Your secret supply," she said.

He told her about hearing a scientist say that cold, in the form of snow and ice, can be stored, but heat cannot. "He forgot about this," he said. Taking it back from her. "To our wives and sweethearts. May they never meet."

The liquor felt wonderful in every part of him.

Eleanor wrapped her arms around her knees. They were completely alone, apart from that passing raven. "My father told me his hair turned white when he was fourteen," she said. "But I hadn't the wit or the curiosity to ask why."

Harry said the same thing happened to Amundsen when he was twenty-one. He spent a winter on a whaling ship in Antarctica and the experience was so appalling, all those months of darkness, that his hair turned white.

"So his white hair was a source of light," Eleanor said.

Another hour passed. Beside him, Eleanor was quiet. "Are you praying?" he said.

"Yes."

Good, Harry thought.

The flask was empty. In an act that would ensure his entry into heaven, he had given her the last swallow.

"They're waiting for us to show up," she said.

"How long will they wait, do you suppose?"

"I wonder."

Her prayer was ongoing and free form. At the moment she was talking to her father. She was saying to him, I have never asked for anything before, and now I do.

Aloud she said, "Maybe this is what happened to Hornby. Maybe he got lost. Maybe that's why they took so long to get to the Thelon." Then she said, "That goose wasn't hurt. The one we saw walking? It's moulting, that's all. Moulting geese can't fly."

Harry put his arm around her. He had not forgotten his boyish sense of a world filled with a divine presence and with many lesser spirits, especially in the woods, especially in the dark; he still believed that just because we cannot see something doesn't mean it is not there, or – more to the point – just because something *is* there does not mean it is seen. Here they were, he and Eleanor, completely exposed, pathetically visible, but unseen, lost. "We're like Adam and Eve," he said, and with those words he began to laugh, for an old limerick had lit up his mind. "In the Garden of Eden lay Adam," he recited, "complacently stroking his madam, And great was his mirth, For on all of the earth, There were only two balls – and he had 'em."

Later still, they made a fire with what sticks they could find, and went on watching the water and a sky that normally was too light for sunsets. But tonight, the prolonged colours of sun under dark cloud echoed the shades of the tiny pink and white flowers near at hand. There grew in Eleanor the sense that no matter what happened it was a privilege to be here, to see this vast tundra landscape that produced one-inch flowers and immeasurable skies. She thought of the Japanese artists who stood out in the weather for hours, simply observing, then went back inside to make their prints of the floating world. We're being visited by the possibility of utter disaster, she thought, but what swept through her was a sense of joy: of dependence on a great personal Being somewhere far off yet nearby, and *our lives are in Your hands*.

Then Harry started to whistle, and suddenly she shivered and rubbed her arms through the sleeves of her heavy woollen shirt. "What's the coldest you've ever been?" she asked him.

He knew the answer without even thinking. Saturday afternoons, bicycling home from playing hockey on the duck pond, his hands on the icy handlebars. His mother would tell him to run cold water from the kitchen tap over his cold hands. Frozen feet too, jumping from foot to foot. The air around the electric light all blue and rainbowy, his eyes so cold. His mother would give him a cup of scalding cocoa and nine times out of ten it took the roof off the top of his mouth. "Nothing holds the heat like cocoa does," he said, "but it doesn't *store* heat the way ice stores cold."

Eleanor said she had a theory that there is something about heat that actually reinforces memory. She broke off, and Harry waited. "When I was about sixteen," she went on, "my friend Jill and I went to a Saturday matinée and when we came out it was dark and freezing cold and the bus didn't come. Ottawa in January. So I decided to walk home and Jill was positive I was going the wrong way. She refused to come with me, she held on to a parking meter with both hands, *no no no*. That was the coldest I've ever been. And all I remember is plodding home and Jill dragging her feet behind me and me trying not to think or feel *anything*. The movie, on the other hand, I remember every detail of, because I was inside and warm."

"*Were* you going the wrong way?"

"No, it was the right way."

"You had better do the navigating from now on."

She was about to tell him which movie it was when a sound – a cough – made them turn around. Impossible to say how long he'd been squatting there, twenty yards away. Unkempt, dark-haired, unsmiling. Cradling a gun in his arms.

Harry stood up, but Eleanor stayed where she was, her arms

around her knees. Where on earth had he come from?

The stranger stood up too and came down the barren slope, and Eleanor thought of Eddy, because the man did not smile and he looked dangerous. The movie on the coldest night of her life was "Teahouse of the August Moon", for which Brando starved himself in order to play the Japanese interpreter Sakini. Now, in one of those uncanny coincidences that guide us through life, if we let them, their wild-looking saviour turned out to be Japanese.

His name sounded like Ee-zay and he was travelling "solo", he said.

By means of a map and some English and a good deal of gesturing, he told them he was coming from Snowdrift on Great Slave Lake and heading to Chantrey Inlet on the arctic coast by way of the Back River. Through his binoculars he had seen their tent, which stood out, being in such an unlikely place. Wanting to stretch his legs, wanting to be sure they were alright, he had hiked the low ridge behind them. His own canoe was out of sight around a bend.

A St Christopher medallion hung around his neck. Eleanor pointed to it in some surprise and his face lit up. "Is your?" he said, and undid the fastener and handed it to her.

After that, Eleanor could not stop smiling. You never know how help will come, or in what form. She felt protected, rather like the Thelon River wildlife sanctuary to which they were headed. *Nothing bad is going to happen to us.* The idea was like a crystal-clear hallucination, the product of a wild coincidence in a wild place.

Tonight Ee-zay would paddle and portage until he reached – he pointed at the map – Ptarmigan Lake, which was their destination too, not that they would get there as soon as this solitary adventurer. He liked to travel all night, he told them, when it wasn't so windy, then sleep during the day, then take off again. They could follow him, he indicated, and they would probably find their companions. By now it was after midnight and the silver lichen had a sheen rising off it like the wavery heat rising from a toaster.

They struck Harry's tent and packed their canoe and the three of them paddled until they reached Ee-zay's canoe. Then he led the way out of the back channel in which they had been lost, and canoeing towards them came the search party of Gwen and Ralph. With that, the lonely Barrens turned into a place of domestic ease and multiple embraces. They beached their canoes and suddenly there was chocolate, dried fruit, conversation, laughter, repeated avowals of never letting you out of my sight. Ralph offered Eleanor morsels of chocolate on his fingertips, and in leaning towards him she caught an old childhood smell of Christmas: nicotine and chocolate and raisins – it was her father at the foot of her bed filling her stocking after he thought she was fast asleep.

They made tea, having a Barren Lands tea ceremony at one in the morning, boiling the water in a billy can, then dropping a bag of black tea into the water and serving it with sugar to their impressive Japanese traveller. Gwen got her tape recorder out of its brown canvas bag and their wild angel talked into it; he had a delightful way of saying pee-nuts ba-ta-, which seemed to be his mainstay along with any fish he caught. They gave him some of their supply of chocolate and dried apricots, then they all returned to their canoes and paddled to the entrance of the Lockhart River, where Gwen and Ralph had set up camp on an island. Ee-zay kept going and they watched his progress into what he called "the big of Ca-na-da".

Watching him disappear, Harry had a sudden intuition and felt somebody walk over his grave. Doug Palliser, Lorna Dargabble's first husband, who had drowned making a trek to the Arctic Ocean, had light brown hair. Lorna, he said to the others, must have gone out into the arctic night, holding in her hand a lock of her dead husband's hair.

THE NEXT MORNING THEY WOKE UP ON THEIR ISLAND IN THE
Lockhart River to fierce winds. The stillness of the night before now
seemed like a mirage. This pattern of a golden evening followed by
its opposite, of silence as the precursor to violent gusts of wind,
would not register in all its significance until it was too late.

What registered instead was the need to ignore bad weather.
From Ralph, Eleanor was learning how it ought to be handled, not as
reason for melancholy, but as material for rough humour; he was
always girding his loins and sallying forth "to be bloody, bold and
resolute", treating as a romp the weather that made Harry so
morose. Before breakfast Ralph had been out filling their canoes with
rocks to prevent the wind from lifting them and tumbling them
hundreds of feet down the shore.

Now it was late morning. Eleanor was in her tent, writing up
the events of the day before and describing the terrible noise of
unimpeded winds tearing at the nylon, the guy ropes, the poles on
either side. *We pass our days in beauty and in drudgery,* she wrote, *like
Cinderella.*

Gwen was beside her, stretched out in her sleeping bag, reading
Eleanor's Bible.

"I'm too resistant," she said, putting it down after a few minutes.

"What are you afraid of?" Eleanor said gently, looking up from
her notebook.

Gwen was staring at the orange ceiling three feet above her head.

"I'm afraid of being taken over," she said at last. "Of having to give up too much."

"Do you have so much?"

"I don't have much at all. But what I have is me."

"You wouldn't be less you, that's what I've discovered. You'd be more you."

"Oh, I'm as much of me as I can stand."

This conversation, once begun, threaded its way through the next little while with Eleanor saying to Gwen that her fear of being effaced was natural, but didn't she realize that her fears already effaced her? "I'm not trying to convert you when I say that Christ saved me from that sort of narrowness."

But there were certain words Gwen detested, among them: Christ, goodness, salvation, sin, saviour.

Gwen tried to figure herself out as the tent billowed sideways in the wind and the sound of flapping worked on her nerves. Earlier Ralph had said the wind sometimes blew steady for weeks, it blew for thirty days straight one year in Baker Lake. He had pointed to willows so minuscule they sat an inch or so above the ground, the wood tough and fibrous and lateral. He said it could take a hundred years for one of those roots to reach the size of a thumb. Now Gwen heard a bird call, only one, in the wind. Later, she would hear the sound of a door banging shut, and recognize it as the sound of her own deep longing for permanent shelter. It must have been a rock falling, she decided.

"Eleanor?"

"Yes?"

"What did you mean when you were talking about blind spots? I mean, being in love and not knowing it?"

"Have you noticed the way Harry looks at you?"

Gwen frowned. "That doesn't mean anything. He's in love with Dido."

"That's what he thinks too. Poor wretch."

On the second wind-bound morning on their island, Gwen picked up Eleanor's *Varieties of Religious Experience* and in the soft orange light of the tent became engrossed in William James. He certainly was a very good writer, and there was something in his spiritual case histories that thrilled her. What she loved were all the outer details that clothed inner change. You knew a change was coming, you even knew what form it would take, but the details varied, the struggle varied, the language varied. One woman said: "I did lie down in the stream of life and let it flow over me."

Gwen closed the book and let herself feel the same marvellous thing.

Harry was beside the fire. He was thinking of Dido's *I love you* as the lift door closed, of the lingering look on her face. He was thinking of her voice, the way she pronounced *Harry* as if it were a problem she could not fix.

After she had gone, there had been a lot of mail from listeners who missed her, who wanted to know what had become of her. One listener wrote that Dido was the first intelligent woman he had heard on the radio. "Her voice was a balm." And Harry wrote back to say that Dido Paris had gone on to greener fields. The word *balm* had stayed with him as a perfect description of her sound. Only a few voices were so expressive. And he remembered an old poet he had heard on the radio once.

"Something's bothering you." Those blue eyes, bluer than ever, searched his face. "What are you thinking about?"

He poked the fire with a stick and Gwen noticed his broken fingernails, his banged-up knuckles. Then he looked up, and discovered an exit from his mood in her sunburnt, teaseable face.

"I was thinking about an old poet I heard reminiscing on the radio years ago. He said he was looking out of the window when lightning struck the tree in his garden, and it threw off its bark, he said, 'like a girl flinging off her clothes'."

Gwen laughed. *"That* I'd like to see. But not as much as you would, I think."

After lunch the wind dropped, and they scrambled to take advantage of it. They left their island and paddled up the Lockhart River. By evening they had reached the rapids below Ptarmigan Lake and camped. July 3. Harry made a supper of "beef stew *isolé*" and Ralph headed up a hill with his binoculars, only to come back with "the foul, dank and dreadful news" that Ptarmigan Lake was also covered in ice.

The next day they moved one mile – over the portage to Ptarmigan Lake and back into a frozen world.

"'O me, my heart, my rising heart,'" Ralph groaned.

But then he put on his sneakers, stepped into the ribbon of icy water at the rocky edge, and began to muscle his canoe forward. The others followed, sliding, slipping, falling, cursing, until they came to a sheltered bay, where they set up camp in a thicket of low willows.

In the morning they woke to what they thought was rain falling on their tents. But it sounded odd until they realized it was snow. Snow falls more lightly than rain, and, if anything, it is wetter, the way it clings and melts. July 5.

In their willow thicket, their little rabbit warren, everything they did soaked them through – brushing against wet bushes to gather wet wood, breaking wet branches, cooking with wet dishes. The snow fell like wet feathers into the pot heating on the fire, it cruised down, Harry thought, knowing from Dido that *cruise* comes from *kruizen* for the zigzag motion of boats evading pirate attacks at sea. He looked up and for one brief moment saw a bush full of roses, orangey-red roses. But it was Gwen's tent in the snow.

Ralph was saying, "A day like today makes me appreciate a day like yesterday."

"Twenty-two more days," Harry grumbled, "and the fifth day

this week we've been weather-bound. Two hours to make bannock."

"An hour and a half," Ralph said.

Harry leaned back. Ralph seemed to be getting younger and fitter with each passing day. He was having the time of his life. He was even sleeping well, as Harry knew from having to endure his freight train of snores every night. "You've always got something to say. I say two hours. You say an hour and a half."

"That's making conversation, Harry. Most people want a response when they say something."

Gwen turned, grabbed Harry's foot. Tugged it. "You really want to know the difference between you two?"

"No."

"I'll tell you anyway."

"I'm sure you will," he said acidly.

But she held her tongue. She turned her face away.

Curious, Eleanor asked her, "What's really the difference?"

"No. Harry doesn't want to know."

A few hours later, when they found themselves alone, Gwen said to Harry, "You don't want to be here."

"You're right. I'd give anything for a plane to come and get me right now. Would you come with me? Would you run away with me, Gwen?"

She gave him a look meant to squelch his nonsense, but not entirely. Not entirely.

Eleanor examined her hands and said they had aged thirty years in three weeks, they were the hands of an old fisherman. She held them out and they were large and cracked, red and rough in patches, swollen and scraped from sun and weather, from cold and wet. She said her father came to Canada and never wore gloves in the winter, they don't in England, and his hands were the mottled blue and red and purple of old books on shelves.

They all glanced at their sore hands with a certain amount of wonder and pity, and Gwen asked if they had ever had their palms read.

No-one had, except Gwen herself. She rolled her eyes. "The fortune teller told me I was a natural healer under a great deal of stress. I almost asked for my money back."

Harry grinned. "You were hoping for fame and glory?"

"At least."

The talk of colours and turns in fortune had Ralph thumbing through his copy of Farley Mowat, looking for and finding an excerpt from *Glimpses of the Barren Lands* by Thierry Mallet, a fur trader with Revillon Frères, who published his little book in 1930. One day Mallet came upon two little Eskimo girls helping their blind grandmother gather willow twigs. "'*Their faces were round and healthy, the skin sunburned to a dark copper colour, but their cheeks showed a tinge of blood which gave them, under the tan, a peculiar complexion like the colour of a ripe plum. Their little hands were bare and black, the scratches caused by the dead twigs showing plainly in white, while their fingers seemed cramped with the cold.*'

"What a painting," Ralph said.

He read on and the story was unforgettable. Mallet encountered a small band of inland Eskimos fishing through the ice one winter. Like Hornby, they had missed the herds of caribou in the fall and they were starving. Mallet and his guide gave them some of their food – the Eskimos were courteous to a fault – and learned their intentions: if the fishing did not improve they would head for a lake twelve days' walking to the northwest in the hope of finding muskoxen. In the spring, Mallet's guide and three others returned to the spot. Finding the camp deserted, they headed northwest and soon came upon the end of the story. First, a bunch of traps. Then caribou blankets. Then a child's grave, followed over the course of several days by a fish spear, a telescope, an axe, a snow knife, pairs of boots, then bodies, singly, or side by side.

They knew there were seventeen people in the band and three rifles. The old leader appeared to have fallen last, but he had no rifle beside him, and only sixteen Eskimos were accounted for. And so they kept on the trail. Five hours later they came upon the last body, a girl of twelve, who had persevered by herself, carrying the rifle, *with nothing but a sense of direction inherited from the old chief*.

How quiet they were when Ralph finished the account. After a bit, Harry joked huskily that they don't make kids like that any more, they won't leave home without a wallet full of travellers' cheques. And Gwen reached for the book and said "Thierry Mallet" slowly, as if memorizing the name, and Eleanor very gently corrected her pronunciation. "Tee-ay-ree, I think it is."

On the Barrens something happened to their sense of time. They were living every second of bad weather in a land that was barely out of the ice age, a place no different from how it had been a hundred years or a thousand years ago. They were seeing what Hornby and Samuel Hearne had seen, what aboriginal hunters had seen when they hunted here, far back. And so seconds ticked forwards and years swept backwards, and they got used to thinking of time passing in tiny increments and huge leaps.

Ralph would say that the long wait for the wind to die down – another two days of being wind-bound and ice-bound – made him think of Agamemnon waiting to set sail from Aulis. The north winds kept blowing day after day until they sacrificed Iphigenia, poor girl; then the winds fell away, the thousand ships set sail for Troy, and one thing led to another, until Aeneas fled his burning city and fetched up on the shores of Carthage, "where he broke poor Dido's heart," Ralph said, throwing Harry a sympathetic look.

With tender timing Eleanor and Gwen then compared the bruises on their legs, rolling up their trousers and exposing shins that looked as if they had been beaten with sticks, but it was the ice they had fallen against and battled through. The bruises filled Harry's mind with memories of his time with Dido. She had been like a stray, a waif that he had found by the shore and brought home. During those six weeks, she had never talked very much. Never really confided in him. The black eye had been her fault, she had said. And the bruise he saw on her arm happened from banging into a cupboard. He had to suppose that when she was with him she was just resting, recovering, biding her time until she was ready to leave.

Finally, at one in the morning, the sky began to clear. They could make out four or five ptarmigans in the meadow beyond the willows. Through binoculars they studied the male, its red markings above the eyes, its plumage a mottled brown until it flew up, and then its wings flashed white.

"What does ptarmigan taste like, I wonder," Gwen murmured.

"Ptough," Ralph said.

Eleanor remarked that seeing ptarmigans on Ptarmigan Lake was rather like seeing Harry on Harry Lake.

"You mean I washed myself in Harry?" Gwen cried.

"How lovely," Harry said.

*   *

It was noon of the next day. They were almost out of Ptarmigan Lake, having broken free of their snow-locked, weather-bound state by throwing caution to the winds. In the morning they had hauled their canoes with ropes across the middle of the frozen lake, making several miles of progress. Gwen managed to tape the sound by hanging her tape recorder around her neck and holding the microphone between her teeth; Harry snapped a picture for what he called broadcasting posterity.

They skirted the blackest ice, the last stretch so rotten his feet did a little dance as he sped across. And then they were in open water. July 7.

In the early afternoon, a line of light blue appeared at the lower edge of the sky and in the distance something moved. A palomino boulder was swimming slowly across the lake. They paddled towards it and saw their first caribou, large and handsome, like a heavily built deer with a rack of dark antlers.

By evening the sky was clear. The light luminous and rich. Not brilliant as in the Mediterranean (where Harry once removed a splinter from a woman's finger on the streets of Sète in light that acted like a magnifying glass). Gentler. Almost autumnal. The hills did not have light on them, they were in light, the way something is in water.

To Harry it seemed the Barrens relaxed. *One day something relaxed inside and I saw things in a new way.* The words came from an old book about an old botanist, and he felt the truth of them as they left behind frozen lakes and entered a land of flowing rivers. On July 8 they were on the Hanbury River, skimming along with the current, running two rapids and making three portages and completing a total of twenty-three miles. A grand day. That night they reached Sifton Lake and it too was melted, the next night they took advantage of an evening with almost no wind to keep paddling, hour after hour, in the pure golden light.

At midnight they beached their canoes and were about to make camp on an invitingly grassy bank when they saw, just across a small cove, something move.

They slipped back into their canoes and paddled closer. The grizzly was smaller than they had imagined and very curious. It came to the water's edge, then waded into the water, climbing atop a rock several feet from shore. From there it stood watching them for fifteen minutes, brownish-blond, face like a wide dish, close-set eyes. At a distance of fifty yards, or less, they took pictures in the evening light. Then the bear turned around, waded back to shore, and ambled up onto a grass-covered knoll, where it lay down and went to sleep. They had no firearms, having failed to take Teresa's advice, and Harry suspected they had been far too trusting, but the charmed evening had emboldened them. Even so, they paddled a full hour before they set up camp.

Several days after that, on July 13, a muskox in the afternoon. The bizarre beast appeared suddenly after miles of nothing. Dark massive head, down-curved horns, a fur coat like a chocolate-brown kilt, except along the uppermost part of the animal's back where it was lighter in colour as if faded by the sun. In the 1920s, Ralph said, after the decimation of the buffalo, muskox furs were in such demand for carriage robes that only protective legislation, inspired in no small part by John Hornby's observations and recommendations, saved them from being wiped off the face of the earth. This fellow stood on the riverbank with the blue sky behind him and sparse leafiness around his feet. After a few minutes he lumbered off into the distance, Ralph in careful pursuit with his camera, Eleanor calling after him to be careful: *Ralph!*

The next day, a group of three muskoxen. The animals thundered off and the humans inherited their flies. At supper mosquitoes plunged into the soup, kamikaze pilots in love with soggy death. Harry's emptied bowl had a dozen dead mosquitoes in the bottom. Eleanor took the bowl, turned it three times, and read the mosquitoes like tea leaves.

"I see a boy stung by bees," she said to Harry. "Six bee stings. No, seven."

"Not a girl stripping off her clothes?" teased Gwen, handing her own bowl to gypsy Eleanor, who turned it three times and said she saw a sudden change of course followed by a wedding.

Ralph instructed Eleanor to see money in his mosquito-leaves, huge sacks of it, mountains of it. But Eleanor saw, instead, a great expanse of water and suggested to Ralph that he might be going overseas.

By now Gwen's hair was sun-streaked and her face ruddy. "'As brown in hue as hazel nuts and sweeter than the kernels,'" said Harry, addressing her with a gleam in his eye.

She blushed and raised her hands, which were too dried and cracked to close. "They feel like baseball mitts," she said.

Harry surprised her by taking one of her hands in his. "I have just the thing."

From his pack he produced a tin of udder balm for chapped and swollen teats, then proceeded to work the ointment into her skin, especially her split fingertips. "What about your feet? Take off your boots," he said.

"What is the smoothest part of Gwen?" He reached for her bare foot, only to exclaim, "Not the heel!" His eyes widened. "You could do permanent damage with this heel."

Gwen's heels had never been so in the limelight, her rough, raspy heels. Harry would see them again when her tent blew down and she was out flying around in the middle of the night in bare legs and white heels and nightie, trying to restake and prop it up, while Eleanor held it down from inside. From his tent door Harry shouted at her to lay it flat and bring their sleeping bags in here, and Gwen shouted something back that he could not make out, for in the wind their voices tore like fabric.

Gwen later admitted she had seriously underestimated the importance of good shelter by bringing "that shitty tent", which sagged like a soft berry picked by the weather and manhandled between its fingers.

That night they lay across the floor of Harry's tent like four slumbering sardines.

WHERE THE DARRELL RIVER MET THE HANBURY RIVER, THEY passed into the Thelon Game Sanctuary. It was not a distinct shape, rather a continuation of what they had seen, yet it took on the shape in Harry's mind of a garden, a garden in the wilderness. Now there were scattered trees again, more and more trees. On a single day, July 15, they portaged around Macdonald Falls, Dickson Canyon, and Ford Falls, about three and a quarter miles in all. Between the first and second carry, they walked back along the edge of Dickson Canyon and saw rough-legged hawks above, and churning water below, as well as three large pools to one side fed by the rapids, each pool feeding the one below, deep green water in which grayling swam. On a hill Harry noticed muskox hair caught in the willows and low trees, the soft wool called *qiviut*, so Eleanor informed him when she came alongside. She picked tufts of it off the twigs and slipped them into her pocket, reminded of poor Absalom caught by his beautiful hair in the branches of the biblical oak, and of Lorna holding that tuft of hair in her dead hand, and of the first Dido whose spirit would not leave her dying body, Virgil said, until Iris descended and cut off a tress of her hair.

When finally they came to a halt that day, Harry soaked his head and feet and sore knee in the Hanbury River. They were on a beautiful sand dune – white sand beyond their tents, white snow above the sand. Fox and caribou tracks in evidence. And Gwen washing her hair.

"Always washing your hair," Harry said to her.

"Always watching me wash my hair," she said back.

She got him to stand behind her and wave away the flies and he felt like a painter with "Woman Shampooing Hair" on his easel.

"Your face is thinner," he told her when she turned around, her head wrapped in a towel. "You've developed cheekbones."

Eleanor looked up and watched the two of them for a long moment. The out-of-doors was the best beautician. Tanning Gwen's skin, lightening her hair, lengthening it (hair grows three times as fast in the summer she had learned from Lorna Dargabble, as do toenails). Gwen's shirt was bone-coloured, bleached by the long light. And now the animals were appearing and the story was coming to an end, the story her father was reading to her when he died, since that would have been what happened: the ostracized, runaway girl would have been helped by the animals in the forest, and then some admirer would have come along, perhaps a secret admirer who had always appreciated her without knowing he was in love. And would not the girl be looking the wrong way at the time, since isn't it the hardest lesson in the world, learning to appreciate people if you have never felt appreciated?

* *

They were finding things, one after the other. A black thread hanging from a low willow. A weathered orange pip on a rock. A lantern base of heavy glass, and some fox traps left behind at the foot of a portage. A hand-made sled runner, or so it appeared to Ralph, who pronounced it made in Captain Back's time. The 1830s. In the absence of trees that shed their leaves in autumn, objects could sit in the open for decades, centuries.

One night Harry caught a sizable grayling, a fish that was dull-brown in the water but vivid out of its element – in its death throes it went through a troubled array of colours from purply blue-black on its body to brilliant red spots on its large dorsal fin. Harry knelt to clean and fillet the pretty fish. He cut across the backbone, but left the tail in place in order to have something to hold on to when he skinned it. The carcass he threw into the river, having first shown Gwen what the fish had been eating: smaller fish, partially digested, the colour and consistency of grey glue. Gwen had her cassette recorder over her shoulder and she taped the sounds of scraping, eviscerating, slicing, rinsing.

This was the night, July 17, Eleanor elected not to go to bed at all in order to experience the brief middle-of-the-night twilight with its profusion of violet clouds directly overhead and its yellow gleam in the northern sky. Dressed in woollen trousers, wool jacket, gloves, with bug repellant smeared on her face and neck, she lay on her back on the warm, mattressy tundra whose thick growth held on to the day's heat. Tweedy smells rose from the soft tangle straight into her nostrils. The colours and textures at eye level, the russets, browns, blacks, reds, formed an embrace so gently erotic she dozed off with a smile on her lips, only to come awake when a ptarmigan whirred by, or a snowy owl flew down and sat on a big stone twenty feet away, or loons cried in the distance. The loon's long call seemed to her like a statement of the hour, a horizontal sound that tapered off into the horizon, while its laughter was vertical, high, flashy, rippling. The Barrens themselves were horizontal, but vertical, too, she thought. A vertical world of air: a country of clouds, an abundance of wind.

"You were the only sleepers," she said in the morning. "Everything else was awake."

The air, she claimed, was ten degrees warmer in among the plants than a foot above, and several degrees warmer still inside the actual blossoms. Ralph, wanting proof, knelt beside her and felt the warm air swell up from the heated plants, the tundra less a riot of colour, he said, to her everlasting delight, than a peaceful demonstration. She thought of the cool air that blows over your skin when you meet someone. Then with some few you feel warmer, as it was warmer by these vivid ten degrees close to Ralph, and close to the arctic ground, to the tussocks of moss and low cushion plants and ground-hugging berries and spreading mats of grasses and flowers and such.

Together they examined the tiny complete world at their finger-tips. Over the last few weeks she had identified flowers like yellow arnica, white-petalled arctic dryad with its look of wild roses, yellow and violet oxytrope and wild sweet pea, pressing them into her pocket-sized notebook and making sketches and lists: of the chick-weeds or starworts with their little white starlike flowers, the violet and yellow louseworts rising up out of the moss, the pink arctic fireweed, yellow arctic poppy, twiggy Labrador tea with its neat, round clusters of white flowers and narrow rolled-under leaves, the buttercups, milk-vetch, white and purple saxifrage, the small, white bells of the arctic heather, the red-violet clusters of Lapland rosebay like miniature rhododendrons, the dwarf pink azalea.

When she and Ralph stood up, their eyes took in the full extent of the boundless northern wastes. Every foot of evenly rising plains and worn-away hills was as detailed as the small bit they were standing on.

A long-tailed jaeger flew overhead, its tail like a dark, slender, beautiful paintbrush. Sometimes, Ralph said, the canny suitor, he felt life ripple through him, connecting him to every other living thing, and his own existence was the least of it and the most of it. Yes, she said.

They came down off the tundra as if hand in hand, and joined Harry and Gwen at the water's edge. The river and the landscape it ran through stretched in immensity on either side – what vastness they had dropped in to visit – yet in each other's company, this fellowship of four souls, they felt light-headedly secure.

The next evening Eleanor came upon Harry sitting by himself on a knoll not far from the campsite, smoking a cigarette. She sat beside him and without looking at her he reached over and took her hand.

The tundra rolled away into the distance, the undulating barren hills, the immense light.

"I want to know something," he said to her. "When Dido telephoned you, did she even mention my name?"

Eleanor did not answer for a moment. "Do you mean, did she say she wanted to see you or talk to you? No, Harry. She did not."

Harry nodded. With a bitterness he wished he could rise above, he said, "I can't figure out what she sees in Eddy."

Eleanor reflected. "Maybe he makes her feel good about being bad."

Harry let out a short laugh.

"There's Gwen," Eleanor said.

They saw her heading off on her own, walking towards a ridge of land a short distance away. Her head was down. Her tape recorder was around her neck and she steadied it with one hand. She waved flies away with the other.

"What will become of her, do you think?" Eleanor said.

"Eddy's going to ruin her life."

"I meant Gwen."

"Ah," Harry said.

Gwen had shortened the shoulder strap on her cassette recorder and hung it low enough on her chest to see the levels on the v.u. meter; easier to walk this way too. She looked down, alert to sounds, but otherwise lost in what Harry would have called a brown study; she was thinking about his soft, swollen ear and about his other appendages, wondering about them idly, not so idly, as the look of the scruffy heath imprinted itself on her eyes.

At the sound of loons, she automatically pressed RECORD and stood listening to birds that mated for life, their beautiful mad laughter. What held her eye, however, was the look of her hand on the microphone. So weathered and chapped compared to the silver-metallic stem she was holding carefully, no rings on her fingers to click against the metal and transfer to the dark spool of tape, her equipment solid and unchanging and Japanese, her veins purply under the roughened, reddish-brown skin. She saw her hand on a doorknob, pushing open a bedroom door, and the phrase "inquiry without walls" came into her head, the Barrens like Berger's commission: you learned a great deal, more than you wanted to know sometimes, more than you knew what to do with. Could there be a more primitive, naked, intimate sound than the heavy breathing, the solitary moan and whimper she had heard from inside Harry's tent an hour ago? The physical side of life, which stretched in utter loneliness and tenderness all around her.

A WOLF, WHITE, OLD, MANGY, ARTHRITIC, SLOWLY STRETCHED
and yawned on the riverbank as they paddled by. A harbinger, had
they but known. By now it was July 20 and they were on the wide,
smooth, east-flowing Thelon River, seven days from the end.

Ralph spotted shapes moving in the distance. Gwen thought they
must be geese, they were used to geese running along the shore. They
drew closer and the scales fell from their eyes. A group of fifteen caribou were crossing the river ahead of them, antlers like high heels
rising from their heads.

They paddled to the south side of the river, as did Harry and
Eleanor, and waited with thumping hearts for the caribou to come
towards them along the shore, but the animals clambered out of the
water and went the other way. Then another smaller group swam
across the river and they too went up the sloping bank through low
willows and spruce, then up over the rocky ridge and out of sight.

They had lunch on the rise of land above the river and realized
they were on the edge of a large herd. Caribou in the hundreds were
all around them, in the distance and moving slowly, or not moving at
all, blending in like boulders on the open tundra of grass and heath
and rounded hills. What they had been hoping for was finally
happening.

La foule. The word came unbidden to Ralph from accounts of
the great migrations of the past. It was like witnessing the arrival of

a myth: the caribou emerged from the land and belonged to it, tentative, purposeful, graceful, shy, their colours buff, brown, grey, pale, Gwen's colours when she first arrived at the station. What they were seeing was the mass arrival of something beautifully recessive and fleeting. They could have missed it just as easily, a few hours one way or the other.

Ralph nestled against the lip of a low hill and looked through long grass at the large herd on the other side. Eleanor was close to him. Not far away was Gwen, her cassette recorder around her neck, her microphone in her hand, when a cow and calf came thundering right up to them, unaware of their presence, then ran off a bit, then came closer again. Soon several caribou were eating willow leaves just twenty feet below them. Gwen taped the sounds of their soft lips pulling off small leaves, the quiet sounds of chewing. A male reached around and scratched his back leg with his antlers. Dark, velvet, bone.

Black antlers above the greenery, the willows, the water. The look of heavy mascara around their eyes. The ripples of movement that occurred when one animal started and the rest followed. They were like camels in the sand dunes, beautiful on the blond hills, moving and gathering, arranging themselves in small, elegant groups around the willows, like a series of almost still-lifes.

Harry called softly. A group of ten was coming down the shore towards their canoes. The others followed him and stood very still under the high-pitched hum of clouds of gnats, watching intently and with enormous excitement. Gwen taped the sound of hooves splashing at the water's edge. Loud, their coming and going, yet subdued, and soon over. The large numbers that gathered on their side of the river all afternoon were spooked at about seven in the evening. Having filed down to the water and along it, maybe five hundred, seven hundred animals, they suddenly drew back up over the bank and over the hill and away across the tundra.

"I think we're in a thin place," Ralph murmured, remembering his father's passion for the Celts. "Where seen and unseen meet."

That being the very definition of this ancient caribou crossing, where the river narrowed and offered passage to the other side. The animals were every bit as sensitive as the witnesses at the Berger Inquiry had claimed, and this was not even their most skittish time. The calving and post-calving had occurred farther north, and now, less urgently, they were engaged in the long return to the timberline.

So quiet, whispered Eleanor. So easily not seen, and then so easily lost. She and Ralph stood together watching straggling cows with their calves, and solitary calves. On the opposite shore a bull and a calf entered the water and began to swim across, a twosome. But halfway, the calf dropped out of sight and did not resurface, no matter how long they kept looking.

They were alone again "in the land of feast and famine". Nothing for so long, and then abundance, and then nothing again, but a nothing haunted by the previous abundance.

That night, thumbing backwards through Whalley's book, Ralph came upon Edgar, raw-boned and white in his photograph. Parted hair and ears sticking out. Then Hornby's emaciated face after one of his starving winters near Fort Reliance. The sunken, glittering eyes. The amiable smile. The head of hair still dark and thick. In 1925, the year before his last journey, Hornby was travelling with James Critchell-Bullock, an ex-army officer turned traveller-photographer-collector. After a squalid winter near Artillery Lake, holed up in a collapsing cave dug into the side of a sand esker, they were making their miserable way to Hudson Bay. On the evening of July 23, they sighted "a large group of caribou moving south-west on the south shore: about two thousand animals, mostly females, 'moving all over the hills making a tremendous noise calling to one another . . . a beautiful sight on the sand hills with the gold of the sunshine reflected on the water'." Another sixty miles and the two men came to the sharp double bend in the river that took Hornby's fancy and sealed his fate, for on the north side rose a fine stand of white spruce that inspired thoughts of building a house and overwintering.

Ralph set down the book, understanding an aspect of Hornby for the first time: he had been seduced by the idea of a well-built home instead of a filthy cave or swampy tent or crummy tarp. The tiny, extraordinarily tough, self-destructive Englishman had actually been seeking a wild kind of comfort.

In himself something similar was going on. He felt a growing desire to be attached, not to a place but to a person. For years he had made a habit of keeping his options open, of not letting himself be pinned down, an approach to life that seemed almost juvenile to him now. They had come such a long distance already, he and Eleanor and the others. They were two-thirds of the way there, two-thirds of the way home, and he felt more sure of his next step than he had ever felt about anything. Eleanor was not even forty and he was sixty-one, but on the last night of their trip he would ask her to marry him.

The next day they paddled on. The air was calm. The mosquitoes ferocious, almost as plentiful as the caribou hair in the bushes and at the water's edge, white, brittle, hollow hairs and some finer fluff, a floating mattress of hair. The shore, formerly flat and hard, was churned up by hooves.

Clumps of Labrador tea among the rocks. A few terns overhead. Ashes from their small tea fire blown about by a sudden gust of wind. And the need to make twenty-two, twenty-three miles a day if they were to reach Beverly Lake on time.

And again they were among the caribou. Thousands of them were crossing the river that afternoon. In their canoes they drifted with the current while the caribou circled around them and continued swimming to shore, then climbed the bank, their dark antlers magnificent amidst the greenery in this paradise of leafiness and sky.

Clumps of trees thickened into woods on the hills, hair covered the water, the shore, the grass. Grunting, so many of them now, like pigs rooting, mud and grass churned up. A heavy manure smell in the air. And Gwen recording.

More and more came, the hillside emptied and filled again. Caribou filed across the horizon on a high ridge, then down the steep slope to the water, a line of strolling players with the sky behind them and a wolf invariably bringing up the rear. The effect was joyous and spellbinding and sobering. Over supper Eleanor said she felt like giving thanks for Judge Berger, who would see to it that these vanishing herds were protected.

"The government must rue the day they appointed him," Ralph chuckled.

"He's a special man," Eleanor said, fingering the medallion's chain around her neck. "I cannot imagine anyone else in the part."

No-one disagreed. For five minutes.

Then Gwen wondered aloud if he wasn't too gullible. He gave the impression of believing every word every native witness said, but were they not as human as anyone else, as capable of self-interest and poetical exaggeration? She wondered if the bond they felt with the land and the animals was as genuine now as in the past, before they had high-powered rifles and snowmobiles.

Harry said she had a point, but insisting on purity was not fair. The natives felt a connection to the land, he said, that was almost incomprehensible to us. He said he had the sense of miraculous brakes being applied. He was betting on Berger, betting he would manage to delay for a considerable time the onslaught of development. "And if that's possible, what isn't?"

The next afternoon they were looking at John Hornby's grave in the sun. Three simple, weathered, wooden crosses shored up by rocks piled at the base of each one. E.C., J.H., H.A. The ruined cabin just to the left, its bottom logs still in place, but the roof fallen in, and the walls. Some caribou antlers inside the cabin and more just outside the door. It was July 22.

They had come 350 miles, from old Fort Reliance to this beautiful spot, an open bank rising up steeply on the north side of the river to the famous stand of spruce. Late afternoon, the warm sun shining, and after an hour of looking and taking photographs, they decided to stay for the night. Gwen wandered around the little makeshift cemetery, the remains of the cabin, and then she headed off on her own, her brown canvas tape recorder bag over her shoulder.

Harry was making supper. He was saying to Eleanor that young Edgar's fate reminded him of what happened to the Eskimo girl in the Thierry Mallet story. The last one left alive carries on.

He had borrowed Ralph's copy of Whalley's biography and read the final pages that described Edgar letting the fire in the stove die out. Edgar placed his companions' papers and his own diary in the cool ashes, then lay down on his bunk and pulled the blankets up and over his head. Whalley imagined the sounds he might have heard, perhaps "the faint sound of ptarmigan feeding outside", and the effect of the silence, "like wings folding about him".

What Harry admired so much was Whalley's restraint in telling the story. Whalley was like Berger in that way. He did not pick on people. He did not ridicule Hornby for his mistakes, or excoriate him. He could have so easily. A journalist would have.

He added another stick to the fire and saw Ralph coming up from the river, but he did not see Gwen. And then he heard her.

Gwen had climbed the wooded slope that rose behind the cabin, looking for signs of Hornby and finding them in the axe cuts in old stumps that she had read about. She had her eyes down to negotiate the branch-littered ground, the thick ground cover. A little farther and she thought she might get a fine view of the river below. In the

251

northwest corner of this fringe of trees between cabin and open Barrens, she expected to find the windbreak of stones Hornby had erected from which they watched for caribou. In her mind she was with Hornby and Edgar and Harold Adlard as they made the same ascent, alone or together, early on when they were healthy and strong, and then later when they were desperate. Once, they saw thirty caribou in the distance and thought salvation was at hand, but the animals disappeared before they could get close to them. She turned to look south towards the river, but the twisted, slow-growing trees, some of them at least four hundred years old, still blocked the view. She turned back and saw something blondish-brown out of the corner of her eye. Fifty feet away? They are not huge animals. They do not have to be huge. It lifted its nose and sniffed.

Experts say to avoid eye contact. To back away noiselessly. Not to turn and run.

Gwen's scream coincided with her seeing a set of small, black, gleaming eyes. She turned and ran.

It was like going full tilt down a flight of stairs covered in books. She felt her feet go out from under her even as she tumbled forward, and instinctively she grabbed at the nearest tree and slowed her descent at the expense of her arm. Her right shoulder wrenched out of its socket. Then she was lying in a small heap, the pain so intense she could not make a sound.

Her head slid forward to rest on the ground and she bit down on the dead branch that offered itself, aware in a flickering part of her brain of an age when biting down on wood offered the only consolation in moments of physical agony. Her shoulder was not there, nauseatingly not there, but her heart was bouncing her off the ground. She heard the bear behind her, then beside her. She heard its heavy breathing. She felt it nose her left leg and she bit harder into the wood. It nosed her leg a second time and she closed her eyes, lay completely still, apart from her thumping, cartoonish heart. She smelled the animal. Heard the saliva bubbling in its mouth. Kept as quiet as she always had at the dining-room table when a wave of fury would darken her father's face. She braced herself for more pain, and heard the bear moving, and realized it was moving away.

When they found her, she was coming slowly towards them like a shell-shocked survivor of the trenches or the highway. She saw them and sank to her knees.

Harry was beside her.

"Shoulder," she managed.

She felt his hands on her shoulder, and with a slight, subtle adjustment her arm was amazingly back in place.

"I thought you were proposing," he would say later, bringing a weak smile to her face.

He helped her to her feet and she breathed out, "We're not camping here."

The next morning, before the others were up, Harry went down to the water. They had paddled two hours beyond Hornby Point (he and Eleanor taking more of the load in their canoe so that Ralph could paddle alone as Gwen rested her shoulder, to say nothing of her mind) and they had camped on a steep bank on the opposite side of the river, to be extra sure. Harry had not slept much, thinking about Gwen and the grizzly, wondering if they were travelling under a lucky star or if their luck had run out. He would never forget the sight of her coming down the slope. She looked damaged, lopsided, wrong. They had to brush twigs and leaves off her cheeks and forehead, but the imprint remained for hours.

They had talked at length about how long it lasted, her encounter with the bear. Not as long as she thought, he was sure of that; a second with a grizzly is an eternity by any measure. He had heard her terrifying scream, they all had, and they had come charging up the hill and through the trees, but she had not heard them. They were downwind for one thing. In Gwen's mind there was only the noise of the bear's breathing, a kind of huffing, a moist huffing, and the powerful reek of animal, and the memory of small, cold eyes. It nosed her leg "like a teacher tapping your shoulder in the hall", she said, and she had tapped Harry's shoulder to demonstrate, not hard: sending a chill down his spine. *Detention, young man.*

Now, as he came down to the water, he saw a tiny calf, its side ripped open, resting under a tree. It struggled to its feet upon seeing him and ran desperately into the water, then tottered back to shore, then back into the water and back to shore, where it collapsed, "all tuckered out", he would tell the others at breakfast. Using the biggest stick he could find, he put the little chap out of its misery with three hard blows. Then he reached for his knife. It took him a long time to dress the meat; he was reminded as he worked of his grandfather, of all the furriers and trappers and woodsmen who constituted a dwindling breed of their own. Often they were the most soft-hearted of men, and it had to do with being on the land so much, something the anti-trappers would never understand. That night they had caribou veal and it was certainly his most delicious and most poignant dish.

Eleanor told them about her father speaking very fondly of a dinner he had had at the Waldorf Hotel in New York. Green turtle soup, double breast of grey partridge, and strawberry mousse. This meal was just as memorable. "But I wonder if I'll talk about it quite so much."

"Gwen?" Harry offered her seconds.

She was hungry, as hungry as someone who has just escaped the firing squad, and she held out her plate. She had done everything wrong, she knew, fleeing when she should have stood her ground, turning herself into prey. Yet here she was, still alive. The world around her tingled with life.

Gwen saw admiration in Harry's eyes, and in Ralph's and Eleanor's too, and she basked in it. But when they told her how brave she was, she shook her head. "You should hear me when I get a paper cut."

Later, she would say the bear's eyes were like Eddy's, small and mean. Harry would turn his hand into a microphone, "Now tell us how you *really* feel." And Gwen would smile, until he dropped his microphone-hand back into his lap. Then suddenly she remembered the shoulder bag containing her tape recorder and tapes. Back there, back where she'd fallen. Back being pawed by the grizzly bear. Thus occurred their first irretrievable loss.

Gwen sat disconsolate on a flat stone and the trip ran like a reel through her mind, erasing itself as it went along. The tinkling ice on Charlton Bay, the songbirds on Pike's Portage, the sounds of paddling, straining, cursing, of crackling fires and roaring rapids and wriggling fish, of mosquitoes being slapped and long tent zippers being opened and more rapidly shut, of gargantuan snores, of foot-steps among the ankle-turning stones and the whish-y tread of boots on tundra. Of Ee-zay saying pee-nuts ba-ta. Of ice-hauling accompanied by the tap of her teeth on the microphone. Most prized of all, the tapes of the Barren-ground caribou, their clicking hooves and strenuous swimming and muted eating, since who had ever recorded them before?

Harry's efforts were good-hearted, if clumsy. He suggested she could re-create what she had lost, using sound effects and words. Gwen let out a despairing groan, but he was patient. He told her what mattered more than sound effects was the effect of sound. He liked remembering car tyres going through puddles and over melting snow on the street outside school, blue jays in the woods, squirrels high in the trees – sounds that evoked the soft days when winter was turning to spring and long summer holidays were around the corner. We had a bell in the Town Hall, he said. Tom Finnegan rang it every day at noon and at five in the afternoon. If it rang hard and successively, it meant fire. Train whistles were wonderful too, and dogs barking in the distance. And the radio. I always loved the sound of the radio. "What's the first sound you remember?" She shook her head. "Come on, Lippy." And she gave in and laughed a little.

"Maybe it was the rain," she said.

"And what about the first thing you heard on the radio?"

"'Blue Suede Shoes.' I was four years old."

That set Harry off. His first piece on air was a movie review he recorded in a bedroom cupboard because he could not stand his roommate hearing him read the script. A month later he was hosting a programme, and two years afterwards he was working in Toronto. "That's how quickly fortunes can turn," he said, thinking as much of what had come after as what had gone before.

This was the evening they saw a strangely beautiful group of caribou emerge from the water and slowly approach, their pattern governed by hunger and available food – by the arrangement of leaves on willows fifty feet away. No matter how they moved around the low trees, reaching up or down or forward or around, the animals seemed exquisitely placed, as if by an Old Master.

Their little group of four was also being reconfigured. In the mornings Ralph took Eleanor a cup of tea, unzipping the door of the tent she shared with Gwen, and singing snatches of songs to her when she arrived at the campfire. One evening he reached for her hand and they moved in three-four time across the widest dance floor in the world.

There were summers in Gwen's childhood when her father's favourite brother came to visit from the States, and the anticipation of his arrival, that keen pleasure, was like this one of watching Ralph and Eleanor together. To witness the two brothers greet each other, to gauge the level of their affection, to watch her sociable uncle take pleasure in her unsociable dad and her dad take pleasure in her uncle – all this was high, ardent drama. She wanted to see every moment of mutual delight and there was never quite enough to satisfy her. Did her uncle know – did he have any idea – how much her father loved him?

Something blossoms in an unlikely place. An oasis of trees miles above the treeline. An arctic river warmer than any other water they had come upon. The four of them bathed in the waters of the Thelon, wading out into it, almost swimming. On shore they towelled themselves dry and dressed, and there was no feeling to equal the splendour of warm clothes on river-cold skin.

The next morning Ralph said to Eleanor within Gwen's hearing, "I was dreaming about you last night."

"What was I up to?"

"You were pointing with your finger at very specific places on your body that you wanted me to kiss, and I obliged you with pleasure."

Then no sooner had all of this closeness come about than it dispersed. That night Eleanor asked Harry what he was going to do with himself next, and he surprised them by saying he wanted to leave Canada behind for a while, not radio but Canada; his friend Max Berns knew people at Broadcasting House in London; he might well move to England.

In thinking it through over the past weeks, turning this way and that in his thoughts, he had reminded himself of caribou at the river's edge. They retreated once, twice, three times. He had never known before that migration was not one unbroken forward movement; it was sideways, backwards, forwards, a passage enlivened with indecision in the face of real and imagined danger. They came to the river, they shied away. He was not like Eleanor, he thought. He felt attuned not to the God within but to the uncertainty within. His connection was with the poor, dumb animals.

Eleanor had her own surprise. She had been thinking about opening up a bookstore just down the street from the post office in Yellowknife, and she had almost convinced Ralph to be her partner. Ralph grinned. "She wants my pretty coins," he said.

And once again Gwen's favourite uncle was back in the States and the first day of school was looming.

BY NOW IT WAS JULY 25 AND THEY WERE MAKING SWIFT AND easy progress to their final destination of Beverly Lake, and their last night on the Barrens. A strong current, almost no headwind. A wolf, perhaps the same one that raked open the side of the little calf, swam across the river ahead of them. A grizzly and her two cubs appeared on the riverbank; one of the cubs stood between its mother's hind legs and watched them as they paddled by. Passing an island on their left, they spotted a magnificent moose in a grassy marsh. Above them soared a golden eagle in the eggshell-blue sky.

They were seeing sunsets now. Mosquitoes became flecks of light in the evening. A rock in the water moved with flies when they approached.

The land continued hilly and pasture-green. They saw semi-palmated plovers and low, protected blue flowers. The wind came back and the clouds and the rain.

That evening they boiled up a pot of soup and one of tea, a fire that would scar the tundra for years. Their effect, just passing through, was not insignificant. And the effect of the trip on them?

They paddled on. The woods thinned out. The sun shone. They were within reach of Beverly Lake now, and felt the swell of the lake reach up the river, waves high enough to splash Eleanor in the bow and chill her through.

They reached the lake on the afternoon of July 26. In time. The float plane would arrive in the early morning hours of the next day.

Their last campsite was on the north shore of a deep bay near the remains of two sod houses on the open tundra, little more than remarkable outlines, and the bushes around them full of muskox hair. The tundra wide, open, forever, the water calm and violet-blue, the light clear and the number of mosquitoes infinite. Eleanor pointed out a tern's nest – or egg, since the beach was the nest, a pretty egg, green and brown with some dark spots; the tern flew off as she approached.

Across the big lake, the rolling plains and undulating hills turned the horizon into a thick to thin line of dark ink. The four of them were the only moving parts in a landscape more remote from settlements of any kind than almost anywhere else in Canada.

At supper Ralph announced that he was going to shave and put on clean clothes. "No need to leave the bush looking like part of it," he said. After he reappeared, looking ten years younger, he asked Eleanor to go for a walk with him and they were gone a long time.

That evening it was perfectly still. Not a breath of wind.

Eleanor and Ralph were in the lee of a knoll on the tundra, lying together, listening to the silence, happy. Ralph told her a special memory of walking in an ancient rain forest and hearing music far away on a transistor radio, a party of geologists, he thought, and he headed towards it, curious, but the sound moved away like a bird. It was sound without a source, he said to her, reaching over to stroke her face and her hair, it was the sound of the forest itself. Here on the Barrens there was not music, but a hum, a vibration, the sound of the earth and she agreed. In moments of silence, she had heard it too. It reminded her of Buddhist singing bowls vibrating at their lowest octave.

She noticed crawling specks of light in Ralph's hair, even the mosquitoes were beautiful. She noticed how smooth his mouth was without whiskers, his lovely mouth, and how their bed was mostly white labrador tea.

The sun was low on the hills when Ralph thought of ending the trip as he began, with a last paddle, a last few pictures. Eleanor was asleep. He took off his clean shirt and arranged it gently over her face to keep away the flies. Then he went down to the shore, grabbed another shirt from his pack, took his paddle and his camera, his life vest, and slid his empty canoe into the water.

Harry saw Ralph's canoe far out on the glassy lake. He had been walking on the tundra, and now his attention was diverted by a young caribou, perhaps a yearling, that came over the hill. It turned and skirted him. He stood still, while flies rained down upon his head and got into his eyes. He raised his hand to brush them away, by which time the caribou was some distance off. Despite the flies, he felt a tranquillity on this piece of tundra that he had hoped to feel more of the time and sooner. He headed back to shore and found Gwen sitting on a rock, tending her driftwood fire. He squatted beside her.

She had made the fire inside a circle of stones, a little stone wall. She loved these outdoor kitchens, these uninhabited places suddenly inhabited – arranged for minimal comfort. Her brush with death was so recent, so vivid that she still felt marked, set apart from the others. It was Eleanor who had suggested the bear might have been Hornby himself, guarding his bit of paradise, an idea that appealed, since it meant she had been visited in a special way, visited and spared. But for what? "I've been wondering," she said to Harry, "if this trip has changed me."

He smiled.

"Has it changed *you*?" she said. "I mean, besides drying you out."

"Wretch," he said, and to Gwen's ears he made the word sound like the most affectionate of endearments. "Ask me in five years."

"Let's meet in five years," she agreed eagerly. "We can be like Hornby and Critchell-Bullock planning to meet up years hence."

"Except they didn't meet up."

"I know," she said sadly.

"Time was so different then," Harry said, musing to himself. "Those were the days of long voyages, long visits, long courtships, long seductions. In some ways I envy Hornby. The man was so busy surviving he didn't have to learn how to live."

"Are you really going to England?"

"I think I might."

"But you belong *here*."

He put his arm around her as he laughed. Her small shoulders were rounded, dejected. In his view no-one belonged to a place unless they were aboriginal. The rest of us were like the dust of the earth blown east, west, north, south.

"Gwen, do you realize we've travelled the last few weeks without setting eyes on another human soul?"

He was poking the fire now and she watched his hands fix, arrange, finesse. In her loneliness she felt her chest tighten, and remembered their world as it was just a few weeks ago, blocked with ice and impassable, as it would be again in several weeks' time.

"Oh, Harry," she said. "I wish I were a different kind of person."

He took off his glasses with one hand, a gesture she loved, and studied her. He was exposing himself to her gaze even as he was seeing her with his own eyes.

What kind of person, he wanted to know.

"Someone," she said slowly, "who truly loves life."

He was still looking at her, still cradling his glasses in his left hand. He said, "You're the kind of person who never stops trying."

She returned his honest gaze. He seemed to mean it. And so she let herself absorb this worthwhile compliment and her place in the world opened up. That is what she would be. The kind of person who never stops trying. And though this was not a moment of pure release, of the ice finally giving way, still, everything in her life would flow from this exchange.

*

On the water Ralph noticed the lake become a little wrinkled. He looked over his shoulder and saw Gwen and Harry, who looked very small on shore. And then the wind hit – a soft blow to the side of his head – an offshore wind out of nowhere, and the canoe started to move. He set his camera at his feet and picked up his paddle. He looked over his shoulder again and the wrinkle was a ripple moving towards him, darkened water, a disturbance of small waves racing in his direction. The wind swung him around. It came out of the north-west and he knew if he wasn't careful it would blow him out into the middle of a lake two miles wide. He slid down onto his knees and moved forward until his belly was against the middle thwart and then he began to paddle hard, trying to swing the canoe into the wind, trying to get back to shore, but his knees slid around, he had nothing to lock his feet under, no way to get a good bite with his paddle. He did his best, he worked hard. There were little whitecaps now, but not too bad. He was thinking he had been lulled by the perfect stillness into coming out too far, and it felt like a bad decision to be alone on a lake this size. *Once a lake is ten miles long it might as well be an ocean.* Some canoeist's voice from another trip years ago. The bow of his empty seventeen-foot canoe was like a weather vane. The wind kept taking it and pushing him farther out. His canoe bounced on the waves, then started to bang, but the sounds were carried off by the wind.

Eleanor did not feel the wind come up, and neither did Gwen or Harry, the one asleep, the others sheltered beside their fire. They intended to bed down in the open air that night, since the float plane was expected in the early morning. Had they pitched their tents they would have been aware of the wind sooner, the slight flapping.

Half a mile out it is a different world.

*

The waves were eighteen inches high now, two feet high, it happened fast. Ralph was exerting all his energy trying to straighten out the canoe, but the errant wind was determined to blow him away. He no longer supposed he was in control, but it took him a few moments to realize he was in trouble. The waves picked up his canoe and surfed it forward, and he felt the sweat pour down his back. Out of a clear sky he was thinking – a rogue wind like a mini-storm, a mini-hurricane, at least way out here. On shore, would they even notice?

The sun goes down so slowly, it hangs on the horizon and goes slowly down. A wave splashed over the back of his canoe, then another, and his knees were in two inches of water. He leaned out far, dug in extra-hard and the paddle gave way and he was in the water before he knew he was going over. In the water, holding the shaft of his cedar paddle in one hand, the blade gone. Gasping from the cold. He grabbed the canoe – it was wallowing upright – he grabbed it with his left hand, but he could not catch his breath, the water barely above freezing, and nothing mattered, except getting out of it. He heaved what was left of his paddle into the canoe and tried to climb in over the side and the canoe rolled over. He tried to pull himself up onto its bottom, but the bow went up and the stern went down under his weight and the canoe slid out from under him. He tried once more from the side and the canoe rolled over again and sat upright. Then he was just hanging on, hands on the gunwales, an iron grip, the shore endlessly far away.

Eleanor had slept for half an hour, perhaps. When she opened her eyes, she felt the warm shirt on her face and stood up and looked around for Ralph, and felt the wind. She walked back to their campsite holding the shirt in her hand, looking around her at the tundra, at the sky, then down at the uneven ground. When she came to some bushes, she stopped and gathered tufts of muskox hair off the twigs, slipped them into her pocket, a gift for Ralph. The sun was going down, it was ten o'clock by her watch, so she scrambled down to shore and saw Gwen and Harry talking by the fire.

She said, "Where's Ralph?"

Harry stood up and scanned the lake. He had forgotten about him. The last he had seen, Ralph was a long way out and the water was calm. Now he could not see the canoe at all and the lake was choppy. It was always worse out on the water than it looked from shore, he knew that. Maybe Ralph was behind that big island. Eleanor was reaching into her pack for her binoculars. The three stood gazing out at the lake, waiting for Ralph to come into view. While they watched, the sun went all the way down and the wind died away.

He had no idea how much time had passed, how much time he had left. So quiet now. So incongruous to be fighting for his life when it was calm and peaceful.

Breathing is loud when there is no other sound. It reminded him he was alive. He rested his head against the side of the canoe and there was the astounding silence and his breathing. He was eating apple pie with his mother. He was looking at the wedding ring on her floury hand. Then he was back in the present, an old man with no feeling in his submerged body, agony in his arms, hands like stone claws from holding on. He was sorry, so profoundly sorry to be losing everything, and so sorry about the trouble he was going to cause. He called for help, unsure whether any sound would come out. It did, and he felt relieved. He was still alive. He called again. His mouth could not form a word, but his throat produced a sound. He heard it. He heard his breathing, and his breathing was not inside him any more, but outside, disembodied. He was lying with Eleanor on the tundra. The warmth, the ecstasy. He was seeing to the bottom of the lake and it was covered in beautiful stones. A camera lay among the stones, his last pictures of Eleanor in the camera, and the camera was so close, the water was so clear, that the metallic parts of it were shining, and he could touch them. He could reach down and touch his canoe, which was glinting too. He could touch the floating man in an orange vest bobbing in the water beside his canoe.

A one-hour blow, that is all it was. The wind died down as they watched, the water went flat, and they kept looking and Ralph did not reappear. Maybe he was fine, probably he was fine.

They took Harry's canoe, he thought to throw in a jacket and a length of rope, and set off down the lake, staying fairly close to shore. Every few minutes Eleanor stopped paddling to raise her binoculars and scan the water. Gwen, with another pair of binoculars, walked the tundra above the shore. She had a whistle around her neck. She would blow the whistle if she saw anything, that was their agreement.

Alone on land, Gwen felt as she had on those Sunday nights when her parents drove her brother back to university and she spent several hours imagining the car accident that would leave her orphaned. Fourteen years old and the radio for company. She became aware that she was not looking for a silver canoe at all. She had her eyes trained on the red canoe, not willing to let them out of her sight, but at a certain point she could not see them any more.

Midnight, and it was perfectly still. The wind comes in the front door, it goes out the back door, and the house returns to a supernatural quiet.

Eleanor and Harry paddled and looked until their eyes hurt. The sun below the horizon, the light duskier, it was harder to see, and they lost track of time. "I'm not an artisan," Eleanor remembered Ralph saying once. "I don't make anything except commotion." Which wasn't true, but she loved him for saying it. This is too much commotion, she was telling him. Please.

The landscape changed before her eyes. A movement here, a shadow over there, a hint of light, a shape that her eyes fastened on with such greed, such greedy longing. She was looking for Ralph and seeing nothing but ghosts. Her arms worked, her eyes were intact, but her soul was coming apart. And when she saw, finally, a spot of drifting orange that receded and shifted and came into being, she recognized that she was seeing her future, and it was a future of infinite sadness.

They were on their way back. Gwen saw how the canoe was lower in the water and how their paddling was automatic, deadened, slow. She headed for their campsite, stumbling, running. She would make a fire, she thought, she would make tea, she would make them something to eat.

Her hands were shaking, but she made a fire, she got water boiling. She rummaged in the packs for tea bags and powdered soup, then went to the water's edge. Eleanor stepped out of the canoe and dragged it a little up. Then Harry hauled it the rest of the way.

It was the sound the canoe made on the gravelly shore that marked the end for Eleanor. She walked a few feet and sank to her knees.

Gwen drew her to the fire, helped her into dry clothes. Put a mug of tea into her shivering hands and remembered her once saying that nothing puts you together like a cup of tea. Eleanor lifted the mug. It hit her teeth. Gwen took it out of her hands and held it for her and Eleanor sipped. Gwen wrapped her arms around her friend, rocked her back and forth.

Later, Harry and Gwen lifted the body out of the canoe. Eleanor watched them lay Ralph on a stretch of sandy shore. She would never forget how they grew in stature before her eyes, head and shoulders above themselves. They took off Ralph's life vest and there he was in his old shirt, and she remembered his wedding shirt, the clean shirt he had placed over her face, but she couldn't remember where she had put it and could not rest until she remembered. Gwen found it for her, folded up, on a flat stone ten feet from the fire.

Harry went to get a nylon groundsheet. He came back and Eleanor was sitting beside the body. The sun was not up yet. She was examining Ralph's small hand in twilight that was bright enough to read by, if you had good eyes. A refrigerated hand. She stroked the back of it, turned it over, and studied the stiff fingers. They were asheny-blue, a little rough, still stained by nicotine.

Harry stood for a moment watching her. Her head looked like the heaviest of peonies after a rain, her body tilted forward over Ralph's. And the thought came to him that it was not just one person who had died, but all the filaments of life connecting that person to everyone he had ever known and to every place he had ever been.

Eventually he persuaded Eleanor to leave Ralph's side. He led her up to the tundra to a makeshift bed he had prepared – their thin insulite mattresses and sleeping bags. She crawled into hers. He and Gwen lay on either side of her, inside their bags and under a tarp. She began to talk then, wondering about Ralph's final minutes, how long he suffered, how much, and Harry said it would have been very quick, he would have drifted off in a stupor. If only I had gone with him, she cried. She meant that if they had been together, two in the canoe, it never would have happened. And what did happen? The wind came up, yes, and the lake was wide and long, but how had he overturned? We'll never know, Harry said. He got into trouble, we'll never know exactly how. Don't blame yourself, he said. Nobody's to blame, Gwen said.

Harry and Gwen slept a little. Eleanor lay awake. After a while she eased herself out of her sleeping bag and went down to the water. It was wrong to leave him alone. He lay wrapped in Harry's groundsheet, a broken body, and she sat on the shore beside him. So cold to the touch when she pulled the nylon sheet away from his dear, lost, clean-shaven face. She found herself repeating the 23rd psalm and why it should give her comfort under the circumstances she could not quite fathom, since she felt real bitterness too. She had lost her father too soon, she had lost Ralph even sooner. But she murmured to herself the words about the valley of the shadow of death, the house of the Lord, and she felt situated in a larger place, so large it held every possible thing, including all the minutiae of every kind of pain.

The sun came up and with its warmth the mosquitoes came alive and Gwen stirred and Harry slept on. Gwen joined Eleanor and they walked together along the shore, listening, waiting for the Twin Otter to arrive. Around seven they heard it in the western sky. Gwen went to wake up Harry and found him folding the tarp, rolling up their sleeping bags. Then they went down to the shore and prepared themselves for the last part of their journey.

They noticed the wind, of course. The stillness of the previous night seemed hallucinatory now. It had been perfectly calm for how long? A few hours? Long enough to fool Ralph into going out alone and too far. Now they knew that the only reason it was calm was because the wind was shifting. The stillness fools you, because it is never really still. The stillness is the time before the change.

Grey clouds on all sides. Blue sky with cumulus clouds above.

And then the Barrens were far below them, glowing in the sun, all vast and distant and bronze. The body of Ralph was inside the body of the plane, which was bouncing over the body of the world, and Gwen reached for a motion sickness bag and quietly threw up. Ralph's canoe was in the plane too. The pilot – older, experienced – had brought reality of a different kind into their midst. He had said they should find the missing canoe. He used the word *evidence*. There would be questions, because there had been a death. He and Harry had set off in the float plane and it had not taken very long to spot what the sun had already picked out. The glinting canoe had drifted almost to shore, not far from where they had found Ralph floating face down in the water.

WHERE THEY HAD BEEN WAS SO VAST, AND RALPH'S DEATH so unforeseen, that their sense of the ordinary died with him. The normal grasses of life never quite grew back. On the day they returned from the Barrens, there was the official business of death. The police took Ralph's body to the hospital, where he was examined by the coroner. For the other three, there were questions by the police and statements to sign. There was Bill Thwaite with his microphone. By late afternoon they were so exhausted they returned separately to their homes, where each of them had a variation of the same almost surreal experience. Harry reached for a can of coffee on his kitchen shelf, then stood delighted by this simplest of things, a wooden shelf at eye level. Gwen stood in her bathroom, enraptured by the dusky light emanating from the porcelain sink and the warm water flowing from the tap. Eleanor listened spellbound for a moment to the whispering slide of wood on wood when she opened and closed a dresser drawer.

Gwen, it was, who telephoned Harry to say that no matter what Eleanor thought she wanted, they should not leave her alone. They arrived at her door soon afterwards, only to find Teresa already there. Teresa, who had kidded them quite rightly about not knowing enough, knew exactly what to do. She got them talking and their impromptu wake began, hours of stories about the trip, about Ralph. His foibles, his turns of phrase, his stamina, his passionate heart.

Around midnight, half-crying, half-laughing, Eleanor said, "Some men will do anything to avoid a wedding."

After the others left, she got into bed and slept for twelve hours. When she woke, she went into her kitchen, discovered the fruit and cheese and bread and ham that Teresa had put in her refrigerator, made herself a small plate of food, and nibbled at it. Then went back to bed and slept four hours more. During that time she had a dream. She was in her father's study on the second floor at home, stuffing paper into a big hole in the wall. She was preparing to sell Ralph's books. She pulled forward a small table, moved the other furniture to one side, and felt a breeze, a cool lake breeze coming from some-where. She went out to the hall landing, then headed downstairs, and on the stairs she felt the breeze even more. Suddenly the front door blew open and Ralph was there in the sort of detail that cannot be recaptured in waking life. She went to him and pressed her face against his neck and felt his whiskers. She could smell him and feel him. He was not big, but he had bulk, muscle. She did not want to let him go, but she wanted to look at him. He was wearing a red and black flannel shirt, a T-shirt underneath it, his old baggy trousers. His grey hair was mussed and plastered to his forehead, and his face was flushed from recent exertion. She told him how overjoyed she was to see him again, and his face brightened and he intimated that she should not worry. Then he said something more, something important. He was passing on the secret of life and she began to realize she was dreaming. But that is not what woke her up. She woke up because she was crying. For a while she lay in bed, going over the dream, struggling to remember what Ralph had said. But she could not.

The next day, as she reached for the hairbrush on her dresser, she experienced a visitation of a more mundane kind. She looked in the mirror and saw her mother.

You pass a photograph on the piano, she thought, a picture of a family member, a face utterly familiar, but bearing no relationship to your own. And then a stranger comes along and sees the resemblance you have overlooked. Staring in the mirror, she was her own stranger, noticing in her altered face something more recognizable than herself, the expression of worn-out grief she had seen on her mother after her father died.

Later, she sat down and wrote to her. I am back from the trip I told you about, the trip Dad would have loved to make. But something happened. Four of us made the journey and only three of us returned. She related everything in detail. She wrote, I find myself thinking of you a great deal.

A week and a half later, she would read her mother's reply. "Something punishing has happened to you," her mother wrote, and Eleanor was struck by the aptness of the word. A single word balanced atop a mountain of feeling.

*   *

After the close-knit intensity of the trip, and the closer-knit shock of Ralph's death, Gwen settled back into herself, into work, and it felt wrong. It tasted off. Compared to Harry, the new young manager was a pipsqueak, she thought, who never looked you in the eye. His only interest was the new building, or so it seemed. Earlier in the summer, construction had started on a building site on the outskirts of town, far removed from the heart of Yellowknife. Things were well under-way, and if plans went as scheduled, they would move out there next June. Everyone around her, it seemed to Gwen, was on edge, poised to see what openings television would bring, and how they might advance themselves.

At Ralph's funeral there had been hymns and old songs and they had spoken to her in some way she did not quite trust. They filled her with what she thought of as easy emotion, and made her feel vulnerable. The church they had used for the service was Eleanor's church, and the pews were filled, not with Ralph's family, which was scattered and distant – he had an ex-wife and no children and only one surviving sister – but with his friends from the radio station and from town. "There is a Balm in Gilead." "Unto the Hills." She listened to Eleanor's quavery, thin voice, a little embarrassed for her, and ashamed of being embarrassed. But why should things be censored and simplified. Why should Ralph's death be softened when it was shockingly hard, and sweetened by hymns when he was not a religious man, not that she had been aware of. For six weeks they had shared a canoe and she had come to know just how strong and stubborn he was, and how gentle and erudite. He knew more things by heart than anyone else she had ever met. She pictured him now, wrapped in a groundsheet, hoisted like a gunny sack into the float plane.

The minister was a short man, clean-shaven, elderly. Without preamble he read a psalm and from the first words, "Lord, thou hast been our dwelling place in all generations", he made the hairs stand up on the back of Gwen's neck. His Bible was open in his hands, but he did not once look down, speaking directly to them as a gifted radio actor might do. "Before the mountains were brought forth, or ever thou hadst formed the earth and the world." And what struck Gwen full force was something she had never really considered before, the idea of a spiritual dwelling place from the beginning of time. Not the idea of God, as such, but the idea of such a dwelling place, and such timelessness over time.

Gwen leaned over and whispered to Harry, "What psalm was that?"

And Harry, the minister's son, knew. "Ninety," he whispered back. "Nine-oh."

The psalm gave her the wider feeling she was after. It captured the sweep of past and present, reminding her of the immensity of the land they had returned from just days before. The endless skies, the rolling tundra, and lakes the size of seas.

The following afternoon, as she was editing a tape, Dido's needling question suddenly echoed in her head. What time do you *want* it to be? And with the question came Dido's insinuation that she, Gwen, did not know. That she was one of those people so out of touch with herself that she could not say or would not admit what it was she wanted.

She could have said, What do you mean by *time*? She could have said, I want it to be bedtime. She could have said, I want you to stop giving me a hard time. But the answer she had actually given still held, even if she wished her delivery had been lighter, less defensive. I want it to be the time it is. I want to be in the here and now.

* *

A few days later, sitting at Eleanor's kitchen table, Harry said, "You don't wear the St Christopher medallion any more."

No. "It didn't quite do the job," she said. She had put it away in a drawer.

"You have to eat," he told her. "Have you been eating?"

"Teresa feeds me. In fact, everybody feeds me." She opened her refrigerator door with a sad flourish. "Abundance," she said.

"Are you sleeping?" he said.

"Harry, you're a sweet man. I'm sleeping enough. I can't look any worse than you do."

She told him not to fret, she would be fine. That day she had handed in her notice to his replacement at the radio station, the boyish-faced man with the small teeth and the nervous smile. She would fulfil her contractual obligation of a month's work, but that was all, for she was going to set in motion her plan to open a bookstore somehow. She hoped to sell new and used books, she told Harry, and she wanted to hang Ralph's photographs on the walls of the shop, his series of weeds floating on water, catching the light.

Harry said, "You're way ahead of me."

He still had not altogether unpacked from the trip, he admitted, although in his mind he was already weighing the next stage of his life and putting out feelers about work. He had been mulling over what he would take with him when he left. He had to decide what to do with Dido's few things, the letter, the watch he had given her, the key chain. Perhaps he would use the key chain, throw away the letter, give the watch to a stranger.

The canoe trip had been medicine of a sort. Once the country opened up and they had entered the flow of water and wildlife, he had been taken past the Dido-wreck in his mind for continuous stretches of time. She receded for a while, several days, a week. But then she returned no less vividly and occupied his thoughts.

IN LATE AUGUST, THREE WEEKS AFTER THEIR RETURN, GWEN was in the station when an older man came looking for Dido. His name was Daniel Moir. He was a close friend of Dido's, he said, and he was trying to find her.

Gwen told him yes, she used to work here, but she had left, months ago. The man nodded and rubbed his lower lip with his knuckle. He was casually well-dressed, late fifties perhaps, tanned and fit, with a strong, successful face, what her mother would have called a fine-looking man. He stared out of the window, and the next thing he said, he said to the window. "How many months ago?"

"In January."

"And she hasn't been in touch since."

"Not with me. But she's been in touch."

At this point Eleanor came back to her desk.

Gwen said to her, "This gentleman is looking for Dido."

Eleanor knew immediately who it was. Dido's description of the handsome father-in-law held true. He looked vigorous, capable, and disappointed. She told him that Dido was in California and had been since January, at least as far as she knew. They had spoken in May, but hadn't spoken since.

He asked what had taken Dido to California. Eleanor replied that the person she had gone with came from there.

"I see," he said. "My timing wasn't good."

Eleanor wondered if he was one of those worldly men who thinks timing is everything, as others believe everything is luck, when it seemed to her everything was fragile, that's all.

In the evening she saw Harry and said, "A man came to the station looking for Dido today. He said his name was Daniel Moir."

Harry raised his head. "The famous father-in-law."

"Yes." So Harry knew. "Poor Dido. But I wasn't sure how much to tell him. I almost gave him her telephone number, but would she want that? I mean, if she wanted to be in touch with him, she would be in touch with him, it seems to me."

"So what's he like?" Harry said, grimly curious.

Eleanor, not to rub salt in the wound, said, "He's in good shape for his age."

Harry tracked him down at the Explorer Hotel. He wanted to meet the man for any number of reasons, the rival for Dido's affections, the fellow loser, the man who had travelled so far on her account, the man who had made Dido wait. *We just looked at each other, we just looked.* How had she gone from A to Z, from this man's son to Eddy? He wanted to know something about the mysterious, self-destructive logic of Dido's love life.

On his way to the hotel, Harry had felt unsettled, at odds with himself. But when he shook Daniel Moir's hand and looked into his eyes, he saw an old man, and his heart lightened.

"I'm Harry Boyd."

"Daniel Moir."

Harry explained that Eleanor Dew had mentioned he was here, and why. "I used to be Dido's boss," he said. "As well as a close friend."

"I'm Dido's father-in-law," Daniel said.

They went into the Snowshoe Lounge together and had a drink, and then another.

To Harry, Daniel Moir looked rich. His hands had known weather, and immediate care afterwards. His way of holding a glass of Scotch in both hands, it was Dido's way of holding her coffee mug. No wedding band, but the white memory of one on his tanned ring finger.

"I was hoping she was still here," Daniel said. "I haven't had a letter in a long time."

Harry nodded. He could have told him he had a piece of their correspondence. "She spoke of you," he said.

Daniel glanced up, a sharp look. But he had enough self-control not to ask what it was that Dido had said about him.

She loved you, Harry thought. Later, he was sorry he had not said it. A person should know he is loved. "We missed her when she left," he said. "She was a natural on air – beautiful speaking voice, tremendous presence. She needed no training at all. She was born to it."

Daniel's face relaxed. "I find that easy to imagine." He asked what she had done, wanting to know in detail, and listened intently.

Harry's lightness of heart subsided the longer he sat across from the man, whose features came into focus the more they talked. Press the Dido button, thought Harry, and the years drop away.

Daniel began to tell him about Dido's other abilities. She excelled as a student, he said. She and his son had studied together, that's how they met. She was one of the only girls in his philosophy class and unlike most of the other students she spoke out. "Well, she was a few years older. My son told us he had met a girl who knew how to play chess. He was impressed, and so were we when he brought her home. His mother and I thought she was an extraordinary young woman."

"His mother and I." He was stating as a simple fact, it seemed to Harry, something that had complicated his life beyond measure.

"What's he doing now, your son?" He did not even know if they were divorced. He assumed not. She had never said.

His son was in Toronto, studying law, Daniel said, and just recently he had become engaged to a lovely girl, a registered nurse. "Someone a lot like his mother."

Harry pointed to the telltale evidence on Daniel's left hand. "You've parted company."

Daniel nodded. "A month ago." By now he was staring into his second Scotch. He began to talk about his grandson, his daughter's child. He had not foreseen how much pleasure having grandchildren would give him. He took the boy sailing, he said. He said he could count on one hand, less than one hand, the women he had met who truly enjoyed sailing. Most women endured it for the sake of their husbands. But Dido had a real feel for it. She was terrific on the water.

Harry had the sudden suspicion that Daniel dreamt of sailing away with Dido. And on the third Scotch Daniel confessed to having done exactly that. He had once taken her aboard his boat and had not brought her back for twenty-four hours. He had been tempted not to bring her back at all. She had joked that she was perfectly equipped for any eventuality. She was wearing pearl earrings. I'm dressed for any occasion, she had told him.

His wife and son had been at a family reunion in Maine and never found out. Or perhaps they had. They knew something. Shortly after they returned, he and Dido went for a long walk on the beach, and then she left, moved away, came up here.

Daniel said, "I once thought my life held no surprises and I was content with that. I knew things might change, but I did not think that *I* would change. I pitied men who ran after younger women. But from the first moment I saw Dido," he said, then stopped. Then picked up again. "At the end of that first visit, she said goodbye and she put her arm across my back – I was sitting at the dining-room table – she put her hand on my shoulder and draped her arm over my back – and it was such a warm gesture. You can't understand it until it happens to you, what it's like to suddenly feel so much. It's a huge gift of feeling," he said slowly. "But I couldn't see my way clear until my son moved on in his life." He stared at his glass and shook his head. "I grow roots when I drink Scotch." Then he said, "Who's the man she's with now?"

Harry had been listening with interest, but no enjoyment as Daniel unburdened himself. "She ran off with the technician," he said.

Daniel eyed him. "Every man I've ever seen her with falls for her."

"She doesn't fall for them, though."

"You're right about that."

"She likes men who are good at what they do," Harry said. He was remembering the drunken party at his house when only Dido remained awake and alert at the end, sitting on the floor in the lotus position, asking him if he thought Eddy was good at what he did. And he should have said, Other things matter more. Or as much. He said, "She likes men who are rough with her." Finally arriving at the heart of the matter.

Daniel did not take his eyes off him. "How do you know that?"

"Not because *I* was rough."

They scrutinized each other. They had finished their jockeying, satisfied their need to talk. They were not ill-disposed towards each other.

Daniel said, "What are you telling me?"

"I was hoping you would tell *me*. You know more about her than I do."

"Maybe. Or maybe I don't know as much as I thought." He looked away. "I gather she's in Los Angeles. I'm sure I could find her if I tried."

"Your son must be in touch with her. If he's getting married again." Divorce papers, Harry was thinking. He did not let on that Eleanor had her telephone number. He considered doing so, then decided not to push the man one way or the other. It was up to Daniel to work out what he would do next.

* *

279

At the end of August, the Berger Inquiry conducted its last community hearing. Over the course of 283 days of testimony, the inquiry
had gathered 40,000 pages of transcripts presented by 1,700
witnesses. Now Berger faced the daunting challenge of completing a
report in six months that would deliver on his promise "to tell the
government and people of Canada what your concerns and thoughts
are".

Harry had put his house up for sale. He sold it within a week,
waterfront lots on Latham Island being highly prized. Then he began
to organize the things he would take to England. He wanted to whit-
tle his life down to its essentials, like Huck Finn, he thought to
himself, and to that end he was confining himself to two suitcases.
Everything else he was boxing up either for the church to give away,
or for the dump.

One night, Eleanor and Gwen dropped in and found him
surrounded by chaos. Help yourselves, he told them. Dig in. Take
anything you can use. Then his tone changed, and he said he was
looking for someone who might be able to use his canoe.

It was early September and the residue of the trip was gone from
their faces and hands, even from their muscles – they had town
faces, town thoughts, town dreams. The Barren Ground had not
followed them into their sleep. It worked on them differently, more
consciously, perhaps. It was a short, atypical chapter in their lives.
They could not quite believe it had happened, even though afterwards nothing was the same.

"Are we ever going to see you again?" Gwen said.

"Ah, Gwen," Harry said. And wrapped her in a hug. He was
drinking again, the sobriety of the canoe trip already a distant
memory. "You're a sentimental soul."

"Can I hide in one of your suitcases?" she said. She was ready to
run off with him now, she said, ready to stow aboard.

Harry just smiled the comment away. His flirtatious banter of the
canoe trip was a thing of the past too, and she could not resurrect it,

not even by telling him the radio station was unbearable without him. He had moved on, it seemed to her. He had already left.

She was right. Ralph's death had worked a change in him, turning his thoughts to Eleanor and her welfare, then to his own future.

Gwen stood in the living room as Harry wrapped up his life in Yellowknife. In one of those paradoxes she found hard to grasp, she felt more isolated in town than when she had been on the Barrens with miles of emptiness around her. Just three months ago in this very room, they had organized their supplies, full of excitement about leaving. How was it possible to feel safer in the wilderness – as safe as she had felt almost until the end – and how was it possible to feel lonelier now?

A week before he was to leave Yellowknife, Harry opened *News of the North* and read a brief article about an exhibition of photographs in Los Angeles that was causing quite a stir. A series documenting young Dene women, unposed, half-naked, and looking as if they were high on something. Canadian Press had picked up the story. The report said viewers had responded with outrage and concern about the lives depicted, but with admiration for the political message and the artistic daring of the photographer. "The disconcerting intimacy of the pictures never feels exploitative," one reviewer said, and Eddy Fitzgerald was quoted. "I can't transform their lives, but I can show the truth of what's happening." He said he wanted to show the underside of life in a far northern town where whites were the majority, where they were racist, where they used and abused young native women. He wanted his pictures to be seen as a warning of what lay ahead if the pipeline went through. A book was in the works, he claimed, and all the proceeds would go to the Dene Nation. There was a small shot of Eddy, looking intense, unsmiling, and next to it one of his photographs: a young native girl sprawled on her side in what looked like a seedy motel room.

Harry realized with sudden and painful clarity that Eddy was going to make a name for himself, a thought that dismayed him almost as much as the pictures did. He could not tell from the article if the photos were true to life, or if Eddy had staged them for his own purposes. He did not know if he should be impressed by what Eddy had done or appalled.

When he saw Teresa the next day in the Gold Range café, he asked if she had seen the article.

"Jesus," she said. "What planet does Eddy live on?"

Harry felt relieved, and grateful for her straightforward reaction. "But it's all in a good cause, apparently," he said. Wanting her to elaborate, to clarify his own thinking. "Art in the service of politics."

"No," she said. "It's art and politics as a cover for – you know. His dick."

A response so unequivocal it blasted away the confusion in his jealous mind.

* *

Eleanor was the only one of their foursome, except for Ralph, who would never leave the North. In early October, Harry moved to England, and not long after that Gwen began to apply to radio stations in the south for work. Vancouver, Toronto, Winnipeg, Ottawa. She wanted more experience, she told Eleanor, she wanted to learn from people who really knew what they were doing, and that meant going "outside", the northern term for anywhere south of the sixtieth parallel. By implication, the North itself was "inside". A distinction that first struck Gwen as an existential riddle, since how could this vast out-of-doors ever be construed as an interior? But then she experienced her first Yellowknife winter.

Winter closed in again with frigid winds, icy roads, longer nights, and, yes, she was inside a place gripped by the cold. Ironically, now that she had made up her mind to leave Yellowknife, she felt more bound to the place, eager to absorb everything she could. She intended to be gone before the station took up its new quarters the following summer. Under the present manager, she was back on nights. She preferred it. She saw less of the man, who, unlike Harry, had no interest in opening up broadcasting to women. Teresa did not get on with him either. "But I've figured out how to handle him. He fires me, then I fire him," she laughed. "I've outlived bad bosses before," she added with a trace of bitterness.

They both kept tabs on Eleanor. She had made an arrangement with the owner of the stationery store to split the rent and devote her half of the space to books. One day Gwen helped her go through Ralph's photographs to select which ones to hang in the store. They discovered that before his summer grasses he made a series on grasses in winter that looked like Japanese calligraphy. The dry stalks were bent over like little sticks, pressed into shapes by weather, half buried under the snow. It was almost too much for Eleanor. Ralph had walked right back into their lives. She told Gwen then about the remarkable dream she had had soon after he died, in which there was the sort of detail – sight, touch, smell – that an ordinary photograph does not have and neither does memory. But these photographs of what he had bent down to look at so closely that he was inches away gave her the sense that she was looking through his eyes. This intimacy with him – so physical, yet intangible – came to her in a rush and made her feel his absence all the more.

As Gwen studied the snowy light in the black-and-white photographs, she was taken back to a winter's day seven years ago when she had driven with her mother to Toronto to see an old friend, a painter named Marta, who had rented an apartment in a high-rise overlooking Lake Ontario. There was just a bedroom, living room, small kitchen, not unlike my own apartment here, thought Gwen, except for one thing. Marta had a view. Large windows overlooked the lake below and winter sun poured in, such white, parched, unsparing sunshine that everything seemed charged with unusual life. All the way home, driving with her mother through the bare countryside under the white winter sky, she had felt Marta's aspirations working like sap running through her, and it wasn't the sap of spring, but the latent sap of winter. She had never forgotten, but neither had she known how to put the feeling into action. Now it occurred to her to use her kitchen table as a work space and try her hand drawing and sketching the things she remembered from her winter walks around town, like the hooded faces obscured by plumes of icy breath, and the makeshift log cabins and wood piles wrapped in ice fog, the skiers coming across the frozen lake, and the occasional dog team that surged over the snow, pulling a toboggan behind them like a snow boat, the dogs reaching to the side to swipe mouthfuls of snow.

At Christmas they received cards from Harry, who told them he was remarkably well for a man in his condition. He had found a job at the B.B.C., producing radio dramas.

That's *my* job, Gwen wrote to him. Eleanor replied too; she would be a faithful correspondent. Gwen wrote again in January when she was offered a job for the following July as a summer replacement at the C.B.C. in Ottawa. Harry sent his congratulations, she wrote to him yet again, and when he did not reply, she let it go.

In February, a hundred miles northeast of Inuvik, a young man working on an oil rig in the Mackenzie Delta was killed by a polar bear. His co-worker said that he had left him alone, but only briefly, to warm up in a nearby trailer, and when he came out several minutes later, his partner was gone. He searched around and found a boot, a sock, and a polar bear paw print. The story ran on the news and inspired Gwen to write a radio reminiscence about her own encounter, and the little body of sound, her bag full of tapes, that lay on the slope above Hornby's quiet cabin. In response she heard from a retired Barren Lands trapper, Gus Daoust, who gave her his droll and terse assessment of the weather in that part of the world. "Every wind is a headwind," he said. He also observed that around

Yellowknife there were two periods in the year when everything seems to stop still. January and June. May, he said, was the month of sounds of all kinds.

Appropriate, then, that Berger released his final report in early May, since it generated so much talk. The report was more hard-hitting than anyone had expected. "No pipeline now," he recommended, "and no pipeline across the northern Yukon ever." He called for a moratorium of at least ten years on the Mackenzie Valley pipeline to allow for the settlement of native land claims. He recommended that measures be taken to protect critical wildlife habitat. He highlighted the need to preserve native culture and to foster the development of an economy based on renewable resources. "TEN YEAR DELAY," trumpeted the headlines.

Copies of the report were flown to every settlement and waved in the air in triumph. Teresa personally delivered a copy to her grandmother in Fort Rae. Her grandmother couldn't read it, but that hardly mattered. There were many pictures, including one of herself smoking a pipe, her hair white, her eyes trained on the distance. She could turn the pages of photographs of the land and of the animals, and she did, repeatedly, until the binding came apart.

By the end of the summer it would be clear to everyone that a huge political shift had taken place. The inquiry and the report that followed had effectively stopped the pipeline. If it was resurrected, native peoples, empowered by their land claims settlements, would have a central voice in the process.

On her last night in Yellowknife, Gwen did her late show a final time. It was June, one of those brief nights we call long because the twilight is so extended. She was in the announce booth, in its very particular light, never more aware of the rest of the world than when she was so completely shut away from it. She opened her little sound-effects door wide for Sleepy John Estes, the blues guitarist, who used to recognize everyone's step, she said, so acutely did he absorb the sounds around him.

Shortly after one in the morning, Eleanor picked her up at the station and they drove to Old Town. The street lights were on and store signs were lit, but it was not dark. They rolled down their windows and the air smelled of the big lake. Harry's canoe was tied to a rack on the roof of the car. They were planning a long paddle on Yellowknife Bay.

They parked near the causeway to Latham Island. When they slid the canoe into the water, there was a slight breeze, but the air was so warm they only needed sweaters under their life vests. The last of the ice had been gone from the bay for just over a week.

They stayed close to shore. It was almost a year to the day since they had set off for the Thelon River, and they had not been on the water since Ralph died. As they paddled, they passed Willow Flats on their right, Jolliffe Island on their left. They passed School Draw, and the shoreline turned wilder. Soon they made out the tower of Con Mine and more islands. Gwen assumed she would never see these things again and she wanted to say goodbye, to sign off, as it were.

After a while, they stopped and drifted. Eleanor in the stern, Gwen in the bow. The air had become perfectly still.

"I've been thinking you should have my fur coat," Gwen said. Everything else she had packed or sold or given away, including the car and trailer she had driven to Yellowknife two years ago. "Would you take it and wear it?"

"You'll need it in Ottawa," Eleanor said. "It's yours."

"It's not really mine at all. I've never thought of it as mine."

"It is yours. Harry gave it to you."

Gwen turned to look directly at her and saw that she was serious. "Why?" she asked. "Why did he do such a thing?" In her mind, besides the surprise, were the arresting words *from a secret admirer*.

"He said it wasn't being used and you needed a warm coat. It used to be his grandmother's, that's what he said." Eleanor smiled. "He wanted you to have a warm coat."

"What a kind and strange thing to do," Gwen said, adjusting herself to the kindness, the strangeness. *From a secret admirer.* Why those words? she wanted to ask. But she knew why. He wasn't being literal. His grandmother's coat, after all. A grandmother's coat isn't romantic.

"I'm spilling the beans," Eleanor said. "He didn't intend for you to know."

"I'm *glad* to know. It's been such a puzzle, wondering where it came from. Harry," she said, and laughed. "He didn't want the coat to go to waste. Or something."

"Or something," smiled Eleanor.

Gwen was remembering when they had all been together a year ago, travelling into a second spring and a second winter. Last year's June had slid backwards into May and they had heard all the sounds of breakup and renewal all over again. Lifting the needle, putting it back at the beginning instead of forward to the next song.

"You've changed," she said to Eleanor. Lifting the needle off herself. "When I first met you, you were biding your time. Not any more."

"We've come a long way together. But I think we're still recognizable."

Somewhere between three and four in the morning, as they were paddling back, they saw a world that Ralph might have photographed had he seen it, and that Gwen would later try to paint. But it was not possible to duplicate the colours except by closing her eyes. Then the islands in the distance became the right shade of jet black, and the sky and the water were an identical, intense, unblemished peach.

TOWARDS THE END OF A WARM SEPTEMBER, A FULL EIGHT years later, Gwen heard Harry's voice again. She was in her kitchen with the radio on and she stopped what she was doing and stood transfixed. His relaxed, gravelly, conversational voice was so familiar that a decade of time dropped away and she was back in a place more vivid than the present. How rare it was to hear someone on the radio who was not glib or pushy or out to impress you. Harry was talking to another man about the direction his life had taken, questioning him about the key turning point. They must be in a studio in Toronto, Gwen thought. The other man had been just thirteen, he told Harry, when he and his mother went to visit some elderly neighbours in a cottage and the couple brought out bread and beer. How can the boy grow if he doesn't drink beer? said the persuasive old neighbour, an amateur musician, it turned out, who then went to the piano and played a selection of musical warhorses – Beethoven's "Moonlight Sonata", a waltz by Brahms, Mozart's *Eine Kleine Nachtmusik* – and the effect on the boy drinking his first glass of beer was electric. This is what he wanted to do with his life, he knew instantly. He wanted to study music. More than that, he wanted to arrange, rearrange, move the notes around.

The radio went from the man's voice to his music and it was Harry Somers, Gwen realized. The boy had grown up to be the composer Harry Somers.

Harry asked Somers about the Newfoundland folk songs he had arranged which every child in a Canadian choir has at some time or another sung, and Somers answered that he was very drawn to them, that now, of course, they represented the memory of something rather than the thing itself, since that sort of life, the outport life, had disappeared or was disappearing. Then a choir began to sing "She's Like a Swallow" and Gwen's eyes filled with tears.

The phrase that came to her mind was "the long and sudden of it". We go on and on through the long months of our lives until we hit a sudden moment that stuns us. This was one such moment and soon there would be another. When the programme ended, an announcer informed listeners that it had been recorded years ago; she had been listening to a tape. Harry was not back in Canada, after all.

Gwen sat at her kitchen table, flooded less with memory than with feeling, as you sit flooded with feeling after a telephone call tells you sad news about someone you love. Hearing Harry's voice had been like slipping on the soft tan glove of the past.

After a while, she stood up and switched off the radio, then went to the window. Autumn crocuses splayed wide in the garden below like mauve, over-the-hill mushrooms. Or birthday candles melted down into a soft, crazy tilt. From here she could see how candle-white the stems were. Autumn crocuses were something she had never known about until she moved into this old house in Ottawa. The small, leggy flowers expired almost as soon as they appeared. At the window she became aware of unhappy crows, their racket outside. Then she saw somebody in what looked like a uniform at the foot of the garden, and someone else, in the same kind of beige shirt and trousers, run across the lawn and disappear around the side of the fence where the mint grew.

She went outside and her neighbour called over the high hedge, "There's a fox!"

"A fox?"

"With one leg missing. It was asleep in our yard and the crows went crazy. It's in your yard now."

Gwen went to the foot of the garden and saw the fugitive, its right back leg missing from the hip, trot leisurely from her garden into the alley. An extraordinary sight – a gaunt, grey veteran of the wild, moving at its own otherworldly pace.

The uniformed strangers were animal control officers and Gwen watched them corner the fox behind a neighbour's gas barbecue, then hook it around the neck with a wire noose on the end of a long pole, and hoist it into the air to hang limp, skinny, twisted, its eyes flat and expressionless, either too weak or too wise to struggle, before they dropped it into a cage. They carried the cage to their van and then drove away. For a few minutes, she remained outside. The crows had dispersed. The street was quiet. The fox had been too mangy, the control officers had said to her, potentially too dangerous to be allowed to continue on his way. By the battle-scarred look of him, he had been fighting against the odds for a long while. There was a time when she would have brought out her tape recorder and taped the whole incident. Not any more. But sometimes she still thought about her lost tapes, imagined how another traveller might stumble over them, and listen to them later, only to be transported as she would have been back to that remote, animal-filled wilderness.

The fox had seemed magical to her. A creature from one world passing through another. But he didn't make it.

Saddened, she went back inside, and telephoned Eleanor at the bookstore. She told her about the fox, told her he had been minding his own business. And she got the sympathetic reaction she had counted on. But was that really what prompted the call? "Another amazing thing happened today," she said. "I heard Harry on the radio."

"It must have been something he did for the B.B.C.," Eleanor said. "He's still over there, I know. Holding the radio fort, tending the broadcasting fires, as he likes to say. You know Harry."

"No, it was a tape recorded years ago." Then she said, "I'm sorry. I should have asked if you were busy."

"It's alright. Things are quiet. How's David?"

"David's great. I've put another one of his masterpieces in the mail to you. We splash colour around when he gets home from daycare."

Eleanor said she was going to bring him some books on her next visit. She would be flying down from Yellowknife in the week following Christmas to spend more time with her mother.

Good, said Gwen, she could not wait to see her, she missed her. And, "I didn't realize how much I missed Harry."

Early the next morning, having spent much of the night talking to Harry in her head, she telephoned the B.B.C. in London and they put her through. "Harry," she said when he answered, "I spent an hour with you yesterday under the strangest circumstances."

"Gwen? Where are you?"

He sounded as pleased to hear from her as she had hoped he would be.

"Still in Ottawa. They replayed your interview with Harry Somers."

"It's so great to hear your voice," he said. Then, "You're up awfully early."

She was. It was six in the morning. She was the only one awake in her house. "Tell me about your life over there," she said. "Are you well?"

"No complaints. They've got me producing audio books now."

"They have you reading them on tape, you mean."

"No, no. We have actors do that. Proper professionals, not old radio hacks. This is Britain."

"But you would be great at it."

Harry chuckled. "I'll pass that on to them." Then he said, "I've been keeping track of you through Eleanor."

"What has she told you?"

"She tells me everything."

"Then she tells you more than she tells me."

Harry laughed. "I should be calling you a traitor for defecting from radio."

"Sometime over a drink, we'll talk. Do you ever come to Canada?"

"I do. Now and again, when I've got a good reason. I've been toying with the idea of showing up at Abe Lamont's retirement party just to give the old grump a surprise. It's in November," he said. "In Toronto, though."

And Gwen gathered from his tone that Ottawa was not on the cards. "When I heard your voice yesterday, I actually thought you *were* in Toronto. I thought you'd moved back."

There was no response. Then, "Sorry, Gwen. Just had to hand something to a colleague. You're asking if I plan to move back to Toronto. Not really. I have things to keep me here."

His personal life. She had been wondering about it. "Things besides work."

"As a matter of fact, yes. Mind you, I'm not as tied down as you are."

"No wife," she said. She heard him reach for an answer and assumed there was someone, but no-one official, and intercepted slyly by asking, "Harry, you're not still relying on self-service, are you?"

There was a moment's silence. Then she heard a huge guffaw.

"You're *very* forward," he said.

They were both laughing, and Gwen felt more relaxed than she had in a long time.

He said, "So let's say I do go to Abe's party. Would it make any sense for me to take a side trip to Ottawa?"

She felt the smile broaden on her face. "It's only an hour's flight. We could have dinner together and catch up."

"Then I'll see what I can manage and keep you posted," he said. "I'm tremendously glad you called."

"I love your voice, Harry. It isn't like anyone else's."

*   *

Five weeks later, in the lobby of the Lord Elgin Hotel in Ottawa, Harry removed his glasses and looked at Gwen.

"I like the blue on blue," he said.

She glanced down at herself and recalled in the same moment her turquoise earrings. She touched her ears.

He said, "The blue blouse, the blue necklace, the blue earrings, and your blue eyes."

"Ah," with a smile.

She surveyed his face, adjusting to the changes of the intervening years. His eyes seemed smaller because his jaw was wider. His skin was ruddier, the cauliflower ear its fat, lumpy self. He was more solid yet more vulnerable. But ageing made everyone that way, not that Harry was so old. By her calculation he was fifty-one or -two, and only somewhat better groomed than he used to be. A comfortable tweed jacket, decent trousers, scuffed brogues.

"What happened to your wrist?" he said.

She glanced at the cast that encased her lower arm and extended beyond her sleeve. "I was making my way through the dark bedroom and I fell over my husband's shoes." She raised her eyebrows, smiled, then looked away. "I used to know that room by heart."

Harry had stepped into *terra incognita*, the state of a troubled marriage. He was not sure how to proceed. "You were going to tell me how you and radio parted ways," he said, slipping on his overcoat. "According to Eleanor, you got tired of asking people about things that were none of your business."

"Eleanor told you that? Well, that's certainly part of it."

293

"And the rest?"

"Let me show you where it happened," she said, buttoning up her coat. "It's on the way to the restaurant."

They walked over to Wellington Street, then made their way across the small bridge that spanned the canal and led to the Château Laurier Hotel.

One day about six years ago, she told him, when she was at work right up there, and she pointed to the top floor of the old hotel where c.b.c. Radio had its studios, she looked out the window and saw that it was snowing, the first snowfall of the year. Around her everybody had their noses to the grindstone while outside huge, lazy flakes drifted down. One or two others noticed the weather and grunted and looked away. For a few minutes she stood by herself at the window watching the snow fall from the sky, and in those few minutes the light flurry of flakes, suspended in the air yet moving in all directions, became a thick squall, blotting out the buildings across the street, and then the snow was over. A big blue swath opened up in the sky. She thought how changeable and infinitely various the air is, and how she was being paid to cram it to the gills with talk, to bury it under endless information, and she could not do it any more. "Has that ever happened to you, Harry? Whatever you were doing you couldn't do it for another second, and you quit?"

"Getting fired was more my line." His tone and manner so wry that impulsively she put her arm around him, openly, easily fond. "Go on with the story of your life," he said to her, his voice a little gruff. "Eleanor told me you married a professor. How did you meet him?"

They had met, she said, when she enrolled in social work and he taught her several courses. She had not finished the degree, though. She had stayed home for a year after their son was born, then she had volunteered at a hospice and found her calling. It was listening to people with real problems tell her their troubles. "It never tires me," she said. Now she was training to be a family counsellor who would work in palliative care, but she was doing it part-time, since

David was only four. So there it is, she said. That brings you up to date.

They stopped at a corner and waited for the light to turn. "Your hair is different from what I remembered. Shorter." He pushed it gently off the side of her face and touched the rim of her ear. It looked delicately chewed, as if by mice, he told her. "My good ear's the same," he said, the result of frostbite as a kid, those hours and hours of playing outside and walking to and from school. He told her he had heard of Prairie kids who delivered newspapers and froze their fingers so badly that although otherwise their hands grew to normal size their fingers stayed stubby, the growth plates destroyed. "If you ever see someone with fingers like that," he told her, "you'll know the reason."

She fixed him with those eyes of hers. "I almost wore your fur coat today. I would have if it had been any colder."

"Then it hasn't fallen apart." He felt caught, but not displeased. "So Eleanor couldn't resist."

Gwen smiled. "The coat's still perfect."

"Well, good. I just took pity on a poor girl who needed a warm coat."

"Thank you," she said. "Thank you, Harry Boyd."

He leaned forward with something in his manner that Gwen had not seen before, an almost beseeching gallantry, and planted a kiss on her ear.

They crossed the street and what came next might have seemed like a *non sequitur*, but it was far from that for them. "Last summer," she said, "my son stepped on a wasps' nest and got stung seven times."

Harry seemed to be wrapped up in looking at her.

"And I got stung twice when he ran into my arms."

"Last summer I was in New York," he said slowly. "I was walking in Central Park, when a woman touched my arm. She said, 'You don't recognize me.'"

From the change in his face, the way it widened in mystified sadness, Gwen guessed who it was. "It was Dido," she said, and her voice was flat.

He nodded.

Gwen turned her head and glanced at the traffic going by. "And what's she doing with herself now?"

"I'm not really sure. She has problems with her health. If I'd never seen her before," he said thoughtfully, "I might have mistaken her for a nun."

Gwen stopped and stared at him. In her mind she saw Dido in her pretty shoes. In a cashmere sweater and leather skirt. Slender, elegant, fresh from her time in L.A. "You could say many things about Dido, but comparing her to a nun isn't anything that ever would have occurred to me."

He smiled. "I don't mean she was wearing a habit. She looked very different, that's all. Thin. Not very happy. Eddy looked much the same as ever."

"So they're still together."

"He's got more work than he knows what to do with, he told me."

Gwen reflected. "I wonder if they have children."

"They didn't say so. I don't think they're even married."

Gwen was silent. Then she said, "Marriage is hard." She had been about to tell Harry something more, about her own marriage, but the moment had passed.

*   *

Harry had been walking in Central Park when he saw Dido after all those years. It was a late summer afternoon and the wide green spaces were full of light and movement. Runners, cyclists, the leaves stirring a little in the trees. To Harry, the park's gentle contours seemed extraordinarily inviting, and he stopped walking to take it all in, then felt a hand on his arm.

"You don't recognize me," she said. She had leaned forward

from her bench to get his attention. She had a book open in her lap.

The sight of her did something to his heart. He felt its exact location and entire size inside his chest.

She had lost weight. She was wearing grey. A loose linen dress with long sleeves. He saw streaks of silver in her dark hair; a filigree of silver, he thought. No wedding band.

"The last time I saw you," he said, "you were wearing a yellow sweater."

She smiled. "We can't be feeling sorry for ourselves, Harry."

He sat beside her on the bench. "Why not?" he asked.

"How many years ago was that? Don't tell me." Her dark–light, buoyant–sad voice. "You were good to me. I haven't forgotten."

And what was he to make of that, he wondered. She had not forgotten, but she could not be bothered to explain.

"You disappeared without a word," he said. "I waited for you to come home. I almost called the police. Then I ransacked the house and realized you had gone. Why the hell didn't you say anything?"

"Kill it before it dies," she said, and sighed. "I'm not saying I couldn't have done better by you. But at least you knew where you stood."

"What are you talking about? I didn't know a thing. You didn't *tell* me anything."

"You weren't listening. You're still not listening."

He shook his head at her, confounded.

"I'm not such a prize, Harry."

"That's not how I see it."

A boy on a skateboard zoomed by so close Harry drew in his feet, looked up, and a girl in jeans and a tank top glanced at them as she strode by. Then he saw himself, a middle-aged man with a hangdog look, sitting on a park bench with the woman who had broken his heart. Snap out of it, he knew Dido was saying in her own way. Snap out of it, Harry.

She was rubbing the side of her face with her hand and *she doesn't look well*, he thought, pulled back into his concern for her. "Has life been good?" he asked.

"I've had better days," she said.

He pressed her with more questions and learned that she had not been able to work since June, a combination of exhaustion and depression; the doctors had suggested an extended leave might help, and N.B.C. was being decent about it. Eddy worked for both of them anyway, she said. He worked all the time.

Listening to her talk, Harry wondered if Daniel Moir had ever contacted her. He wanted to ask, but it was really none of his business. If Moir had gone all the way to Yellowknife but no farther, it would not do Dido any good to know about it. And if they had been in touch, it had not amounted to anything, obviously. Why meddle, he said to himself. Why open old wounds.

She and Eddy had been in New York for two years, she was telling him. Eddy was directing a television series now, a police show that was very popular. "But *you* wouldn't know that," she said in a tone that had in it something of her old manner, flirtatious, cutting. "Not being one for television."

"That doesn't sound like Eddy," he said, "a police series."

Dido shrugged as if she had no opinion on the matter, or as if Harry's opinion was of no interest. She said Eddy had other things on the go too. His photography for one.

"So." Harry lifted the cover of her book. "What are you reading?"

"You won't know it," she said again, and she told him it was an old volume by A. E. Coppard, one of the English books her father had struggled with. He had kept them in a row on a shelf beside his bed, and she had brought some of them back with her after a recent visit to her mother. She had been perusing them to see what it was that had occupied her father for so many hours. "This one's very old style. Not easy either. I wonder how much my father understood. Shall I tell you what it's about?"

There was something a little mocking in her voice, challenging, aggressive. "Sure," he said.

Well, she went on, it was about two women who go into the woods to gather dead branches for firewood, and while they work they reminisce about the same man. "The same long-lost man," she smiled. "Then the wind rises in the forest and they listen to it."

When she had come to that passage, a certain phrase had made her pause and read it a second time: the description of the wind in the treetops "as of some lost wave seeking a forgotten shore", and she had become aware of the breeze in the trees around her and raised her eyes and there was Harry Boyd, large as life.

She raised her shoulders and let them drop. "Life is a bit of a joke," she said.

As if, thought Harry, he needed any more reminding that he did not cut it as a long-lost man.

Then she sat forward, pushed up her sleeve to check the watch that fitted her wrist exactly. "I have to meet Eddy in ten minutes." She stood up. "Why don't you come and say hello to him."

"Eddy doesn't want to say hello to *me*."

"You mean *you* don't. Come on, Harry. Keep me company."

The breezes had stopped and the air was heavy. Beads of sweat had gathered on his neck. They walked quickly through the park, Dido saying it was not far. A friend of theirs was having a show in a gallery and they had been invited to the opening. Beside him, despite the heat, Dido looked cool, and quite at home in the city. They came to the address on West 57th and went up a flight of stairs and through a glass door into a sizable gallery. He saw Eddy at the back, talking to a younger man with a brush cut. Dido went to them and Harry followed in her wake. Eddy had a long, deep scratch on the top of his nose, red and recent.

Dido said, "Look who I found wandering around Central Park."

Eddy stared at him without a glimmer of recognition, it seemed to Harry.

Dido kissed the young artist on both cheeks. "You're a genius," she said. And introducing him to Harry, "He's going to be very famous one day."

Then she said, "Look at Eddy. The cat swiped him. Well, he deserved it."

"It's been a long time," Eddy said, shaking Harry's hand. "I can't remember half the things I've done since I left Yellowknife."

So he *does* know who I am, Harry thought. Eddy's eyes still looked absolutely neutral. It gave Harry the weirdest feeling.

"But I've always got more on the go than I can handle," Eddy said.

He wore black jeans and a black T-shirt, and he looked more substantial, Harry thought, more muscled. He had been working out. His face had the old chiselled confidence. His haircut must have set him back a few bucks. "Dido tells me you're still taking pictures."

"Yeah. I might have a show here," he said, glancing around him. "It's not really my kind of space, though."

The gallery was filling up. Another admirer collared the artist and pulled him away, and for a moment, Harry and Dido and Eddy were their own little unit. Harry ventured to say he had left Yellowknife not long after they had, but an older woman, wearing half her weight in gold jewellery, had approached Dido and begun to bend her ear, and Eddy excused himself and started to work the room. So Harry made his way around the gallery as best he could. It was hard to see the paintings for the people. The canvases were big, bold, abstract. He rather liked them. Once, in the early sixties, he had flown into Resolute Bay in the Far North after a fresh snowfall, and the buildings around the airstrip were like these pure bands of orange and yellow. The people, however, were not his type at all. In some cases their clothes were so elegant and well fitted he was tempted to say, "Who's your tailor?" He looked around for Dido, but the room was too crowded, he could not see her. And so he left, taking the stairs down to the street and stepping outside into the warm evening air. He turned east and walked for quite a while before it occurred to him that he was going the wrong way. He stood for a moment on a corner, trying to orient himself. Then he turned south and walked to the bar in his hotel.

*   *

Harry and Gwen located their restaurant near the market and took a table by the window. After they ordered glasses of wine, Gwen drew a snapshot out of her purse and showed him her son.

Harry studied the picture. "He's lucky," he said.

She laughed. "Because he doesn't look a bit like me."

He handed the picture back to her. "I was thinking of his father. He's a lucky man to have the two of you. Maybe he doesn't know how lucky he is."

Gwen's face was suddenly warm.

Harry asked her if she had told her son about her time in Yellowknife and their trip on the Thelon River. "The delicious taste of Coffee-mate on porridge," he said, and smacked his lips. "And all the animals. The herds of caribou, the muskox, your encounter with the grizzly. Our slog across the ice when you held that microphone between your teeth. You wouldn't want him to grow up thinking city life is all there is."

"You seem just the same, Harry. Well, maybe a little balder."

"Wretch."

She laughed. He was easy to talk to, he always had been. And no, she had neglected to tell her son stories about the North, but she would correct the oversight. She said she wondered if she could remember all the lakes on their long route, and began to list them. Artillery, Ptarmigan, Sifton. "Burr Lake," threw in Harry. French Lake, she continued. Kipling Lake. Harry Lake, she said with a smile. Beverly Lake, they did not say, but knew each other was thinking. A look of understanding passed between them.

"You sound like a radio announcer," he said, "listing all the places the signal carries to." All the faraway towns, he thought, filled with listeners who are only half-listening, their minds on other things. *I used to know that bedroom by heart.*

He said, "You were saying that marriage is hard."

"Yes." She looked up. "I find it so." Here was the moment again. "But my mother-in-law is coaxing me to give it one more chance, for David's sake."

"So you're thinking it over."

"I'm thinking she's probably right."

"Yes," he said heavily.

When their food arrived, they occupied themselves with eating, hardly looking up. Then Harry thought to tell her about the special trip he had made to Dover, to Edgar's school, to see the original red leather diary that lay inside a glass case in the headmaster's study, also the plaque to Edgar's memory in the school chapel. It felt profoundly circular, he said, that having stood in the very spot where the diary was written and then preserved in the cold ashes of a stove, he had caught up with its final resting place. It made him wonder if the two places were separated – or if they were connected – by those several thousand miles.

Later, they walked back to Rideau Street. Harry offered to see her safely home. No need, she said, she would grab a taxi, and she flagged one at the corner. She hugged Harry, then slid into the back seat as the light turned red, giving her a chance to watch him jay-walk across Sussex Drive, then continue up the slope past the Château Laurier. She had always loved the way he walked. Never in a rush, hands in his pockets turning a lighter or jiggling a few coins, shoulders square from having played rugby and from years in his father's church choir. His left foot a little pigeon-toed. She liked the outward curve of his left shin and she could not have said why, except that it seemed erotic.

A year passed before she telephoned him again. This time she said, "Harry, when are you coming into my bed?"

ONE SUNDAY MORNING, DURING A LONG, WET SPRING, HARRY opened the paper at the breakfast table and glancing through the obituaries almost missed Dido's. He read the short paragraph that summarized her life and early death, while the rain came down. It was almost tropical, the sound of the rain. All around them the steady beat, the full gurgle of water flowing off the roof, through the pipes, into the ground. Last night he had heard voices outside at ten o'clock, laughter despite the weather and the hour, then a series of bangs that puzzled him until he remembered. He had called to Gwen and she had joined him at the bedroom window. Through a gap in the trees, they watched fireworks transform the rain-soaked sky into brighter and bigger cascades of colour until the final all-out volley and the sudden lights out. The twenty-fourth of May, the Queen's birthday. Always an occasion for firecrackers. A constant, he had thought, since boyhood. A reassuring custom that knit together a whole span of years.

He passed the newspaper across the table to Gwen.

Her "oh!" then silence while she read about Dido's death "on May 17, after a long illness. Born 1947, in the Netherlands, only child of Johan and Griet. Cherished companion of producer and experimental photographer Edward Fitzgerald. Adored aunt of Tracey, Erin, Joshua. Seven years at N.B.C. Filing cabinets filled with clippings about social justice, ideas for films, plays, screenplays, stories. Passion in search of a vehicle. An erratic, emotional, beautiful woman who never quite found herself."

Gradually the rain stopped, but the sky stayed heavy and grey. Everything brimmed – the rivers, the canal, the lakes. Harry threw open a window and they heard the trickling away of water and the birds.

In the afternoon, while David played next door, Gwen and Harry went out for a walk. At first they were silent, skirting puddles, occupied by their own thoughts. Gwen mulled over the words Eddy had chosen, perhaps self-serving in some way, but they had the ring of truth. An erratic, emotional energy – quick to leap and quick to subside. Dido's beauty had been the main event that summer when light made them tireless, like children playing outside till dark, but there was no dark.

"I'm astounded they stayed together," Harry said. "I never thought they would." He had been remembering Dido in the art gallery, how she had more than held her own.

"They must have loved each other," Gwen said.

Too pat, thought Harry. Too easy. It doesn't tell you anything. "Was it love, or something else," he said. Some unhealthy need, he was thinking.

"She was loyal to him, he was loyal to her," Gwen said simply. "They had a bond, call it what you will."

Harry nodded slowly, and for some reason the tangle in his heart let go a little. He felt his view of the pair, not reverse itself but widen – a bond, call it what you will. He slid his arm through Gwen's and they kept walking. They turned a corner and two boys were biking through puddles on Euclid Avenue. It began to spatter rain and they headed back.

That night, when she woke at three and could not sleep, Gwen did what she often did, she went north in her mind, into the summer air, down the road to Latham Island and out onto the pre-dawn waters. Usually Harry was sound asleep beside her, but now he spoke to her in the dark. The sound of his voice was the sound of that place, and it took her all the way back and brought everything forward. His voice was as dark as a plum, and the darkness in their room was the shade of a plum tree. He spoke to her again, and she felt held by his voice and taken under the wing of that faraway place.

In the morning, it was raining again. They heard it when they woke up, and Gwen murmured that they were lucky not to be in a tent. Or a boat, Harry said. The rain beat against the roof and slid down all the windows facing west. They felt vulnerable and protected, lying there, listening to the sounds the world makes in the month of May. How the earth could hold any more water they did not know.

ACKNOWLEDGEMENTS

Always in the background as I wrote this novel was George Whalley's marvellous biography, *The Legend of John Hornby* (Macmillan of Canada, 1962), a book that has stayed with me since I first read it thirty years ago. The quotations from it, including "Garden of Desire" and "Country of the Mind", have been used with the kind permission of his widow, Elizabeth Whalley.

The quotations from George Whalley's radio drama, "Death in the Barren Ground: A Narrative of John Hornby's Last Journey", broadcast on C.B.C. Radio on April 10, 1966, have been used with the permission of C.B.C. Radio and Elizabeth Whalley. To suit the chronology of my own narrative, in these pages the broadcast occurs five years earlier.

Ken Puley of C.B.C. Radio Archives was unfailingly helpful in finding the material I needed. I thank him most gratefully.

The thought on page 219 that "the robin in the egg doesn't know that the robin's egg is blue" comes from Margaret Avison's *A Kind of Perseverance* (Lancelot Press, 1993), and is used with her generous permission.

The quotation on page 7 from Alden Nowlan's "The broadcaster's poem", included in his collection *I'm a Stranger Here Myself* (Clarke, Irwin, 1974) and reprinted in *Selected Poems* (House of Anansi, 1996), is used with the kind permission of Claudine Nowlan.

Other books that were of great help to me were Knud

Rasmussen's *Report of the Fifth Thule Expedition, 1921–24* (Copenhagen: Gyldendal, 1930), E. W. Harrold's *The Diary of Our Own Pepys* (The Ryerson Press, 1947), and *In a Sea of Wind* by Yva Momatiuk and John Eastcott (Camden House Publishing, 1991).

I am deeply grateful to Mark Fried, Bella Pomer, and Mick Mallon for reading this manuscript at various stages and for giving me invaluable advice. My editor, Ellen Seligman, has been her usual astute, imaginative, and tireless self; it is impossible to give her enough credit for bringing this book into being. Heartfelt thanks, also, to Anita Chong and Jenny Bradshaw. For the British edition of this novel, I had the great good fortune to work with Christopher MacLehose. Grateful thanks to him and Laura Palmer.

In the absence of a good memory, one needs old and good friends. I lived in Yellowknife from 1974 to 1978, I canoed the Thelon River in 1978, but I have turned to many others, many of them friends, to add detail and accuracy to my shaky recall. Without their knowledge I could not have built a solid fictional world in which all of the characters, except historical figures, are fictitious. I thank everyone most gratefully who answered my questions. Let me name, in particular, Mick Mallon, John Stephenson, Peter Gorrie, Craig McInnes, Roy Thomas, Stuart and Peter Kinmond, Elizabeth Whalley, Diana Crosbie, Dave Devlin, Doug Ward, Hal Wake, Sheila McCook, Linda Russell, Wendy Robbins, Catherine O'Grady, Eric Friesen, the late Lister Sinclair, Rosemary Cairns, Matthew Crosier, Richie Allen, Huguette Léger, Sheelagh Teitelbaum, Conny Steenman-Marcusse, Marian De Vries, Parker Duchemin, Stewart Chadnick, George Grinnell, Max Finkelstein, and David Kippen.

I gratefully acknowledge the financial support of the City of Ottawa.